Safe Now - 2nd Edition

Heroes of Grant's Crossing
Book 2

H.M.S. Brown

Leaux Cay Press, LLC

Also by H.M.S. Brown

Heroes of Grant's Crossing Series

Wayward Guilt

Safe Now

End of a New Life - Coming Summer 2025

Grant's Crossing M/F Romance

Don't Call Me Sugar

Author's Note

Safe Now was a tough book to write. It spans from the early 2000s to 2016.

I put my characters through an awful lot, starting in the fictional small town of Halston, MO, through Chicago and Detroit, and landing in my beloved, fictional small town of Grant's Crossing, Ohio.

Steve and Nick sure have it rough, but the love between brothers gives these men the strength they never thought they'd need. Thank you for joining them on this journey.

Happy reading,

- Heather / H.M.S. Brown

Contents

To Mom,

Thanks for turning my complaint into creativity.

Content Warning

This book contains situations that may act as triggers for some readers, including an interrupted sexual assault scene at the beginning of the prologue. While the assault is not on the page, the reaction and subsequent escape are there.

There is on-page domestic violence, discussion of a death in the family, religious-based homophobia, discussion of abuse, combat violence, PTSD, and brief drug use.

If you or someone you know is in an abusive relationship, please know that you are not alone and that you have options. The National Domestic Violence Hotline is a 24-hour confidential service for victims, survivors, and all those affected by domestic violence. Help is available 24/7 at 1-800-799-SAFE (7233). Texting is also available.

Text "START" to 88788. Online chatting is available via https://www.thehotline.org. All calls are free and confidential. Texting charges may apply.

If you or someone you know is a victim of human trafficking, call the National Human Trafficking Hotline at 1(888)373-7888.

If you suffer from PTSD and want help, please reach out to https://www.ptsd.va.gov.

In addition, the Veterans Crisis Line offers 24/7, confidential crisis support for Veterans and their loved ones. You don't have to be enrolled in VA benefits or health care to connect. You can dial 988, then press 1. Or you can text 838255. Texting charges may apply.

Online chatting is also available. For more information, visit https://www.veteranscrisisline.net

Reach out to family or friends.
Reach out to someone.

You are not alone.

Prologue

Columbus, Ohio - September 2015

Taking a deep breath to control his anger within this rundown 1920s-era bungalow, Steve Cook turned toward the back room, where he heard grunting sounds from inside. He threw the door open so hard against the wall that an old picture crashed to the floor, revealing the only semi-clean spot in the entire house.

As he stepped inside the room, a balding man jumped back from the bed and yelled, "Hey!" His angry eyes glared at Steve before gaining control of his expression and aiming his sleazy smile at the man on the bed. He pulled out his wallet and tossed some cash on the bed just as he caught sight of a second man standing in the doorway.

"Leave it," Steve growled.

"Leave what?" The bald man scoffed.

"Your cash. Leave it all."

The man sneered as he put his wallet back in his pocket. "I paid the going price. Fair and square."

In a flash, Steve drew his knife and pointed it at the man, who nearly went cross-eyed while focusing on the sharp blade mere inches from his eyes.

In a deep and steady voice, Steve lowered the blade down the man's body and spoke. "I don't give a flying fuck what you think is fair. I said leave it, or I'll make sure you leave something else."

The bald man's eyes widened in fear as he felt the push of the knife point against his unzipped fly. He emptied the cash out of his wallet, stumbling backward until he bumped into a scratched-up chest of drawers. His face winced as the sharp corner dug into his back. "Ow," he moaned.

Steve stepped back and glanced down at the nearly passed-out victim lying face-down on the bed.

His shoulders slouched the moment he laid eyes on the slender, half-starved man.

Robert Nicholas Cook.

His brother.

Chapter 1

First Kiss

HALSTON, MISSOURI, OUTSIDE ST. LOUIS - FALL 2003, 12 YEARS earlier

Steve ground his cigarette into the ground with his tennis shoe and looked through the stands at the Halston Junior - Senior High School football field to catch a glimpse of the scoreboard. "Fourth quarter," he muttered to himself. He ran his fingers through his neatly trimmed, dark blond hair.

"Where's Marissa tonight, Steve?" Bryce asked before taking a drag on his cigarette and handing it to his girlfriend, Dani. She pulled her hand from his shoulder to take it and inhaled.

"She's at her dad's tonight. Said he'd probably be passed out cold since he started drinking at noon."

"Pretty rich, considering how much he rails against drinking when he fills in for the minister," Bryce said.

"Except wine, of course," his girlfriend laughed. She handed the cigarette back to him. "Glad I don't go to his church."

"Me, too," Steve said. "I've gotta get my jacket out of my locker, then take my little brother home."

"Bet you can't wait for him to be old enough to drive," Bryce said.

"It's not so bad. Besides, it lets me watch out for him."

"Too bad we can't say that about our parents." Bryce flicked his lighter for his girlfriend to light another cigarette.

"Yeah. I just wish Dad wouldn't be so tough on him, you know?"

"Yep. He's a good kid. I don't get why Uncle Gregory's always been hard on him."

Steve's eyebrows shot up as he slowly shook his head. "I don't either." Steve had his suspicions as to why his Dad was so hard on his brother. Nick was such a sweet, sensitive, barely teen-aged boy, which pissed his father off. Steve didn't care; It was his job to protect his little brother as best he could since his parents couldn't be bothered.

"Yeah. Sorry. Nicky likes orchestra, though, right?"

"He loves it. Being in the band didn't take for me, but man, Nick loves anything with music. Especially the guitar. He's playing Sunday morning."

"He is?" Bryce's face lit up. "That'll make your parents happy. Who knew my cousin had so much talent."

"He's nervous because he's the soloist for communion for both services, but I know he'll be great."

"What's he playing?"

"Bach and something else. I don't know, but he listened to the CD, and now he's playing it." Steve's face lit up with pride. "He's amazing. I can barely read music, but he can just listen to something once or twice and then immediately bring it to life on his guitar. He's so good."

"Can't wait to hear it." Bryce stayed silent for a few moments. "Will he be singing, too?"

"Just in the choir."

"You know Nicky's music'll get him out of here someday."

"I hope so." Steve extended his hand and gave his cousin a half hug. "I gotta bounce. See you on Sunday."

"Yep. See ya."

Steve hugged Bryce's girlfriend, too. "See you later, Dani."
"Bye, Steve."

———

Steve jogged up the stairs and rounded the corner to the hallway where his locker was located outside Mrs. Winston's English classroom. He grabbed his jacket but hesitated when he heard sounds coming from the classroom across the hall. He tilted his head to the side, straining to hear what sounded like voices, but couldn't make out what they were saying.

Closing his locker door, he spun the dial on the combination lock before slipping his arms into his jacket. He had just shrugged it over his shoulders when he heard a familiar voice. He creased his brow. "Nicky?"

When no one answered, he inched closer to where the sounds came from, stepping lightly so as not to give himself away. He heard a second voice, and upon hearing the first voice speak again, he was sure it was his brother.

Steve stopped just shy of the doorway when the voices stopped. He turned to step inside the classroom just in time to see his brother kissing another boy. They were hesitant, unsure of themselves.

Yep. Definitely their first kiss.

He backed up against the wall of lockers, but the clang of the metal door echoed loudly in the empty hallway. He closed his eyes and swore under his breath.

Nicky and the other boy gasped in surprise and whisper-yelled to each other to stay quiet.

Steve started to call out to his brother to offer fair warning, but he heard voices heading in their direction. He thought he recognized one of them, too: a bully at school and at church, namely a bigoted kid who came from a bigoted family. He and his friends acted like they hated everyone, yet still showed up at church every

Sunday. Steve's dad wasn't much better, but his mom's influence made sure that he and Nick weren't like that, probably her only saving grace.

A quick peek around the corner confirmed his suspicions: Cabot Larszin and Joshua Maylock. And, of course, the other kid who usually tagged along with them, Malcolm something? Marvin? Merlin? Whatever his name was, the scrawny kid probably thought hanging out with the school bully made himself look bigger and stronger.

Steve's heart skipped a beat, and he looked down at his shaking hands. He turned his head toward the room Nick and his friend were in, then down the still-empty hallway as the voices drew nearer. His brother was probably scared shitless. Steve had to get him out of there. "Shit."

He darted inside the classroom in time for Nick and his friend, Danny, to jump away from each other like the two like-poled magnets they played with in physics class earlier that day. Steve couldn't understand why his mind went to a science class and, normally, might even have laughed at the reaction if one of his least favorite people weren't drawing near. "Quick. Grab your jackets," he commanded.

When they just stared at him like frightened deer in headlights, he grabbed his brother's jacket off a desk and tossed it to him. "Don't be afraid, Nicky. It's okay. I promise." He tossed the other jacket to Danny. "Hurry up and put them on. Somebody's coming." He motioned with his hands to urge them to move faster. "Put them on. We'll say you guys followed me to my locker since I left my jacket there, anyway."

Finally, the two boys snapped out of their trance and shoved their arms in their jackets. Steve made it a point to straighten his brother's collar. "Breathe, Nicky. It's okay. Just breathe. I've got your back." He placed his hands on Nick's shoulders. "You believe me, right?"

Nick tried to smile, but it didn't last. He was small for his thirteen, almost fourteen, years and still frightened easily. "Yeah, Stevie."

Steve then turned his attention to Danny and confirmed his jacket was on right. "You, too, Danny. It's gonna be alright." He shot a quick glance toward the hallway, then motioned for the boys to follow. "Let's get out of here. Just follow me and let me do the talking."

When they both nodded, Steve gave them a borderline-cocky smile to share some of the confidence he wasn't sure he possessed and led them out. "I got this."

Chapter 2

Confrontation

They stood by Steve's locker, which Steve smacked so it would sound like they'd just arrived there. With his back to his brother for a few seconds, he clenched his fist a few times, then turned the combination lock again when the three upperclassmen appeared at the end of the hallway.

"Stay close," Steve whispered over his shoulder. Steve remained a step or so in front of his brother, ready to confront the trio of boys heading in their direction.

Cabot, Joshua, and their friend sneered at Steve, Nick, and Danny.

"What are you doing here?"

Steve didn't answer. "Cabot," he said in acknowledgment.

"I said, why are you here?"

"I'm a Senior. I don't answer to you."

"Yeah, well. They're not." Cabot tried to get past Steve, but Steve's hand shot out and grabbed him by the arm.

"Whaddya want, Cabot?"

Cabot shrugged out of Steve's grip. "What are they doing in my school?"

"Your school?" Steve scoffed. "The junior and senior high schools are all in the same building."

"He's right, Cabot," Joshua agreed.

Cabot turned back and yelled. "Shut up!"

"This is my part of the school. My locker's right there." Steve pointed over his shoulder.

"Yeah? Why are they here, then?"

"You mean my brother?" Steve held the collar of his jacket as he battled down the butterflies in his stomach. "Nick came with me to get my jacket, and we ran into Danny." While Nicky may have been his nickname for his brother, he didn't let anyone else call him that. To everyone else, it was just Nick.

"Yeah. Right. Can't say I'm surprised to see you with two wusses like them."

Pulling his shoulders back, Steve stood as tall as he could, making his five-foot-nine-inch frame seem just a bit taller. Steve lifted his chin and leered at the bully. Cabot still had him by an inch or two, but Steve didn't care. He would do what he needed to defend his brother. His menacing gaze dared the bullies to try something. "They're with me, Crabbit."

Cabot sneered upon hearing the nickname.

"Stevie." Nick's shaky whisper was barely audible.

Steve put his arm around his brother's shoulders while he spoke calmly. "I need to get them home." He did his best to exude confidence because, while he was in shape and worked out with a punching bag at his cousin's place, he'd never fought an actual person before. He knew he'd be shit outta luck if they actually planned to fight him.

His lips curled up into a goofy smile. "They'd almost talked me into stopping for milkshakes before you losers showed up."

"How cute," Cabot said while Joshua and the other guy chuckled.

Marlin? Was it a fish name?

Steve didn't care. He placed his other hand on Danny's shoulder, partly to steady himself. It was mostly to give strength to the two boys who stood there frozen in fear, wide-eyed, mouths gaping open. Steve turned just enough to give them a reassuring nod. Nick closed his mouth. Danny didn't move.

Cabot narrowed his gaze and sneered again. "So you're a little faggot-lover now, huh? Those little pussies were probably just -"

Steve dropped his arms and strode forward, cutting him off as he got right in Cabot's face. Steve may not have had the height advantage, but he had more muscle; and right now he was pissed off. Playing confident was one thing, but he would not let Cabot call anyone that word, much less his brother.

His voice dropped way down and didn't shake one bit despite how hard his heart was pounding inside his chest. God, he hoped Cabot didn't catch on that he was just as scared as Nicky. "You might want to take a long... hard... look in the mirror before you finish that sentence, Crabbit. You insult my brother, you insult me. I honestly don't think you have the fucking balls to follow through. Shit. You wouldn't even make it to the second punch."

Nick gasped behind him at the language Steve used.

The scrawny kid, whose name Steve couldn't remember, stepped backward. His gaze bounced back and forth between Cabot and Steve. "Dude. I... I... c...can't fight."

Joshua put a hand on Cabot's shoulder, which he immediately shrugged off. "Samerlin's right, Cabot. We didn't come up here for a fight. My parents will kill me if I get into a fight."

Samerlin. That's it.

Cabot's eyes darted from left to right as he realized he wouldn't have the backup he expected. He cleared his throat. "Well. Good thing Josh and Sammy are here to talk me out of wasting my time on you."

If looks could kill, Cabot would already be dead, but Steve maintained his hard glare. He could probably take a punch. Sure, he'd sparred with Bryce during their workouts, but he'd be damned sure Nicky never had to take one.

Cabot took a step back.

Steve released an annoyed exhale. "Yeah. I didn't think so." He looked both Joshua and Samerlin in the eye. They each took another step backward, too.

"We done here?" Steve exchanged his anger for annoyance.

"Yeah," Cabot agreed as he yielded to the side. "We're done."

Joshua and Samerlin moved as well and stood with him by the lockers. Clearly, they weren't looking to start one of their usual fights tonight. Cabot preferred to outnumber his opponents to the point where they just gave in. So, if his two cohorts didn't want to fight, he had to back down.

"Good." Steve gave a gentle nudge to both Nick and Danny, putting himself between them and Cabot's crew. "Come on. Let's get outta here."

Chapter 3

I'll be Bach

Nervous energy had Steve walking a fast clip to his grandpa's old beater of a car. "Get in," he told Nick and Danny. He took a few seconds after they got in to stand outside the driver's side door to close his eyes and catch his breath. Resting his forearms on the roof of his car, he held his hands palms up and clenched them a few times as he slowed his breathing. He wasn't winded from hurrying to the car. It was from the pounding in his chest that did not want to calm down.

After a few more deep breaths, he opened the door and let his body drop into the driver's seat. He flashed a smile of confidence he didn't feel so Nick would see him as the strong big brother he was supposed to be.

He fastened his seatbelt and locked the car doors, then turned to face the two frightened boys sitting in his car. Nick in the front seat, Danny in the back. "Are you two alright?"

They nodded more at each other than at Steve, who exhaled, keeping any frustration to himself. "Are you sure?"

They each mumbled something in response, but Steve didn't want to force the issue. He had more pressing concerns at the moment. "Danny," he said with what was probably too stern of a tone. "Do your parents know?"

Danny's wide eyes shot up in fear. Steve felt sorry for the poor kid. Danny may have been fourteen, but he looked like he was about to wet his pants.

"Look," Steve tried again, keeping his voice gentle but firm. "You're both safe with me. I won't say anything, but do they know?"

Danny gave another nervous glance to Nicky. "It wasn't... we didn't..."

This time, it was a look of disbelief that Steve shot toward the back seat. "You can tell me, Danny. It's okay. Like I said, you're safe here."

Danny's shoulders slumped forward. "No. They don't know."

Unsurprised, Steve slowly nodded. Danny's parents were horribly closed-minded, much like Steve and Nicky's parents.

"Okay. Best not to say anything then."

Danny's wide eyes finally met Steve's. "Are...are you gonna tell them?"

"Stevie." Nick reached for Steve's arm. His voice shook as he spoke. "You can't tell his parents. They'll make him go to one of those camps..."

Steve's stomach dropped. Both boys were scared. "I know." He turned his attention to Nick and covered Nick's hand with his own. "So might ours, Nicky." Steve could feel Nick's hand shaking. "I'm not going to say anything to anyone. I promise. I would never do that to you." Steve looked at both boys, "I am going to tell you this. You can always trust me. Both of you. No matter what, you can count on me as a friend, alright?"

When they didn't respond, Steve asked again. "A'ight?"

The boys released a collective sigh of relief as they muttered their thanks.

"Now," Steve raised his lips into a smile. "Let's go get milkshakes. Sound good?"

"Yeah?" Their faces lit up with hopeful smiles.

"Yeah." Steve's smile was genuine at their reaction. "I want one, too. Besides, it'll help you both calm down because you look like you just shit yourselves."

"Stevie!" Nick admonished his big brother while trying not to giggle.

Danny's mouth hung open. Apparently, swearing wasn't a thing in his family, either.

"Sorry, Nicky." Steve turned the engine and revved it a couple of times before putting it in reverse, but he couldn't pass up an opportunity to send a sly grin to his brother. Steve paused a second, then gave a friendly push to Nick's upper arm before resting his arm on the back of the seat to look through the rear windshield. "We won the game, by the way," he told them both as he backed out of his parking spot. "17-14. We got a last-second touchdown to win. Our parents may want to know."

He turned to face the front, shifted the car into gear, and drove off.

After they enjoyed milkshakes at a local fast-food restaurant, Steve dropped Danny off at his home about fifteen or so minutes from where he and his brother lived. On their way home, he pulled into a small strip mall where the shops were all closed for the night. He shifted the car into park in between two of the tall, brightly lit light poles. He kept the engine running with the heat on low but didn't say anything at first.

"Stevie... I didn't mean... I don't..."

He shifted in his seat to face his brother. "Nicky, it's okay. I will always have your back." Nick's face lit up in a smile. "Always."

"You're the best, Stevie."

"And don't you forget it, little brother." He gave Nick another playful push on the shoulder. "So you like Danny, huh?"

Nick's fingers tapped on the seatbelt strap as if he were playing a musical number in his head. "Um..."

"You can tell me anything, you know."

"Um...yeah?" Nick gave his brother a sideways glance. "He uh... let it slip one day that he liked boys. And... I like boys, too, but..."

Steve didn't push his brother. He sat in silence, remaining patient while Nick came up with the right words.

"But he's a grade above me and well..." Nick furrowed his brow and turned to face Steve as if just now discovering he was there. "He's really cute." Nick giggled but pressed his lips together to stop.

"First kiss?"

"Yeah." Nick dropped his gaze down to the floor. "It was..."

"Awkward and wonderful all at once?" Steve suggested, thinking back to his own first kiss with Melinda Cartwright.

This time, Nick's smile grew. "Yeah."

Steve tapped Nick's arm with the back of his hand. "Mine, too." He breathed out a quick laugh. "I didn't know what I was doing, but I'm the guy, so I thought I had to at least pretend I knew what I was doing, right? Turned out okay. Well," Steve winked at his brother. "Better than okay, but it was still weird at first. I've definitely gotten better with practice. You will, too."

Nick laughed. "I hope so."

The flickering lights of one of the overhead lights danced across their faces as they sat there.

"Yeah, but I'm your big brother. So, I hope you wait a while, but make sure you stay safe, okay?."

"Stevie!"

Steve pretended to defend himself against Nick, who was laughing now while trying to push an unyielding Steve by the arm. Steve loved his brother's laugh. He loved seeing him happy.

One of the overhead lights went out, drawing his gaze and casting a shadow in their section of the parking lot. He let his smile drop and then turned a serious eye toward his brother.

"Mom and Dad can never know, okay? I mean, never. You know what they think of anyone who isn't... well... anyone who's different.

And I swear to you, I'll never tell them. You have my word, but you have to be careful, Nicky. I mean, really careful. I've heard them talk about what happened to a kid in a neighboring church a few years ago."

"They sent him away."

"Exactly. And it sounds like Mom and Dad weren't too upset about it."

"I know."

"I think Uncle Clint may have had something to do with it. You know how he has all those cabins on his property."

"Yeah." Nick shuddered. "They creep me out."

"Me, too."

They sat for a few minutes until Nick broke the silence. "What about Bryce and Marly? And Aunt Linda and Uncle David?"

"I think our cousins would be fine. And Uncle David would be fine with it, but I don't know about Aunt Linda. She's really close to Mom so I'd rather be safe. I don't want you to get hurt."

"Okay."

"At least our church is far more accepting than our parents even though Mom and Dad complain about that sometimes. I'm just worried about what would happen if they found out before you finished school."

"What if..."

"Don't...," Steve cut him off. "I will always protect you, okay? Always."

"But what if they send me away."

Steve placed his hand on Nick's shoulder and gave a gentle squeeze. "I'll find you, Nicky, and I'll help you get out. If it ever happens, just agree with whatever they say if you have to. Try to look like you're sorry. Make them believe you see the... the *error* of your ways."

Nick pulled his face back in surprise. "You think I should lie?"

"Only long enough to get out and get somewhere safe. I've only heard stories about places like that. They're awful places, Nicky. Horrible places. But whatever you do, stay strong, as strong as you can. You're not a pushover. Just play your music in your head. I know how you like to do that when you're scared or nervous, how it calms you. Trust in that. Trust your music."

"Okay."

"And trust in me."

"Okay," Nick mumbled while staring at his feet again. His fingers were tapping, this time on his jeans.

"Hey."

"What?"

"I swear, I'll do my best to always take care of you," Steve exchanged another sly look with his brother, "Until you get sick of me, of course."

"I'll never get sick of you. I love you, Stevie."

"I love you, too, Nicky."

Steve took one last look at his brother before putting the car in gear and pulling away. "Tell me. What was the score?"

Nick recited the score and told Steve all about the final, last-second touchdown in the fourth quarter.

"Now tell me about this Mozart piece you'll be playing on Sunday."

"It's Bach!" Nick exclaimed. "And I'll be playing more than one."

"So, you'll be Bach?" Steve asked in his best, really bad Arnold Schwarzenegger impression.

Steve couldn't see Nick rolling his eyes, but he could hear it in his brother's tone when he started talking about the Bach pieces, something Steve was happy to listen to the entire way home.

Chapter 4

Nick's Solo

ST. MARK'S EPISCOPAL CHURCH, HALSTON, MO - SUNDAY *morning*

Steve stifled a yawn as he held the church door open for his brother, who juggled carrying a guitar almost as big as he was in one hand and a guitar stand in the other. Someday, he'd grow into it; but for now, Steve was happy to be his brother's roadie, even if that meant sacrificing a couple of hours of sleep on a Sunday morning. Knowing how important this day was, Steve made sure his brother arrived in plenty of time to warm up and calm his nerves.

Steve yawned again as he walked inside and back to the choir room where Nick could get some last-minute practice in, not that he needed it. Nick could play this music in his sleep.

Still, Nick had fought off his nerves the entire drive, worrying about this note or that phrase. On the way to St. Mark's Episcopal Church in their hometown of Halston, Missouri, a little southwest of St. Louis, Nick talked about the pieces he would play. Steve's own ability to read music left much to be desired, but he was okay with that. He could at least offer encouragement to Nick, whose playing was going to be fantastic.

It always was.

Steve walked around the hallways between the Sunday school rooms and their large Fellowship Hall to get his blood pumping and to keep himself awake before the service started. He forced a few smiles and good mornings to anyone who passed him in the hall in an attempt to appear more awake than he really was. He wasn't a fan of coffee but didn't want to fall asleep in the middle of the sermon, either. He downed a small cup of the bitter brew along with a piece of cinnamon coffee cake set out each Sunday by one of the women's groups. Boring sermon or not, he wanted to be there for his brother when he was ready to play. He'd volunteered to take Nick to church for the early service so he could be there for both performances. Sure, he told his parents it was so they could just show up later for Sunday school after a leisurely morning to hear him play in the late service, but selfishly, he just loved to hear Nick play.

A few minutes before the choir donned their robes and lined up for the procession, Steve found his brother struggling with his tie while another choir member held his hymnal.

Nick grunted in frustration. "Ugh. Help me, Stevie. Please?"

"Sure." Steve tied and straightened Nick's tie, then helped pull his robe over his head and zipped it up. Steve straightened the robe, too.

The pews in the early service were already filling up with its usual assortment of retirees, parents with young kids at home, and anyone not wanting to miss the opening kickoff of their favorite NFL team. Parents of older kids tended to wait until the later service since getting teenagers out of bed this early on a Sunday was nearly impossible.

Steve curled his lip up on one side. "You've got this, little brother. You're gonna be great." He grabbed both the guitar and the stand. "I'll set these up behind the pulpit so you can get to them when you're ready to play, okay?"

"Alright." Nick smiled up at his brother for a second before frowning. "I'm nervous, Stevie."

"I know you are, but you know the music," Steve assured him. "Trust in the music, alright?"

Nick craned his neck to get an idea of how many people were already seated in the sanctuary. "Yep."

"Do that, and you'll be fine."

"He's right, you know." A short man with thinning gray hair wearing a matching choir robe handed Nick his hymnal with a smile as they lined up side by side for the procession. He spoke up as Nick opened it to the correct page. "You'll be just fine, Nick. The music you played was simply glorious in our practice this morning."

Nick's face lit up with a smile that morphed into a yawn. "Thanks."

"See?" Steve asked his brother. "Like I said. You'll be great."

Nick let out a long exhale.

"Okay, Nicky. I'm taking these up. I'll be right up front, so concentrate on me when you play, and you'll be great."

"Thanks," Nick said through another big yawn.

"Stay awake, little brother!" Steve gave Nick's shoulder a brotherly squeeze. "See you in there."

Everything about the service was normal despite being a couple of hours earlier than what Steve was used to. His brother made it up on stage with the rest of the choir but kept glancing over at his guitar.

Steve set it up exactly how Nick asked him to that morning, the night before, yesterday afternoon, and...well, there was no way he could have messed it up after all the times Nick explained just how it was supposed to be.

Everything was perfect until the communion was about to start. The plan was for Nick to go up and get his communion first so he could then sit down and play while the rest of the congregation took theirs. The minister had already given Steve permission to go up at the same time since Nick was probably more nervous about taking communion by himself than he was about playing.

Steve and Nick dipped their bread in the grape juice and said their amens before going their separate ways. "You've got this, Nicky," Steve whispered to his brother before returning to his pew. The minister gave them both a reassuring smile.

Without making eye contact with anyone, Nick sat on the chair in front of the choir and nervously adjusted one of his strings. Right after the minister invited the congregation to stand and join him in communion, he started playing J.S. Bach's Bourrée in E Minor.

As soon as the notes started flowing, Nick's confidence took over. His eyes closed while his fingers pulled at the strings, eliciting the most beautiful tones. Steve always loved to watch his brother get lost in the music, the one language anyone could understand. The world could be tumbling down around him, but once the first string vibrated and dulcet tones flowed, Nick was in his happy place.

Pride filled Steve's chest, deadly sins be damned. He hoped his parents would like Nick's playing as much as he and the other people in the congregation. He especially couldn't wait for Bryce to hear his brother play at the late service. Sitting on the aisle, he received warm smiles and friendly pats on the shoulder from the congregants standing in line to take communion. As Nick transitioned to his next piece, a few people even leaned over to compliment Steve on the beautiful music filling the sanctuary. Their effusive comments about how such a young man could play so well warmed his heart. Steve beamed a proud smile that only grew with each successive request to pass their thanks to his brother for playing today.

Steve and Nick's parents arrived in time to greet them and ask how the first service went before they all went their separate ways for Sunday school. Afterward, Steve found his parents and sat down next to them near the front of the church.

Nick wasn't nearly as nervous about the late service now that he had one performance under his belt He could thank the great performance earlier for that. Their parents lapped up the compliments they received about their son's playing. Steve knew they would, but he also knew that Nick played even better the second time around.

When an older gentleman turned around in his pew to pay a compliment to his parents, Steve nudged his cousin's arm so Bryce could hear it as well. He leaned closer and whispered. "I told you he'd be great."

"Never doubted you for a second."

Chapter 5

The Smell of Rain

THE REST OF THE LATE SERVICE WAS THE SAME AS THE FIRST. Surprisingly, Steve stayed awake for the repeat of the sermon. Afterward, they gathered in the Fellowship Hall for coffee and snacks, where Nick, no longer in his choir robes, joined them. He received hugs from his cousins, Bryce and Marly, his Aunt Linda and Uncle David. Then, his parents got to show him off and bask in the compliments they received from the other parishioners about his playing.

Steve and Bryce grabbed a few cookies and cold slider-sized sandwiches and sat at a table in the corner with a few of their friends while Nick escaped to the other side of the large hall to hang out with boys and girls his own age.

While talking about the upcoming youth group retreat to a nearby state park, Steve noticed his parents talking to Cabot Larszin's parents about something. Cabot stood by his parents and gave an occasional sneer in Steve's direction when no one was looking.

So did Cabot's father.

Steve elbowed Bryce to catch his attention. "This doesn't look good."

Bryce agreed. "No. It doesn't. I wonder what they're up to."

"Probably talking about what happened after the game."

"After the game?"

"Yeah. I uh... met up with Cabot, Joshua, and Samerlin after getting my coat." Steve gave him a quick rundown of what happened, leaving out a few details he promised his brother he'd keep secret.

"Why would they pick on eighth graders? What did they ever do to them?"

"They pick on them because they can, but...." Steve turned to his friend, still speaking in a low voice. "I'm probably going to hear about this when I get home."

"Yep." Bryce tapped Steve's shoulder. "Here's hoping he goes easy on you. Doesn't sound like anything was your fault. You were just defending your brother. I've never known you to start a fight. I can't even imagine you throwing a punch at anyone."

"I was tempted the other night."

"Yeah, well." Bryce glanced over at Nick, who was laughing at something his friends were saying. "He touched on the one thing that would bring out that side of you. Lord help the one who ever pushes you over that edge."

"Nick's a good kid, but he doesn't have a mean bone in his body."

"No, but he's got a big brother."

"That he does."

Nick's father gestured to Steve and Nick that it was time to go. "Gotta go."

"Good luck, Steve."

Steve hugged his cousin goodbye and caught up to his brother.

After church, when they were back at the house, Steve and Nick changed into casual clothes. Steve hung out in his room for a while before heading downstairs for a relaxing Sunday.

"Did you hang up your suit," Steve's mom asked when he came

downstairs. She was reading a daily devotional while his dad read the newspaper.

"Yeah," Steve said.

"Yes, ma'am," his father corrected him.

"Yes, ma'am," Steve said.

His mother nodded in response without looking up from her reading.

"I'm heading outside." Steve was almost past him when his dad called him out.

"You can go outside after you clean out the garage."

"But Dad, it's a Sunday."

"Don't talk back to me. Nick's already out there."

Steve released a frustrated exhale.

"Come back when it's finished."

"Yes, sir."

Steve opened the door to the garage and saw Nick struggling to move a heavy box over to the side so they could move some things around to make space for their cars. Steve rushed over to help.

"Dad said he wanted this moved up on the shelves." Nick pointed to the shelves in the bay for the third car they didn't actually own. It had become a collect-all for everything that didn't have its own spot.

"Let me get that, Nicky."

"Thanks, Stevie."

"So you didn't escape either, huh?"

Nick smiled and reached for a broom. "He caught me just as I was coming downstairs."

Steve laughed. "Yeah. I was within a few steps of the door when he snagged me." He scanned the area until he caught sight of the old transistor radio on a high shelf, he reached up and set it on a lower shelf. "I can't believe we still have this."

The dial clicked, and static came through the tiny speakers.

"Hey. It actually works." Steve turned the dial past talk radio until finally finding a music station.

Steve and Nick cleaned the garage for the next couple of hours. Leaving the garage door open, they worked while a storm dropped some much-needed rain. The scent of petrichor permeated their senses.

"I love the smell of rain."

"I do, too, Nicky. It smells good."

Steve held the dustpan while Nick swept the last of the dirt into it. Steve dumped it into their trash can, where it would wait until the garbage truck came through on Wednesday.

"You played really well today, you know." Steve hung the dustpan up on a nail while Nick clicked the broom into its designated hook on the wall.

"I was really nervous."

"You couldn't tell."

Nick scoffed.

"Okay. *I* could tell, but nobody *else* could tell. A ton of people even told me how much they loved your music."

Nick grinned. "I love playing."

"I know. And everyone could hear how good you are." Steve laughed. "Mom and Dad ate it all up."

Wiping his hands a few times, Steve surveyed the newly cleaned garage. "Well, it looks a lot better. I'll see if Dad wants to check it out." He opened the door and called their dad.

They waited in silence for a minute or two until their dad came out to inspect the garage. He looked at it for about a minute before grunting. "Looks good. Thank you. Now, come inside and clean up. Dinner will be ready at five." He turned and shut the door behind him.

The rain stopped falling, but the water still flowed down the street and poured into the storm drains. Water was dripping from the maple and oak trees on the edge of their yard, and the lawn itself had several pools of water from the rain that came down too fast to soak into the ground. The birds were singing again as the sun attempted an appearance from behind the dark gray clouds.

Steve held the door open for his brother. "So much for going outside," he said.

"That's okay. It's still a good day."

Steve followed his brother inside the house and left their shoes inside the door to head upstairs and clean up for dinner. "Yeah, it is."

Chapter 6

Sunday Dinner

STEVE'S PARENTS MADE NO MENTION OF THEIR CONVERSATION with Cabot's parents with dinner going so well. Their mom cooked a standard Sunday dinner with baked chicken, mashed potatoes, green bean casserole, and salad. They talked about the church service and all the compliments they received about Nick's playing.

Then, it happened.

"I heard some disturbing things about you before our Sunday school class today, Steven." His father said, his deep voice carried a stern note as he wiped his mouth with a cloth napkin.

Steve swallowed hard before sticking a bite of green beans in his mouth. He made eye contact with Nick.

"I spoke to Ralph Larszin, who told me you cornered his boy at school."

Steve choked on his food. "I what?"

"Don't interrupt me! I heard you said some nasty things to Cabot and his friends." He took a sip of his iced tea and then faced Steve. "What do you have to say for yourself?"

"For starters, that's not what happened. He was picking–"

"I'm not looking for excuses."

Taken aback, Steve stretched his hand toward his brother.

"Excuses? How about the truth? He and his friends were picking on Nick. They were calling him names. I never cornered them."

"I was told quite a bit of swearing was involved."

Steve couldn't deny that, but he'd be damned if he didn't get out what really happened. "They called Nick and his friend horrible names, Dad. They're bullies. They were scaring them. All I did was stand up to–"

"Bullies?" His dad raised his voice. "Are you saying Ralph Larszin's boy is a bully?"

"Yeah. I mean, yes, sir. He's probably the biggest bully in the entire school. Everyone knows that."

"Nick needs to learn to take care of himself. If he gets beat up a few times, then so be it."

Nick's fork clinked against the plate. Receiving a stern look from his father, he picked it up and continued eating. "Sorry."

"So be it? But Dad - they're seventeen," Steve pleaded. "They're juniors. Nick's just in eighth grade. Besides, they're practically a foot taller. It would never have been a fair fight."

"Life's not fair, but he's gotta toughen up sometime."

"Toughen up?"

"Plus, I learned you used the Lord's name in vain, and you should never do that."

"I did not use the Lord's name in vain!"

"Don't lie to me, Steven."

"I didn't. I swear. I never said that," he argued. "I may have used the F-wor..." Steve trailed off as he realized what he had given away.

Nick and their mother both froze. Nick in fear and their mother in feigned shock. Had their sanctimonious mother been wearing her pearls, her fingers would have turned white, considering how tightly she'd be clutching them.

Gregory Cook glared at his son. He was a man accustomed to getting his way, and he certainly didn't appreciate his son's sass. No one talked back to him, and no one ever told him no. No one argued with him, and no one disagreed with him. Ever. People took him at his word. Always. And always, without question.

Steve knew his father didn't like it, but he was not about to let his father suggest that he should have let his brother get beaten up by a bunch of boys a lot older, a lot taller, and a lot bigger than he was. That wasn't right. Maybe when Nick was older, he could fend them off, but as a scrawny, happy-go-lucky young teenager against a bunch of upperclassmen? No way. Steve loved his brother, and Nick was many wonderful things, but a fighter wasn't one of them. He would have been outnumbered and outfought.

Sadly, all that was secondary to the fact that Nick and Steve's dad hated swearing. He hated it with a passion and wanted to make sure his boys never swore at all. But if someone even hinted that one of them had said the Lord's name in vain, he believed them. The truth, oddly enough, no longer mattered.

Steve spoke again, attempting to keep his inevitable punishment to a minimum. "All I was saying is that Nick is family. I'll always protect my family."

"I will too, Steven, but I'll not have my sons disrespecting their parents either."

Steve exhaled, knowing his father would never see reason. "That was never my intent." He closed his eyes and dropped his chin to his chest, his shoulders slumping in defeat. "I never used the Lord's name in vain, Dad," he whispered. "Never."

He stabbed a few green beans and had just started chewing them when his dad proved that reason was not going to be considered.

His proof came quickly when his dad forced his chair back with a loud screech.

Steve's stomach lurched when his father reached down and wrapped his fist around a chunk of Steve's T-shirt, pulling it upwards. "Get up."

"Stevie!"

Their mother shushed Nick as soon as Steve's name escaped his lips.

Steve quickly swallowed his green beans. "What? Dad!" Steve's fork and knife fell to the floor with a loud clang as he tried to free himself from his dad's unyielding grip, all while avoiding being yanked out of his seat.

"Come on," his dad said while pulling Steve away from the table. "We're going to have a talk."

Steve struggled not to land butt-first onto the floor when he was pulled out of his seat. The dishes rattled as he fought to find purchase on the kitchen table to avoid falling.

His father's deep voice bellowed out. "Don't make me wait on you, boy. It's bad enough you're disrupting the dinner your mother worked so hard to make for us."

Steve offered a pleading look to his mother and was met by a cold stare. Nothing. No support.

Nothing new.

"Finish your dinner, Nick," their father commanded.

Nick's eyes flew wide open. Too scared to utter a single word, his lips formed his brother's name. Silently, this time.

"Steven James." His dad released his now-wrinkled T-shirt. "Now."

Steve stood all the way up, his height nearly as tall now as his father's, but his breathing was rapid as his shoulders moved up and down from being yanked out of his chair and nearly dragged onto the floor. He straightened his shirt and schooled his fearful expression long enough to offer a reassuring nod to his brother. "It's alright, Nicky. We're just going to talk," he lied.

Chapter 7

Just a Talk

RELIEVED AT THE HALF SMILE HE RECEIVED IN RETURN, STEVE headed through the door to follow his father outside. He did his best to calm himself on the long walk to the large workshop they keep in the back of their two-acre property. It was more like a super-sized, rectangular-shaped shed, about 1,000 square feet in all, with a small loft that Steve used to play in as a little boy.

Before he died, his grandpa used the workshop to make furniture and wood carvings that he would sell to support his family. Nick would have been too young, but Steve could remember back to grade school when Grandpa Joe would teach him how to properly sand the wood or build a dresser, making sure all the angles were just right. He would display his creations in his shop in Halston, the shop that their father now owned.

Grandpa Joe died when Steve and Nick were eleven and six years old, respectively, but not before he made the bedroom furniture they still used.

While their father was taught to make furniture, he no longer maintained the tradition of handcrafting anything they sold in the shop. Now, it was all factory-made, mass-produced stuff. It's higher-end, sure, but it's not the same as what their grandpa could have made. Their dad was a sell-out in order to make more money and brag about how successful he was.

That was no consolation as Steve approached the old workshop, no longer kept up as it once was. His grandpa took care of everything inside as if his tools, benches, and finished pieces were his own children, but his father treated it all like an annoyance. He just let it go. The outside hadn't seen a fresh coat of paint in years. The inside was dusty, full of cobwebs, and being overrun by mice. Steve would occasionally head out to fix up holes where they got in, but they were determined creatures, as his grandpa would say. They always found a way in, no matter how much they tried to keep the little critters out, especially now as the weather started turning.

His father used the workshop as an oversized dumpster to hold all his junk. The no-longer-wanted pieces of furniture Steve's grandpa never had the chance to finish were tossed in the corners. Corrugated boxes filled with old toys were piled on now-broken table legs and spare chair seats. Wood that once held so much promise and potential would now probably end up as kindling. His dad only kept the front area clear for when he brought Steve back for a *talk*, as he called it.

"Get inside," his father's stern voice ordered. The rusty hinges creaked as he pulled the door open.

He pushed Steve through the doorway, forcing him to take a few extra steps to maintain his balance. Steve turned around when the door slammed shut behind them.

Steve swallowed hard as his dad unbuckled his belt and pulled it through his belt loops, pulling the ends tightly with a loud pop before bringing them together to hold in one hand.

"Drop them," he commanded.

"Dad!"

"You know how this works. Do it."

His dad was right. Steve knew all too well how this worked.

His father kept speaking as Steve unfastened his jeans and pulled them down below his butt. "To the knees."

Steve gives his dad a pleading look. "But..."

His father's hard stare never wavered. "That just earned you more."

Reluctantly, Steve dropped his jeans and underwear to his knees.

"Now, lean against the table, Steven."

Steve hesitated a fraction of a second before his Dad yelled again.

"Do it now, boy."

"Yes, sir." Steve leaned forward, resting his forearms on the dusty workbench in front of all his grandfather's old tools that still hung on the wall.

This was what Steve hated most of all, the period of time after he leaned forward but before he felt the first sting of his father's belt. Only today, he knew he'd feel it on the back of his legs.

SLAP!

"Remember you asked for this."

SLAP!

Steve's face grimaced with each successive blow to the back of his buttocks and thighs.

"Every time you disrespect me, you get a beating."

SLAP!

"You'll never learn, boy."

SLAP!

Steve opened and closed his hands in an effort to keep his wits about him and not cry out, focusing his gaze on the row of crescent wrenches his grandpa used to use. Though dusty, they still hung on the same particle board that kept them organized.

SLAP! To the buttocks.

SLAP! To the thighs.

SLAP!

Over and over, his father struck him, breaking his skin in a few places this time, all while lecturing him on how he made him look bad.

Steve winced with each blow but never cried out. He never cried out. He wouldn't cry out, but an occasional silent tear spilled down his cheeks as the pain became harder and harder to bear.

A drop of blood dripped down one of his thighs, but he still never cried out.

Then, it stopped.

Risking a look, he turned his head in time for his father to pull something out of his back pocket.

With a cloth handkerchief, the older man wiped the sweat off his brow. He then wiped a few drops of blood off his belt, pausing to inspect it to make sure he got it all.

It landed on the dusty workbench, drawing Steve's gaze. He stared at the sweat-marred cloth spotted with a few drops of blood.

"Wipe off the blood so your mother doesn't have to clean it off your jeans," he ordered while slipping his belt through the belt loops.

It took every ounce of energy Steve had to remain standing.

"I'll write you a note to keep you out of gym class this week," he said as he buckled his belt.

This week. Usually, it was just 1-2 days, but Steve felt a drop of blood dripping down as far as his knees.

"Did you hear me, boy? Look at me."

Steve stood up, biting the inside of his cheek to prevent himself from shedding more tears.

"Stand up straight and look at me."

Trying not to show his pain, Steve pressed his lips together and forced himself to stand up straight. He let his arms hang slack by his sides, but his pants and briefs had fallen in a bunch around his ankles, forcing him to shuffle just to face his father.

"I said I'll write you a note to keep you out of gym class."

Steve's voice cracked as he forced out an obligatory thank you.

His father grunted at his response while opening the door and muttered, "Good talk."

Chapter 8

A Good Day

When the door finally closed behind his father, Steve exhaled with a whimper and caught himself on the workbench, barely preventing himself from hitting the floor. It took a minute or two to let himself feel relieved that it was over. His shaking hand drifted to the back of his leg with his father's handkerchief. He winced in agony as he clutched the back of his leg to relieve himself of some of the pain.

"Bastard!" he whispered to himself. A sound drew his gaze to the floor, where a small mouse scurried along the floorboards.

"Too bad he didn't hear that, huh?" Steve's weak voice sounded out to the junk-filled workshop. He brought up his hand and stared at the handkerchief that was much redder now that he'd cleaned the backs of his own legs. He struggled to bend down and pull his briefs and jeans back up, wincing again as the coarse denim fabric rubbed against his tender skin. Pursing his lips together, he buttoned his jeans and pulled up the zipper. After a few moments of leaning against the workbench to collect himself enough so his brother wouldn't know how much he truly hurt, he wiped his eyes one last time. He pulled his shoulders back and walked across the yard and toward the house.

His mother stood at the back door with a sour expression marring her once beautiful face.

"Your father said you'll do all the dishes tonight." She uncrossed her arms before turning around and letting the screen door shut behind her.

"Yes, ma'am." Steve opened the door back up to let himself inside the house.

His mom paused as Nick stood up to help. "No, Nick. He'll do it himself." She gave them both a warning look and then left the room.

Without a word, Nick gave an apologetic look to his big brother, which turned into a smile as soon as Steve smiled back at him. "It's okay, Nicky. You can go play your guitar if you want." Steve jutted his chin toward the stairs. "Go on."

Later, after Steve finished the dishes, he passed by the living room, where his parents were watching a TV show, and shuffled upstairs to his room. As soon as he was in his own room, he closed his door. His legs still raw and in pain, he traded his jeans for sweatpants, but first took time to bandage up a few of the more tender spots where the skin had broken. He staggered into the Jack and Jill bathroom he shared with his brother to relieve himself. When he pushed the handle down to flush the toilet, he paused to listen to the new music his brother was playing on his guitar.

He leaned against the doorframe to Nick's bedroom. "That sounds really good, Nicky. What is it?"

Nicky greeted him with his usual carefree smile. "Spanish guitar."

"I like it."

"Thanks."

Steve carefully worked his way to the bed, the pain from the lashings slowing his movements. Placing his hand on the bed to ease himself down and into the least uncomfortable position he could manage, he gave his brother his full attention.

Nicky set the guitar down and hugged his brother. "Are you okay, Stevie? Tell me you're okay."

Steve flinched at the sudden movement but gave in, wrapping his arms around his brother's shoulders to return the hug. "I'm fine, little brother. I promise!"

Steve shifted his position, pursing his lips to hide his pain as he gently straightened Nicky back upright. He reached to the other side of his bed and handed his brother his guitar. "Now, what were you just playing? I want to hear it again."

"Really?"

Steve laughed. "Really."

Like an open book, Nick wore his happiness on his face. He grabbed the CD case that was sitting on his pillow and held it up for Steve to see. "I checked this out from the library. Andres Segovia, or however you pronounce it." He flipped it over so he could read off the back. "Albeniz or, well, I don't really know how to pronounce the composer's name, either. The people on the classical radio station pronounce it like Albenith. Maybe I'll take Spanish next year when I start high school."

"Maybe." Steve cracked up as Nick talked a mile a minute, explaining everything he knew about the music. Then he positioned his fingers above the strings and strummed a few notes.

"Anyway, I'm not very good yet and don't even know it all, so I have to go really slow, but..."

"That's okay. I like to listen."

"Really?"

"You know I do," Steve assured him with a friendly shove to the shoulder. "In fact, I loved hearing you play at church today. So did Bryce. Now, come on. Let me hear you play."

Nick's fingers met the strings, and even a brand new song that Nick was still learning was amazing. Nick learned simply by playing the song over and over again in his CD player, then practicing a little bit at a time. He wove the notes together so beautifully that Steve forgot all about the supposed talk he and his dad had in the workshop after dinner.

Steve grabbed a pillow and leaned on his side while he listened to his brother play. His day was ending on a literal high note because Nick's music could make even the worst day a good day.

Chapter 9

At the Movies

20 MONTHS LATER, SUMMER 2005

Steve pulled at the Velcro strip to open his wallet to pay the cashier. He handed the large bucket of popcorn to Nick and two drinks to Danny. Once he received his change, he shoved his wallet back into his pocket and grabbed his own drink and candy.

"Come on," he said, encouraging Nick and Danny away from the counter. "We're in theater two."

"May the force be with us," Danny joked as they headed toward the entrance below the marquee with bright red lights announcing the latest Star Wars prequel was starting soon.

Nick laughed and tagged along next to him. "Oh wait, we forgot straws."

"I'll get them," Steve offered. "You guys go on in."

Steve had been working at a local warehouse since he graduated from high school a year ago, saving his money for when he started his Fire Academy Training after his birthday in a few weeks. He'd already passed the preliminary exams and medical screenings and was happy to celebrate the start of summer with his little brother, who wasn't so little anymore.

During his freshman year, Nick had shot up to five feet eight inches and was still growing. Steve finally peeked at six feet tall, a little taller than Danny, who was ready to start his junior year in the fall. Nick would be a sophomore.

Grabbing straws and a few napkins, Steve felt a shove in his shoulder. He turned and found himself face-to-face with Cabot Larszin.

"They let you out, huh?"

Steve nonchalantly unwrapped a straw and stuck it in his own drink, discarding the paper wrapper in the trash by the drink counter. "If you mean graduated, yeah."

Cabot was trailed by his usual entourage of Joshua and Samerlin, though he wasn't nearly as intimidating as he once was since Steve was just as tall, if not taller than he was.

"I see you're still hanging out with those two queers," he sneered. "Do you have to spend time with them since Marissa isn't around anymore?"

"She's in college." Steve didn't feel it necessary to also mention he and Marissa broke up nearly a year ago when she went off to the University of Nebraska.

Cabot tried again. "What would your parents say if they knew your brother was a queer?"

Only he didn't say queer. He said something much worse.

"They were looking pretty cozy while they were in line getting popcorn," Cabot continued.

Steve made a face and shook his head. He knew they were always careful when he took them to the movies. He scanned the immediate area to make sure no one was too close since he didn't want to create a scene, then kept his voice low as he leaned closer to Cabot. "Are you sure that's what you saw? Because I don't think it was."

Grateful to be there on a weekday rather than a far more crowded weekend, he confirmed Joshua and Samerlin were still fixing their drinks, then spoke right into Cabot's ear. "After all, just because two men are close to each other doesn't mean they're kissing. It could just be that one is talking to the other." Steve noisily licked his lips, taking advantage of Cabot's reaction. He released a slow exhale onto Cabot's neck.

Cabot shuddered but remained frozen in place.

"But from a certain angle, maybe even Josh and Sammy's angle, someone might think I'm kissing you." Steve pulled back just enough to make eye contact with Cabot, but in such a way that the casual observer might think that he and Cabot were having a romantic moment themselves.

"Would you like for *that* rumor to start spreading? Hmm?" His lips curled upward.

For a split second, Cabot's eyes went wide.

"So, no. You didn't see what you think you saw. Because if anything happens to my little brother." Steve glared at Cabot. "Anything at all. I will come after you." Steve thought back to the night of Nick and Danny's first kiss. "You see, it might not be a punch in the face. And it sure won't be *allegedly* cornering you in the school hallway, but I will come after you."

Cabot swallowed hard.

"You see, someone could make an anonymous call about the *threesome* you, Josh and Sam are having." Steve smirked.

"What? We're not..."

"Aren't you? I mean, how would you prove it?" Steve grinned as he spoke. "You three are *always* together."

Gathering the courage, readily available to him whenever his brother was involved, Steve walked away and disappeared into the theater. He clenched his shaking hands a few times while letting his eyes adjust during the preview playing on the big screen. He found his brother and Danny in their usual spot in the middle of the last row. With school ending the week before, there were still a fair amount of kids in there, so he slid his way through the second to last row, stopping in front of Nick and Danny, who were already holding hands.

Their hands snapped apart the moment they realized someone was watching.

"Don't scare me like that, Stevie."

Placing his knee on the seat in front of them, Steve handed them their straws, but kept his voice low as he spoke. "Be careful. Cabot, Josh, and Samarlin are here."

"Shit," Nick whisper-yelled. "I mean, shoot!"

A laugh escaped Steve's lips, but he was quickly shushed by the people sitting in front of him. He ignored them since the previews were still playing. He turned back to Nick and Danny. "I'll keep an eye out for them. I think I overheard Josh say something about seeing *The Longest Yard,* so hopefully they won't be in here." He reached down and grabbed a small handful of popcorn out of their bucket before sidestepping through to the end of the row.

"Thanks, Stevie."

"Yeah. Thanks, Steve," Danny added while his head turned left and right as if looking for impending danger.

True to his word, Steve had never once told anyone about Nick and Danny. While a theater concession ad started playing on the screen, he took his usual spot in the last seat of the back row so he could keep an eye on the place, effectively standing guard for his brother and his boyfriend so they could enjoy some time together as a couple. He opened his bag of Twizzlers as the lights turned dark, signaling the start of the movie, though Steve never cared about the movie. He just liked to get out of the house. Still, he would always pay enough attention to give off the impression he went for more than just his brother.

Chapter 10

Don't Get Into Trouble

"THAT WAS SO GOOD," NICK EXCLAIMED IN THE CAR AFTER Steve dropped Danny off. When he was excited, his entire face lit up. He was incapable of hiding his feelings.

Steve laughed. "Glad you liked it, Nicky."

"I so liked it," Nick gushed. "And that final lightsaber battle between Anakin and Obi-Wan? WHOA! So awesome!"

Steve kept laughing. At the next stoplight, he said, "Hey, Nicky. Open the glove box."

"What?"

"Just open it."

"Okay." Nick opened up the glove box and started rifling through the papers. "What am I looking for?"

"It's on top."

Nick tilted his head to one side. "The envelope?"

"Yeah. Open it up."

Nick opened it up and nearly bounced in his seat. "You got tickets?"

"Yep! Tomorrow's game against the Red Sox."

"That's awesome! I hope we win."

"Obviously! Thought I'd treat myself for my birthday before I start at the Fire Academy."

"I can't believe you're going to be twenty this weekend."

"And I can't believe you're going to be in the tenth grade this fall."

"It comes after ninth, Stevie," Nick said casually as he checked out every detail on the tickets.

Steve threw a sideways glance at his brother. "Good math skills you've got there." The light turned green, so he pulled into the intersection. "It's an afternoon game, so it'll just be me with my favorite brother."

"That's so great. I can't wait. Thanks!"

"You're welcome."

Steve took the corner onto their street only to discover his uncle's minivan had taken his usual parking space. He pulled up in front of the house and peered through the passenger-side window as he put the car in Park. "Wonder what Uncle Clint is doing here."

"Stevie," Nick said, his voice barely audible.

"It's alright, Nicky. We'll go in together, okay?"

"Okay."

"Maybe we should leave the tickets in the glove box."

Nick placed the envelope back inside and snapped the glove box shut.

"Ready?" Steve asked with an encouraging smile.

Nick smiled back. "Ready."

Walking into the house, they were met with the stares of their parents and their father's brother, Clint.

"Hi, Mom. Hi, Dad," Steve greeted them as they stepped into the living room. "Hi, Uncle Clint."

Uncle Clint sneered behind his dark brown glasses, greeting

them both with his usual contempt for children who are heard and not just seen. The fact that Steve wasn't a teenager anymore made no difference.

"Dinner's in the oven," their mom announced. "Clean up, then set the table. And take the trash out while you're at it."

"Yes, ma'am," they both responded on their way up to their rooms.

At the double vanity in their shared bathroom, they started washing their hands.

"How was the movie, boys?" Steve mimicked his mom's voice, pretending she actually cared. "It was great, Mom. Thanks for asking," Steve tilted his head back and forth as he lathered his hands. He passed the soap to Nick, who did the same in between giggles.

"Did you enjoy your time with your friends, Nick?" Nick mimicked their father's deep voice and creased his brow. His shoulders still shook with laughter.

"Yes, Dad. I had a great time." Nick stuck his hands under the running water. "Maybe we can invite my boyfriend over for dinner some...time..." his voice trailed off as he stared down at the water pouring out of the faucet. Nick paled.

"Nicky?"

"Stevie..." His breathing quickened as his face turned green. "I... I'm gonna be sick." Without turning off the faucet, he did an about-face and dropped to his knees in front of the toilet, where his body expelled his lunch and the popcorn he ate at the theater.

Steve turned the faucet off and grabbed a towel. He dampened it with water and got on his knees next to Nick, who had started dry heaving since he didn't take long to empty his stomach.

No wonder he was always slender.

Steve rubbed gentle circles on his back to help calm him. "Breathe, Nicky. Breathe. You're okay. You're okay."

Whether it was the flu or the fear of being sent away merely because he liked boys, Nick always seemed so helpless whenever he got sick, but Steve was always there. Nick was family, and Steve would take care of him, no matter what.

Well, Nick was the only family he actually loved.

Steve was nice to his parents because it was expected, but he loved his brother. Steve hated when Nick had this kind of reaction rooted in the deep fear of discovery. Their parents were supposed to love them, not make them so scared they became physically ill.

Clearly, they didn't get the memo.

Then there was Uncle Clint. God. He was ten times worse. Uncle Clint always railed against gays. He preached about wanting to help them, but if they couldn't be healed, he wanted to *eradicate* them.

"There's no excuse," he always said before diving into a long diatribe about how horrible and unworthy they all were. They just needed to *decide* to be straight, he said constantly.

Right. As if they could actually choose who and what they were.

They couldn't.

The worst part was, if their uncle had his choice, he'd try to beat the gay out of them.

Steve shuddered at the thought.

Asshole.

No doubt his uncle had probably already tried on other kids. Uncle Clint lived down by DeSoto with his own compound on a few hundred acres of land. He called it a religious retreat and campground, but Steve heard of other activities when his parents thought he wasn't awake.

Uncle Clint switched churches a while back. He felt the Episcopal church, where his parents still attended, was too open-minded and *inclusive*, a word he used with contempt.

With a damp towel, Steve gently wiped Nick's face, which was as pale as a sheet. "Just try to breathe, Nicky. You'll be okay. Here. Take the towel so I can fix you a cup of water."

Nick barely lifted his hand, so Steve pressed the towel in his brother's fingers. "Be right back."

Steve stood up and grabbed Nick's cup by his side of the sink. Sticking his finger under the faucet to make sure the water was cold, he filled it about half full, then sat back down on the floor. "Here you go. Take a couple of sips."

Nick wrapped his fingers around the cup, but Steve kept his own hand underneath it since he was unsure of Nick's own grip.

"I hate that you feel like this," Steve whispered as Nick handed the cup back. Steve set it on the floor and pulled his brother into a tight embrace when he heard sniffles. "I love you, little brother. And I'm always here for you."

Nick sniffed again. "It was such a good day."

"I know," Steve assured him. "And it'll be again tomorrow when we see the Cards play." He looked his brother in the eye. "Think you're done?"

When Nick nodded, he flushed the toilet and stood up. He held out his hands to help his brother up, pulling him back into another hug. When they pulled apart, he straightened his brother's hair and cupped his face.

"Come on. I'll be right there with you. They don't know anything, remember?"

"Are you sure?"

Steve wasn't sure why Uncle Clint was here, but he didn't need to stoke any more fear in his brother. Nick was already shaking. "Yeah. I'm sure."

"I hope he doesn't stay for dinner."

"I hope not, either." Nick's chest was heaving as he tried to catch his breath.

"Just take it easy. You'll be alright."

A car engine turned outside.

"You're strong, Nicky. Remember that. Hang on. I'm going to take a look outside." Steve hurried to his window in time to see his Uncle's mini-van backing out of the driveway. Nick stepped up beside him. Steve put his arm around his brother and pulled him close as the tension left both their bodies. "He's leaving."

He put his hands on Nick's shoulders and squeezed. "Look at me, Nick." When Nick still didn't make eye contact, Steve tried again. "Nicky?"

Nick finally raised his face to meet his brother's eyes.

"We'll go down together." Steve forced a smile to get his brother to cheer up enough so his parents wouldn't suspect anything. "After dinner, you can play your guitar for me while I start reading up on firefighter stuff, okay?"

"But you haven't started yet."

"Yeah, well. I want to get a heads-up on that stuff. We'll have a written test at the end, and I'm already nervous about it."

"You're nervous?"

"Hard to believe, huh?"

Color started returning to Nick's face.

"You're looking better."

"I feel a little better."

"Take a few more deep breaths, and then we'll go down. Together, a'ight?"

Nick pulled a face. "Ah-what?" He always called his brother out when he said that. If nothing else, he liked to give his big brother a hard time about it.

"Alright?" Steve scoffed but enunciated the word for his brother anyway.

Nick's face turned serious. "Don't get in trouble for me today, Stevie, please?"

"I promise."

Chapter 11

Don't Act Up

"Uncle Clint decided not to stay for dinner?" Steve asked while scooping some potatoes out of the bowl and dropping them on his plate. He tried not to sound too excited at his uncle's absence when they sat down to dinner.

"No," his father answered. "He has a lot of work to tend to."

"Oh. Okay." Steve couldn't bring himself to answer more than that.

"He's doing some wonderful things with those children," Steve's mom chimed in, delighted.

Steve tried to stay nonchalant despite his own curiosity to learn what his uncle was really doing. "With what children?"

"All those troubled children," she said. She took a moment to pat her lips with a cloth napkin. "They're lost or... or misguided, and he helps them find their way."

"Find their way?" Steve repeated.

"Yes."

Steve and Nick exchanged a look. "Where do they come from?"

"All around St. Louis. He helps bring God into their lives so they won't be so lost." Her smile lit up her face. "Isn't it wonderful?"

Steve grunted.

His father cleared his throat, so Steve jumped in with more. "Um, yes. That's really great." Steve and Nick both kept their heads down. "Are they mostly runaways?"

"Some, yes," his father answered while slowly cutting a piece of chicken. "Some are from parents whose children won't be good no matter how much they provide for them. Some children just aren't grateful."

His mom cast a warning glance at Nick and then at Steve. "They just need the Lord, and then the world opens up to them. I wish you could be more like him, Steven."

Steve tried not to shudder at the thought. "Oh, I don't know," Steve said in an attempt at humility. "I don't think I could make that much of a difference."

"Probably not," his dad added.

Shit!

Steve shot a brief, wide-eyed glance to Nick, who concentrated on his dinner. His dad wasn't supposed to agree.

His dad continued, "I don't hold out much hope that you'll be as great as my brother, Clint."

Steve choked on his food. "What?"

"Nick is still young enough to be molded into a good man."

"A good man?" Steve set his fork on his plate. "Wait. You... you're saying I'm not a good man?"

"What are you doing with your life but working a dead-end job? You can't even tell me the truth about where you were today?"

"What the..." Steve leaned forward. "We were at the movies. Weren't we, Nick?"

"Yeah," Nick croaked out.

"Then why weren't you sitting next to your brother?"

"We were in the back row."

His father set down his silverware.

Steve continued, "And I just got accepted to the St. Louis Fire

Academy, Dad. I'm gonna be a firefighter. That's not a dead-end job."

"It's not much of a job. Maybe you should start thinking about moving out on your own."

Nick's eyes flew wide open.

Steve's stomach dropped. "Moving out?"

His twentieth birthday was this week. He wasn't ready to move out on his own. He just used all his savings to fix up his car. Where would he go? He wouldn't leave without Nick, and Nick wasn't yet old enough to move out with him.

"Something to think about." His father took a sip of iced tea. "In the meantime, you won't be taking Nick to the movies with Danny ever again."

"How..."

His father turned smug."How did I know? Well, let's say I'm also told you had words with Cabot at the movie theater."

Fucking Crabbit.

Steve clenched his fists beneath the table in an attempt to remain calm. He'd been taking them to the movies for over a year, and this was the first time anything was mentioned.

Dammit!

Steve met his brother's eyes and forced a smile. Nick had stopped eating and appeared to be hanging on by a thread.

Hang in there, Nicky.

"How long have you been covering for your brother?"

Steve gave Nick a reassuring nod and took a few deep breaths in the silent hope his brother would follow suit.

"We've just been going to the movies, Dad. That's all."

"That's all, huh?"

"Yes."

"Well, I spoke to Danny's parents last week."

Last week?

"And they think it's best to move him to another school. In fact, they're sending him to live with his grandparents out in St. Joseph."

"What?" Nick finally spoke.

"St. Joseph is practically in Kansas," Steve exclaimed.

"Almost." His father picked up his fork and knife to cut another piece of the baked chicken. He shoved a large bit in his mouth, so their mother spoke up.

"You and your brother have been lying to us. The Bible says you should never bear false witness," she snapped. "It also says you should always honor your father and mother."

"But we–" Steve started, but his father's curt tone stopped him mid-sentence.

"Don't talk back to your mother."

"I didn't..."

"Maybe Clint can help Nick become a better man because you're clearly not the example he should follow." His father gave Nick a sideways glance, reeking of disappointment, and spoke directly to him. "Maybe he can toughen you up as well." He turned his attention back to his plate as if he hadn't just struck fear into the hearts of both sons.

Steve shot a look at his brother, but he didn't say a word. Nick's eyes widened, and his shoulders rose and fell with every breath.

Their father narrowed his eyes at Steve with a satisfied smirk. "Well, that's one way to keep you both in line, I suppose."

As much as he tried, Steve couldn't hide the fear in his heart. "Please don't send him there, Dad. Mom?" he whispered. "Please?"

"Stevie."

Steve cleared his throat. "It's okay, Nicky." From across the table, Steve assured his brother with a lot less confidence than he would have liked.

"Then maybe you'll not act out against your mother again."

Steve was met with a stern glare. "Yes, sir. I won't, sir."

"That's better." His father gave Nick a derisive look. "I guess we'll keep him here for now."

Steve's mouth turned dry, but he swallowed. "Thank you." Hard. "Sir."

"Provided you don't act up, that is."

"Provided I..."

His father arched a brow.

Steve did the only thing he could in defeat.

Accept it.

"Yes, sir."

<hr>

After he and Nick made it through that horrible dinner with their parents, forcing down food for which they no longer had an appetite, they cleaned the dishes and retreated into their rooms. Nick played the guitar while Steve read whatever he could about being a firefighter. Nick made it through dinner without a major incident, but he didn't begin to get back to being himself until his fingers touched his guitar strings. Steve knew that would help him cope. The music flowed while Nick worked through an acoustic version of a new song by Rob Thomas. Nick was definitely getting better at playing and singing at the same time.

He was still playing in his room when Steve closed his book and wished him goodnight. Summer vacation had just started, so Nick didn't have school, but Steve had to work a few hours in the morning before they went to the ballgame.

At least they had that. They could get away for a few hours and just be brothers and remove themselves from their worries. This summer would be rough for Nick. And once Steve started at the Fire Academy next week, he'd have a lot less time to watch out for him.

And without Danny in the picture, how would Nick fare? Nick

had that uncanny ability to retreat into himself, but it could be too much. He could go too far.

As he pulled back the covers and crawled into bed, Steve's worries weighed heavy on his mind. He was already a year out of high school and didn't know how much longer he could keep living in his parents' house. He was biding his time until he could get his own place, but Nick wouldn't be able to come with him, so he stayed. Nick wasn't even old enough to drive yet.

Steve's thoughts wandered to his parents.

No. He stayed because he could never leave Nick here alone.

Not with them.

Chapter 12

Disappointment

Summer 2005

"Thanks, Stevie!" Nick's face lit up as he accepted the framed picture. He held it with both hands as if it were something delicate, something to be revered.

Steve had taken his old digital camera to Busch Stadium when he and Nick watched the Cardinals trounce the Red Sox, nine to two.

"I thought you might like that." Steve sat next to his brother on the front stoop and gave him a little nudge with his shoulder. "I have the same picture in my room."

He smiled at the picture showing them both modeling the new Cardinals T-shirts they bought just before the ceremonial first pitch. The picture made a perfect souvenir for a great day at the ballpark. It also served to cheer Nick up. He'd been having a tough time the last few days after Danny was now living on the opposite side of the state.

The grin on his brother's face made it all worthwhile. They sat outside in the hot summer sun, talking about the next time they'd be able to go to a ballgame together. It was their favorite thing to do, even if they only got to do it two or three times a summer. Now that Steve was old enough, they could go without their parents, without any worries about what they talked about or who they saw.

Just as they were reliving one of the homers from the game, their mom stepped onto the front porch. "Steve?"

He turned to respond. "Yeah, Mom?"

An arched brow conveyed her disapproval at his response.

Shit.

"Yes, ma'am?" He stood up.

She thrust a piece of paper with some writing on it. A shopping list. "I need you to go to the store for a few things." She handed him some cash. "I need it for dinner, so go now."

"Yes, ma'am." He stuck the cash in his pocket. "Nicky, wanna come along?"

Nick shot up from where he sat, ready to tag along.

"I need Nick's help here."

Nick's smile dropped.

"Okay." Steve clapped his brother's shoulder. "I'll be back in a while." He read the list and stopped. The items on the list were basics. Sugar? Milk? Flour? Napkins? His mom never ran out of them. "Mom? I think we have most of these, don't we?"

"Just go, Steven. I think I know better than you what we need in the kitchen."

"Yes, ma'am."

"And pick those up at Markle's, not the chain store."

"Yes, ma'am." He did his best to hide his dubious expression as he walked toward his car. Markle's was farther away; but not wanting to make waves, he left.

Steve returned almost an hour later with his small bags of groceries and dropped them on the kitchen counter. The house was silent. He couldn't even hear music coming from Nick's room upstairs, so he called out. "Mom? Dad? Nicky?"

Figuring they were probably outside, he went about putting the groceries away. He stopped in his tracks the moment he opened the pantry. "What the..?"

He furrowed his brow and set the new package of napkins on top of existing napkins. "I knew we had some in there." He opened the refrigerator to find a nearly full gallon of milk inside. He placed the new gallon of milk his mom asked him to buy right next to it. Same with the flour and sugar.

After everything was in its place, he trotted up the stairs to Nick's room to find it empty.

"Nicky?" He called out, receiving no response. He stopped to listen... for anything.

Something wasn't right.

With his hand on the door frame, he gave his brother's room another scan to confirm his suspicions. The guitar was on Nick's bed, but it was turned upside down. Nick would never leave it with the strings facing down. Even Steve knew that much. Scanning the room, he stepped over to the bed and grabbed the guitar by the neck to right it. When he turned it over, his heart sank.

The strings on Nick's guitar had all been cut.

"What the..." Steve's shoulders sagged. "Oh, Nicky. What happened?"

Heavy footsteps and the sound of rattling keys drew near, prompting him to freeze in place. A few moments later, he faced his father's imposing figure, filling the doorway.

His father rattled his car keys another time or two, then dropped them in his pants pocket. "Your brother will be staying with your Uncle Clint the rest of the summer," he said without even making eye contact.

Steve's jaw flew open. He was so stunned that it took him a few attempts before he could make a sound. "Wha... what?" He shot up off the bed and chased after his father. "Why? Why is he with Uncle Clint?"

"Not now, Steven," his father said while loosening his tie.

"No." Steve grabbed his father's arm and stopped him. "That's not good enough! Why did you send him there?" Steve almost collided in the back of him when he stopped. "You promised you wouldn't send him there."

Enraged, his father practically growled at him. "I don't owe you any explanation. This is my house, and what I say goes."

"No."

"What?"

"I said, NO! YOU PROMISED!" Steve was no longer shorter than his father. In fact, he stood just a little taller, and thanks to working out with his cousin, Bryce, he was almost bigger. His father ate well, and it showed. Steve was in much better shape, especially because he was preparing to start at the St. Louis Fire Academy. "Why, Dad? Why did you send him there?"

"Because he's sick. He needs help. He needs healing."

"Sick?" Steve scoffed. "Healing?"

"He's not healthy, Steven."

"What?" Steve couldn't believe what he was hearing. "He's perfectly healthy."

His father shook his head and mumbled something under his breath. "No, Steven. He's not."

"Yes. He is." He started to exit Nick's bedroom but was blocked by his father. "I've got to go get him."

"No. Your mother and I have prayed and prayed for a solution, but your brother needs to be able to have a family, and he won't get it with boys!"

Steve's stomach sank at his father's words.

They knew. They fucking knew.

"What?"

"Your brother's a queer, Steven."

Like Cabot, his father didn't say queer.

"He's sick." His dad frowned. "Clint is going to heal him and then whip him into shape because I will not have a queer living under my roof." He turned a hard glare to Steve, poking him in the chest. "And you're no better because you've been helping him."

Steve backed up to keep his balance. "Helping him?"

"Yes. You knew, and you said nothing!"

Steve pulled his head back when spittle flew from his father's words. "There's nothing to say. There's nothing...wrong... with him, Dad."

His father scoffed. Then, not caring, his father laid into him. "You said nothing. YOU," he dragged out the word, "You even took him to the movies."

"Of course, I took him to the movies, Dad. We go to the movies all the time. I have a car, and Nick isn't old enough to drive yet."

"You encouraged him. With that... that BOY."

"With his friend, yes, but you seem to have gotten rid of him already."

His father waved him off as if it were no big deal. "Of course I did. His parents needed to know that their son was ruining mine."

"Ruining yours?" Steve was taken aback. "Danny wasn't ruining anything. He's a good kid."

"I already have one son who's a disappointment, Steven." He stepped away and then paused to speak over his shoulder. "I'll be damned if the other one is, too."

Chapter 13

I'll Go

SUMMER 2005

"Have you heard from Nick?" Steve asked his father after he rushed inside from mowing their lawn. "Is he back?" He wiped his face with the bottom of his sweat-soaked t-shirt after having had to finish with the push mower. "I saw Uncle Clint's car and thought–."

His father grunted.

It had been four weeks since Nick had been taken, and Steve still hadn't heard from him. He hadn't even heard anything about him. His parents usually gave him the silent treatment, which, normally, would have been fine.

This summer, it was anything but.

His relationship with them, if he could call it that, was never what he'd call great, but this summer was so much worse. Desperation to hear anything about his brother ate him alive. It hurt to live without his little brother around.

Attending the fire academy was his one shining light. It was a lot of hard work and a great distraction. He was doing well and getting a lot of positive feedback, something he was not accustomed to receiving at home.

Steve wished he could talk to his cousin, Bryce, about what was going on. Whenever he saw him at church, he could tell that Bryce knew something was going on. He had noticed Nick's absence but Steve couldn't talk to him since his parents constantly hovered.

Steve's dad was keeping a tight rein on his movements, and it was getting old pretty quick. When he wasn't at the academy learning his new job, his father gave him all sorts of extra work to do, even going so far as to volunteer Steve to help paint the interior of the church or make some minor repairs as needed just to keep him busy.

"Nick's getting the help he needs, Steven." His father's stern voice announced. "There will be no more talk of him from now on."

"No more..." Steve's voice trailed off when he received a glare from his father. "Yes, sir."

The following weekend, Bryce had a rare Saturday free where he didn't have to work the same day Steve was at the academy, so they met up to watch the Cardinals game.

At a pizzeria not far from Busch Stadium, Steve and Bryce sat down together for the first time since Nick was sent away. They snagged the last available booth at the end near the hallway to the restrooms but away from the noisy bar.

After ordering a sausage, onion, and pineapple pizza with extra cheese to eat while the Cards game played on all the large-screen TVs around the restaurant, Bryce took a sip of his Coke and spoke to his cousin for the first time in a long time without Steve's parents in the vicinity. He leaned forward and rested his arms on the table. "What happened to Nick, Steve? Where is he?"

Steve had always shared everything with his cousin. They were lifelong friends - best friends, and he hoped they'd stay that way, but he was worried about how revealing Nick's truth would go over.

Would Bryce shun Nick like his parents did? Or would he accept him as readily as Steve had?

With Nick having been sent away, he didn't have much of a choice.

Bryce prompted Steve again when he didn't respond. "Steve?"

Steve blinked a few times and focused on his cousin. He took a sip of his root beer and let out a slow exhale. He looked his cousin in the eye and let the truth out into the open. "They sent him to Uncle Clint."

Steve and Bryce's Grandpa Joe had three sons: Steve's Dad, Gregory; Bryce's Dad, David; and Clint, a religious zealot who had never shown an ounce of kindness as far as Steve could remember.

How Uncle David, the kindest and most open-minded of the three, became the only one who was like their Grandpa Joe, they'll never know. Bryce sure lucked out. Steve once thought his own Dad wasn't quite as bad as Uncle Clint, but now he wasn't so sure.

Bryce's jaw fell open. "Why the hell would they send him there?"

Steve shrugged. "Why do they send anyone there?"

"Clint mostly takes in runaways or problem kids," Bryce said. "Nick is neither."

Steve shook his head as if trying to wake up from a bad dream.

Bryce continued. "And from what my dad says, he doesn't treat them the best. He makes them work hard labor all day long, chopping wood, or clearing brush to create space for more cabins. Shit, sometimes, he has them stack the firewood next to a building one day, then move it all to the opposite side of the compound the next. He probably had about 200-300 acres or something like that, so that's no easy trek. The kids have to do their own cooking and their own cleaning. Dad hasn't been able to shut him down because of... of religious freedom or some bullshit like that. Uncle Clint calls it a church camp." Bryce spit out those last two words as if they were rancid.

Tears welled in Steve's eyes. He clenched and unclenched his fists atop the table, something that didn't go unnoticed by his cousin.

"Steve?"

"Yeah," Steve answered.

"What he does is really bad."

It took all of Steve's energy to admit his next words out loud. "My parents want to join him, to be honest."

"Seriously? Dad says the kids there are basically beaten into submission. It makes me sick."

"Yeah."

"Dad's even heard about solitary cabins where they put the worst offenders, whatever that means. We usually keep our distance from him. I don't think Dad's talked to him in a few years unless he absolutely had to."

The bell on the front door sounded, drawing their gaze to a raucous group of fans, all in Cardinals shirts, appearing at the bar to snag their seats before the ceremonial first pitch for today's game.

Bryce returned his attention to the conversation at hand. "So why did they send Nick there? He's not a problem."

"Depends on your definition of problem," Steve choked out.

Bryce furrowed his brow. "If he's not a runaway and not in trouble with the law, why? I mean, the only other kids Clint takes in are..."

A crease formed in Steve's brow, confirming what Bryce was probably thinking. Steve pressed his lips together.

"...are..."

"Are gay," Steve said, dropping his head into his hands.

"Shit."

They sat in silence for a long minute before Bryce spoke up again.

"I didn't know. I mean, it's not as if I've seen him anywhere but church since we graduated."

"I've known for a while, and, well, to say Dad wasn't happy is an understatement."

"No offense, but your dad can suck it."

Steve pressed his lips into a humorless smile.

"I can't get to him, Bryce." Steve leaned forward to vent his frustration so Bryce could still hear him in the noisy restaurant. He shook his head. "I've never gone this long without seeing him. I drove down there, but they wouldn't let me in. I need to know he's okay."

"If he's there, he's not okay."

Steve was about to say more but froze the moment Bryce's words hit his ears.

Nicky's not okay.

"I'm sorry," Bryce started. "I didn't mean..."

Steve splayed his fingers for a moment before pressing his fingertips against his temple. He squeezed his eyes shut for a few moments. When he opened them, he rested his elbows on the table and clasped his hands together as if pleading. "You've gotta help me, Bryce. I have to know how he is. Mom and Dad... they don't seem to care. They won't even let me ask about him anymore."

Bryce was taken aback. "What?"

"I don't get it either." Steve's eyes darted all around the booth. "I overheard them talking once, and Dad said that Uncle Clint would send him back in time for school to start, but he may have to go back if it doesn't take. Whatever *it* is. Nicky needs to know somebody cares about him."

Steve turned his gaze back to Bryce. His voice turned raspy. "We have to do something, Bryce. We have to."

Bryce closed his hands around Steve's, directing as earnest an expression as Steve had ever seen on him. "I'll go. And I'll burn that fucking place down if I have to."

Steve smiled for the first time in ages.

He wasn't alone.

Chapter 14

A Promise

A few hours later, Steve shook the hand of Lynn, a young woman in her early 20s. They stood in the parking lot of a fast food restaurant on the edge of town, the easiest place to meet up.

"Nice to meet you, Steve." About 5'6" with a long, black ponytail, she wore denim capris and a yellow cotton top. "Bryce tells me you want to check up on your friend?"

"My brother."

She nodded slowly.

"I'm not sure how you can help, though. I mean, I appreciate it, but aren't you studying to be a pastor or something?"

She laughed. "Not quite. Religious studies, sure, but it's a double major with criminology. I won't be able to do much except look around. I've heard of this camp. Bits and pieces, and none of it good. So if your brother is in there, I hope he's out soon."

Bryce laughed "She also volunteers at inner-city homeless shelters and doesn't take crap from anyone, so she and I can go in there."

"So, what's the plan?" Steve asked. "What do I need to do?"

"Lynn and I will go in and find Nick," Bryce said. "It's been a couple of years since I was there, but I remember it pretty well. Lynn's going to be able to ask all the right questions. I'll just tell Uncle Clint how I've always wanted to help or some shit like that, and just want to see how he's changed the place. She'll keep him distracted while I find Nick."

"Good. I'll help you with that."

Bryce stuck out his hand. "No, Steve. You can't go with us."

Steve stopped like he'd had the wind knocked out of him. "What?"

"We need you to wait here."

"But, I..." Steve was stopped short by Bryce's held-out hand.

"I know," Bryce said in a soft voice. "But you can't go with us, Steve. They've already seen you try to get to your brother. So, I'm sorry, you just can't."

Steve dropped his gaze and kicked at the ground. Reluctantly, he nodded. Uncle Clint would see right through them if Steve were to show up on his proverbial doorstep.

Lynn observed them in silence, sympathy showing on her face.

"It'll take us about fifteen to twenty minutes to get there, then give us an hour or two to look around, provided they don't kick us out first."

Steve exhaled. "I'll be here."

Bryce pulled him into a hug. "We'll be back soon." He gave a hard pat to Steve's shoulders, then slid into his car.

Steve's shoulders sagged as Lynn and Bryce drove away. It was an otherwise beautiful day. The sun was shining, ducking behind an occasional cloud while the birds sang and flittered about. A gentle breeze kept the summer heat to tolerable levels but, even if he could spend the day at the beach or watching his Cardinals play, nothing was going to improve Steve's mood until he received word about his brother. He parked in the back of the restaurant parking lot, only going inside to buy a quick soda and take a piss. The rest of the time, he paced back and forth next to his car, constantly checking his watch in a futile attempt to make time pass quicker.

Steve whipped around when a car pulled into the parking spot next to his, but it was just a group of boisterous high school kids talking about whatever movie they'd just watched.

His stomach churned at the thought of the last time he and Nick saw Star Wars. It was the last time he and Nick had seen Danny. He was such a good kid, Steve hoped he was doing well.

Another half hour went by before Bryce and Lynn finally pulled up. Steve rushed to the driver's side door, but their somber expressions stopped him dead in his tracks.

Chapter 15

One More Thing

Out of fear or worry, he wasn't sure which, Steve threw out a slew of rapid-fire questions at his cousin and Lynn while they clambered out of the car. "Did you see him? How is he? Did he ask about me? Did you tell him what I said?"

"Slow down, Steve." Bryce grabbed Steve by the shoulders in an attempt to calm him.

Steve's eyes welled with tears. "But did you see him?"

"Yeah," Bryce whispered. "We saw him."

Steve smiled and hugged his cousin. He started to pull back, but Bryce kept him in a tight hold while Lynn leaned against the car, focusing her attention on the two men.

"He's... not good," Bryce admitted sullenly.

"What do you mean?" Steve blinked back tears. "What do you mean, not good?"

Bryce hesitated before responding. "All the kids are forced into non-stop prayer. And the chores never end."

"What do you mean?"

"The kids have a set schedule every day which allows for no down time at all," Bryce explained. "The chores are based on stereotype. The boys do outdoor chores such as mowing the grass, chopping firewood, or washing the vans they use to transport the kids to and from the camp. The girls are forced to do all the cooking and cleaning."

Steve shook his head.

"And, for any LGBTQ kids, it's tougher," Lynn said.

Steve's head popped up. "Tougher? How?"

"They pair the boys and girls together," she explained. "They have bible study together and they even room together in the same cabin. Different beds because they're young, but within the same tiny room. They're not allowed to go anywhere without the other, and they're required to hold hands whenever they walk anywhere. The only exception is when they're carrying their food trays to their table or performing a chore. They say that it creates worth along with a sense of love for a union between a man and a woman."

Bryce dropped his hand on Steve's shoulder. "There's more. When they don't submit or answer as quickly as Uncle Clint and his acolytes think they should, they get punished, which can range from doing dishes by themselves to being beaten or sent to solitary. In Nick's case, his solitary is with a girl named Skye. They punish them both. They're not allowed to be separated except when taking showers or going to the bathroom. The only privacy they get for that is a small curtain that separates their bathroom from the beds. There's no door or even a full wall."

"Jesus."

"Yeah," Bryce said. "It gets worse."

Steve's body tensed as he braced himself for what came next.

"They're brainwashing them," Lynn spat out with disgust.

"She's right," Bryce agreed. "In addition to all the preaching about how evil and worthless they are," he said with undisguised contempt, "they gave each kid a small pocket knife and..." Bryce swallowed hard, unable to continue for a few moments. When he did, his voice cracked. "They told them to use it on their arms if they question anything... or still have what they called 'unsavory' thoughts. They force the kids to do it to themselves until they start doing it on their own." Bryce swallowed. "They told Lynn that the fewer cuts they have, the sooner they can be redeemed or some shit like that."

Tears spilled down Steve's face as he shook his head from side to side. "No... No..."

Bryce reached for Steve's arm. "He had cuts up and down his arm."

Steve shook his arm free, and his shoulders shook as he cried.

"It's not your fault, Steve." With a sigh, Bryce pulled him in for a warm embrace. "Uncle Clint is a sick fuck."

Lynn stepped forward. "I'm already reaching out to people I know to see what the process is to shut him down. Sadly, there are a lot of exemptions for..." she made air quotes, "*religious institutions.*"

"Tell me." Steve wiped his nose with the back of his hand as he sniffed. "Did you talk to him?"

"Yeah," Bryce said, "I told him everything you told me to, but... I don't know, Steve. I'm not sure how much got through."

"He's just a kid. All he wants is to study music." Steve sniffed. "I mean, who cares who he loves, right?" He lifted his gaze, but his voice was weaker. "Right?"

Bryce and Lynn both nodded in agreement but neither one spoke.

Steve ran his hands down his face and then through his short blond hair. He took another couple of minutes pacing, attempting to pull himself together.

It didn't work.

"How could they do this to kids?" He wiped his eyes with his palms and gave one last sniff before his eyes turned eerily dark. "How could they do this to Nicky?" A single glance at Bryce and Lynn caused them both to step back. He pointed toward the sky. "I swear to whatever fucking god is up there that I will do whatever it takes to get Nicky out from under our parents."

He stepped around his car and took a few steps into a narrow, grassy area that separated the parking lot of one fast-food restaurant from another. He opened his shaking hands, then clenched them tight to keep them still. Shaking his head from side to side, he mumbled to himself, running calculations in his head the whole time. He punched his fist into his other hand and turned around.

"Nicky will be fifteen in a few weeks. He'll be a sophomore. He can run away, and I'll take care of him."

"Can't do that," Lynn said, matter-of-factly. "He needs to be at least sixteen, and you'd want to take him to Illinois."

"What?" Steve snapped as he and Bryce both furrowed their brows and stared at her.

"Since you're over eighteen, it would be felony kidnapping to take him out of state, so he'd have to take the bus."

Met with blank stares, she huffed out a breath and explained. "Sixteen-year-olds can legally emancipate themselves from their parents if they move to another state and remain there for 90 days. He'd just have to get there on his own."

"What?" Steve folded his arms. "How?"

"Well, in Nick's case, he'd have to get away and prove he can provide for himself. It can be with help, but he would need to stay away and establish himself at another residence." She rolled her eyes. "He can open a bank account or something, but after 90 days, he can file for legal emancipation from his parents, and there's nothing they can do about it."

"That's over a year away."

"Better start planning."

"Wait," Bryce stood ramrod straight. "Don't you have grandparents or something up near Chicago?"

"No," Steve shook his head.

"No. No. No." Bryce pointed his finger at Steve. "On Aunt Gwen's side. Aren't your mom's parents up there? They're not here very often because they have a farm or something?"

Steve's eyes went wide. "Yeah. Up in Joliet or Mendota or someplace. But they're not our grandparents. They're our great aunt and uncle or something. Aunt Evelyn and Uncle Sam. Mom doesn't talk to them anymore, but they still send us Christmas presents every year. I haven't seen them in a few years, but they were always nice to us."

"Do you think they would help?"

"I don't know, but I can ask." Fierce determination crossed his face. "In the meantime, Bryce, I need your help with one more thing."

Chapter 16

Nicky

Lynn offered to keep in touch with Steve, but as she was still just a student, she couldn't make any promises. They all said their goodbyes before she got in her car and left.

Bryce turned to Steve. "What do you need?"

Steve took a few moments before speaking. "Two things, actually."

"Name it."

"First, I need to go to Carmen's Music Shop back in Halston and then to Knight's on Fifth Ave," he said, pulling his keys out of his pocket.

"Knight's?" Bryce gave his cousin a sideways glance. "Isn't that a tattoo shop?"

Steve rounded his car and opened the driver's side door. "Yep."

Bryce cocked his head to the side. "Okay." He opened his car door.

"And Bryce?"

Bryce turned back to Steve before getting into his car. "Yeah?"

"Thank you. For today." Steve cleared his throat. "I..."

Bryce nodded. "You're welcome." He smiled. "Let's go. I'll follow you there."

Steve's parents were at the family's furniture shop, so he was able to retrieve Nick's guitar from home without incident. And since they were about to close, the guitar tech at Carmen's said he'd get it restrung and tuned in time to pick it up the following day. Once that was taken care of, Steve and Bryce parked in front of the tattoo shop.

"So what's your plan?" Bryce asked.

"To support my brother," Steve said matter-of-factly.

Sitting in a chair toward the back of the shop, Steve's first arm was stenciled and ready for ink.

"Going for both wrists, huh?" Bryce asked from a chair opposite the tattoo artist.

"Yep." Steve winced the first time the needle hit the inside of his wrist. "One for me, one for Nicky."

After a while, words in a dark, navy blue were formed on the inside of his right forearm just below the wrist. *WHATEVER IT TAKES* was written out so Steve could read it simply by flipping his palm up. Direct below, he added the date: *17 JUN 2005*.

"What's that date?"

"It's the date they took Nicky away."

The tattoo and piercing-covered artist wiped off Steve's arm and spread something on it before wrapping it in a plastic wrap. After a couple of minutes, the artist traded places with Bryce to work on Steve's other wrist. He took a minute or two to stencil Steve's wrist, then started to work, this time with black ink.

"What's this, Steve?"

There were three words on Steve's right wrist: *DISAPPOINTMENT* followed by *NO HOPE* directly below.

He took a few moments to respond to his cousin. "It's what Dad said to me the day they took Nicky. It's what he called me." Steve winced again as the artist hit a tender spot. "I plan to prove him wrong."

Another month went by, and Steve stuck to his guns. He kept his head down and worked his butt off in the fire academy, loving every minute of it. Then he'd come home to a house filled with tension so thick you could cut it with a knife.

His parents became more standoffish than usual ever since they sent Nick away. It was almost as if they'd already written Steve off as a family member worth loving, not that he ever knew what parental love was like, having never truly experienced it. No sense in worrying about that now, he supposed. The way he saw it, they provided him with genetic material. Beyond that, he wanted nothing else to do with them except to maintain what little access he had to his brother.

As a result, he begrudgingly started paying them rent now that he was more than a year out of high school. They no longer acted like his parents, but like landlords, tolerating him as a tenant who did extra chores in exchange for a cheaper place to live. Sadly, Steve was already accustomed to being treated like the hired help, doing everything his father had neglected in years past. Odd since his dad had plenty of money to keep up the place, thanks to owning a successful furniture business.

Despite the family business, his father spent more and more time at prayer groups than at the office or at home. His mom spent more time away as well. Steve didn't mind. He used to enjoy going to his youth groups when he was younger, but for now, he liked when his parents were out of his hair. And when they were home, Steve kept his head down, doing his best to not provoke his father's rage, though when it reared its ugly head, he didn't give in to it, either.

As hard as he tried, it couldn't always be avoided. Within a week of tattooing the inside of his wrists, his father went into a rage about the evils of covering one's body with the devil's markings. He even recited Revelations 13:16 at dinner one night. Exasperated, Steve threw his hands up and agreed, raising the possibility of another tat on his forehead. His father practically spat out his dinner at the mere suggestion.

Steve had never seen his father's face turn so red. How he didn't have a coronary right then and there, the world will never know.

Though his father demanded answers, Steve refused to tell him the meaning behind the date and the words. He received punishment, of course, but since he was now taller than his dad, being marched to the workshop outback didn't carry the same results as when he was younger and smaller.

There was no belt.

There were no lashings.

No cuts.

No bruises.

No emasculation.

Steve had had enough, and this summer, things changed.

Instead, he received the monumental task of cleaning out and painting the entire workshop on the back of their property. For nearly four weeks during the hot summer, in between taking care of the lawn and any other odd jobs his dad could think of, the workshop became Steve's place of refuge, an escape from the parents who were glad to get him out of the house. It was also the main thing keeping his mind off the fact that his brother wasn't there.

A huge undertaking, he went through years and years' worth of boxes stacked as high as the ceiling in some corners. He split it up between keeping, donating to the church, and trashing. Little by little, he spent his weekends and evenings chipping away at the mess until the fruits of his labor began to take shape.

On an overcast Saturday morning, when his parents were out of town on a week-long deacon's retreat, Steve carried the last of the boxes destined for the landfill out to the garage. The forecast called for a steady rainfall that would turn into thunderstorms overnight, so he took the boxes as far as the garage so they wouldn't get soaked overnight. He could run them to the end of the driveway the next morning.

He dropped the last box onto the floor of the garage, giving it a push so it didn't get in the way of the garage door when it closed. He wiped the sweat off his forehead with his forearm and stared up at the cloudy sky.

The air was thick and warm, and a storm was definitely brewing but hadn't blown in yet. He wiped his mouth and strolled out to the edge of the driveway by the road. Their home was off the beaten path, on a county road surrounded by cornfields on all sides.

Already taller than Steve, the corn would be ready to be harvested soon, meaning they'd start seeing the combines working their way through the fields any day now. For some reason, he always found that sight comforting. As a young kid of thirteen and fourteen, he detassled corn for extra cash in the late summer before school started. The farmers markets were already beginning to sell this summer's sweet corn, some of the best food in the Midwest.

A pickup truck came into view on the horizon. The sun was high in the sky, and it shone in his eyes as he watched the vehicle approach. He held up his hand to block some of the brightness.

The truck slowed to a stop about a hundred yards down the road, just beyond the edge of their property line. Steve craned his neck to see what was happening on his sparsely-traveled road.

The driver got out and walked around to the passenger side and opened the door. The truck itself blocked his view, but after a minute or two, the driver returned to his side of the truck and climbed back in. He drove forward a few truck lengths, made a quick K-turn, and sped off in the opposite direction.

Something dark stood in contrast to the yellowing stalks of corn along the edge of the straight, long road. With the sun in his eyes, Steve squinted to see what it was.

"What the...?"

He quickly checked both directions and saw no other cars save the truck disappearing in the distance. To get a better look, he crossed the street and took a few steps in the direction of where the truck stopped.

"Is that?"

It was a person. And from a distance, they stumbled forward into the road, seemingly disoriented.

Steve increased his pace until he recognized the Halston High School T-shirt he had handed down to his brother last spring. It looked dirty, like it hadn't been washed for a week, and was worn the entire time.

"Oh, shit." He started running. "Oh, shit. NICKY!"

Nick stopped and turned toward his brother. He took one more step but stopped and stared, tilting his head to the side as Steve approached.

"NICKY!" Steve raced up and pulled his brother off the road and into his arms. "Oh my god. You're back."

"Stevie!" Nick hiccuped a couple of times and burst into tears as they both collapsed to the ground.

Steve's heart broke as his brother fell to his knees and bawled.

Chapter 17

Nothing at All

"Let it out, little brother," Steve rubbed circles on Nick's back. "Let it out."

While he cried, Nick leaned against Steve. He didn't wrap his arms around him. He didn't try to speak anything other than Steve's name. He just cried. And cried.

And cried.

"It's alright, Nicky. I'm here. You're safe now." Steve held him tight and offered soothing words. What else could he do? They must have known their parents weren't at home, but they just dropped him off in the middle of the road anyway. Thank god it was on the weekend and not when Steve was at the academy for the day.

A few raindrops landed on his forehead. Steve looked above him to find the clouds had darkened.

How fitting.

The storm was about to arrive.

Nicky still cried in his brother's arms. Holding onto his fifteen-year-old brother with one arm, Steve pulled his phone out of his pocket and flipped it open with the other. He pressed Bryce's speed dial and held it to his ear.

"Steve?"

"He's home. I need help."

"On my way."

He snapped his phone closed and stuck it back in his pocket. With both hands, he cupped Nick's face and forced a smile. "Nicky."

Nick still cried, but he made eye contact with his brother. More raindrops landed on their faces, but Nick didn't seem fazed by it at all.

"Nicky. We need to go inside, okay?"

With no change in expression, Nick responded with nothing more than a slow nod okay.

"Can you stand up?" Steve asked him the most basic of questions. One thing he'd already learned in the fire academy was that people trapped in a fire or accident or other traumatic experience would freeze up. Their brains wouldn't function in the same ways they would when everything was normal.

Nick gazed off into the distance as Steve helped him to stand. Steve knew Nick was like a zombie, moving only because someone told him to move, not because he actually wanted or felt the need to do it.

"Good, Nicky." Steve wrapped his arm around Nick to hold him up. "Think you can walk?"

Nick gave the slightest of nods. His step wasn't steady, but with Steve's help, he put one foot in front of the other and moved forward.

When they were across from the driveway, Steve looked both ways and urged Nick across the street.

The rainfall fell steadily now. Steve didn't care if they got wet, just that they eventually made it inside.

"Come on, Nicky. We're almost there, okay?"

Nicky still hadn't spoke as as they started up the driveway at a glacial pace. Nick's feet shuffled along as Steve urged him forward toward the garage. They were almost inside when a car pulled into the driveway.

"Jesus!" Bryce jumped out in a hurry and ran up to the other side of Nicky to help. "When did he get here?"

Nick flinched when Bryce grabbed hold of his arm to support him but didn't fight it at all.

"Right before I called you," Steve said as they reached the door inside. He turned the knob and pushed the door open. "They just dumped him on the side of the road. He was wandering into the road when I got to him."

Nick's crying softened to whimpers and sniffles as they pulled him inside the house.

"Let's get him upstairs," Bryce said. "I'll help you clean him up and get him into bed. He looks exhausted."

By the time they got Nicky inside the bathroom, it was pouring outside. A flash of lightning brightened the darkened sky, followed about ten seconds later by a loud rumbling of thunder.

"Storm's about ten miles out, Nicky," Steve said as they set him down on the toilet seat. For the most part, Nicky was despondent. He'd stopped crying, but his face was still tear-stained, and his nose ran. He'd occasionally sniff, but otherwise, snot ran down his lip. Steve grabbed a tissue and wiped his brother's nose.

He breathed out a low chuckle. "Never thought I'd have to take care of you like this, did you?" He tossed the tissue in the wastebasket by the toilet. "Don't worry. I'll do whatever it takes for you, little brother. You can trust me on that, okay?"

Nicky didn't respond, but his eyes followed every move Steve made.

Bryce leaned against the doorway. "How can I help, Steve?"

Steve rested his hand on Nick's forearm. Nick stiffened for a split second but didn't otherwise pull away.

"Can you get the first-aid kit out of the hall closet?"

"Sure."

"Then can you heat up some food for him?" Steve wiped his mouth with the back of his hand. "We... uh... should have some cans of chicken noodle soup in the pantry. He looks like he hasn't eaten in a while, so maybe we can get a little something in his stomach. But grab the Homestyle one with the small noodles. It's his favorite."

Bryce disappeared long enough to bring back the oversized first-aid kit and set it on the bathroom counter.

"I'll get that soup heated up."

"Take your time," Steve said while pulling Nick's shirt up and off him. "This may take a while."

"Holy shit," Bryce exclaimed.

"That son of a bitch," Steve muttered as he saw Nick's chest.

Nick was not muscular at all, but what little muscle he had on his chest was covered in bruises. He was way too skinny, too. The outline of his ribs was prominently on display on his slender body.

Steve slowly reached for one of Nick's bruises, causing his brother to flinch. He snapped his hand back. "I'm so sorry, Nicky."

Bryce dropped his hand to Steve's shoulder. "I'll get that soup now."

Steve could only nod in response.

"A'ight, Nicky." He forced a smile up to his brother. "We're going to get through this. Right now, let's start with getting you out of the rest of these clothes, okay? Then we can get you cleaned up."

"Ah-what?" Nicky whispered.

Nick's voice was so faint that Steve almost missed it. "There you are," he whispered back with his first genuine smile since seeing his brother on the side of the road.

Steve helped Nicky into the bathtub since he didn't trust him to be able to hold himself upright in a shower. With help, Nick went through the motions of cleaning himself. Steve washed Nick's hair, which probably hadn't felt a drop of shampoo in weeks..

Lightning flashed, and the thunder sounded only a few seconds later.

"Storm's almost here, Nicky."

Steve helped Nick dry off and then inspected his arms. They were covered with fresh cuts; some had opened from being cleaned. "What did they do to you, Nicky?" Steve said, more to himself than to his brother.

"They made me do it, Stevie."

Steve gulped down a sob in a vain attempt to appear strong. "I know they did." Steve disinfected Nick's arms and wrapped them up so they'd stay clean while they healed. He'd learned that much first aid in the academy, at least.

Except for bringing in a pair of sweats and a t-shirt, Bryce waited in Nick's bedroom while Steve took care of Nick in the bathroom. He also made sure Nick's bed was turned down and had extra pillows.

"Come on, Nicky." Steve settled him on his bed. Keeping his voice as calm as possible, Steve prompted his brother to eat a little something. "Think you can eat a little bit of soup?"

Nick nodded, which Steve and Bryce agreed was a good sign. When Nick ate about half the can of soup, they took that as a better sign. Steve placed a glass of water on the nightstand by Nick's bed. When he could barely keep his eyes open, Nick leaned over and rested his head on the pillow.

"Stevie?"

"Yeah, Nicky?"

"What did I do wrong?" Nick closed his eyes and drifted off to sleep before Steve answered.

"Nothing, little brother. Nothing at all."

Steve pulled the covers over his brother's shoulders and turned out the light. It was still raining outside, but the main storm had passed, relegating the thunder to a low rumble in the distance.

Steve made his way through the shared bathroom and into his

own bedroom, where Bryce waited. He pulled the door closed and leaned against it with a pronounced exhale.

Within seconds, tears ran down Steve's own face. His shoulders shook as he brought his hands to his face.

"Hey." Bryce jumped up and hurried to his cousin. He placed his hands on Steve's shoulders. "Hey."

Steve sniffed and wiped his eyes with his palms. "What?"

"He's out," Bryce tried to cheer him up. "He's home."

"Yeah," Steve sniffed. "But what's to keep them from sending him back?"

"I can't answer that," Bryce said. "We can only hope they don't."

Steve sniffed. "He asked me what he did wrong."

"He didn't do a damned thing wrong, Steve, and you know that."

"I really hate them, you know. Mom and Dad."

"Yeah," Bryce agreed. "I know."

Chapter 18

Shine is Lost

STEVE WOKE UP THE NEXT MORNING AND LIFTED HIS HEAD OFF the pillow he'd laid out on the floor next to Nick's bed. The last thing he wanted to do was let his brother out of his sight.

"Nicky?" Steve blinked a few times to wake up, then sat up on the floor. He turned to find his brother lying on his side with his eyes open. "Hey, Nicky."

Nick watched his brother with no change of expression.

On his knees, Steve worked his way to Nick's bed and smoothed his hair off his face. "You okay?"

"Hmm," Nick said. His eyes showed nothing. No curiosity. No sadness. No life.

"I'm going to head down and fix you some toast," Steve said as he stood. He curled his lips into a smile. "With raspberry jam, too."

Steve was happy to see Nick's lips twitch into what might have been a smile. He'd take any sign of life from his brother that he could get.

He came back up with the toast and jam that he promised. "Here you go, Nicky."

Nick took a few bites and, with a bit of prompting, finished the first piece of toast.

"Nicky."

Nick didn't respond while nibbling at the second piece of toast, but he met his brother's gaze.

"I have something for you." Steve stepped over to the wall, reached for Nick's acoustic guitar, and handed it to his brother. Nick froze with the toast halfway to his mouth. Without a word, he set it on the plate, wiped the crumbs off his fingers, and accepted the guitar Steve set in Nick's lap.

"I had it restrung for you," he said. Steve opened the top drawer of the nightstand and pulled out a small package. "I even picked up an extra set of strings. Just in case."

Nick strummed a few strings, paused to adjust the tuning, then strummed a few chords. With a bit more tuning, he seemed happy with what he heard. He ran through a classical melody. Maybe it was some J.S. Bach again? Steve didn't know for sure, but Nick was playing, and that's all that was important.

"They didn't let me have my music," Nick said while strumming a light melody. "They didn't let me have anything, and they said I might have to stay."

"You made it through. You were strong. You did what you had to do, and I'm so proud of you for that."

"I kept asking for you." He continued playing. "Bryce came once."

"He went to see you when they wouldn't let me in. I tried, Nicky. I really tried."

After a few minutes, Nick stopped playing and looked up at his brother. Steve was thrilled to be on the receiving end of Nick's first genuine smile since coming home.

Nick played for another couple of minutes before stopping and staring up at his brother. "Thanks, Stevie."

Steve returned the smile. "You're welcome."

The rest of the week went on the same way. Nick slowly came out of his shell. He spent a lot of time playing his guitar as if re-familiarizing himself with the concept of music. He even started playing some of his Spanish guitar again, which made Steve happy.

They were both grateful their parents were at that stupid retreat for the week so they wouldn't have to deal with them. In the meantime, Steve did everything he could to reassure Nick that he didn't do anything wrong and that he didn't deserve anything that had happened to him. It wasn't easy.

While they talked a little bit, Nick didn't say much about what happened while he was at their Uncle Clint's compound.

Steve only knew what Bryce had told him, but he didn't want to push Nick at all. He just knew it was bad. There were times when Nick would wake up from a nightmare. He called out the name Skye from time to time, but the one time Steve asked about it, Nick only referred to her as his friend and then went quiet.

Maybe someday he'd say more.

The thing Steve could do was reiterate to his brother the need to submit to their parents just to get through each day until they could move out on their own. "Keep your head down, and don't talk back to them," Steve smirked. "Let me do that."

They talked about their relatives up in Mendota, near Chicago, whom Steve called before Nick had returned. There wasn't a lot they could do right now, but when Nick was old enough to get away on his own, they'd happily take him in. He just had to get there.

With their eventual plans in place, Steve checked Nick's arms, which were healing nicely. Hopefully, they wouldn't leave obvious scars. The new school year was about to start, and Steve foresaw an awful lot of long-sleeved shirts in Nick's sophomore year.

Their parents returned home the following weekend with hardly a word. They didn't even acknowledge the fact that both of their sons were there when they brought their bags inside.

"Nick's home," Steve said as he met his parents by the car.

His father just grunted in response and headed into the house.

"He has clean clothes again," Steve spoke behind them as they all walked inside. "He's eating again, too," he added defiantly, in an effort to prove to his parents that his uncle mistreated their son. "In case you wonder how your younger son is doing."

Nick was sitting at the table, watching his parents walk right by on their way up the stairs.

"Are you going to say hello to him at least?" Steve yelled from the bottom of the stairs.

No response.

Nick met Steve's gaze but said nothing.

Chapter 19

Just Curious

DINNERS WERE QUIET FROM THAT POINT ON. CONVERSATIONS were kept to a minimum with the exception of the occasional 'pass the potatoes' or 'help your brother with the dishes'.

School started again, and even though Danny was gone, Nick could at least be with his other friends. He wasn't the same, though, and it killed Steve to think about what Uncle Clint might have done.

Steve still didn't push for more details. Nick opened up to Steve more than anyone else, but it wasn't with the same level of enthusiasm or optimism as before.

Nick lost his shine.

Music helped, and Nick's playing improved. He sought solace in the melodies he could strum out on his guitar. The songs he played were typically more melancholy in nature or far more intense than what he used to play. His ability to play the Spanish guitar music was incredible. Nick was talented, and for that, Steve was grateful.

Steve went on with his academy training, which was just about finished. His graduation day was on a weekend, so Nick was able to attend and see Steve in his dress uniform.

Their parents didn't attend.

Much to his parents' dismay, Nick was letting his hair grow out. It was one way he could push the limits. Otherwise, he never spoke up. Anytime he was addressed, it was *Yes, ma'am. No, sir.*

No inflection.

Nothing extra.

The worst part is that their parents seemed happy with that. Blind acceptance. Blind obedience. Too bad they were the ones who lacked sight. Steve hated that they didn't see that their wonderful and talented son wasn't the same.

After graduation, Steve started working at a fire station in the southwest corner of St. Louis, closest to where they lived in Halston. He worked 24-hour long shifts. One day on and two days off. It was a tough adjustment, but Steve was doing well, all things considered.

He took Nick to school on the days he was off, and Nick would take the bus on the other days since he wouldn't be old enough to drive the following school year when he became an upperclassman.

While Nick acquiesced to their parents, Steve fought with them. With each argument, Steve almost dared his father to try to take him out to the shed to beat him, but he never tried anymore. Instead, his father made non-physical threats, such as hinting that Steve should get his own place, but he hadn't yet forced it.

Steve was biding his time until then.

On days he wasn't at the station, Steve worked at his father's shop, helping with repairs along with shipping and receiving. It gave him the extra money he needed to save up to eventually get his own place. Being a firefighter didn't pay enough to get a place on his own, and with Bryce in college living in the dorms, they couldn't be roommates.

Steve's father was at the shop less and less and left the day-to-day management of the company to Les, who had been there since Steve and Nick's grandfather ran the business. He was an older guy who knew his stuff but often clashed with their father about how the place should be managed. Steve thought Les did a better job and was far more genuine with the customers than his dad, but he didn't have any say in the business. So, Steve kept his head down and did his work. The only reason he didn't look for another job is because of the days when Les was in charge.

Steve signed the bill of lading and then shook the hand of the driver delivering some new dinette sets. It was a cool, windy day in October, so once the driver pulled away from the dock, he shut the large bay door to keep the cold air outside the small warehouse.

Les walked up to him. "Is that everything, Steve?"

"Sure is. I think we're all set for a while. We just need to get these loaded when Wayne and Mike are back so we can get them delivered."

"Sure wish we could get you in here more than a few days a week," Les said, "but I know you've always wanted to be a firefighter. How's that going, by the way?"

"I'm learning the ropes. We had a big warehouse fire on my last shift that was pretty intense. Luckily, there were only minor injuries."

"Thank God for that!"

"No kidding," Steve agreed. "I'm back on tomorrow."

"I hope this winter is mild, so you guys don't have to be out in the cold so much."

"You and me, both."

Once Wayne and Mike were back on their way out for the final deliveries of the day, Steve swept out the loading area with a large push broom.

"Looks like everything is in order. We're set for the rest of the day. Deliveries are done. Why don't you head out early today and enjoy a little time off," Les said while perusing some paperwork on his way back to the shipping office. "Bryce is up front asking for you anyway."

"You should have told me Bryce was here," Steve laughed.

"I just did." Les gave Steve a friendly shove. "Now, get out of here."

Steve grabbed his coat off the back of the rolling chair by the shipping desk. "I'm gone. Thanks, Les!"

Steve shrugged on his coat while walking toward the front of the store to meet his waiting cousin. "Hey, Bryce." He shook Bryce's hand and exchanged a half hug.

"I'm starving," Bryce exclaimed while holding the door open. "Let's get some burgers."

Steve playfully bumped his cousin's arm. "I'm in the mood for wings."

"I'm good with that."

They both started down the street when Steve caught sight of two men in formal military uniforms walking past a storefront. They wore crisp navy blue trousers and dark navy jackets trimmed in red, covered in medals and colorful pins. Their uniforms were set off with chevrons on the sleeves, along with white belts and white hats. He nudged Bryce and stopped. "Hey, look at them."

"Look at who?"

Steve pointed across the street. "Those two guys in uniform. They look sharp."

Bryce's gaze followed where Steve's arm pointed, "Pretty sure they're Marines."

Steve looked both ways and started across the street. He was halfway across before Bryce noticed he'd left him.

Bryce jogged to catch up. "Hey! Wait up."

The two uniformed men entered the Marine recruiting office. Steve nudged Bryce again. "Let's go in."

"What?" Bryce stopped. "It's a recruiting office. You thinking of enlisting?"

Steve opened the door and walked in. "Nah. Just curious, that's all. Come on."

Chapter 20

What It Takes

Steve and Bryce entered the Marine recruiting office and were greeted by two men wearing navy trousers and tan shirts. They both sported the typical military high and tight haircut. Their sleeves contained chevrons as well and their chests were covered with a name tag and a few lines of multi-colored pins. Each man had a serious air about him that could probably turn on a dime if you ever crossed them. Steve had no doubt they knew about seventeen different ways to kill someone.

The men in the formal uniforms were nowhere to be seen, The two Marine recruiters shook Steve and Bryce's hands and invited them to sit down. Before he did, Steve toured a wall covered in pictures of men in full combat gear holding weapons and looking like nothing in the world could stop them.

How great would that be?

A picture on the far wall caught his eye, so he crossed the room for closer examination. It was a picture of what looked like a firefighting crew battling a fire on a runway caused by an airplane that seemed to have crashed, like a larger version of the car crashes he'd seen while serving as a St. Louis firefighter. The burning plane was surrounded by rescue vehicles and firefighters in the military equivalent of turnout gear, aiming a fire hose at the flames. A man was pointing at something beyond the confines of the picture. His mouth was open, so Steve figured he was probably the one in charge of the scene, their equivalent of the fire chief.

Steve couldn't tear his eyes away from the photo as his now-trained eyes were confirming everything they were doing in the scene as everything he'd do at a crash scene.

"I see something has grabbed your attention."

Steve turned to find one of the uniformed recruiters standing behind him.

How long had he been standing there?

"The Marines have the best rescue crews in the world," he explained. "These men are the first ones to run into danger and pull our men and women out of the flames if need be."

Steve kept staring at the picture on the wall. "So they're trained to fight fires instead of going into combat?"

"Oh no. Every single Marine you see in any of these pictures can pick up a weapon on a moment's notice and join their fellow Marines in combat. There's not a single one I wouldn't trust with my life."

Bryce stood back while Steve took in what the Marine recruiter was saying.

"Think you have what it takes to join the Marines? Think you could fight fires with the best of the best?"

"Oh, I know I could." Steve finally turned and met the Marine recruiter's gaze. "I'm already a firefighter."

The recruiter nodded in response, then proceeded to tell Steve about ARFF, which stood for Air Rescue and Fire Fighting. He explained how the men and women serving as Expeditionary Firefighting and Rescue Marines worked both on bases and on aircraft carriers with their emergency and rescue operations. The recruiter also told him how they go through the same basic training and learn the same combat techniques so they can join any fight, anywhere, anytime.

Bryce stood in the corner while Steve asked a slew of questions.

Bryce waved them off the offer of more information, but Steve left with several pamphlets. He was invited to a recruiting event the following week where he could learn more and ask additional questions of the active-duty Marines who would be in attendance.

On their way to get their burgers and wings, Bryce laughed as he made sure Steve didn't run into anyone walking in the opposite direction while he perused the pamphlets.

"Watch it, Steve. Wait until we sit down so you don't cause one of those accidents you take care of on the job."

"What?" Steve lifted his eyes in time to narrowly avoid walking into a light pole. "Oh yeah. Right."

Laughing, Bryce held the door open. "Come on, let's get a table."

***

They sat down and placed their orders for wings, Steve going for the Buffalo and habañero sauces. Bryce opted for the sweet BBQ and parmesan garlic. They split a double order of the teriyaki. Topping it off with a basket of fries and a couple of sodas, they leaned back in their seats to relax.

After the server returned with their drinks, Bryce leaned forward. "You seemed awfully interested in what that recruiter had to say in there."

"Well, yeah. Can you imagine working on an aircraft carrier?"

Bryce shook his head. "No. I'm perfectly happy staying on dry land."

"Even on land, they're like firefighters on steroids," Steve said, unable to contain his excitement. "Did you see those pictures in there?"

Bryce laughed. "You just became a firefighter. Are you already itching for something new?"

Steve took a drink of his root beer. "I don't know. It's just nice to dream, you know?" He rested his elbows on the table. "Can you imagine serving your nation doing the exact job you want to do?"

Bryce tilted his head in acknowledgment. "I suppose so."

"I mean, you could serve as a lawyer. What do they call it? JAG or something?"

"I'll have to get through law school first."

"Minor detail," Steve huffed out. "You're already on your way, so you'll get through it."

The server returned to their table with six baskets of wings, some celery stalks, and blue cheese and ranch dipping sauces.

They ate in relative silence, watching whatever game was on one of the large flat-screen TVs up on the walls.

"It's not like I can go, anyway," Steve finally said.

"Why not?"

"I can't leave Nick." Steve sucked the last hint of chicken off the bone and dropped it in one of the empty food baskets on the table. "You know that."

"Right. What if he gets to your great aunt and uncle's place up by Chicago?"

Steve grinned. "That would let me do it, but more importantly, it would get him somewhere safe."

Chapter 21

Tie the Knots

Summer 2006

Bryce's advice all those months ago still gnawed at Steve. *"You're allowed to make plans for yourself, you know."*

"No, I'm not," he said to himself, walking into the fire station for his next shift.

"What was that?" Chief Brayden said as he walked by Steve toward his office.

"Uh, nothing, Chief," Steve mumbled. "Good morning."

"Morning, Steve. I'll see you at the morning rundown."

"Yes, sir."

Steve stuffed his duffle bag into his locker and headed out for the morning meeting to get the day started. After greeting his fellow firefighters and paramedics, they took their places to go over the morning rundown.

Today, they planned to visit an elementary school to teach fire safety classes. They were always fun because kids asked the best questions. As the candidate, or newest member at the station, Steve always ended up being the person who had to be rescued, or rather, the person tied into the basket when they demonstrated how they saved people.

Naturally, the kids didn't know that since Lieutenant Starkman, or Starks, always announced how Steve had been good enough to volunteer.

"For the purpose of this demonstration, we're going to secure our patient in what we call a Stokes Basket." They showed the students a large basket, big enough to hold an adult, then had Steve lay down inside to the sound of snickers from his fellow firefighters. Naturally, the students couldn't hear those. Steve groaned when Starks invited some students to come over and check the knots and determine whether or not Steve was secure enough to move.

After Steve was pronounced safe from the fire, they taught the students how to tie some of the knots they used. Once a few kids got the hang of things, they opened them up to questions.

"Why are your lights red?" One child asked.

"Yeah," another kid chimed in. "Why aren't they purple?"

Just as Steve and the other firefighters started to answer, ten more students would yell out questions. Trying not to laugh at the wonderful curiosity of children, they did their best to answer all the questions in some semblance of order. With the younger kids, chaos reigned at least once during the presentation, and the teachers would have to step in. The best part was when the kids could walk up to the fire engine and turn on the sirens.

Letting them try on the hats and turnout coats was fun, too, because their adult-sized coats were always way too big for three and four-foot-tall kids who ultimately found themselves covered from head to toe.

As much as Steve loved fighting actual fires and pulling civilians out of danger, he had a blast working with the kids. Answering their questions and teaching them how to stay safe made his day and reminded him why he always wanted to be a firefighter.

Once they left the school to a large crowd of cheering students, they went about their day of cleaning and running drills to improve their response times for future fires. That night, they responded to a fire at an abandoned house not far from a strip mall in a rundown part of town.

Steve and Nick grew up out in the country in a conservative part of St. Louis County, but he wondered what it would be like to live in his own apartment or even his own house where he had actual neighbors rather than cornfields.

Someday.

"Good morning," Steve said the next morning, walking through the front door of his parent's house after he got off shift.

His father grunted a good morning in between reading a bunch of papers that looked like bills. His mom pointed at one paper and mumbled some sort of suggestion that his father didn't agree with. "No, but we can sell it."

"You're selling something?"

"Did I ask your opinion, Steven?"

"No, but what are you selling?"

"And we want you to start paying more rent," his father said. "We've talked about this before, and your mother and I have decided that you've lived off our good graces long enough. Either pay more rent or move out."

Pay more rent or move out? Steve needed to stay close to Nick, at least until he was old enough to emancipate himself from their parents. Steve was making his own money now, so paying rent wasn't entirely unfair, though it would slow down the amount he could save. Still, if it meant staying near Nick, he was okay with it.

"Sure. How much?"

"Your measly $100 isn't enough, so make it $200."

"Okay." Steve grabbed an apple and a bottle of water. "I'm heading upstairs for a bit before I head to the shop. I'm on at noon."

His father merely grunted in response as he turned his attention back to whatever they were discussing. Steve still didn't know what they were talking about, but they definitely arguing over the funds for something.

"Maybe we can use the insurance money," his father said to his mother.

"How much more do we have to pay him, Gregory?"

His mom's question was the last thing he heard before heading upstairs to his room. Who needed money from them? And why were they worried? They'd never worried about money as far as he knew.

Walking by his brother's room, he smiled at the picture of the two of them on Nick's nightstand. That day at the ballpark was a great day. Inside his own room, he changed into shorts and a T-shirt and tossed his other clothes into the hamper. He took a sip of water and set the bottle down on his nightstand next to the Marines pamphlets he'd read many times over and crawled under the covers. As he drifted off to sleep, he wondered what had his parents so worried and what was going to happen to him and his brother.

Chapter 22

We Don't Need You

FALL 2006

Steve pulled his car up to the curb in front of Halston High School and put his car into park. "I can't believe you're already starting your Junior year, Nicky."

"Did you ever think I'd make it to eleventh grade?"

Steve scoffed. "Of course, I did."

"I wish I didn't have to take math though," Nick said with a grimace. "I just can't get it."

"You made it through geometry last year, didn't you?"

"Yeah. Barely. I think I'll need therapy for a while to get over the trauma from doing proofs."

"Nah. They're just detective work. They're like solving a mystery."

"They were easy for you."

"Easy? Don't know where you get that idea. Bryce and I both struggled with that." Steve rolled his eyes. "We had to stay after school with Mr. Clements just to keep up and get a C."

"He helped me, too. This year, I have Algebra two / Trigonometry." Nick let out an exhausted sigh and tugged his long-sleeves down. "It'll be awful."

"Yeah well, it's a right of passage," Steve assured him. "We all have to suffer through."

"At least I have music class right after. I may even help with the school musical, assuming Mrs. Tapman will allow a guitar to infiltrate her orchestra."

Steve laughed. "She's heard you play before. There's no way she'll keep you out."

"I'll be sixteen in a few weeks, Stevie."

"Yeah. You will."

The first morning bell rang out.

"You've got to get in there. I'll be working at the shop today, so I'll get you when school is out."

"Okay." Nick opened his door and got out of the car. "Bye!"

Steve waved as Nick headed toward the front door with all the other students rushing to get inside.

***

Steve and Nick arrived home that afternoon to find a for sale sign in the front yard of their home.

"What the hell?"

"Stevie!"

"Oh come on, Nicky. Like you're not thinking the same thing." Steve put the car in park and leaned back in his seat while he collected his thoughts. "Let's go in."

Steve's heart sped up and his breathing quickened. He needed to be able to stay near his brother. If his parents were moving, he wouldn't be able to stay home with him.

He opened the door with a bit more force than intended, but he was beyond caring at this stage. "We're moving?" He called out as the storm door hit the wall. Nick was right on his heels, carrying his backpack.

Their father glanced up and scowled. He quickly schooled his features and responded as if nothing had happened. "We have company, Steven."

"So I see," Steve responded while narrowing his eyes at the man sitting at the table going through a stack of papers.

"This is the last thing I need, Gregory, then you and Gwen will be all set," the realtor said as he accepted the last paper they both signed. "I'll get the listing written up and online by the end of the week. We'll have someone from our office stop by tomorrow to take pictures. I see you keep your lawn in good shape so that'll help with curb appeal."

They all stood up and shook hands while Steve glared at his parents.

A much thinner version, but nearly as tall as his brother, Nick stood beside Steve in the kitchen without uttering a single word. They stood in silence as their parents showed the realtor out the door. As soon as the door closed, Steve broke the silence. "So, we're moving?"

His father stopped directly in front of him. "You're not, but we are as soon as the house sells."

"What the..." Steve exchanged a look with his brother. "What does that mean?"

"It means, your mother and I and..." he paused to sneer at Nick, "your pansy brother will be moving to DeSoto."

"DeSoto? What?"

"Clint has an extra cabin we can move into. I've hired someone to manage the shop, so we can concentrate our efforts on helping Clint with his ministry."

"Ministry? Is that what he calls it?"

"We'll be doing the Lord's work, Steven," his mother said. "Maybe someday you'll see that and be able to join us, even with the devil's markings on you."

Steve's heart raced as he barked out a laugh. "They're tattoos, Mom, not the devil's markings." He turned toward his father.

"Nick's in school. You can't just pull him out in the middle of the school year."

"He'll be homeschooled. Clint can teach him."

"Yeah. He did a real stellar job the last time he was there."

"Maybe he'll learn–"

"I'm not going!" Nick's loud voice silenced the room.

"You'll go where I tell you, boy," their father snapped at Nick.

"No."

Steve was both proud of and afraid for his brother. Their father had that look on his face like he did before he'd beaten Steve in the past. Being bigger than his father, Steve was no longer the target.

No. It was Nick, the skinny kid with a desire to make the world a better, more beautiful place through his music. He wasn't a fighter.

"No, boy. You'll learn how to be a man, take a wife, and take care of your family." With no warning, their father raised his hand and backhanded Nick in the face. Nick tumbled to the floor with a yelp.

Steve lunged forward and shoved his father against the wall. He pulled his fist back, ready to strike. "You will never hit my brother again, old man, do you understand me? If you want a fight, you fight me."

"How dare you threaten your father, Steven."

Steve turned his glare to his mother. "Oh now you care when someone threatens violence in this house? I've seen bruises on you before, too, Mom. Don't think I haven't."

She at least had the decency to appear sheepish and look away.

Steve shoved his father against the wall again then stepped back. He received a glare in return before he helped Nick up to his feet. "Are you okay, Nicky?"

Their dad cleared his throat. "Looks like I've made you a man, at least. Too bad your brother isn't as worthy. It's not right for him to like boys."

"It's not right for you to hit your sons," Steve said.

"Your father's right, Steven. It's not natural," their mother chimed in again.

"It's who he is, Dad. There's nothing wrong with him, Mom. He's my brother,and I'll always look out for him."

"If you looked out for him, you'd teach him how to be with a girl so he can get married and have a family."

"But that's not who he is." Steve grabbed a towel and dampened it with a bit of water from the kitchen sink. "It's okay, Nicky. This may sting a bit." He dabbed at the blood on Nick's mouth.

With tears welling in his eyes, Nick winced a bit as Steve cleaned the blood off his lips.

"There. It's not so bad," Steve said softly while inspecting his brother's face. He grabbed a few ice cubes and placed them inside the towel for Nick to use as an ice pack. "Here. Hold this against your mouth. It'll help."

He turned his attention back to his dad, making sure his body was between Nick and his parents. "Nick will live with me. I'll take care of him. If we won't be living here anymore, he can stay with me."

Their father scoffed. "Good luck with that on just your firefighter pay."

"What?"

"I don't think the new manager of my store will want to employ people who encourage such aberrant behavior. If only your brother would do as God commands. You may be a man, but you're a lost cause, Steven." He grunts. "Looks like Nick is, too."

"He's never been a lost cause. He's just a kid." Steve grabbed Nick by the shoulders and raised his chin. "And we'll make it work. We don't need you."

"Don't need us, huh?"

"Fine. You're both out when the house sells."

"Fine."

The next day, Steve dropped Nick off at school and went to work at his father's furniture shop to find a work crew changing out the sign in front. He walked in and headed to the back to find Les packing up a box.

"What's going on, Les?"

"I've been let go, Steve. Turns out there are new managers."

"New managers?" Then it hit him. "Dad said something yesterday about hiring a new manager. They'd be a fool to let you go. You know more about this business than anyone. I don't get it."

"Of course, you don't." A familiar voice sounded behind them. "It means your family no longer manages the store. I run it now."

Steve turned around to see Ralph Larszin standing in the doorway. His stomach dropped. "You have got to be kidding me."

"It also means that you can pick up your last paycheck next week. You've worked your last day here."

Cabot showed up behind his father. Ralph put his arm around Cabot's shoulder. "Cabot will be taking care of shipping now."

Les shook his head. "I'm sorry, Steve."

"Not your fault, Les. I wish I weren't surprised."

Steve scanned the restaurant full of fans in St. Louis Blues jerseys before he looked back at his cousin. "We haven't had any showings yet, so I hope that means we can at least make it to Nick's sixteenth birthday next weekend before it sells."

Bryce met Steve's gaze from across the table. He refrained from speaking as the server dropped off their pizza and drinks. "I talked to Dad. We've got the guest room all set up for one of you. The other can sleep on the couch until you figure things out. Either way, you're welcome to start bringing clothes and such over."

"Thanks, Bryce," Steve said. "I really appreciate what you guys are doing for us."

"You're family, Steve. There's no question. We have the room, and I think Dad likes to stick it to Uncle Greg a little bit, too. They've never gotten along," Bryce admitted. "Have you talked to your aunt and uncle up in Mendota?"

"Yeah," he said, taking a gulp of his root beer. "Nick is scared, but they're ready to take him in as soon as he's able to get up there." Steve laughed. "They've even talked to some friends about enrolling him in school, though I know they won't be disappointed in getting extra help around their farm on the weekends."

Steve took a slice of pizza and took a large bite. After he swallowed, he took another swig of his drink and continued. "Uncle Sam told me that he and Aunt Evelyn were disgusted with Mom and Dad." He laughed. "He said that they may be a couple of country bumpkins with a farm but family is family. They don't care about Nick. Well, they care. Obviously. But they don't care that he's gay. Aunt Evelyn said she can't wait to see the man the delightful boy has become."

Bryce laughed. "Delightful boy, huh?"

Steve joined in the laughter. "Yeah."

Bryce smirked. "And how did she describe you?"

"Uh..." Steve hedged a bit, but breathed out a laugh, thinking back to his childhood. "Not so delightful, but I think the word handsome came up a time or two."

They shared a conspiratorial smile.

"I'll be honest, Steve," Bryce said, turning serious. "I hate to see you both go, but I get it. And I support you both 100%. You need to get away from your parents. You need a chance to live without being in constant fear that something awful will happen."

Steve nodded. "Thanks, Bryce. I've barely been out of Missouri before and now I'm talking of heading up to Chicago."

"Well, Mendota isn't quite Chicago."

"True, but it's much closer than where we are now."

"You know... they'll have Cubs fans up there."

Steve pulled at his shirt. "Don't worry. I fully intend to take my Cardinals gear with me."

"Good. Make sure our guys are well-represented up there."

"Absolutely!"

They spent a few minutes eating in silence. Bryce glanced up at one of the many large-screen TVs on the wall to catch the Blues' left winger shoot the puck in the net. "Blues just scored."

Steve glanced up to watch the replay.

"Steve."

Steve dropped his gaze to give his full attention to his cousin.

"It's a good thing you're doing. Not easy, but it's a good thing. It's the right thing."

"Yeah." Steve started to take another bite of his pizza, but then thought better of it. He set it on his plate and grabbed his napkin to wipe the sauce off his fingers. "I just hope Nick doesn't hate me for it."

"That'll never happen, Steve," Bryce promised. "Never."

Chapter 23

Conflagration

STEVE DROPPED HIS BAG INSIDE HIS LOCKER THEN HEADED OUT to the lounge. He'd already told his chief about the situation on the homefront and, fortunately, received his support.

"Hey, Steve," Starks tapped Steve's shoulder. "Chief needs to see you."

"Thanks." Steve headed to the chief's office. He was always nervous when Chief Brayden asked to see him, as if he were being called to the principal's office or something. He squeezed his hands a few times to control any shaking that typically accompanied his nerves.

He took a deep breath then knocked on the door frame. "You wanted to see me, Chief?"

The chief's smile put him at ease. "Yes. Come on in, Steve." Still seated, he motioned to the chairs in front of his desk. "Have a seat."

Steve sat down across from the chief, who was writing something on a piece of paper.

"I've made some calls, and it looks like there are a few stations outside of Chicago that have openings."

Steve leaned forward. "Oh yeah?"

"Yes. Chicago proper has several, but Naperville has a couple, and so do some other places, like Des Plaines, Schaumburg, Evanston, etc. Some of those are pretty far north. The closest one to you may be Joliet."

Steve turned his head to the side. "Isn't there a prison there?"

"Well sure, but you won't be in the prison."

"I sure hope not," Steve said with a laugh, a bit more at ease.

"I've put in a good word for you. You just need to decide where you want to be." The chief handed Steve a paper with some names and numbers on it. "Do you know when you'll move up there?"

"Not yet. Soon, though. I'm still working on getting guardianship for my brother since he's still a minor. He's old enough to emancipate himself from our parents after 90 days, but to get him out of the state... he needs to either be in my care, legally, or he needs to run away."

"Neither is an easy option."

"No," Steve agreed. "And Mom and Dad aren't making it easy on us, either. We'll file charges if we have to, but we don't have much of a recorded history at this stage. That's uh... not really the thing we ever wanted to advertise."

"Have you ever retaliated against your father?"

"Never." Steve shook his head again. "I've been tempted, but I've never hit my dad back." Steve leaned back in his seat. "I won't lie. There have been times when I wanted to. I even came close once, but I didn't follow through. Dad doesn't lash out as much anymore since I'm bigger than he is, but I can't imagine what he'd do to Nicky."

"That's a tough situation, to be sure," The chief admitted. "I don't envy you. You've always done good work here, so whatever you need, I've got your back."

"I appreciate that, Chief. Thanks," Steve said. "But you've already done more than I could ever ask of you."

A loud siren roused Steve from his nap on the couch at the station.

"Let's go, everybody," Starks called out to everyone in the lounge. "Let's do our jobs!"

Everybody jumped up and rushed to their respective spots by their trucks, pulled up their turnout pants, grabbed their turnout jackets and helmets and jumped into their seats. Both trucks and the ambulance were all pulling out with sirens blaring and lights flashing within a minute.

Steve's station wasn't far from the small town of Halston, where he lived with his parents and brother. Even though they were in St. Louis itself, they often responded to fires or paramedic calls just outside their area to create a little overlap and help the smaller fire stations in the vicinity.

Steve didn't catch the address of the emergency, just that it was a house fire. Looking out the window, the route they were taking seemed rather familiar. Steve turned around to talk to the Lieutenant in the front seat. "Hey, Starks," he called out. "Where are we headed?"

Starks gave him the address.

Steve's eyes widened and his stomach dropped. "Where?"

Starks repeated the address.

"Shit!" Steve's stomach churned.

"Steve, you've gone as white as a sheet. What's wrong?"

"That's my house!" Steve grabbed the lieutenant's shoulder. "THAT'S MY HOUSE! We've gotta hurry!"

"Keep your cool, Steve. We'll get there."

"Keep my cool? My family's there."

Starks turned serious. He grabbed Steve's wrist from his shoulder. "Breathe, Steve. Breathe, or I'll make you stand down."

"Stand down?"

"BREATHE, STEVE. CALM. DOWN."

The other men in the truck were watching intently. Carver spoke up first. "What's up, lieutenant?"

Then, Drake said, "Steve. You okay?"

The driver started down the road to Steve's house. The lieutenant turned to talk to the men in the ladder truck with him, then he said the same into the radio to the other truck and ambulance. "The fire's at Steve's house. Take care, men. This is for one of our own. Let's keep him safe."

"Always."

"You got it, Lieutenant."

"We'll be the second company on site. We do not control the scene. Do NOT go in until I give the word. Do you understand?"

"Yes."

"Steve. Do you understand?"

Steve's head was already at the fire. "I have to make sure Nick is safe."

The trucks arrived at the scene, and the men jumped out. Steve secured his gear and turned to the house.

"Fuck!" Steve couldn't believe what he saw.

The house was fully engulfed in flames. They could feel the heat from where they stood by the trucks. The house itself was already being reduced to rubble with flames stretching out of what remained of the windows. Even a few trees were on fire. Pieces of wood were strewn all over the lawn like matchsticks. And right after Steve scanned the scene from the front, the roof collapsed onto itself. The Halston Fire Department was already on the scene with hoses pointed toward the house, but at this stage, they could only prevent it from spreading. Nothing could be saved at this point.

"Cook!"

Steve turned toward his lieutenant, head tilted to the side, heartbroken. "Starks."

Starks pointed over there. "Get an update from the Chief."

Steve ran toward the chief who was already coordinating with the Halston fire chief already on the scene. "Did you get anyone out? Was everyone okay?"

"Get back to your truck, Cook," Chief Brayden commanded.

"Starks sent me," Steve replied. "Is my family alive? Are they okay?" Steve demanded again. "Are they okay?"

"Is your fam..." the Chief stopped speaking mid-sentence.

"I live here, Chief."

He turned to his Halston counterpart who gave them an update. "We took a woman with second-degree burns to the hospital."

Steve's heart was beating so hard, he felt his chest would burst. "What about..." His voice shook. "What about..."

The Halston chief exchanged a look with Chief. "We recovered one body out back and a kid made it outside. He's being treated now, but we think he was in the outbuilding when it caught. ETA on the second ambulance is four minutes."

Steve looked left and right. "The kid? Nicky? Where is he?" He grabbed Chief Brayden's arm. "Chief, I've gotta see him!"

The Halston chief called over one of his men and ordered him to take Steve to the kid they pulled out.

The man took Steve to the far end of the farthest truck, what seemed like miles away from the fire itself. He saw a soot-covered teenager sitting against the end of the ladder truck, coughing. A guitar was propped against the truck next to him.

"NICKY!"

Nick's head snapped around, and he jumped up to run toward his brother. "STEVIE!"

Steve ran up and pulled him into his arms. "Oh my god, Nicky. Are you okay? Are you hurt?" He backed away to inspect his brother. Nick had black soot all over his face and a few cuts, but he seemed otherwise unhurt. "How?"

Nick coughed. "I heard an explosion, Stevie. Then it was so hot."

Someone handed Steve a bottle of water. He twisted off the lid and handed it to his brother. "Here, Nicky. Sit back down and talk to me."

Nick took a long drink and then poured some on his face, allowing some of the black soon to drain off. "Mom and Dad were inside, arguing about something, so I took my guitar out to the workshop." He coughed some more.

Steve glanced toward the backyard to see the workshop his grandfather built that he'd fixed up, going up in flames. Two pairs of firefighters were starting up a hose to douse the flames.

"I was out there playing and then BOOM!" He splayed out his fingers and then opened his arms wide to emulate an explosion. "I grabbed my guitar, got out, and started running. Then, another explosion happened, and a big fire broke out in the workshop, so I ran to the street and crossed to the cornfield on the other side."

Despite the sun setting far in the horizon, Steve turned toward the cornfields across from their house. The corn had been long harvested already, but it seemed the safest option for someone scared out of their wits who was fleeing from an explosion.

"You did the right thing, Nicky. You did the right thing." He hugged his brother again. "I'm so glad you're alright."

"What about Mom and Dad?"

"They took Mom to the hospital." Steve swallowed. "I don't know about Dad," he lied. Technically, he didn't, but they found a body. Who else could it be?

Nick fell into another coughing fit as the second ambulance arrived on scene. "Let's get you checked out, okay?" He grabbed Nick's guitar and escorted him over to the ambulance so the paramedics could make sure he was okay.

They gave Nick some oxygen so he could help clear any excess smoke from his lungs. He coughed a little less as he breathed it in, but was still not breathing easily. Overall, he ended up with a few cuts and scrapes, and a cough that might last a few days. Otherwise, he was pretty lucky, all things considered.

Nick pulled the mask away from his mouth. "Stevie?"

"Yeah, Nicky?"

"Where are we going to go?"

Steve took in a deep breath and released it as a very slow exhale. "We'll live with Aunt Linda and Uncle David for a while. After that? We'll have to figure it out."

"Will I have to go back to Uncle Clint's?"

"No." Steve shook his head and turned to his brother. "We may be on our own, but we'll figure it out together, okay?"

Nick put the mask back against his face and dropped his chin to his chest in exhaustion. "Okay."

The sound of their house collapsing drew Steve's gaze. "You'll never go back to that place again, Nicky. I promise."

Chapter 24

Worst Betrayal

With Chief Brayden's blessing, Steve accompanied his brother to the hospital for further care by a doctor. The paramedics suggested taking Nick to Barnes-Jewish Hospital in St. Louis since his coughing wasn't letting up as much as they'd like. Steve appreciated their caution. Maybe Nick was more affected than he thought. Rather safe than sorry.

"Steve?" One of the emergency department nurses recognized him and called his name when he stepped through the sliding doors. "Are you okay?"

"It's my brother, Keisha," Steve answered as he followed behind the gurney his brother was on. He was in full turnout gear and awkwardly carried Nick's guitar as he followed.

Keisha instantly turned to his brother and received the rundown from the paramedics who described Nick's breathing. He was still wearing an oxygen mask, but his eyes darted all around in panic.

"I'm here, Nicky," Steve called out.

As a firefighter, Steve had been here several times, though once he got the paramedic certification he wanted to get, he'd probably see the inside of hospitals a lot more often. He'd already started shadowing the paramedic team to learn as much as he could, so he and the emergency department doctors and nurses were getting to know each other.

"Your name's Nick?" she asked.

"Yes," Nick answered, pulling back from her.

Don't worry, Nick," Keisha said as she took over Nick's treatment after the paramedics transferred him onto the gurney in the ER. "We're going to take good care of you." Nick was able to help shift himself over, which confirmed he was in decent shape, at least.

A pregnant nurse came in. "Hi, Steve."

Steve glanced in her direction but maintained his attention on his brother. "Hey, Lauren. Still with us, I see."

"Yeah." She rested one hand on her stomach but patted his arm with the other. "Got another six weeks to go." She gestured toward Nick. "Need some help, Keisha?" Before waiting for an answer, she cleaned her hands, donned some gloves, and started helping.

"What's with the guitar, Steve?" Keisha asked as she communicated Nick's vitals to Lauren.

"It's the only thing that didn't go up in flames at home."

She met his gaze with concern, then shifted her attention to Nick. "At home?"

Steve filled her in on what happened in Halston.

"I'm so sorry, Steve. We can put Nick's guitar behind our desk to keep it safe."

"I've got it," Lauren said. She took the guitar and carefully stored it behind the front desk with strict instructions for no one to harm it. She returned with an iPad. "Steve, can you help me out with his information, please?"

"Sure," he said. "Full name is Robert Nicholas Cook." He turned to her and spoke softly. "He's never been in a hospital before, Lauren. Our parents never took us to doctors."

Steve and Nick weren't inoculated against anything growing up. He didn't start receiving any vaccines until he joined the fire department and got actual medical benefits. He was able to get some for his brother, too. The ones that were free or relatively inexpensive anyway. He didn't want his brother to get sick because of their parents' neglect. Fortunately, neither he nor Nick had any reactions to any of the shots. Somehow, their immune systems welcomed them.

"They what?" She met his gaze and immediately nodded. "Got it. Any allergies?"

"I don't know." He closed his eyes for a moment. "I don't think so. Not to food, anyway, that I know of."

"It's okay, Steve. We'll take good care of him."

"I know you will." He grabbed his brother's hand to reassure him.

Nick was sitting up in the gurney, wide-eyed and panic-stricken. Keisha gave Nick assurances that he'd be fine. She raised the back so he would be more comfortable while breathing in the oxygen. "Your blood pressure is a bit elevated, but considering what you've just been through, it's perfectly normal."

She answered a few of Steve's questions and stuck around while a doctor performed a more thorough check. The doctor instructed Nick to continue his breathing treatments for a while to be on the safe side, and then he could be released.

"You're okay, Nicky," Steve said when the doctor and nurse stepped out of the trauma bay. "It's pretty scary in here, but they're all really good people. They're smart, and they know what they're doing. You can trust them. Especially Keisha. She's like a pitbull and won't let anyone hurt you."

Keisha gave a knowing glance and smirked. "Even doctors are afraid of me, so I'll keep you safe."

Nick pulled the mask away from his face long enough to whisper. "Thanks, Stevie."

"You're welcome." Steve tousled his brother's long hair, receiving a friendly glare in return. Steve knew Nick was probably still unsure about Keisha, but she would watch over him. "Hey, I'm gonna check on Mom, okay? They said she was brought here, too, but I think she might be hurt."

Nick's eyes started darting around as if their mom were about to walk through the sliding glass door.

Steve squeezed Nick on the shoulder. "Nicky, look at me. No one's going to hurt you in here, alright? I'm just going to check on her. I'll ask Keisha and Lauren to check in on you. You'll be fine."

"How's he doing, Cook?"

Steve was startled but turned to find two of his fellow firefighters in the doorway in his same full turnout gear. Steve took a deep breath, happy he wasn't entirely on his own. Except for Bryce, they'd never had anyone in their corner. His parents certainly never checked up on them. They'd only punish and reprimand them. The relief he felt washed over him, easing his own fear about what would happen next.

Chief Brayden appeared in the doorway and spoke up. "Your older brother was worried about you, kid." He walked into the room. "Looks like you're doing okay, all things considered."

Nick visibly relaxed and then nodded, though not without a few glances toward his brother. He had met Chief Brayden and the other firefighters on multiple occasions, so he was comfortable around them. As comfortable as he could be while wearing an oxygen mask and sitting in an emergency department hospital bed with two nurses doting on him.

"Don't crowd my patient too much, boys," Keisha's voice broke through from behind the men, who quickly cleared a path for her like the parting of the Red Sea.

"Just watching over him, Nurse."

She pursed her lips and gave the chief a disapproving look; then she smiled at Nick. "How are you doing, sweetie?"

Nick nodded in the affirmative.

Her smile never waned. "You be sure to let me know if you need me to shoo these boys out of here. I'll take care of them for you."

Now, it was Nick's turn to smile.

Steve lifted his gaze to his firefighting brethren. "Hey, Chief. Think you guys can watch over Nicky for me while I check on my mom? I haven't had a chance to see her yet."

"We'll take care of him, Cook," Starks spoke up with a mischievous smirk. "Maybe we'll even tell him a few stories about you while you're out."

The other men laughed at this and surrounded Nick's bed.

The Chief followed Steve out just as Starks started a story. "Did Steve ever tell you about the time he…"

Two police officers were standing by the nurse's station as Chief Brayden led Steve outside to a quiet place in the corridor by the vending machines. Seeing police officers in an emergency department wasn't in and of itself unusual, but Steve couldn't stop his eyes from following their movements.

"Steve," the chief said as he stood at the end of the hall.

Steve turned his attention back to his boss.

"Steve, I'm so sorry about what happened to your home, and I'm glad your brother is okay." He took a deep breath and continued. "I don't know much more about the body we found, but…"

"It's my dad, isn't it?" Steve asked in earnest, though his heart pounded away like a jackhammer.

"I don't know. But you should know…" the chief paused for a moment. "Chief Michaels started taking a look at the home, and it looks like it may have started in the laundry room."

"Laundry room? How?" Steve's brow furrowed. "Do you know how often I go in there to make sure the vents are cleaned out?"

The chief nodded. "And it may have been deliberately set."

"Deliberately?" Taking in the chief's words, Steve slowly nodded. "So, it was…" He didn't want to say the word.

"Arson, yes," Chief Brayden said. "Most likely. Michaels said they're going to have to do a full investigation."

"Shit."

"Do you think Nick–"

"NO!" Steve's eyes turned cold as he glared at his boss. "Don't you even think about suggesting..."

"I didn't think so, Steve, but..." He stopped himself and put his hand on Steve's shoulder. "I'm so sorry."

Steve blinked a few times. "Yeah. Well. I've gotta find Mom." He left the chief in the hallway and found Keisha again, who led him to his mother.

The policemen stood in the room, apparently asking his mother questions. She was being treated for first and second-degree burns on her arms and legs. Her face had some minor burns on it as well. The moment Steve walked into the room, she flew into a rage.

"YOU KILLED HIM!" She pointed to Steve. Her bloodshot eyes glared at her son as if he were the devil incarnate.

Stopping on a dime, Steve met the gaze of everyone in the trauma bay. "What?"

"MY HUSBAND IS DEAD BECAUSE OF YOU!"

"Dad's dead?" Steve swallowed. A part of him thought the dead person must be his dad, but to hear it confirmed was shocking.

A nurse grabbed his mom by her shoulders, struggling to keep her down. "Ma'am, please calm down. I don't want you to pull out your–"

"I don't care about these." His mom cut her off. "He's the reason we did this!"

"Reason you did what?" Unsure of what his mother was railing about, Steve stepped into the room.

"If it weren't for you, our son would be cured. You encouraged him. You made him what he was. YOU ARE THE SINNERS WHO SHOULD BE DEAD, NOT YOUR FATHER."

Steve's eyes widened at the accusation.

She clenched her teeth and scrunched her face. Her cheeks puffed full of air, and the moment she spoke, spittle flew through her teeth. "YOU have the devil's own marking on your body. YOU ARE EVIL!"

"What are you talking about, Mom?"

A doctor pushed him aside as the nurse and police officers held her down.

"He said it wouldn't go up until we were gone. We weren't supposed to be there when it happened. We weren't supposed to be there when it blew."

The doctor tapped a syringe and stuck it in the IV attached to her arm.

Her bandaged hand shook as she raised it one last time. "You were."

Chapter 25

In Shock

THE ROOM FELL EERILY SILENT AS HER EYES FLUTTERED closed and she fell back on the gurney. No one else spoke for the longest time.

They all shifted their gaze to Steve, who stared at his mother. She was in a deep sleep, but Steve couldn't move. A hand rested on Steve's shoulder. From a nurse, his chief, he didn't know. Not wanting to turn around, he could feel the weight of it, but could only stand by and listen to the sound of his own heartbeat after his mother admitted in front of everyone that she and her husband had tried to kill their own sons.

Steve knew they'd all heard it. Everyone in the emergency department. They had to have heard his mother screaming. Nurses, a doctor, two police officers, Chief Brayden, and every other firefighter on his shift who had come by the hospital to show their support.

It didn't even register with him that a police officer had already cuffed his mother to the railing on her hospital bed.

"We'll keep a uniformed officer posted outside her room," an officer said to the doctor and nurses inside the room.

Steve stood up straight. "Oh, shit," he exclaimed as he spun around. His panicked gaze met Chief Brayden's. "Nicky!"

He pushed his way through the crowd that had gathered. "Shit. Let me out!" They parted to let him through. He hurried to where his brother was being treated, only to find the rest of his firefighting crew standing outside while Keisha comforted his brother.

"Thank you," Steve whispered to her.

She spoke in a calm, controlled voice. "His heart rate spiked when she started yelling." To Steve, she mouthed a silent apology.

Of course. She'd heard it, too.

Inside the mostly quiet trauma bay, tears ran down Nick's face. Keisha leaned in and spoke softly. "Nick, your brother's here."

Nick turned his head in Steve's direction. The oxygen mask was still in place. Steve dropped his turnout jacket onto the floor and rushed to the gurney. "Oh, Nicky."

She backed away so Steve could take her place. He instantly wrapped his arms around his little brother and held him close. Nick responded in kind, clinging to Steve like the lifeline that he was.

A police officer stepped into the room, but Keisha instantly shooed him out.

"They can't be disturbed right now," the nurse said in a calm yet stern voice that was not to be questioned. She reached for the door handle.

"We need to ask them a few questions," the officer insisted.

"I don't care." She held up a hand when he started to protest and gave him a no-nonsense look that even doctors feared. "Whatever it is, Officer, it can wait."

Steve glanced up just as she closed the sliding glass door behind her, dampening the volume of their conversation but not blocking his view.

The officer finally yielded and backed away. It wouldn't last, but Steve appreciated Keisha now more than ever.

"They tried to kill us, Stevie." Nick's voice sounded weak in between the sniffles and residual coughs.

He wasn't wrong.

Steve's stomach churned at the thought, but he stared up at the ceiling, blinking a few times to keep his own tears at bay. His voice broke as he responded the only way he could.

Truthfully.

"Yeah, Nicky. They did."

They held each other and cried as the firefighters stood shoulder to shoulder with their backs to the glass to give them what little privacy they could in a busy emergency department. For whatever luck sent Nurse Keisha and his fellow firefighters into his world, Steve would be eternally grateful.

Nick sniffed and pulled back from his brother's embrace enough to look him in the eye. "What do we do now?"

"I don't know, little brother," Steve said honestly. "I don't know."

Chapter 26

Ends of the Earth

IMMEDIATELY AFTER THE FIRE, UNCLE DAVID AND AUNT Linda insisted they move in with them, having rearranged things so they could be together. It was a bit crowded, but Nick and Steve were able to share the basement.

The house was gone. Their possessions were all gone. Their grandfather's workshop in the back of their property was gone. It was a total loss, with everything reduced to ash.

All they had left were whatever Steve had with him on shift that day, Nick's guitar, and their lives.

Nick retreated into his music, hardly talking to anyone but Steve. He hadn't gone back to school since the fire, so they sent his homework assignments home to him once a week. Nick didn't make any effort to do the work, and Steve didn't have the heart to make him. Uncle David and Aunt Linda kept promising that he'd come around.

Steve added another date to the tattoos on his left arm. 07 *OCT* 2006. He already had plans to add more. His mother had been arrested for arson, murder, and conspiracy to commit murder. So much for celebrating the holidays this year.

The holidays. What a joke.

She was currently being held in police custody, awaiting a trial that would probably take place sometime in the spring.

***

Nick started to go back to school, and he was slowly getting caught up. It was tough, and it was going to take a miracle for him to salvage a few of his grades.

Steve was going to be twenty-two soon and needed to get his own place. He just didn't have the money. He and Nick would probably split their dad's life insurance payout if their mom ended up being convicted. It wouldn't be enough to set them up for life, but it would be enough to make a difference. For some reason, the insurance company didn't want to write a check to the person who caused the death in the first place. If the life insurance couldn't pass to their mom, then it would pass to Steve and Nick.

In the meantime, they had a roof over their heads. Steve pitched in wherever he could to help cover the extra expenses.

"You're family, Steve," Uncle David insisted. "Stay as long as you need. We have room, and you and Nick are always welcome here."

Still, Steve would buy groceries to help cut some of their expenses so he could feel like he was contributing. His fellow firefighters passed the boot around all the shifts at the fire station. A couple of neighboring stations did the same thing, donating clothes and money to help cover their expenses needed to replace everything they lost.

Steve wanted to leave and take his great-aunt and uncle up on their offer to take them in near Chicago, but needed to stay through the end of the school year. At least Nick didn't have to be afraid in Uncle David and Aunt Linda's house like he was with their parents. He wanted to leave, too, but even though their mom was in jail pending trial, she might regain custody of Nick pending the outcome of the trial. Guilty? Steve could take custody of his brother, but only if he could get his own place. Not guilty?

Well. Best not to think about that.

Steve visited his mom once, where she was being held. Her burns had mostly healed, except for a scar on her left cheek and arm. She promised him that she'd take Nick to her brother-in-law's camp in DeSoto as soon as she was out, and Steve would never see his brother again.

"I hope you rot in here, Mom," Steve sneered. "But if you don't, I swear I will go to the ends of the earth to keep him from you."

With a determined set to his shoulders, Steve walked away and never looked back, not even while she yelled obscenities at him.

A few months later, on his day off, Steve adjusted his collar to ward off the cold while walking down the street in the old part of downtown. Arriving at the door to the Marines recruiting office, he stomped the snow off of his boots and stepped inside. When he came here with Bryce, he was curious. Then, he came here to kill time before picking up his brother after school, but every couple of weeks since then, he returned for the possibilities. The reputation the U.S. Marines had as the world's best fighting force was second to none and Steve longed for a sense of purpose even stronger than what he had as a firefighter.

Simply put, the US Marines were the best, and he wanted to be a part of that.

"Good afternoon." The uniformed man recognized Steve from previous visits. He extended his hand in greeting. "Back with more questions?"

"Yes," Steve answered the recruiter and sat down. "Just one, really. How soon after enlisting would I leave for basic training?"

Chapter 27

No Remorse

The trial ran for six days. Steve, Nick, Uncle David, Aunt Linda, and Bryce were all there. Uncle David and Aunt Linda were both there for every minute of it. They listened to testimony about anything and everything: the forensics, their father's autopsy, and first responders on the scene, including the Halston fire chief and arson investigator.

They were joined by Steve, Nick, and Bryce after they each testified to establish their parents' history of abuse.

Steve testified about how their parents raised them. He testified about the *talks* he and his father frequently had out in their grandfather's workshop and how his mother did nothing to stop them.

When Nick testified about the day he was sent away, Steve almost lost his lunch. While he was on a fool's errand buying groceries they didn't need, their parents had driven Nick to a farm outside Halston. They abandoned him at a dilapidated old house surrounded by tall weeds. While wandering in the direction he thought would lead him home, two men drove up and forced him into the back of a van. He was taken to Uncle Clint's compound and was kept in a solitary cabin.

After Nick's testimony, Bryce was called to the stand to answer questions about the treatment Nick had received in that compound.

The look of abject horror on their Uncle David's face during their testimony made it obvious he had no idea what his two nephews had seen and experienced. Steve never told his aunt and uncle about what his parents had done and clearly Bryce hadn't said anything either.

Nick hadn't told anyone.

Closing statements were given on the sixth day of the trial. After five hours of deliberation, the jury found Gwendolyn Cook guilty on multiple charges: arson and second-degree murder among them. Steve assumed she must be grieving the loss of her husband, but throughout the entire trial, she never showed any remorse over what she and their father had tried to do to their sons. Despite their own parents' betrayal, Steve and Nick made no outward show of emotion either. Their father was dead and their mother would be going to prison for an extremely long time. The sources of their pain and fear were finally being removed from their lives.

Hands on both shoulders, Steve looked his brother in the eye in the now sparsely populated courtroom. "It's over, Nicky. We're free of them."

Nick glanced toward the door through which their mother had just been taken. "Good," he said in a quiet voice. Nearly the same height now, he returned his brother's gaze. "I can't stay here anymore, Stevie."

Steve pressed his lips together. "I know."

The prosecuting attorneys spoke a few words to them and shook Steve's hand. The judge and bailiff left the room, leaving just a few people in the spectator seats Uncle Clint glared as he started toward them. "It should never have come to this. They're already snooping around my retreat center. You two were–"

Uncle David cut him off. "You're right, Clinton. It shouldn't have come to this. Greg and Gwen should have loved and taken care of their family. Better leave now, before you're the one they have to testify against." He waited for Clint to leave the courtroom before turning back to Steve and Nick. He gave them both a hug. "I'm so sorry all this happened to you. I'm glad it's over."

Steve could only nod at first, but after a few moments, he lifted his chin. "We won't be staying here, Uncle David." He glanced over at Nick, who had remained silent throughout the trial. "We're going to head up to Chicago after the sentencing."

Uncle David took a few moments to take them both in. Recognizing the determination in their expressions, he nodded. "I understand. Whatever you need."

They stepped into the hallway outside the courtroom to continue their discussion.

"I've already contacted Aunt Evelyn and Uncle Sam."

"I thought you might. I've only seen them a couple of times, but they always struck me as good people." David smiled. "We'll hate to see you go, but it'll give you the fresh start you need."

"Uncle David, it's not..." Steve paused, worry plastered on his face. "I mean... we both appreciate everything you've done."

"I know you do." Uncle David placed a calming hand on Steve's shoulder and smiled at both of his nephews. "Steve, Nick, it's okay. I know you would do anything for us, especially Bryce and Marly. We'll always be here for you, alright? That'll never change."

Two weeks later, Steve and Nick declined to make a victim's statement at the sentencing, but the judge had no qualms about making his own thoughts known. He didn't take too kindly to a woman who tried to kill her own children. After a stern talking to, the judge sentenced her harshly: life in prison with the possibility of parole after 27 years.

In other words, Gwendolyn Cook would be at least 70 years old before she might breathe free air again.

The moment the judge announced the sentence, his mother started yelling and screaming at the judge, saying he would be damned to hell for going against God's wishes. After plenty of choice words for him, she turned her rage toward her sons. *You'll be damned* and *you'll never be worthy of love* were among the more memorable things that came out of her mouth. The judge pounded his gavel and called for order in the courtroom.

With his arm around Nick's shoulders, Steve remained stoic as his mother was forcibly removed from the courtroom in her prison garb, screaming at her two sons for being taken over by the devil. Nick just stared at the ground. Like at that trial, Nick never once attempted to make eye contact with their mom. He kept his eyes on the judge or the floor but never her.

Their Great-Aunt Evelyn and Uncle Sam had made the trip down for the sentencing as well, taking the opportunity to reacquaint themselves with Uncle David, Aunt Linda, Bryce, and Marly. They had only met prior to this at a few family occasions before cutting all ties with their niece, who was now headed for a long prison stay.

Most of their mother's side of the family had already cut off ties with her, limiting communication to birthday and Christmas cards for Steve and Nick but otherwise making no effort to interact with her and her husband.

Since Nick was still a minor, it had taken a lot of paperwork for him to be able to leave the state. Fortunately, it was all worked out by the sentencing. Steve didn't have a place of his own, but their great-aunt and uncle offered to take them both in, allowing an opportunity to get away from all the bad memories.

"Goodbye, Uncle David. Aunt Linda." Steve gave them both a warm embrace, receiving an extra tight hug from his aunt. "Thanks for everything."

"We love you both," Aunt Linda said as she gave Nick the same warm hug. "You boys take good care of each other."

"We will, Aunt Linda," Nick said, giving her one of his rare smiles. "I promise."

She leaned in and hugged Nick again. "Now, be careful when you're driving on the interstate. I've packed plenty of sandwiches and snacks for you, so you shouldn't have to stop except to fill up your tank."

Steve laughed. "We'll be just fine, Aunt Linda," he said. "It's only about four or five hours up to their place in Mendota. Aunt Evelyn has promised us a hot meal the moment we arrive." That tidbit of information about a warm meal seemed to put his aunt at ease.

"Well," she said with a forced smile. "Let us know when you arrive so we know you're safe."

"We will," Steve said.

They exchanged hugs with Marly and headed to the car with Bryce.

Bryce wrapped Nick in a tight hug. "Take care of yourself, Nick. And," he tilted his head in Steve's direction. "Take care of this guy. He may seem like he has his act together." Bryce was met with Steve's arched brow. "But he needs you just as much as you need him."

"I will, Bryce," Nick promised, returning his embrace. "I'll miss you."

Nick got into the car.

Steve pressed his lips together, then pulled his cousin into a tight hug. "I'm gonna miss you, too, Bryce."

"Yeah. Me, too." He pulled back. "You're doing the right thing, Steve. We all understand why you have to go. It's the best thing for both of you." He glanced through the door to see Nick waving at Marly again. "Have you told him your plans?"

"He's smart. I'm sure he has some idea, but I won't actually sign until the school year starts."

"I don't like where you'll probably go, but I understand."

"Have you told your parents?"

Bryce laughed. "Hell, no. They'd drive up to talk you out of it." He stuck his hands in his pockets. "I still want to talk you out of it, but I get it."

Steve kicked the gravel at his feet.

"None of that was on you. You did what you had to do for your brother, and you're doing that again now." Bryce dropped his arms. "You're doing the right thing. Evelyn and Sam seem like good people. Hell, they have a farm. You know Nick's going to love that. I can see him now." Bryce laughed and glanced at the guitar, carefully stowed in the back seat of Steve's car. "He'll probably sit on a bale of hay chewing on some straw, playing the classical guitar to whatever animals they have up there.

"Cows," Steve said. "They have cows."

"You're doing the right thing," Bryce repeated. He pulled Steve back into another hug. "And I'm gonna miss the hell out of you."

"I'm gonna miss you, too, Bryce."

Steve held his cousin for a few extra seconds, then opened the car door. With a final wave to his cousin and his family, he got in and started the car. He turned to his brother. "Ready, Nicky?"

"Yeah, Stevie." Nick waved as they backed out of the driveway. "I'm gonna miss them, too."

Chapter 28

A Warm Welcome

SPRING 2006 - MENDOTA, ILLINOIS

Their Great Uncle Sam and Great Aunt Evelyn Sullivan, or Aunt Evie as she insisted on being called, greeted Steve and Nick with warm hugs. They took them into the house and introduced them to some of their mom's cousins and their families. It was going to take Steve a while to remember all their names, but they were all friendly and welcomed him and Nick.

One cousin, a tall, clean-shaven man about the same age as their parents, was the town mayor. "I'm Boone Sullivan," he said by way of greeting with an outstretched hand. "As Mayor, let me be the first to officially welcome you to Mendota."

Some of the cousins started booing, startling Steve and Nick until another cousin said they were just calling out 'Boone'.

It was all a bit much to meet so many people. Steve had never been in the company of so many genuinely friendly people before. They grew up under the shadow of their parents, who would shoot them strict, disapproving glances anytime they looked like they were having too much fun with their youth group friends.

Or even their cousins.

Here, everyone was happy to be together and enjoy each other's company.

"Stop smothering them, everyone." Aunt Evie snapped Steve out of his daze and broke up the hugfest. "Let these boys relax a little bit before you start crowding them."

Aunt Evie pulled Boone closer. "Take them upstairs and show them to their room so they can get settled in before we all have dinner."

"Sure thing, Mom."

"And as their cousin, Boone," she called out as he started for the stairs. "Not as Mayor. No politicking up there."

"Yes, Mom," Boone rolled his eyes but smiled at his cousins. "Come on, boys. Let's go upstairs."

Steve was grateful Aunt Evie stepped in when she did. He was having a tough time taking it all in, so he knew Nick had to be overwhelmed.

Nick grabbed his guitar and clutched it tight as Boone led them up the stairs to the third level.

"This was the attic, but it used to be my brother's and my room. You'll want to run the fans when you sleep since the AC doesn't work too well up here. It gets kind of hot. Great in winter, but not the best in summer. That said, there's plenty of room for two."

Steve stepped into a large attic space. In one corner near the front of the house were a bunch of boxes and an old table or two. At the far end, the space had been laid out symmetrically, with one bed and one desk on each side. Area rugs covered the floor and blended in with the medium gray-painted walls. There was a full bathroom with a shower just off the stairs on one side and then a small living room area with a couch, cushioned chair, and a TV on the other. They even had a small refrigerator and cabinet for snacks.

In other words, it was just what they needed.

"We didn't know if you're into video games or not, so my kids hooked up a Playstation up here with a few games in case you needed some space to yourselves. We figured you'd probably want to stay together - at least at first. If you'd prefer separate rooms, we can make that happen." Boone laughed. "My younger brother and I went through a phase where we couldn't stand to share anything and," he pointed to some boards leaning up against the wall by the boxes. "We made a makeshift divider to give the appearance of separate rooms. The fridge is there because the stairs squeak. We'd always wake up our parents going down to the kitchen for snacks at night, so they put a small one up here so they could get a good night's sleep!"

"Dad," two teenage voices sounded out as what sounded like a herd of elephants rushed up the stairs. "We brought their stuff," they yelled out.

Boone laughed. "My kids, Arya and Blake," he made introductions as they set down Nick and Steve's belongings. "I think they're about your age, Nick. They're finishing up their freshman and sophomore years at Mendota High, so Blake will be a junior next fall like you."

Nick nodded, offering up a shy smile without saying anything. Aunt Evie and Uncle Sam knew, but Steve and Nick weren't planning on telling everyone that Nick was going to retake his junior year after missing so many days after the fire, their father's death, and the trial. He was having such a tough time adjusting to everything that he couldn't keep up with his homework. Best to start over in a new town.

"Go on downstairs, kids," Boone said to Arya and Blake.

As they disappeared, Boone headed for the stairs that led downstairs. He turned back. "I know you've been through a lot, so I hope you'll feel at home here. If you need anything, just say the word, and we'll do whatever we can to make things more pleasant for you. Anyway, dinner should be ready soon. We'll come get you if you haven't come down yet. I imagine you want a little downtime."

"Thanks," Steve said. He turned and released a long exhale.

Nick plopped down on one of the beds and scanned the room.

The accommodations weren't fancy or even overly spacious, but it was warm and comfortable. Uncle Sam and Aunt Evie made them both feel welcome, as welcome as two young men whose parents tried to kill them could be.

"It's not bad," Steve said, scanning the entire upstairs area.

"I'm glad you're here, Stevie."

"Me, too. I can't believe how everyone on Mom's side of the family is so nice," Steve said as he unpacked what few belongings he had. Packing had been a lot easier when all they collectively owned was Nick's guitar and some donated clothing from their church and fellow firefighters.

Nick didn't respond right away as he stared out the window. "They have a workshop, Stevie," he said. "Do you think they'll take us back there..."

Steve looked out the back window to see what Nick was staring at. They'd been told a little bit of what was on the farm when they'd first arrived but hadn't had a tour of all the outbuildings. Steve remembered that some of the farmhands lived out there during the planting and harvest seasons.

"Not a chance, Nicky," Steve assured him. "For starters, they're not like that. And second, Uncle Sam said that some of the farm hands lived on the property and rented rooms in the outbuildings." He tapped on the window and pointed. "See those guys going in and out? I'll bet they work for the farm. Wanna go down later and find out?"

Nick cast a worried glance at his guitar.

"Your guitar will be safe up here while we wander around. I bet we'll get a full tour tomorrow."

Steve and Nick returned downstairs and, for the first time, were truly getting to know some of their cousins on their mother's side. They'd heard about them in passing while growing up but had never met any of them in person.

Aunt Evie mentioned something about how they were actually first or second cousins once removed, which confused everyone in the room, resulting in a few moments of shrugging before they all broke out into laughter.

Still laughing herself, Aunt Evie, the family's self-proclaimed expert genealogist, waved them all off. "We're all family, and that's what matters."

"What about Ezra over there?" One of their younger cousins pointed to the middle-aged man leaning against the kitchen wall who laughed at being called out. "How does he fit in?"

Aunt Evie walked over and squeezed his shoulder with a smile.

Ezra had already been introduced as the foreman who had worked at their farm since he was a teenager himself.

"Ezra's been around here so long; he's as good as family. Anyone who says otherwise has to go through me and remember; I'm the one who feeds you all."

Ezra leaned in with a smile to give Evie a peck on the cheek. "And we'll never forget it!"

Chapter 29

Some Peace

STEVE SLEPT BETTER THAN HE HAD IN MONTHS, MAYBE YEARS, that first night at his great aunt and uncle's in Mendota. The old farmhouse cracked and creaked, especially when anyone climbed the stairs; but otherwise, he and Nick slept to the sounds of the fan and the croaking frogs outside.

Located more than an hour outside of Chicago, Mendota was actually a small town surrounded by rich farmland that was just beginning to turn green with sprouting corn and soybeans. Uncle Sam, Aunt Evie, and their youngest son and daughter-in-law ran the dairy farm and took care of all the livestock which included a handful of chickens and baby goats. Sam told Steve that Evie loved animals and he could never say no to her. It is how they ended up with an obnoxiously loud pair of donkeys.

In the back paddock, they had twenty or so alpacas, along with a pair of trained guard llamas. Steve never knew guard llamas existed, but he learned they could be a really nasty yet effective means of keeping unwanted critters away from the alpacas. The last of the animals, besides a plethora of cats and dogs, were a few horses, who lived in the barn with the other animals but were clearly pets.

Sam's oldest son, Chuck, ran the adjacent farm. It produced

corn, soybeans, hay, and pumpkins. According to his middle son, Boone, the farmer's festival in the fall was a big deal with all the families in the county. The whole family worked together for the fall pumpkin farm activities, which included a big corn maze and hayrides. They even brought out the horses for one weekend in late October so families could go on horse-drawn hayrides. They used the tractors for the other weekends. Sullivan's seasonal, pumpkin-flavored ice cream was the best and only available until it ran out.

After the first few weeks of living there, Steve eventually fell into a schedule. He worked at the local fire station full-time and then helped out on the farm where he could.

Nick was gun-shy, having been the subject of their parents' ire for so long, staying close to his brother when Steve wasn't working and deferring to Steve for most of the decision making. On days Steve was at work, Nick usually retreated into himself and stayed close to the animals he was learning to take care of.

The tension Steve and Nick grew up with living under the cruel hand of their father had always been high and was hard to shake when they moved up to Mendota. Despite the friendliness of the distant relatives they never before had a chance to know, Steve was friendly, but took a while to feel comfortable enough to open up to any of them.

Aunt Evie did her best to make them both feel welcome. "Good heavens," she would say. "You boys are so quiet."

While she was probably the best at coaxing their voices out of them, Nick would smile but hardly spoke. He let Steve speak for the both of them. Aunt Evie assured them that while they might feel overwhelmed at first, they'd eventually adjust to life on the farm.

One night, when Steve was helping to clean up after dinner, he watched Nick head out to the barn with his guitar in hand. When an arm fell on his shoulder, he turned to find a friendly face.

"He'll come around," Aunt Evie said.

Staring after his brother, he cleared his voice so it wouldn't crack. "He thinks everything that happened was his fault."

"I know." She rubbed circles on Steve's back. "None of this is his fault. None of this is your fault, either, sweetie."

"I don't know," he said. "Maybe if I didn't talk back as much. If I'd taken one more punishment for Nicky... I don't know. There's got to be something I could have done or said. Or..."

"No. You don't..."

Steve didn't stop. "Or maybe I could have seen it coming and prevented it. I could have gotten him out. He couldn't get away until he was sixteen, and I..."

"That's enough, young man." Aunt Evie stopped him with a hug. "None of this is your fault. There's nothing you could have done to change anything. Your parents took their own path. They made their own decisions. None of that is on you, and it's certainly not on your brother, either."

Steve stared at the floor after she loosened her arms. "Yeah."

"And you've done everything you could to make sure your brother is safe. More than a brother should have to do."

"He's my brother. Of course, I had to."

"Then, at least let us help you. You don't have to do it all on your own."

Steve met her gaze. The sheer warmth of her smile was so different from anything he'd ever known growing up.

"You're not alone."

"But what about when he starts school next month?" He took a shaky breath. "He'll always be the kid whose mom killed his dad... because she missed... us." He dropped his head on her shoulder and nearly melted into the loving arms of a mother figure who genuinely cared about him.

"You don't have to protect him anymore."

"Yes, I do." He pulled back to look her in the eye. "I just can't do it from here."

A crease formed on her brow as she studied him intently. "You're planning something, aren't you?"

"Yes," Steve confessed. "I just need to make sure he's taken care of first."

Nick worked with the farm foreman and some of his crew to take care of the animals. He was drawn to the animals from the start. They never had an ulterior motive. They just wanted to eat, be warm, make messes, and receive an occasional scratch behind the ears, which Nick was happy to give. More often than not, he would take his guitar out to the barn and play for them.

While Steve preferred metal or harder rock music, Nick was partial to classical guitar or alternative music. Still, he was always willing to play almost any song the crowd that gathered at the barn doors requested. As long as he heard the song once, he could play it for them. One night in early August, Steve got roped into helping to install a new door on the milking barn while the rest of the family and hands set up a large fire pit surrounded with bales of hay for seats. He planned to join them as soon as the new door was in. Steve didn't want to miss eating a few s'mores. In the distance, Nick was actually laughing, a sound Steve hadn't heard in... he didn't know how long.

The family knew Nick was gay and didn't care one bit. Turns out the farmhands didn't care either.

They became overly protective of Nick. They all went out of their way to teach him what they could about life on the farm.

One of the seasonal hands cozied up to Nick while he played. Seth was harmless, and Nick deserved to have actual friends his age, but Steve was sure there was something more going on between the two of them. They talked and laughed together the whole evening.

Regardless of their relationship status, seeing Nick come out of his shell was a beautiful thing.

Applause broke out around the bonfire when Nick stopped singing. He was getting so much better at playing and singing at the same time and was growing into a gorgeous tenor voice. A few of the farmhands discussed it with their girlfriends and concluded that Nick sounded like a teenage version of a cross between Patrick Wilson from the Phantom of the Opera movie and the singer Jason Mraz. Steve hadn't heard of either singer, so he took them at their word.

———

Later that summer, on a hot August morning, Steve arrived home from yet another uneventful shift at the fire station, something that seemed to be the norm in small-town Illinois. He was still getting to know all his fellow firefighters, who, like the men and women he worked with back in St. Louis, never tired of sharing stories from previous fires and rescues. Steve ate it all up, but he couldn't stop thinking about what it would be like to serve in the Marines. He wanted to wear the uniform and serve, though Aunt Evie still made the argument that, as a firefighter, he was already serving.

While in St. Louis, Steve started working toward his EMT certification with the goal of becoming a firefighter paramedic. He was just shy of completing it prior to moving to Illinois. Thanks to a few phone calls from his old fire chief, his new chief in Mendota helped get him restarted in Illinois. He had to take some extra exams to make sure he met all the Illinois requirements, but as of his most recent shift, they were all done.

Tired as usual after working at the station, he dropped his backpack in his room and rushed back downstairs to snag a few pieces of bacon from the plate Aunt Evie kept warm for him.

"Guess what?" he asked around a mouthful of bacon.

Aunt Evie dried her hands and hung the towel on the handle of the stove. "I don't know, but judging by your expression, it's got to be something good."

"I heard."

"You heard..." She stopped mid-sentence before squealing and capturing him in a tight embrace. She rocked back and forth, pulling Steve with her as she swayed. "You passed your exams?"

"Yep," Steve hugged her back and laughed at her reaction.

"Ohhhh, I'm so proud of you, Steve!" Still holding his arms, she turned her head and looked at him from the side, unable to contain her smile.

"Thanks!" He glanced out the kitchen's screen door. "Where's Nick?" He shoved another piece of bacon in his mouth. "I wanna tell him."

"Where do you think he is?"

"With the horses."

"He sure loves those old horses," she said with a laugh before giving a friendly pat on his upper arm. "I'm sure he's got them all fed and cleaned up."

"Saving the mucking for me, I bet."

"He's a smart one, but I'm sure he has the stalls all cleaned up by now, too. He takes such good care of them. Go on and say hello, then get back in here for the rest of your breakfast. I want to hear all about it." She shook her head. "We have a paramedic in the house!"

He snagged one last piece of bacon and grinned. "Yes, ma'am," he called on his way out the back door.

Steve rushed out of the house to the barn that held all the livestock, greeting the various hands along the way. He found Nick exactly where Aunt Evie said he'd be. As predicted, the horses' stalls were spotless. Nick had a bucket of cleaning tools, brushes, curry combs, hoof picks, and other tools Steve hadn't yet learned the names of. He leaned down to grab the bucket just as Steve entered the barn.

Nick's smile was wide as if he'd already just had the best day of his life despite it only being nine o'clock in the morning. "Hey, Stevie!" He carried the bucket over to a large sink in the corner of the barn and started rinsing off the tools.

Steve was never this excited. He was the calm kid, the serious kid. But today, he couldn't wait to tell his brother his news. "Nicky, guess what?"

Chapter 30

Your Own Dreams

Mendota, Illinois - September 2007

Steve helped a few of the hands hose out the dairy barn. The last of the cows had just worked their way out to the pasture when Steve cleaned the last of his row. He finished as his Uncle Sam approached with a wave.

"Hey, Steve. You have a minute?" he asked. "Come help me out with something. I'd like to talk to you."

Steve swallowed. "Uh, sure, Uncle Sam." He handed everything off to one of the other men and followed his uncle outside.

It was late September, and the sun was shining bright. The air was still warm enough to not need a jacket.

Uncle Sam slid open the door to the garage that held the heavier equipment and an old car or two that didn't run so well. Sam Sullivan loved cars and motorcycles. He motioned for Steve to follow him inside.

Thinking back to all the times his dad led him to his grandfather's workshop caused Steve to hesitate for a split second.

Uncle Sam offered up a comforting smile. "I figured we could work on my motorcycle while we talked."

Just that small bit of reassurance was all Steve needed to finally exhale and step inside.

Curious, Uncle Sam paused again. "What did he do to you…" He stopped himself and waved it off. "Nevermind. You don't need to tell me unless you want to. Come on back."

Steve followed his uncle past a tractor and a few cars, including his own, to the opposite side of the building. When they stopped, Uncle Sam turned with a mischievous grin on his face. "This is my baby."

He stood behind a motorcycle and placed his hand on the seat, caressing the leather. "It's a Harley Davidson FXR. Built in the early '80s before you were even born, I imagine. It's a sportier version of those clunky things they sold in the '70s. Great bikes, sure, but this was a lot more fun to ride." He pulled a chain overhead to illuminate the area. "Grab that toolbox on the workbench behind you, would you, please?"

Steve turned and did as he was asked, setting it down on the floor where he was told. His uncle scooted one of two creeper seats around for Steve to sit on while settling on one for himself. He grabbed a wrench and started working on something. Steve didn't know what.

Steve could change the oil in his car, but that was about it.

"Hand me that wrench on top." His uncle said.

 Steve handed it over.

"Nope, the other one."

Steve traded it out.

Uncle Sam kept working, occasionally asking Steve for different tools as he talked about the different Harley models he thought were the best. He answered some of Steve's questions along the way until they worked in silence for a bit.

"Whatcha thinkin' over there?" His Uncle asked after the silence went on for a bit. "While you answer, hand me that three-quarter-inch wrench to your left."

Steve handed it over and breathed out a smile. "This reminds me of when Grandpa was still alive."

"Your dad's pop, right?"

"Yeah. Grandpa Joe." Steve smiled at the memory. "He used to have this workshop out back where he'd make furniture to sell in his shop. Yeah. Dad turned the retail shop operations over to a friend of his. Don't know what'll happen to it now, but when I was a kid–"

Uncle Sam scoffed. "You may be old enough to have a beer now, but you're still a kid to me."

"Yeah, I guess."

Uncle Sam motioned for Steve to continue. "Sorry. Go on."

"But Grandpa would work on his furniture, some chair or a table or something, and he'd let me hang out. I really miss that, you know? I miss him."

"I remember meeting him at your parents' wedding. Good guy, as I recall."

"Yeah, he was."

Uncle Sam pieced something back together and started screwing it in place before moving on to another part of the motorcycle. "You know how to ride?"

Steve eyed the motorcycle from front to back like he'd eye a new car. "Nah, I don't. I've never even been on the back of one before."

"We'll have to change that. Uh... if you want to learn, that is."

"Yeah. I would. Thanks!"

"I've got this old Harley that we can finish fixing up for you to ride if you want. I hardly ever get back on the road these days...."

"You rode this?"

"I used to. My bones may ache and creak, but I'm not that ancient. I have some adventure left in me. I married Evie, didn't I?"

Steve couldn't help but laugh at his great-uncle's words.

"Yeah. This baby handled really well." He grunted as he tried to loosen something on the motorcycle. "Was a lot more comfortable to ride, too."

"You and Aunt Evie are really nice to us. She's especially nice to Nick. He needs that."

"She's got a soft spot for kids who have had to fight harder than most. Our foreman, Ezra? He was a little scrawny kid who slept in our barn for two weeks before we even knew he was there." He removed the gas tank and set it on the ground as he spoke. "Evie and I hadn't been married for more than five or six years. We took him in because he had nowhere to go." He rested his forearms on his knees and paused for a moment, as if thinking back to a time gone by. "The sheriff couldn't find any reports of missing kids. He called all around the country. Well, Ezra stayed with us while he looked into it. Unbeknownst to me, Evie had gone into town to gather the necessary paperwork to foster him. I came in one night after a long day, and she told me to sign it."

"Told you?" Steve laughed.

"Yeah. Told me." Sam chuckled. "As if I could ever say no to her or to that poor kid who just needed a few bites to eat and a roof over his head. I guess you can say we take in strays."

"Like us, huh?"

Uncle Sam scoffed with a wave. "However distant, you're family, but even if you weren't, you'd still be welcome here."

They resumed working in silence for a while until Uncle Sam spoke up again. "You're doing well by your brother, you know. He told me how you've always stuck up for him. He said he's able to stick up for himself now."

"He's never been allowed to be himself. Dad would never let him, and Mom did exactly what Dad told her to do." Steve took a deep breath. "He hit her, too, you know."

Uncle Sam set the wrench on the ground and wiped his fingers with an already greasy shop towel.

Steve continued. "She never spoke up, never spoke out. She only looked down on the two of us like we were some damned inconvenience or something."

Sam just listened.

"It was easier to just take whatever punishment he doled out than to try to fight it. The punishment would always come, anyway. Once I was taller than he was, he threatened to take it all out on Nick."

Uncle Sam muttered a profanity under his breath. "And that's how he kept you in line?"

"Yeah. What could I do? I had to toe the line without pissing him off too much and have him take it out on Nick or kick me out of the house... and then take everything out on Nick."

"I'm so sorry you had to live like that."

"Yeah. Sometimes I wonder, though, if I remind Nick of what life was like before we got here."

Uncle Sam picked his wrench back up and started tinkering on his bike again. "I don't think that's an issue, but I do know that Nick seems to like it here."

Steve breathed out a smile. "Yeah. He does."

"You can't ignore your own needs and dreams. I've seen those Marines pamphlets you try to hide."

"You have?"

Uncle Sam chuckled.

"What's so funny?"

"You're not the best at cleaning up after yourself, you know. You've left them out a couple of times."

"Oh, shit. I mean, shoot. I'm sorry."

"If you're old enough to consider the Marines, you're old enough to cuss." He wiped his hands on the towel again, then on his jeans. "You do good work here. So does Nick, for that matter."

"Thanks."

"So, when are you looking to enlist? We've already given you both our word. We'll take care of Nick no matter where you are. Your parents can no longer hurt him."

"Yeah." He stood up and rolled the seat back underneath the workbench.

"And they can no longer hurt you."

They put the tools away and covered up the motorcycle.

"You've got your own life to lead," his uncle said. "It's time you did that. Nick is safe here. He's happy. I'd appreciate it if you could stay through the farmer's market and Halloween if you could, but understand if you can't."

"I can do that."

"By the way, your ballgame has been rescheduled."

"What?"

"Cardinals vs. Cubs. The rainout? It's been rescheduled for Monday. That's Nick's birthday, right?"

"Yes. Uh... Yes. It is."

"Still have your tickets?"

"Yeah." Steve blew the air out of his cheeks. "Wow. I can't believe he'll be seventeen already."

Laughing, Uncle Sam patted Steve on his back, then pulled the chain to turn the light off. "I'll write a note getting him out of school for the day. I think you two will need the time alone to talk over some things."

Chapter 31

Not a Goodbye

"Finally!" an exasperated Steve exclaimed, his red Cardinals shirt standing out in a never-ending sea of blue Cubs jerseys. "I thought that inning would never end."

He offered a disparaging look at the scoreboard after four innings to see his Cardinals had just given up another four runs to their hosts, the Chicago Cubs. He scanned their section in the stands. He and Nick weren't the only discouraged Cardinals fans wearing disappointed expressions among the sea of exhilarated Cubs fans. "I can't believe they scored four runs on us. I mean, it's bad enough we were just swept by Arizona, but to give up four in one inning?" Steve stood up. "Want another hotdog?"

"Yeah," Nick answered as he followed his brother up to the concessions.

They got their hotdogs and another drink to take back to their seats. As they enjoyed their second round of food at the game, they watched the Cubs beat the crap out of their Cardinals.

"I'm getting pretty sick of Ramirez. If he scores one more run..."

Ramirez's bat hit the ball and sent it sailing into the outfield, where the Cardinals couldn't make a play to save their lives. The crowd went wild as more runners rounded the bases.

Nick started laughing.

Unamused, Steve stared at him. "What's so funny?"

Nick took a deep breath before he answered. "You are."

"I am?"

"Yeah. You're so into this game."

Steve extended his arms. "Well, of course I am. We won it all last year, and now we might not even make the playoffs."

Nick kept laughing, so much so that Steve couldn't help but join him.

"We're happy to go to the playoffs in your place," the guy sitting in front of them turned around to say.

"No, thanks. Besides, aren't you guys planning on going next year on the century mark?"

Ever an optimist, the man adjusted his blue Cubs hat and smiled back at Steve. "Hey. This could be our year. It could happen."

Steve shook his head and leaned into Nick. "So, how are you liking your new school so far?"

"It's okay."

"Just okay?"

"I don't like being the new kid."

"I can see that," Steve said as the inning ended. "How about the farm?"

"I like taking care of the animals." Nick's face lit up. "Ezra is going to show me how to hitch up the horses so I can drive the hayrides."

"That's great, Nicky."

They watched as one of their Cardinals got a hit, but he was thrown out at first.

"POPCORN!"

Steve's head snapped toward the aisle, and he flagged down the concessions guy and bought them each a box of popcorn.

Settling back into his seat, he took a deep breath. "So, uh. I want to talk to you about something."

"Are you gonna do it?"

"I uh... wait. What?"

"Enlist."

"How do you...?" They both paused long enough to see an outfielder catch the batter's fly ball.

"You're always reading those things about the Marines."

Another out and the inning was up. Nick chewed a handful of popcorn, then turned to Steve. "I can take care of myself, you know."

"Nick–"

"I can. Mom and Dad are gone. You don't have to stick around for me."

"But..." They both stood up to let some people walk by. "But I want to make sure you're alright."

"I'm alright, Stevie. I can stay here and take care of the animals."

"And go to school."

Nick released an exasperated breath. "I don't like school."

"You have to go to school, Nicky."

"Steve!"

Steve smirked. "A'ight."

Nick rolled his eyes. "Aw-what?"

They both laughed. When the laughter died down, mostly because the Cubs scored another run, Nick turned serious.

"You really can go, you know. I really can take care of myself. I'll be okay." Nick chewed some more popcorn. "Do you want to go? Into the Marines, that is?"

"Yeah, Nicky. I do."

"Then go."

"If I go, I may be gone by Thanksgiving."

"That's okay," Nick said matter-of-factly. "The holidays have never been any fun, anyway. "

"You'll have to write me, you know."

"Can I e-mail you?"

"Sure," Steve said as the Cardinals finally retired the side. "You can call me, too, though I'm told I won't be able to access my phone during basic training."

Nick nodded without taking his eyes off the field. "I think you'll make a good Marine."

Steve turned to Nick, ignoring the game completely. Nick's expression couldn't be more earnest if he tried. "Thanks, Nicky."

They turned back to the game, no longer caring that their St. Louis Cardinals were on their way to a 12-3 trouncing by the Chicago Cubs.

After talking everything over with Uncle Sam and Aunt Evie to finalize the details of how Nick would be taken care of, Steve went to processing in the middle of October. He took his ASVAB exams, passed with no problem, and enlisted on the spot. He was given a time slot for three weeks later.

Steve was happy he wasn't going to leave before Halloween, but with President Bush pushing a new troop surge, it wouldn't be long after before he left for Parris Island for Receiving Week. The timing was perfect since he was able to be with Nick and his extended family for the Farmer's Fall Festival, which was going to be way better than Mendota's summer corn festival. He even got to enjoy a horse-drawn hayride with Nick behind the wheel. Well, with Nick holding the reins.

He received lots of hugs and his favorite meal of meatloaf, mashed potatoes with gravy, and corn on the night before he needed to take his oath and head for the airport. The next day, he said his goodbyes to Aunt Evie, Uncle Sam, and Nick at the recruiting station.

"I'm gonna miss you, Stevie."

"I'm gonna miss you, too, little brother." Steve pulled his brother into a tight embrace. "Now you take care of yourself, a'ight?"

Nick grinned, though Steve could tell it was a bit forced. "Aw-what?"

Steve laughed. "I just want you to be happy, Nicky. I want you to be safe. There's nothing more I can do for you, and you're in a good place."

"I'll be fine here. Don't worry." Nick stared at the ground for a few seconds, then looked his brother in the eye. "This is not a goodbye."

"No." Steve drew his brother in for another quick hug. "No. It's not. Just remember my number and e-mail. I'll never change them."

"Don't worry, Stevie. I know them."

"We'll take good care of him, Steve," Uncle Sam said, extending his hand. "You have our word."

"Thank you." Steve shook his hand but pulled him in for a hug as well. "For everything." He said his goodbyes to an emotional Aunt Evie, then stepped onto the bus, his large envelope with his enlistment papers in hand.

He took his seat and waved through the window. As the bus pulled away, he stared down at his hand and clenched his fist a few times. Life was about to change in a big way.

Chapter 32

Snickerdoodles

P*ARRIS* I*SLAND* - B*ASIC* T*RAINING*

Receiving week for basic training was a chaotic and tough welcome to the new Marines. Steve and the other recruits arrived in the middle of the night, were given haircuts, and started with their basic training. They were all instructed to call home to let their families know they'd arrived safely. Except for a couple other opportunities to touch base with their loved ones, they would be on their own for the next twelve weeks.

What stood out to Steve at first was all the yelling, but it didn't come with the accompanying beating he received growing up, making the military a far cry better. Once he accepted the yelling, he learned what it meant to be a Marine. It was hard, much harder than the fire academy in St. Louis, but much better. They weren't just called in after something awful happened. He had the chance to make a preemptive difference in the world.

Steve's fellow recruits came from all over the country. They quickly learned they all did better when they worked together. The bonds of brotherhood were forged early on, even if they didn't always like each other. When it came to becoming combat-ready, Steve didn't care if someone liked him. He just cared if they had his back, which was something drilled into them from sunup to sundown.

There was no rest for the weary, even on Sundays. The drill instructor just barked orders at Steve and a few others to prepare their barracks for yet another inspection.

Mason, a fellow new Marine, walked in looking happy and relaxed when someone tossed a broom his way. Only quick reflexes had him catching it before it smacked him on the forehead.

"What's this?" Mason asked.

"Got an inspection at 0930," Janson explained in his thick Boston accent. "And why are you so fucking happy over there? Get to work. I'm sick of getting screamed at all day."

Falkner tapped Janson on the back of the head. "This is basic training. It's their job to scream at us."

Janson shrugged him off. "Can it, Falks, and get cleaning!"

Mason started sweeping the non-existent dust off the floor. "I just got back from church."

"Aw shit, Mace," Janson whined. "Are you gonna start preaching to us now?"

Steve snickered while he remade his bunk, which was already perfectly made.

"Nah. I'm not into all that God and worship stuff."

Steve's brows shot up. "Then why'd you go?"

Mason laughed as he kept sweeping. "They don't yell at me there. It gives me a solid hour each week to myself. Chaplain thinks I'm praying when actually I'm napping or thinking about my girlfriend back home."

Janson perked up. "They don't yell at you there?"

"No, Jans. Best place for a little privacy, besides the latrine, that is."

"And even there, they want you to shit by the numbers." Tolbert added.

Continuing their cleaning, the men all laughed.

"You're right about that, Toley," Steve agreed.

Mace continued. "My older brother is a Marine, and he said that church was probably the only time during basic where you could relax and think."

Janson gave Mason a friendly tap on the arm. "I'm going with you next week, then."

A few of the others muttered their agreement.

The next Sunday, Jans, Mace, Toley, Falks, and Steve all went to church together, reveling in the fact that they had at least one hour of quiet.

"From what I understand," Toley said on their way back to the barracks, "We're all going into the infantry. With President Bush's Iraqi surge, they're gonna want us over there as soon as we get trained."

"Can't say I'm surprised, but I really wanted to be part of the ARFF," Steve said.

Mace clapped Steve on the shoulder. "Sorry, man. Looks like they need more warm bodies in the sandbox, so the Aircraft Rescue and Fire Fighting is on their own."

Though disappointed, Steve nodded. "Still get to make a difference." That's what he told himself, not truly wanting to go into combat but always knowing there would be no way to avoid it.

"Hey," Mace said, pulling Steve's attention his way. "I've got your back just like you've got mine, bro. We're gonna do our jobs, then get back home to our loved ones."

Steve returned Mace's gaze and was met with a smirk.

"We've got this, bro."

Afghanistan - Summer 2008

Steve had never spent so much time on an airplane before. He followed his fellow Marines of the Twenty-fourth Marine

Expeditionary Unit, or MEU, into their new barracks. They were in a forward operating base or FOB, so it was nothing fancy, not that they expected five-star accommodations in the middle of Afghanistan.

Mace dropped his duffle on the bunk next to Steve's. "Apparently, the concierge is on break, so we'll have to find our own entertainment for the evening."

"Welcome to Helmand Province, Marines," an officer said as a greeting as he walked into the room. He immediately assigned them their entertainment which included standing guard along the perimeter of their base. They were the newest additions to the 24th MEU, already in the middle of an ongoing deployment, so they were assigned the majority of the grunt work, though they all did their fair share.

Mace leaned toward Steve. "Sergeant Naismith needs to work on his concierge skills. I can think of better things to do than clean latrines."

Steve laughed. "Sorry to break it to you, Mace, but we both signed up for this."

"Did we?" Mace paused as another officer walked by. "Because I seem to remember someone signed up for ARFF."

"That's true," Jans said. "But look on the bright side: we all get to travel."

Steve snorted. "I doubt we'll get to go hiking here or do anything fun."

Jans started the fire in the 50-gallon drums. "Oh, we will. They just call it going on patrol. And look." He extended his arm toward the barracks. "We get to go camping, too."

"Too bad there aren't any women," Steve added, drawing laughter from his friends.

"Something funny, Marines?" A stern voice asked.

They all spun around to find their sergeant standing behind them. "No, sir," they all responded in tandem, stifling their laughter.

"Didn't think so," the sergeant responded, then walked away.

"At least nobody's firing on us yet," Mace said, keeping his voice low.

"Oh, they will," Jans responded while staring at the flames.

Steve's stomach dropped. He was prepared, but when his eyes met Mace's, he swallowed hard, knowing Jans was right.

"RPG," a voice yelled over the sound of weapons fire.

Steve and Mace ducked behind what was left of a wall of a home in the small village. The goal was to clear out the Taliban, but the indigenous fighters were putting up one hell of a fight.

"Jesus," Mace exclaimed. "How did these fucks get to be so well-armed?"

"Pretty sure those are American-made RPGs they're firing at us," Jans responded from his position behind a neighboring wall.

The explosion was far enough away from them that it only dropped dust and small rubble on them, but it was still too close for comfort. The moment it hit, they turned and fired back at the Taliban fighters, taking out a few along the way.

"Fucking Company," Steve muttered to himself. "LOADING!" He loaded a new magazine into his rifle and started firing again.

The fighting continued for another long while until they heard the order to hold their fire. They maintained their position until receiving the call to break cover.

These skirmishes were getting old. They were winning them, but not without a cost in both money and blood. The Taliban had moved into homes and community buildings, which the Marines had mostly destroyed, but then, in agreement with the families needing to live there, they helped pay to rebuild the town. It didn't make sense to Steve, but then again, he wasn't used to an enemy hiding among the citizenry and putting them all in such danger.

As for blood, several of his fellow Marines needed to be medevacked in Steve's first few months. Sadly, he'd also seen two men sent home to their families in boxes. Those were definitely not the memories he wanted to keep from his time serving, but they would probably be what he dreamed about for the rest of his life.

War doesn't care who lives and who dies.

People just die.

It's war.

Steve was grateful for the paramedic certification he earned prior to enlisting, though they all learned basic first aid as part of their training. The corpsmen in their units were the best of the best, able to save even more lives now than they did when the Marines first went in after 9/11. Necessity was the mother of invention, and years of war allowed for many advancements in combat medicine.

That night, they were surprised to find that the mail had found its way to their barracks. They all returned to letters on their bunks.

"Yes," Mace called out as he snatched up the letters on his bunk. "Sheryl wrote me one..." he paused to count. "Two...three letters." He kissed each one, then leaned back and opened the first one.

Mace cleared his throat and sat up. Pausing, he looked around and stood up. "Uh... I may need to read this one in private."

Jans scoffed. "Like we haven't already heard you jerking off to Sheryl's letters before."

Settling into their own bunks with their own letters from home, all the men laughed.

"Yeah, but this time she sent a picture." Mace hurried toward the door.

"Looks like you've got somethin', Steve."

Steve picked up the letters and read the names before looking at the package. "Here's one from Aunt Evie and Uncle Sam, though mostly from Aunt Evie." He shook the package and tore it open, all but ignoring the letters he'd received. A grin broke out on his face when he opened up a cookie tin. "Snickerdoodles. Yes!" He stuck one in his mouth and started chewing as several of the guys swarmed him on a quest for cookies. Steve took a minute to savor the cinnamon and sugary deliciousness, then swallowed it down. "When did she send this?" He shoved another cookie in his mouth while taking a look at the date on the package. "Ha! Three weeks old. Not bad."

Mace did an about-face when he heard people talking about cookies. "Are these cookies from your aunt?"

"Back so soon?" Falks asked Mace, receiving a punch in the arm for his efforts.

"Well?" Jans asked him, ready to pounce.

Steve pulled the cookie tin closer to his chest. "What?"

"Come on, man," Jans pleaded. "You gotta share your cookies."

Steve took a bite of one more cookie before responding. "Why?" He smiled.

"Because we know how to kill you in at least seventeen different ways," Falks deadpanned.

"Yeah," Steve laughed and passed the tin to the men surrounding him, snatching one more cookie for himself. "And I know how to defend myself in at least eighteen different ways."

"THANK YOU!" The men yelled.

Within two minutes, Steve's cookies were ancient history, but someone else was offering up some summer sausage and other snacks they received from their families and friends back home. Any taste of home was welcomed out in the middle of nowhere. Anything to take their minds off the realities of war and the desperation of the people they were there to help while searching for bin Laden.

Of course, letters from home, including one from Nicky, always made the day better.

Chapter 33

News From Home

Steve opened Nick's letter and double-checked the date. It was from April, and it took over two months to get to him. He started reading and then stopped. "What the fuck?"

"You okay, Steve," Mace asked. "You don't usually drop f-bombs when you're not shooting at somebody."

"My brother dropped out of school." Steve read on, the crease in his brow deepening with each passing word. "Said he didn't want to tell me earlier because they didn't want me to worry."

"Didn't want you to worry? What do you mean? Why'd he drop out?"

Steve kept reading. "Said it wasn't for him. He wants to work on the farm. Our great-aunt and uncle are taking him on as one of the regular farm hands, though he still gets to live in the house."

"High school isn't for everybody, but we still go."

"Yeah, well, he's had it tougher than most."

"You mean what you guys went through with your folks?"

Steve and Mason Albright hit it off during basic training. They talked about anything and everything from their first girlfriends to what it was like growing up in St. Louis with the Cook family versus growing up in Detroit with the Albright family, their second girlfriends, and their current girlfriends, who, for Mace, is a young brunette named Sheryl.

"She's super smart. Went to Michigan State and got a business degree," he said when he first started bragging about Sheryl. "She wanted to get out of the U.P.," which, thanks to some weird hand motions by Mason, Steve learned was Michigan's Upper Peninsula.

For Steve's part, he shared a lot about himself and his brother growing up in the home of two religious zealots who believed the only way to raise kids was to beat them into submission rather than actually pretending they loved them.

On the long patrol missions, Mace talked about everything he loved to do to his girlfriend. Steve thought it was a bit too much detail, but he did learn a few things he'd have to try out the next time they were stateside.

Steve's own exploits weren't nearly as extensive as Mace's or the other guys, but he shared everything he'd done so far to protect his brother. Surprisingly, neither Mace nor anyone else in their unit balked at the fact that his mom was in jail for killing his father. Sure, they agreed it was messed up, but Falks never knew his dad because he could never get out of jail long enough to visit his own kids. Jans' parents were divorced and moved across the country to California when he was in grade school, leaving him behind with his grandparents.

"Yes," Steve finally responded to Mace's question. "He should have been able to go through school, date whoever he wanted, and be happy. Well," Steve chuckled at the thought. "As happy as any high school kid is who wants to spend time with friends instead of doing homework."

Mace laughed at that. "You've got that right."

"What are you going to do?"

"He's somewhere safe for now," Steve said as he finished the letter. "He's got family around him, albeit extended family. And they let him work with the animals. He says he's been a lot more involved with the dairy farm itself and can't wait for the farmer's market and fall festival." Steve folded the letter. "I have to trust him to make the best decisions he can."

Iraq 2009

Steve wiped his forehead with the back of his hand as he dropped his duffle next to his bunk. "Fuck, it's hot!"

"Welcome to Iraq," Mace responded, sweat already darkening his shirt below his neckline.

They sat down on their bunks, which were even dustier than those they had at the FOB in Helmand Province, Afghanistan. Mail was already waiting for Steve, so he tore open a letter from Nick that started with the words *'SHE'S HERE! SHE'S OKAY!'* that had Steve grinning from ear to ear.

It took him over a year, but Nick finally told his brother about the girl named Skye, whom he was paired up with at Uncle Clint's horrible camp that has since been shut down. Apparently, she was sent back because her parents didn't want her anymore, so Clint kept her. When they closed down the camp, she was interviewed by the authorities; then she ran away. After a while, she found a way to get in touch with Nick and worked her way up to Mendota. Their great-aunt and uncle had taken her in and was now helping out in the ice cream shop they run on weekends as Sullivan's Ice Cream's newest employee. She never finished high school either, but she's working toward her GED, which Nick is doing as well.

"They're talking about moving to Chicago, Mace."

"Is that good?"

"I hope so. He'll be with friends."

"I thought he was dating that Seth guy?"

"That was one or two boyfriends ago. Pretty sure my brother's turning into a player."

Mace smacked Steve in the arm. "Taking after his big brother, huh? You must be so proud!"

Steve shook his head. "Yeah. Yeah. Yeah. Fuck you!"

Mace guffawed. "Nice to know you can drop f-bombs without shooting me."

"CORPSMAN!"

Steve yelled for the corpsman while attempting to fire his weapon with one hand and support Jans with the other. Mace and Falks took up a position to cover them so they could get out of the line of fire. Jans' yells were drowned out by the sound of bullets flying overhead. Steve got him far enough back to where he could be treated by the corpsman, who took one look at Jans' leg wound and turned around.

"He'll have to wait," he said while moving to treat a more serious wound.

"Doc," Steve insisted while carefully setting Jans down on the ground at the casualty collection point. "He needs help. Now."

Jans' yells dropped down to groans. "Stay with me, Jans."

"Gotta wait your turn, Marine," the corpsman said through gritted teeth as he had one hand in the gut of another Marine, desperately trying to save his life.

"Fuck this shit." Steve pulled another tourniquet from his own pack and tied it around Jans' leg to stop the bleeding from the bullet he took to the inside of his upper thigh. Once secured, he felt for Jans' pulse. It was hard to detect. "He's not in good shape, Doc, and he's already lost a lot of blood. I need an IV."

"You need a what?"

"An IV, dammit," Steve repeated. "He took a bullet to the leg and was going to bleed out. Tourniquet is applied, but the pulse is thready, and he's barely conscious."

"How do you know what that is?" Hands still on his patient, the corpsman looked over to visually assess Jans' situation. "Shit. It'll be a minute before I can get to him."

"I can do it."

"I can't just let you–"

"Doc, I was a paramedic. I know what I'm doing."

The corpsman paused long enough to make eye contact with Steve. He nodded. "Okay." He tilted his head to his medic pack. "They're in there. Gloves, too."

"Stay with me, Jans."

Jans' groans continued.

Conditions were anything but ideal. Dust was flying from nearby explosions and weapons fire. And what was left of the roof where they took shelter would probably collapse any minute, but Steve did what he had to do. He donned a pair of gloves and grabbed one of the IVs. He cleaned off Jans' arm as best he could and inserted the needle into the vein. Getting the IV going was just like riding a bicycle. He shouldn't have been surprised, but he never expected to use his paramedic training while serving with so many capable corpsmen.

"Yo, Steve," a weak Jans said after the saline solution started working its way through his body.

Steve clapped him gently on the shoulder and grinned. "Welcome back, asshole."

"Fuck you." Jans bent his arm at the elbow so he could grab Steve's hand on his shoulder. "Thanks, man."

Steve nodded.

Jans coughed, and his voice remained weak. "Your bedside manner sucks."

Steve coughed out a laugh. "I'll be sure to work on that."

They'd have to move him soon, but for now, Jans was going to be okay.

Knowing he now had someone who could help, their corpsman recruited Steve to help with all the casualties they took in until the air support gave them the upper hand.

Chapter 34

Better Nickname

On board the USS Nassau, en route to Haiti - January 2010

Jans never fought again. The doctors did their best, but they couldn't save his leg. He went home to his family, who were all grateful to have him back home safe, but that was the last Steve ever saw of the man he saved on the battlefield that day. Six months later, Steve received a Bronze Star for displaying heroic action and meritorious service during combat operations the day he carried Jans out of the field of fire while also taking down at least two enemy combatants. He later saved the lives of his fellow Marines after their corpsman was shot and incapacitated during an extended combat engagement with the enemy. His citation noted how his selfless commitment to his comrades-in-arms had saved lives and reflected the high standards of military tradition.

Steve learned it was the corpsman himself who initially recommended him for his actions on that day. The day he received his Bronze Star, he was also promoted to Lance Corporal.

Two months later, while on their way to Haiti to provide humanitarian assistance after a 7.0 magnitude earthquake, Steve opened a letter from Jans. Inside was a picture of Jans and his pregnant wife, excited to be starting the next chapter of their lives. Steve passed the picture around to Falks, Mace, and Toley. None of them could resist making fun of his much longer hair.

"I can't believe he has a beard," Toley said while rubbing his jaw. "I bet I could grow one like that."

"Bro," Mace laughed. "You could barely get that peach fuzz of a mustache to come in. How do you think you could get a beard?"

The guys were still laughing as Steve opened his latest letter from Nick. Nick was living in Chicago now, working part-time at a local hotel and playing his music at local clubs. He planned to get a Street Performer License so he can play by the L stations before baseball games in the spring. He's heard that people made pretty good money doing that.

Nick wrote that he'd get around to getting his GED, someday. Steve scoffed at Nick's words. Life was hard enough as it was, but it had to be harder for a nineteen-year-old kid without a high school diploma living and working in a big city. At least Nick was rooming with Skye and her girlfriend, so they'd all be sharing expenses and could look after each other. It didn't prevent Steve's heart from sinking.

"Out of the frying pan and into the fire," Steve mumbled as he read.

Mace must have heard him. "What was that?"

"Ah, nothing. Just worried about my little brother, is all."

"What happened?"

Steve gave Mace the rundown about Nick, voicing all his worries and concerns.

"He's an adult now, Steve. You can't control what he does," Mace argued. "He's got to learn to do things on his own. School isn't for everybody."

"But what kind of a job is he going to get?" Steve asked. "He's only nineteen."

"Same one you have?"

"Not without his GED, you know that."

"True," Mace acknowledged. "But you said he's working on that, right?"

"Kind of."

"Again, Steve. You can't control him. He has to live his life."

"Yeah. I suppose."

"Control what you can control, man."

"It doesn't feel like much."

"Of course not," Mace laughed. "We enlisted in the Marines, remember?"

A cocky smirk spread across Steve's face, and he extended his hand to Mace. "Best damned fighting force there is."

"Oorah!"

Camp Lejeune - Autumn 2011

"Can't believe my little brother is now 20," Steve said while scrolling through the pictures Nick emailed him. "Next year, I'll be able to take him out for a beer for his twenty-first birthday."

"Assuming you're out of here," Mace said, sitting down on the steps at the entrance of their barracks.

Steve laughed. "Oh, I'll be out next spring. They're drawing everything down right now. Should be done in Iraq by the new year."

"I'll believe that when I see it."

"Why wouldn't you believe it? Falks and Toley are already out."

"Toley doesn't count, though," Mace countered. "He got an early out after spending a few months at Walter Reed."

"That's fair." Steve nodded. "Fucker. Can't believe he made it."

"Me neither, but I guess his girlfriend's thrilled to have him back. Last I heard, they were planning a wedding, though he's still trying to talk her into eloping."

"Ha!" Steve's laughter was contagious. "So true. How's Sheryl doing?"

"I'm gonna marry her." Mace's face took on a dreamy expression. "She wants a big church wedding. Whatever she wants, man."

"Can't say I'm surprised." Steve gestured with his arms. "You guys have stuck together through all this."

"She's pretty amazing." Mace's grin lit up his whole face. "But I hope to get out the same time you do."

"Hard to believe it's been four years already." Steve released a loud exhale. "I can't wait to see Nick for more than a week at a time. And then kick his butt back in school."

"Are you sure he's going to have time for you?" Mace motioned toward Steve's phone. "There are a lot of pictures with the same guy in there. What's his name again?"

"Mac. It's short for something, I think." Steve scrolled through his email from Nick, but couldn't find what he was looking for. "Well, Mac something."

Somewhere in the middle of the Atlantic, April 2012

"So much for getting out in the spring," Steve said while trying to keep his dinner in his stomach. Traveling by ship usually didn't bother him except when the seas were especially rough like they were today, and it had been a long while since it had been this bad.

The sound of someone in a rack across the room retching into a bucket drew his gaze. He winced and shut his eyes, trying to think of anything but hurling.

Mace's face was already in a bucket. He wouldn't stop groaning. "All I wanted to do was go home and fuck my girlfriend. Then I'd propose, but..." he swallowed. "Oh god...." He retched into his bucket again. "Fuck. That's gross."

The motion of another guy running out of the room caught Steve's attention. In the meantime, he tried to stay in his rack, laying on his stomach with his eyes closed. "How do they expect us to fight if we keep puking our guts out?"

Mace groaned. "I don't know, bro, but I'm hungry."

Steve shot a look of disgust in Mace's direction. "How the fuck can you think about eating right now?" Steve's hand shot out to steady himself as the ship lurched to one side, his knuckles turning white as they gripped the edge of his bunk. "Ugh." His stomach mirrored the motion in his effort to keep his dinner down. "This has got to be over soon. Fucking squids. How do they take this?"

Camp Lejeune - December 2012

"Well, at least we got back on dry land in time for Christmas," Mace said as he packed his duffle for the last time.

"Yeah," Steve said in between laughs. "Too bad they didn't process us in time to get home."

"We didn't exactly plan to have our final tour extended twice to spend extra time around Libya of all places."

"True, but Gaddafi's gone now."

"Yep. People there took care of that."

"Well, you're all done now. Can't believe it's been five years."

Mace took a final look around the barracks. "Can't believe you're staying in."

"Not too long. Should finish up in the spring." Steve laughed. "They've got me training recruits. Can you believe that?"

"I think you just want an excuse to show off your Bronze Star."

"That was nothing."

"I think a few men alive today would say otherwise, Lance Corporal Cook."

They stood in silence for a few long moments before Mace

extended his hand to Steve. "You take care of yourself, man. And if you're ever in Michigan, look me up."

"I sure will." Steve took his hand and pulled him in for a hug, slapping him hard on the back. "Same goes if you're in Chicago. It's not too far."

"I'm gonna miss you, bro."

Steve nodded, unable to speak at first. Mace knew everything about him. He stood by him when he was scared out of his mind. Hell, they stood by each other when they were both scared out of their minds. They'd stuck by each other through explosions and with bullets flying over their heads. They'd saved each other's lives and worked together to make sure as many men and women as possible made it home to be reunited with their friends and families. They'd held each other when it got too much, bought drinks to toast their return home, and changed their buckets when they couldn't keep their food down during rough seas.

"You know," Mace started. "They're not going to understand anything we went through over there. You've got my number, so don't you dare be a stranger, bro. Okay?"

"Goes both ways, Mace."

"I mean it. Anytime. Day or night. And if you or your brother need anything, anything at all, just call. You're family now." Mace grabbed his duffle and shrugged it over his shoulders and gave one last nod to Steve.

Mace walked out, stopping just short of the door. He grabbed the handle and opened it but turned back at the last second. "Steve Cook. How the fuck did you never get a better nickname than Steve?"

He lit up in one final smile and walked out the door.

Chapter 35

On Call

M ENDOTA, I LLINOIS - E ARLY SUMMER 2013

"WELCOME HOME, STEVE!"

Loud cheers erupted and never-ending hugs and handshakes from everyone at Uncle Sam and Aunt Evie's farm greeted Steve the moment he arrived back home. No one looked any different. An extra wrinkle or two, perhaps a little more gray, but the same smiles and the same warm hugs.

He dropped his duffle at the door and shed a layer down to his Marine-issue green t-shirt to stay cool on the hot summer day.

Boone shook his hand and pulled him in for a hug. "Good to see you, Steve." Boone noticed his new art. "You have some new tattoos, I see.

"Yeah." Steve grinned. "Quite a few, actually."

"No piercings, though."

"Oh no. I've got some of those. Just couldn't wear them in uniform on the way home."

A loud and happy squeal broke through the cacophony of noise from all the well-wishers inside the Sullivan farmhouse.

"Oh, sweetie, I'm so glad you're home for good," Aunt Evie said with a hug. "I could just squeeze the pudding right out of you."

Steve laughed. "It's good to be home, Aunt Evie."

Uncle Sam greeted him with a hearty handshake and a manly hug. "Good to have you home."

Steve couldn't remember such a happy homecoming. He scanned the room, accepting more welcomes from everyone, but couldn't find his brother. "Where's Nick?"

"He's out with the horses." Uncle Sam led him toward the back door. "Come on. I'll walk out with you."

"Is everything alright?"

They stepped outside when Uncle Sam stopped and sighed, taking a moment to find his words. "I don't know, Steve. He's become more withdrawn lately. Whenever he comes home, he goes straight to the animals. I think they help calm him."

"Is he okay?"

Uncle Sam bobbed his head side to side before responding. "Yeah...I think so."

When he hesitated, Steve asked, "What aren't you telling me?"

"He's been..." Uncle Sam shook his head. "How do I say this? He's been really distant. And he comes around less and less often. Always cancels at the last minute because he's called into work or something. It's always work. He says he doesn't have to work and will be here for dinner, so Evie fixes his favorite meal. Then the next thing you know, he calls or texts, usually texts, to say he's been called in and has to work. A couple of times, he had something going on with his boyfriend that he forgot about."

"Is he really that tight for money?" Steve asked. "Because I've been sending him some to make sure he's okay. Chicago's really expensive."

"I know, but... he's kind of cagey about his job. I know he works in a hotel, but don't know much about his second job. I'm just..." he turned to meet Steve's gaze. "I'm just worried about him, is all."

Uncle Sam put a smile on his face and clapped Steve on the back. "He'll be happy to see you. That much I'm sure of."

Steve nodded and made the rest of the way to the barn on his own. When he slid the door open, he thought the barn was empty except for a voice coming from a stall by the opposite door.

"Nicky?"

A head peeked out of the stall and broke into a grin. Steve would never be able to get over the fact that Nick was now as tall as he was. Still slender, Nick slid through the stall door opening and jogged closer. Steve ran to meet him.

"Stevie!"

They held each other without a word for the longest time.

"I've missed you, Stevie."

"I missed you, too, Nicky."

Nick didn't let go.

"Hey. Hey. It's okay. I'm home now."

"For good?"

"Yeah. For good." Steve pulled back so he could look his brother in the eye. "I'm gonna go back to being a firefighter paramedic." He breathed out a laugh. "Maybe we can even see the Cardinals play again."

"It's been a while since I've been to a game."

"We can look at the schedule and see them at Wrigley again."

"As long as they don't lose 12-3 like they did the last time we went."

Steve's head fell back in laughter. "That one really sucked, didn't it."

Nick joined in the laughter. "Yeah. They're in town next week."

"The Cards? That's it. We're definitely going." Steve hugged Nick again. "So, tell me everything. How are you? What's new?"

"They have a new horse for me to take care of." Nick walked Steve over and told him everything about the new mare they were now boarding at the farm. Once he started talking, Steve couldn't get a word in edgewise.

Steve loved every minute of it, too. To him, everything was happy and there was no shooting involved. He knew Nick was holding something back, but the sheer joy of being with his brother again could allow that conversation to wait for another day. Right now, he was an honorably discharged veteran Marine re-entering civilian life. All he wanted was to kick back and enjoy his brother's company and sleep in a real bed.

Steve checked his watch as he stepped into the local restaurant recommended by some of his fellow firefighters. It was a hole-in-the-wall place not far from the Chicago fire station at which he has been working since returning to civilian life. He and Nick planned to meet here for an early dinner and a movie. Nick had to work early this morning but should have been off in plenty of time to take the L the few stops he needed to travel to get here.

Steve: I'm here. Where are you?

Nick: Still at work.

Steve: ETA?

Nick: Not sure. Might be a while.

Steve: I'll be at the bar.

An hour later, Nick walked in to find Steve at the end of the bar, watching a ball game on one of the large-screen TVs. "Hey, Stevie." Nick was wearing a nice button-down shirt, a pair of gray slacks, and gray shoes.

Steve smiled and greeted his brother with a half hug. "You look great," he said as Nick took the seat next to him. "You hungry?"

"Starving. I haven't had a chance to eat all day."

"Why not? What have you been doing all day?"

"Working."

"No kidding," Steve laughed as the bartender walked over. Nick ordered a beer and winced as he took his first sip. "Something wrong with your drink?"

"Nah." Nick took another sip. "I just don't like it."

"Then why did you order it?"

"The guys always order it for me."

Steve flagged the bartender for another drink. "Can we get another drink, please?" He turned to his brother. "Get something you actually like, Nicky."

Nick ordered a Sprite and drank it without making a face. He smiled. "Ahh. Much better."

"Nicky," Steve asked with a look of concern on his face. "Why don't you order what you want when you're out with your friends? I mean, Skye doesn't make you do that, does she?"

Nick waved his hands. "Oh no. No. No. Not Skye. It's just... sometimes we go out after work, and they've already ordered drinks for everyone. That's all."

"Do they ever make you do more than that?"

"Sometimes they buy extra rounds."

"Well, you don't have to–"

"I can handle myself, Steve."

Steve was taken aback at not being called by his nickname. "Okay." He handed Nick a menu. "Well... If you ever decide you don't want to, call me, okay? Anytime. Even if I'm on shift, a'ight?"

Nick stared at his Sprite and let out a long exhale. Then he shook his head and turned to Steve with his lip curled up on one side. "Ah-what?"

The bartender set their dinners in front of them and asked if they needed anything else. After being assured they were fine, he left to take care of other customers.

"I've missed you, Nicky."

"I've missed you, too, Stevie." Nick took a couple of bites. "How was it over there? Really?"

Steve finished his bite, wiped his mouth with the napkin and took a drink of his beer. "It was hard. It was really hard. I loved it. I was doing something important, you know? And the men I served with." He shook his head. "I've never been around a better group of men."

"What about that one guy? Mason or something?"

The thought of him brought a smile to Steve's face. "Mace. Yeah. Great guy. He's married now."

"Maybe you'll get married someday."

Steve's head fell back in laughter. "I seriously doubt that."

Nick's phone buzzed, and his lips tightened into a line as he checked the text message. "I've gotta go."

"What do you mean you've gotta go?" Steve asked. "I thought you didn't have to work tonight."

"I'm on call."

"On call?"

"Steve. Please don't." Nick slipped off his stool and slid his arms through his jacket. He read another text on his phone and dropped it in his pocket. He reached out to hug his brother. "I'm glad I got to see you. Love you, Stevie."

"Love you, too.

Chapter 36

Standard Issue

CHICAGO - SPRING 2014

Steve and Nick got together whenever they could, which wasn't very often. Nick sometimes canceled at the last minute because of work or what he said was work. And when he did show up, he almost always left earlier than originally planned. Steve was happy for the time together but felt something was pulling Nick away from him. One time, Nick had plans with Mac, who arrived early to pick him up. Steve dropped cash on the table and ran out to follow Nick. He peered into the open window of the Town Car to meet Nick's elusive boyfriend, Mac, a well-dressed man with blond hair and a short beard. During the brief conversation, he came off as rather charming.

He wrapped his arm around Nick's shoulders when he tossed out the socially acceptable pleasantries. Nick didn't speak, opting instead to snuggle up to him in the back of the car while Mac did all the talking. Nick said goodbye and waved as Steve quickly backed away from the window that was quickly closing. The tinted windows prevented Steve from seeing anything else inside the car as he watched them drive off.

After they took a turn at the next intersection, Steve pulled out his phone and dialed a number he didn't call nearly enough.

"Hi, Steve," Bryce answered. "Glad to hear from you. How are you doing?"

"Hey, Bryce," Steve said while stepping aside to let someone walk by. He ducked into a recessed entryway of a business already closed for the day to continue the conversation. "I just had dinner with Nick... and..." Steve could hear voices in the background.

"Hold on a sec, Steve," Bryce said. Muffled voices spoke in the background as if Bryce covered the phone with his hand. He came back to the call after a few minutes. "Sorry about that. We're working on a big case right now and go to court in a couple of weeks. Is everything okay with Nick?"

"I'm not sure." Steve proceeded to tell Bryce about Nick's situation. "He's cagey about so much, especially his job and his boyfriend. He's also canceling our meetups or having to leave early. Conveniently, his boyfriend never seems to be able to join us. Mac looks like he's got his act together, but I wonder if he's controlling Nick somehow."

"Oh, man. I don't know what to say," Bryce answered. "What has Nick said?"

"Nothing. I mean, I let him choose where we meet. You know, places he wants to try but never has a chance to. He says his friends always choose where they go." Steve scrubbed his face with his hand. "I just wonder how much is actually legit, you know."

"Yeah. I understand," Bryce was interrupted again. "What are you thinking?"

"I want to know more about his boyfriend. Something about him," Steve shook his head. "I don't know. I just don't trust him."

"You know who you should call?"

"Who?"

"Lynn Reintz."

"Lynn... wait." Steve stood up taller. "Is that the same Lynn you went to college with?"

"Even dated for a while, yeah." Bryce laughed. "We didn't work out as a couple, but we're still great friends. She's working for the Bureau now in the Detroit office. She might know something. I know she travels to Chicago from time to time. I'll text you her number and give her a heads up that you'll be calling."

"Hey, Steve," Lynn said, leaning up to give him a quick kiss on the cheek. "It's good to see you."

They met at a dive bar not far from his apartment. He had a longer-than-usual shift thanks to an overnight house fire that spread to two other houses. One would need a little repair work. Another would need a lot, and the third was completely destroyed. At least they were heading into summer, so they wouldn't have to fight fires in the freezing cold.

"How are you, Lynn? Thanks for meeting me." He looked her up and down, appreciating the form-fitting jeans, tank top, and blazer that he was sure hid a weapon of some sort since she was now an FBI agent.

"Sure thing." She smirked and then checked him up and down. "You don't look so bad yourself."

"I..." Steve paused and then laughed. "Not so subtle, huh?"

"Not at all." She tilted her head toward the opposite wall lined with tables spread out along one long bench that spanned the length of the entire room. "Let's get away from the bar. Too many ears."

Lynn led him to a small table in the corner, big enough for two people, and sat down next to him on the bench. They each ordered a beer, and then, turning serious, she leaned in so close their legs and shoulders were touching.

Steve didn't object, but his body threatened to give something away if it lasted too long.

"Bryce got me up to date on what's going on with Nick."

"I'm not sure what's going on to be honest, but..."

"But you have your suspicions."

"Uh..." Steve pressed his lips together. "Yes. I do."

"What's he like?"

"He was doing well for a while and was really happy or..." Steve exhaled. "Seemed really happy when we were over in Mendota, but after I enlisted..."

"Makes you wonder if that was just for show?"

"Yeah." Steve exhaled. "He dropped out of school, then he moved to Chicago with his friend, Skye, and her girlfriend–"

"Maisey. I went ahead and checked them out. They're both clean. No criminal records. Their families are shit, but they're just doing their own thing in spite of everything."

"Like ours."

"Your parents, yeah, but you've got some good eggs in there, Steve."

Steve chuckled. "Good eggs, huh?"

"Like I'm ever getting rid of my Midwestern roots. Quantico didn't change me that much! I have some suspicions, too, though."

"Tell me."

"I want to check some things out first, but they're not so great." She paused a few moments as if gauging his readiness to hear what she thought.

"I know you're thinking something, Lynn. What is it?"

"I'm worried..."

"About?"

"There's been a lot of trafficking activity from here to Pittsburgh."

A crease formed on Steve's brow. "Trafficking activity?"

"Human trafficking."

"Fuck."

"You say he's short on details about his job. He cancels plans or cuts them short. Has a boyfriend you've never met?"

Steve started to say something, but she cut him off. "Not really met, anyway." She took a swig of her beer. "There's a big network we're beginning to see that stretches throughout the Midwest from here to Baltimore, but the majority of the activity has been between here and Pittsburgh. Now, I don't know if Nick is in this at all. He may just be on the periphery, which is why I didn't want to say anything at first."

Steve took a deep breath, not wanting to consider what may be happening to his brother.

"They say it even goes as far as St. Louis."

"Wait. Do you think that my uncle is involved in some way?"

"No." Lynn shook her head. "He's what we consider a fanatic. He's not a businessman. He's not organized. He's also not been out of the St. Louis general area. We broke down his camp, but that's about it. He's out of jail now, but he's the type to preach misogyny and hatred. He's not able to organize something this big. The men and women who do this would chew him up and spit him out."

"So, what does this mean?"

"It means I'm going to keep looking and try to find out the truth." She put her hand on Steve's. "I won't give up. I know what he's been through, Steve. I won't give up until we know the truth."

"I thought he was somewhere safe, you know?"

"Yeah. I know, but he's also made his own decisions."

"Yeah." Steve took a drink of his beer and leaned back in his seat. "Doesn't mean I have to like it."

"No. It doesn't."

They shifted the conversation to lighter topics when a server showed up with another beer delivered directly to Lynn.

"What's this?" Lynn asked.

"Gift from the guy at the bar." The server pointed over her shoulder.

Lynn leaned to the side to see behind the server and saw three different men sitting at the bar. "Which guy?"

Just as she asked, a man wearing a baseball hat, a dress shirt, and slacks lifted his chin in her direction. He looked to be in his 30s and had already had a drink or two, though nowhere near being sloppy. Lynn scoffed, then checked out the beer again. Seeing it was light beer, she curled her lip up in disgust.

"Seriously?"

"He's a regular, and from time to time, he likes to hit on the female patrons, but he has the worst taste in beer. He insisted on sending you what he was drinking. I tried to talk him out of it."

Steve shook his head and laughed.

Lynn smiled up at the server. "Thanks, but please tell him no, thank you. You can take that back, please. Mind telling him I prefer real beer?"

"Oh, hell no. I don't mind." The server shared a conspiratorial smile. "I knew someone would turn him down someday."

"Wait," Lynn stopped her. "This actually works?"

The server shared her disbelief. "More than you might think." She picked up the beer and placed it on her tray. "I'll take this back for you."

"Add it to my tab if he gives you any trouble."

"You got it!"

The server left and returned the beer.

Lynn snuck a glance toward the bar.

The man was visibly upset and started to head in their direction.

"Well, shit." She leaned into Steve. "Quick. Kiss me."

Steve's eyes widened. "What?"

"Kiss me."

"Huh?"

"Dammit." She placed her palm on Steve's cheek and pressed her lips against his, pulling him into a deep kiss.

"Now listen here, lady," the man growled, getting Steve's hackles up enough to pull away from Lynn. He'd already cataloged exactly how many exits there were and where, how many other people might join in a fight if it came to that.

Once a Marine. Always a Marine.

Right now, though, he was stuck in the corner behind Lynn. And she was between him and this dick of a man in front of her, his crotch about level with her face.

The man placed one hand on their table and the other on the wall and leaned within inches of her face. "When I buy you a drink, I expect–"

The man's speech was cut off in an instant, unable to move as if he were in pain.

"You expect what?"

Steve glanced down to find the knuckles on Lynn's right hand turning white from the vice-like grip she had on the man's balls and her left hand holding a switchblade against his throat.

Where the hell did that come from?

Steve never saw her move.

Both her hand and the blade were obscured from the rest of the bar since the man leaned into the corner, but their effect was indeed felt. "You really think you come back here and challenge a Marine?"

He struggled to swallow, and when he spoke, his voice squeaked. "You're a Marine?"

"No." Lynn tilted her head toward Steve. "He is. I'm just the one in control of your balls and if you had any smarts, you'll never offer up light beer to another woman again. Got it?"

He nodded and moaned in pain. "Uh-huh."

"Good." She released him and put away the blade as if nothing had happened.

Unable to stand up straight, the man hobbled toward the hallway leading to the restrooms.

She turned to Steve and dropped her gaze to his lips again, then back up to look him in the eye. "Wanna get outta here?"

"I live a couple blocks away."

"I know. I parked outside your apartment behind your motorcycle. You'll have to take me on a ride sometime."

"How'd you..." Steve licked his lips. "A ride. Yeah. Let's go."

Lynn dropped some cash on the table. "Drinks are on me."

"Yeah."

The moment Steve opened the door to his small apartment, Lynn threw herself against him and claimed his mouth.

"You are not in control here, Lynn."

"Then prove it."

They frantically pulled off their clothes, unbuttoning each other's shirts and jeans. Lynn dropped her jacket on the way to Steve's bedroom.

He paused when he saw her shoulder holster. "Glock, huh?"

She kissed him again and she slid it off and set it on his dresser. "Mmhmm. Standard issue," she panted. "Condoms?"

"Nightstand."

She grabbed one and ripped it open the moment he unzipped his fly. He shrugged out of his jeans and pulled her down on the bed, unfastening her bra as soon as they landed. "Hang on," she said as she shrugged out of her pants. She rolled the condom on and straddled him.

"Nope." He rolled her onto her back. "I'm doing this."

"Then do it now!"

Steve thrust inside her, stopping long enough only to check on her. "You good?"

"Very good."

"Good."

He claimed her mouth again, not caring about the fingernails scratching their way down his back as he moved.

"Harder, Steve."

"Huh?"

"Harder!"

He pulled out and rolled her onto her stomach.

"Oh yeah. Just the way I like it," She moaned.

He thrust back inside her and pumped as hard as he dared.

"Oh, come on, Steve. You can do better than that."

"I don't want to hurt–"

"You won't."

Steve stopped long enough to meet her gaze. "On your knees."

"Yes!"

He got on his knees and pounded into her over and over again until they both screamed out their release. Steve dropped his head on her shoulders, and she leaned back against him. He rested on his knees with his arms wrapped around her while they caught their breath.

After a few minutes, Lynn pulled away and lay down on her back, her arm resting over her eyes. "I needed that."

"Yeah." Steve backed off the bed, leaving long enough to throw his condom away. When he returned, he sat down on the bed and rested his forearms on his knees.

"Do you have a switchblade?" she asked.

Steve shook his head as if to clear it. "That's the first thing you ask after–?"

"You need one if you don't." She swallowed and breathed in and out a few times. "I love mine. It comes in handy."

"Not a bad idea," Steve leaned in for a kiss. After coming up for air, she had more suggestions.

"And you should get your nipples pierced. You know how hot that would be with all your tattoos?"

"My nipples?"

She reached up and sucked one into her mouth. "Oh, yeah." She pressed her hand against his chest and dropped it down his abs. "And maybe even..."

Steve's Adam's apple bobbed up and down. "I'll... uh... consider that. Thanks."

Chapter 37

Not for Months

Chicago, Illinois - Summer 2014

Steve held his phone to his head while resting on his bunk at the fire station. Nick's excitement about his upcoming trip bubbled out of him that he talked a mile a minute.

"Mac's taking me away for the holiday weekend. It'll be fun. We're going to see a baseball game," Nick said. "Then we're going to see fireworks. I can't wait!"

Steve worried about Nick. He was his little brother, after all, despite being nearly 24 years old, but he couldn't prevent him from going anywhere. He had nothing concrete to try to keep him home, so he had to let him go and just see him next week.

"Well, have fun, Nicky, but be careful."

"Stevie, I'll be fine."

"Hey," Steve attempted to keep his tone light. "I'm your big brother. I'm allowed to tell you to be careful."

"I will be. Promise."

Steve could only take him at his word.

"Alright. See you soon."

Steve was on shift on the fourth. They were inundated with small fires caused by fireworks being set off improperly. They had one or two bigger fires, too.

People could be such idiots. A few colorful bangs are not worth the cost of losing your house.

Steve tried calling his brother the following week, but ended up having to leave a voicemail. When he texted, he received a response saying they were still in Detroit.

> Nick: You'd love this hotel. It used to be a fire station.
>
> Steve: Sounds great.
>
> Nick: We're staying an extra week or two.
>
> Steve: What about work?
>
> Nick: Taking vacation time.

At first, Steve heard from Nick every few days, but after two weeks, he heard from Nick less frequently. The text messages grew shorter and shorter. They were usually just about how Nick was heading out with people and places unknown.

After his last message, which was nothing more than *heading out*, Steve called the hotel where Nick worked.

A woman's voice answered. "Meridian Hotel. May I help you?"

"Nicholas Cook, please."

"Do you have his room number?"

"He's not a guest. He works there."

"Hmm. Doesn't sound familiar. Let me ask."

Staticky hold music played in Steve's ear for a couple of minutes. When she returned, she confirmed Steve's suspicions. "I'm sorry, sir, but we don't have anyone here by that name."

"He probably went by Nick."

"Let me ask."

She came back a minute later. "My manager says we used to have someone named Nick Cook, but he hasn't worked here in a long time. I'm really sorry."

"Thank you."

Steve dialed a different number. "Uncle Sam?"

"Oh hey, Steve. How's things in the big city? Job going alright?"

"Job's great, thanks." Steve paused a moment before speaking.

Uncle Sam picked up on his hesitation. "Steve? What's wrong?"

Steve hated the amount of worry in his voice.

"Steve? Talk to me."

"Did you know that Nick doesn't work at the Meridian?"

"Did he find a new job?"

"I just talked to them. He hasn't worked there for months."

"Oh." Uncle Sam paused. "There's something else, isn't there?"

Steve scrubbed the scruff on his chin. "He and his boyfriend went to Detroit for the Fourth."

"Okay?"

"They haven't come back. Nick says he has vacation time. He's lying, Uncle Sam."

Uncle Sam groaned. "Damn."

"What is it, Sam?" Aunt Evie's voice sounded in the background. Uncle Sam caught her up.

"I've got some time off so I can head over there," Steve offered.

"Not a bad idea," Sam said, "but is he giving you any updates?"

"Yeah, he's texting, but it's all pretty vague."

"Well, ask him."

"I have a friend in the area who can check up on him. I'll start with that."

"Good idea. Keep us posted."

"I will."

Nick: I'm home

Steve: Chicago?

Nick: Yeah

Steve: Dinner tomorrow?

Nick: Can't. Have a new job through a temp agency. Maybe next week?

Steve: Sounds good.

Steve knew something was off, but he also sensed that he should tread carefully. Steve didn't want to scare him off.

In early August, Steve was at the station, rolling up some hoses after getting back from a fire, when he was told he had a visitor. "Nicky?"

"Nah, man. A girl with purple hair. Said her name was Skye or something."

"Oh shit. Thanks."

Steve headed to the visitors' area and found Nick's roommate sitting on a chair with a box next to her feet on the floor.

"Hey, Skye. What brings you here?"

"Hi." She popped out of her seat when Steve spoke her name. "Nick's disappeared, Steve. He hasn't been at the apartment in over a month. He said he was taking a trip, but then he didn't come back. And..." She bit her lip and stared down at the floor. "I'm really sorry, but we need a paying roommate."

"So, he's not there now?" Steve asked. "I thought he was back in Chicago?"

Skye pressed her lips together and shook her head. "A couple of weeks ago, two young men showed up at our apartment. I'd never seen them before. They asked for Nick. I didn't let them in." She rubbed her hands together. "They kind of scared me at first, to be honest. I'm glad Maisey was there."

Steve narrowed his eyes in confusion.

"My girlfriend," Skye clarified.

"That's right. Sorry. Go on."

"Well, they said they didn't mean any harm, and they didn't try to force their way in at all. They said they were worried about Nick since he didn't show up for an appointment."

"An appointment?" Steve tried his best to remain calm. "What do you mean?"

"I didn't know," she said. "So I asked them, and their answer was kind of strange. They said he was always reliable when it came to his appointments with clients. They said that they've even gone on appointments with him. The agency they worked for called them double dates."

Steve closed his eyes and shook his head. "The agency?"

What had Nick gotten himself into?

Steve motioned toward the chair, and she sat back down.

"Um..." Skye continued to rub her hands together. "They... uh... they said the weirdest thing. They said Nick had a regular client - a guy named Mac. I told them he was Nick's boyfriend. They looked surprised and suggested that I stay away from him."

"I don't follow."

She looked around as if seeking an escape route. "Um... Nick liked to pretend things were better than they were. He always told me to be positive."

Steve pulled another chair around so he could sit across from her. "What do you mean, better?"

"Mac wasn't his boyfriend, Steve." Her eyes watered as she shook her head. "He was Nick's client."

"Client?"

"Um, yeah."

She took a moment to collect her thoughts.

"It was hard, but he would always try to cheer me up." A hint of a smile appeared on Skye's face but disappeared just as quickly. "It was really hard after we left the farm, but we made it work. He had the hotel job, and Maisey and I work at the restaurant. We make good tips, but... Nick helped us out because his job paid really well."

"He didn't tell me that."

"You were in the middle of a war, Steve. People were trying to kill you. He didn't want you to worry."

"Didn't want me to worry?" Steve scoffed. "He's my brother. He can tell me anything."

Skye arched a brow.

Steve held up his hands in surrender. "Fine. I just worry about him."

"Me, too. He's been such a good friend to me. He helped me down at the compound when we..."

Steve squeezed her shoulder when she trailed off. "I know. Nick's told me some of it."

"Anyway, we thought it was his hotel job that paid really well." She stopped to take a deep breath. "I don't really know much about Mac. I never met him, but..." She smiled as if remembering a fond memory. "Nick always talked about him like he was the best thing, you know?"

"I met him once, but he made a quick exit."

"Well. they said to stay away from him." She sped up as she spoke. "At first, I thought they meant Nicky, which would have been crazy because he wouldn't harm a fly. I wasn't about to stay away from my friend, but then..."

"Then what?"

She returned Steve's gaze. "They said they discovered this Mac guy was associated; they used the word associated." She paused as one of Steve's fellow firefighters walked by. "Um...with some guy named Jett who did bad things out in Michigan or Ohio or someplace. They said they told Nick and the others to stay away from him, but Nick was the only one Mac would request. Nick didn't tell anyone that he started to set up dates outside the system. Mac paid him extra."

"Outside the system," Steve repeated under his breath.

"Yes. Apparently, he paid him a lot because last spring, he paid for three months' worth of rent all at once."

Steve's stomach dropped. He had paying clients.

Nick was an escort.

"Anyway, before he left, he was so excited. Maybe he's still there? That Mac guy was always rolling in cash. Bought Nick all sorts of nice things. Clothes, tickets, took him to fancy dinners. They went to Detroit a couple of times, too, which makes me think."

"Wait. They've been to Detroit before?"

"Yeah."

"Do you know where he stayed?"

"Where?"

"In Detroit."

"Somewhere fancy. Always the best with Mac. Nick once showed me where they were going to be staying in Detroit. It's a cute boutique hotel. I don't remember the name, but it's in an old fire station or something. I remember he told me once that you'd like it because firefighters used to work there. He was so proud of you. I think he was always impressed with his older brother."

Steve smiled.

"He was able to save me. I wouldn't have made it there if it weren't for Nick. He befriended me at a time when I had no one. I mean no one, Steve."

Tears fell from her eyes. "You have to find him. I just know something bad has happened. I told Nick he shouldn't put all his eggs in one basket, but I think he fell for Mac. Mac's no good for him. I didn't even know him, but I don't trust him."

"Nicky said Mac was going to take him to a ballgame in Detroit. I wonder if they ever made it."

Skye wiped the tears from her cheeks and then forced a smile. "I don't know about that. He probably wouldn't mention it to me. I'm not much into sports, though my girlfriend loves it all. She's trying to teach me."

Steve offered up a weak smile. Skye was still fragile, but she was trying.

"Oh, speaking of sports..." She reached her hand inside her purse, struggling to open an inside pocket. "Ah!" She smiled in satisfaction. "Here it is. This was on our refrigerator." Steve accepted a well-worn picture of Nick and him at Wrigley Field from the first time he was on leave and got to visit Nick at their aunt and uncle's farm.

Steve warmed at the memory of taking Nick to his first game at Wrigley. He stared at the picture for a few moments until Skye cleared her throat.

"Um... I'm really sorry, Steve." She placed her hand on the boxes. "I'm sorry to bring this to you, but he left with most of his clothes and stuff. I don't know what to do with the furniture. There's not that much, but we have someone who wants to move in and... well... we can't really afford the place without the extra rent money coming in. And since it's been over a month..."

Steve cleared his throat. "No. I understand." He reached back for his wallet. "Does he owe you anything?"

She stared at the money. "Um... His share of the rent for this month, but... I went ahead and paid it."

"How much?"

She told him. Steve dug it from his wallet and gave it to her. She hesitated.

"Go on. Take it. You've been a friend to Nick, too. I don't want anything coming between you."

"Are you sure?" She started to reach out but pulled her hand back.

Steve grabbed her hand, pressed the cash into her palm, and

closed her fingers over it. "Take it. It's ok. I'll make arrangements to pick the furniture up when I'm off shift."

"Okay." She sniffed. "Look... I'm really sorry about this. I just... I... I hope he's okay, you know?"

"Yeah. Thanks."

She stuffed the cash inside her purse. "Okay." With a half wave, she turned. "Bye. Oh, wait..."

Steve raised his eyes and met her gaze.

She reached into her back pocket and pulled out a shiny green business card. She flipped it over and back again. "The men who stopped by left me this. And they seemed to really care. I hope. But, maybe it'll help?"

Steve read the card. Three words and a phone number. Have you called?

Windy City Gentlemen
312-555-6996

"Yeah."

"What is it?"

Her eyes darted around the station. "You should call them. Tell them you're looking for Robert. It's the name he went by."

"Robert's his first name. Nick is his middle name."

"Oh. Well. When you find him, please call me. If for nothing else, to let me know he's safe, ok? My number's on the box."

Skye turned and walked away.

Steve lifted one of the box flaps to find a number written in Sharpie. He programmed her number into his phone, then sat back down on his chair.

A few minutes later, he pulled out his phone again and dialed.

Lynn answered. "What happened?"

"I need your help. Nicky's in Detroit."

"What are you saying, Steve? You think he's running away? I mean, he's 24."

"He was supposed to go there for July Fourth weekend, but he hasn't come back," Steve spoke quickly, then stopped long enough to take a deep breath. "Lynn... he's not running away. He told me that Mac was taking him away for a weekend. Then, he texted that they were staying for a week. Now they're staying indefinitely. He says he's using vacation from his job at a hotel that told me he hasn't worked there in months."

Steve took another breath. "Then, for the last couple of weeks, he's been texting me, telling me he was back in Chicago, but his roommate just brought a box of his stuff to me at the station because he hasn't been there in so long that they had to find a new roommate."

"Don't do anything rash. Text me the details. And I'll check it out."

Chapter 38

Old Friend - New Mission

Ypsilanti, Michigan - Two months later.

Steve knocked three times on the freshly-painted door of a two-story home in a neighborhood full of well-kept homes and freshly-cut lawns. His old Marine buddy, Mace, opened the door with longer hair and a stomach that wasn't nearly as lean as when they were active-duty.

"Is that your friend, Mason?"

"Sure is, Sher," Mace said over his shoulder. He turned to Steve. "Leather jacket? More tats?" Mace scrutinized Steve with a curious eye. "And is that a piercing I see? You're looking pretty ragged, Steve."

"Good to see you, too, Mace." Steve grabbed Mace's hand and pulled him into a brotherly hug. "Hard to believe you're a cop now."

"I know," Mace said while laughing. "Can you believe they trust me to catch the bad guys?"

"Not how I imagined your life would turn out."

Mace laughed and patted him on the back. "Come on inside and meet the family."

Steve stepped inside the house to find a beautiful blonde woman checking on an infant in a bouncy seat in the corner of the room. Smiling, she greeted Steve with a warm hug. "So you're the man who got my husband through all those combat missions. Welcome to our home."

"No, Sheryl," Steve said while returning the hug. He pulled back to meet her gaze. "*You* were the one who got him through all those missions."

"I'm so glad to finally meet you." She motioned to the kitchen table. "Mason has told me all about you. He said you were here to find your brother? Something about him being in trouble or something?"

"Yes," Steve said. "I'm taking a few months off to track him down."

"I certainly hope you find him soon. I can't imagine how difficult this must be for you."

Mace handed his wife a glass of iced tea, then grabbed two beers out of the fridge and handed one to Steve. "We've converted the garage into a studio apartment." Mace paused, receiving an encouraging nod from his wife. "You're welcome to stay as long as you like, and you can pay us what you can."

"I hope I don't have to be here for too long."

Sheryl covered Steve's hand with her own. "Steve, you're family. You'll stay here as long as you need to."

"Thank you," Steve said.

When a loud knock sounded at the door, the baby instantly started crying. "Dammit," Mace whisper-yelled. "They *know* they're not supposed to wake up the baby."

Steve couldn't stop himself from laughing.

"I've got him," Sheryl said on her way to their son as if it were nothing unusual. "You go on out."

"Let's meet the guys." Mace led Steve outside to where three men waited. "Listen up, men. Steve is going to be staying with us while he takes care of his brother." Mace turned back to Steve.

"These are my friends, Mike, Nathan, and Andy, from the local VFW. Air Force, Army, and Marines, respectively. They're going to help you move in. I promised them pizza and beer afterward, but you're buying."

Steve shook their hands while Mace made the introductions. "No problem. Appreciate your help."

A short while later, after all of Steve and Nick's things had been moved into his new studio apartment, they sat down and waited for pizza. Mace pulled a six-pack out of the fridge. "There's more in there, Steve, but you get to replace these. They're from a good microbrewery in town."

Steve held up his bottle in a toast. "Thanks a lot."

"Mace said your brother was in some sort of trouble," Andy said. "How can we help?"

"Oh," Mace added, "did I mention they're also cops?"

Steve shared what he knew of his brother's situation, including the information that Lynn was able to dig up. First, they had him work with a sketch artist to put together a rendering of the man known as Mac. Mace helped him file a missing persons report at the station so the officers would know to look for Nick as well as treat him as a victim of a crime rather than an actual criminal.

As the weeks dragged on, Steve gave up on returning to Chicago. He took a job at a local fire station that welcomed an already-trained firefighter paramedic.

Lynn popped in from time to time since she was based out of Detroit. Once, she even brought pictures taken of Nick having dinner with Mac. Unfortunately, the undercover agent didn't know who they were when he took them since he was surveilling someone else entirely.

Nick had stopped texting entirely. But, keeping the promise he made back in high school, Steve never changed his phone number or email in case Nick ever needed to use them.

In the spring, Steve and another firefighter from his station went up to St. Ignace near Mackinac Island to help a station that lost two firefighters in an industrial fire. They returned three weeks later. As Steve was settling back into his life, he received a text message from an unknown number. He traced it back to the Boutique Hotel in Detroit.

Lynn checked it out and learned that a man meeting Mac's description paid for a room two months in advance. He was frequently in and out, but a young blond man only went out on occasion. They recognized the picture of Nick, but after checking, Lynn confirmed he wasn't there.

Lynn's undercover contacts started following Mac, who left town for Baltimore, leaving Nick behind. When they raided the room, Nick and all their belongings were gone. The front desk confirmed the room was paid up for another month, but they'd checked out early without asking for a refund of any kind.

When Mac returned a week later, he was questioned. He denied knowing where Nick was or even that his name was Nick. Mac told them that a man named Jett was going to kill him for talking to the police. The man was scared.

Two weeks later, Mac's body was found in the Michigan Theater parking garage.

In June, after being in Michigan for eight and a half months, Steve received a text message.

Unknown: Stevie - 2673 N Hill Street

"Lynn, take a look at this text."

She took his phone and read the message. "Who else calls you Stevie?"

"No one else. Only Nicky."

"Let me make a call." Lynn stepped outside of Steve's apartment while he and Mace sat at his small kitchen table.

"Let me see that address," Mace said. "Hill Street? That's a real shitty part of town."

Steve flinched at the thought.

"Why the hell would Nicky be there?"

Lynn returned. "He would be there in holding because they're moving."

"What?"

"Jett's organization has safe houses in every city they operate in. According to my source, he has two in that area where they keep people for a few days before moving them to another city."

"How soon can you get someone out there?"

"Within the next few days."

"That's not good enough."

"It's the best we can do, Steve," she said. "I'm sorry."

"Fuck that."

Steve grabbed his boots and laced them up. He strode to the opposite wall and grabbed his leather jacket. It was early June, but the evenings were cool. And if he was going to take his new motorcycle out, he wanted to be protected.

"What are you doing?" Lynn asked.

"I'm heading to Detroit."

"You can't go," Lynn scolded him. "We'll conduct the search."

"You can't do it for a few days."

"This is not your jurisdiction," she glared at him.

"Bullshit, Lynn. You go do your paperwork, then you can have your little turf war with Andy and Mace if you want, but as a civilian, I can go wherever the fuck I want. And whenever I want."

"Not if I arrest you, you can't."

Steve picked up his helmet and stared her down. "Are you going to arrest me?"

She didn't respond.

"I didn't think so."

Steve reached into the top of a closet and pulled down a gun safe. Opening it up, he pulled out his Sig Sauer and two magazines. Ensuring everything was fully loaded, he strapped it in a small holster that fit into the waistband of his jeans.

"Well, you're not going alone," Mace said.

Usually the silent type, Andy spoke up. "No. He's not, but you're not the one going with him."

"You're not keeping me home."

"Yes. I am," Andy insisted. "Nighttime news is already on. You have a wife and kid at home. You have another kid on the way. You would be way out of your own jurisdiction in a very dangerous area. I know the area. Plus, I do a lot of liaison work with Detroit PD. I can get away with it, not that I plan to flash a badge."

Steve offered him a nod of thanks.

"Besides," Andy added as he slipped his arms into a leather jacket. "Steve and I will go in as bikers." Andy turned to Steve. "Mind stopping at my place so I can switch out my wheels? It's on the way."

"I'll follow you."

"Be careful," Mace said as they left.

Steve turned back to Lynn, who didn't say a word.

Andy tapped Steve on the shoulder. "Come on. I'll have a plan by the time we get to my place. We're going to a rough neighborhood."

At the last second, Andy grabbed Steve by the arm. "You're not going there tonight as a firefighter, Steve. You're going there as a Marine."

It took a few seconds to sink in that Andy was as serious about finding Nick as he was. "Yes, sir," Steve said. "I'll be ready."

Chapter 39

Near miss

DETROIT, MI - JUNE 2015

According to Andy, Hill Street was the worst part of the worst neighborhood. Everyone knew to avoid it. Its glory days came and went before the first rock 'n roll tunes ever played at school dances. Once World War II production slowed down and then came to a sudden halt, people sought out other options. In the late 1940s, families moved to the suburbs. One by one, businesses closed their doors forever, only occasionally being re-inhabited by fly-by-night businesses that opened one week but closed the next. Soon after, schools consolidated and bussed students farther and farther away.

Pawn shops and bail bondsmen moved in where grocery stores, salons, and dressmakers once sold their wares. What were once family homes became tattoo or massage parlors. Other homes had windows covered with plywood rather than curtains. Storefront churches popped up on one end of the street, only to close and reopen on the other end under a new name with the hope of rebuilding their meager congregations. Much to the dismay of hotel management, the churches did their best mission work next to the places that rented rooms by the hour.

Street cleaners came in from time to time, but newspapers,

cigarette butts, and empty bottles decorated the streets and uneven sidewalks. A police car drove by at least once per shift. Sadly, they couldn't do much to curb the petty thievery and prostitution running rampant on these blocks. The graffiti-covered doors and peeling paint of foreclosed houses offered ideal curb appeal to squatters and drug pushers who would move in for a month or two until the police ran them out. But once the police drove away, they set up shop again in a neighboring house, offering an addictive escape to the working girls and boys who walked the streets after the sun went down.

Dressed in blue jeans, a black leather jacket, and black boots, Steve pulled his motorcycle up to the curb next to a woman wearing a short skirt and torn fishnet stockings. He pulled out a phone and held it up to her as he took off his helmet.

"Hey baby." The long-haired brunette wobbled up to him on her way-too-high heels while chomping a big wad of gum. Her thick red lipstick provided a marked contrast to her chipped, yellow teeth. "Ya wanna take me on a date?"

He held up his phone and showed her a picture. "Have you seen this man?" he asked in his deep baritone voice.

She never fully closed her mouth while chewing. The smacking sounds grated on his nerves like nails on a chalkboard.

Her eyes skimmed the picture. "Or are you into boys?"

Unfazed, he held it back up to the woman.

"Look again. He'd be older now. In his mid-20s." He popped the stand of his motorcycle and rested both feet on the ground.

In front of the flickering neon lights of a payday loan store, the young woman took a better look at the picture. Leaning forward to showcase her wares on display behind a sheer, low-cut tank top. Her caked-on makeup made her look about ten years older than she probably was. She popped her gum and repeated her answer. "Nah. I ain't seen 'im."

She put her hand on Steve's chest, and her bright red lips broke into a smile. "But if you want, baby, I can pretend I have." She nodded toward the open door of the seedy motel.

He gently gripped her wrist without changing expression and pushed it away. "No thanks."

"Another time, then." She turned and strutted to a car that had just pulled up, propositioning the driver as if Steve never existed.

"I don't think so," he muttered to himself. He secured his helmet to his motorcycle, unzipped his leather jacket, and stepped onto the curb. A small piece of paper blew down the street in the late-night breeze the moment he lifted his boot.

Steve asked the next woman and got the same answer. "Nope. Don't know him."

He repeated the question to everyone working the street that night, turning down several offers. He desperately wanted someone to say they'd seen his brother.

A short, round man he spoke to suggested he try the next block over at the all-night diner. "Ask for Lenny. He's a skinny guy. Kind of skeevy, but he knows people. He may know him." The man gave him a nod then walked to a parked car where a woman waited in the passenger seat. Her head disappeared below the steering wheel the second he closed the door.

Steve put his phone in his pocket and made the short walk to the aptly named Corner Diner. He was grateful for his military training on nights like tonight. His ever-vigilant eyes scanned the area, seeing anyone and everyone who lurked inside recessed doorways or behind windows.

The neon sign was partially burned out, making it read as Corn rather than Corner Diner. He shook his head, but it seemed par for the course in this neighborhood. He glanced up at a burned-out street lamp that eliminated any shadows on this side of the street. Finding a spot without chewed pieces of gum stuck to it, he leaned back against the welcome sign by the front door and waited for the lone customer to walk out.

Nearing 2 am, the all-night diner kept its lights on for anyone looking for a cup of coffee or a piece of leftover pie.

After a few minutes, a middle-aged man slinked out of the diner's double doors. With greasy, slicked-back hair and two-day-old stubble, he pulled a pack of cigarettes out of his pocket. His shifty eyes darted around as if he were being followed.

Steve leaned back against the door frame with his hands in his pockets and one knee kicked up against the weather-stained wall.

The other man tensed and gave him a suspicious sideways glance that didn't go unnoticed despite trying to play it cool. Tapping the pack against his palm a few times, he stuck a cigarette between his lips and returned the box to his pocket. He brought a lighter up to his face. Cupping his other hand in front to block the light breeze, he tried to light it. No matter how many times he flicked it with his thumb, he couldn't get it to spark a flame.

Moving slowly so as not to spook him, Steve pulled a box of matches out of his jacket pocket and held it up for the man to see. He lit one to help the man light his cigarette. After taking a few quick puffs, he narrowed his eyes while taking a long drag. "Thanks," he muttered while holding the cigarette in his mouth.

"Nice night," Steve uttered as he slipped the matches back into his pocket.

The lanky man grunted, releasing tendrils of smoke from between his narrow lips.

"It's Lenny, isn't it?" Steve added.

The man stiffened.

Steve was close enough to grab him if he tried to bolt, but neither man moved.

"Do I know you?" He seemed short of breath, but his shifty eyes never made eye contact.

"No," Steve admitted with narrowed eyes. He surveyed each corner of the intersection and turned to face Lenny. "But I'm told you might help me find somebody."

"I don't know anybody."

Steve stuck his phone in front of the man's face. "This man."

Lenny's eyes looked everywhere but at the phone. Steve gently placed his hand on the man's shoulder and gave him a slight squeeze. It wasn't enough to hurt him, but it was enough to convey that he could.

He dropped his voice. "Look at him. He'd be a little older now."

Lenny looked at a smiling young man wearing a St. Louis Cardinals T-shirt. His wavy, blond hair stuck out from underneath the ball cap. Recognition flickered in his eyes. "Yeah," he breathed. "I know him."

Steve's heart raced, but he kept his cool.

"That's Robert," Lenny whispered.

"Where is he?"

"Not here. They moved out last night."

"Moved out? Where are they going?"

"Columbus."

"Ohio?"

"Yeah."

"Where in Columbus?" Steve squeezed tighter.

Lenny shrugged.

"Who's he with?"

He looked away. The end of his cigarette glowed bright orange as he took another long drag. He didn't answer.

"Who?" Steve tightened his fingers.

"He was with Mac, but now he's one of Jett's people." He cringed and tried to free himself from under Steve's tightening grip. "But you didn't hear it from me."

Steve dropped his hand off the man's shoulders and dropped his chin to his chest. He released a long breath and turned to face the wall. With no warning, he smacked it. Hard. "FUCK!"

He didn't care that he made Lenny jump and scamper down the

street. He strode to his motorcycle without another word, glaring at anyone who dared look in his direction. He was as close as he'd been to his brother in months.

And he'd missed him.

Chapter 40

Grant's Crossing

"Welcome to Grant's Crossing Fire Department," a tall, round man with a crew cut boomed out from behind a desk that seemed much too grandiose for the space it occupied.

"Thank you, Chief." Steve shook Chief Travis' hand, nearly worried that he might end up being greeted with a big bear hug in lieu of a handshake. He'd been through this before, moving to a new town and working at a new fire station. He hated all the happy-go-lucky introductions that came with being the new guy. He just wanted to come in, do his job, and ignore everything else.

Chief Jordan Travis stood up and led Steve out of the office with an overzealous pat on the back. "Let me introduce you to the men you'll be working with here at GC Fire."

They strolled toward the heart of the station where the firefighters on shift could relax between calls. It was a rather sizable area with two well-worn blue couches and a trio of recliners forming a semi-circle around a large-screen TV currently playing a Cincinnati Reds baseball game. On the far side of the room were a galley kitchen, an island with a separate coffee station, and a pair of rectangular banquet tables, each surrounded by six chairs.

"Can I have your attention, please?" The chief announced, causing the chatter to stop. Heads turned as he spoke. "I want to introduce the newest member of GCFD, Steve Cook. He's new to town and will start next shift. Like all of you, he's a certified firefighter paramedic."

A tall, slender man of Indian descent stood up and extended his hand. "Abhishek Battacharya,"

"Pardon me?"

He laughed at Steve's knitted brow and open mouth. "I'm one of the volunteer firefighters. Call me Shek."

"Ah. Thanks!" Steve offered a smile as they shook hands.

"And this..." the chief started.

An alarm sounded, cutting off the rest of the Chief's sentence. Everyone straightened, and with a chorus of welcomes, they rushed out.

A man wearing a GCFD Lieutenant t-shirt turned around long enough to point at Steve. "Be at Jo's tomorrow night. We'll meet you then."

Steve lifted his chin. "Yeah."

The man waved and disappeared out the door, leaving Steve alone in his new fire station.

***

The next evening, Steve met the guys from the fire station at Jo's Bar & Grille, a popular sports bar and restaurant in the heart of Grant's Crossing, for an early dinner. Still maintaining a pub-like atmosphere with dark wooded booths, tables, and a large bar in the center, Jo's was made less like the speakeasy it originally was with large flat-screen TVs lining the walls, and a small dance floor with an old jukebox in the corner.

"I'm Juan Palacios," a tall, olive-skinned man with silver laced jet black hair and dark brown eyes stood to greet him with a handshake from across the table. "It's nice to meet you, Steve."

"Juan may be our lieutenant now, but he's been Tank ever since high school." Another man who was about Steve's height, with dark wavy hair and green eyes, said as he patted Tank's back and offered his hand. "I'm Derek Mitchell. And this," he pointed his thumb back to another man standing up from the table, "is Kiro Marinov."

"Kiro Marinov, you said?" Steve said as he repeated *KEER-oh* carefully in his head as he shook the man's hand. Since the last name was close to *Marine* with an *off* at the end, he figured that would be easy enough to remember. "Russian?"

"Nah, man. Bulgarian." Kiro, a fair-complected man with short, spiked black hair and whiskey-brown eyes, corrected him with a grin. "And it's good to meet you. Welcome to Grant's Crossing."

"Thanks."

"We're the primary paramedic team on B-shift," Derek explained as he gestured with his hand to Kiro and continued around the table. "You've met Shek already." Steve shook his hand again as Derek spoke. "That's Tiny Tim."

Steve's own six feet of height made him feel short by comparison when shaking hands with a bald, solid wall of muscle who had at least another five inches on him.

"Tim Ellis." Tim's deep voice sounded out. "Welcome."

"And this is Emerson," Derek introduced the last person at the table before settling back into his chair.

"RJ Emerson," A man, who was an inch or two shorter than Steve and a tad more slender, said. Emerson had a mop of messy, dark red hair and friendly, deep brown eyes. "Glad to have you with us."

"Thank you."

Someone ordered a beer for Steve as he started answering a myriad of questions. "After the Marines, I spent some time in

Chicago, then almost a year outside of Ann Arbor before moving down here."

"Ann Arbor? Really? Tell me you're not a Wolverine fan. I mean, you're in Buckeye country now." Emerson laughed. Ohio State University campus was located in nearby Columbus. They were the rivals of the University of Michigan.

Steve scoffed. "Nah. Navy."

"This should make the Army-Navy game more fun this year." Kiro took a pull of his beer.

"Why's that?"

He tilted his bottle toward Derek. "D and Tank are both Army guys." He glanced up and pointed toward the man standing behind the bar, who gave a quick wave. "So is Mike Porter. Mike and Jo Porter own this place."

"I think I'll be fine. Besides," Steve smirked. "Three to one isn't exactly outnumbered."

Tank rested his drink on the table. "What did you do in the Marines?"

"Usually saved you Army boys' asses."

"Uh. Oh. Them's fightin' words." Emerson joked in his best cowboy accent, drawing laughter from around the table.

Tank and Derek shared a conspiratorial grin; then Tank leaned forward. "We may just have to make a friendly wager this year."

Steve tipped his bottle in a friendly salute. "You're on."

A couple of hours later, most of the men had gone home to their families, leaving only Steve, Derek, and Kiro behind. The three of them all lived within walking distance of the popular downtown watering hole. Steve didn't comment on the fact that Derek was still putting down beers while he and Kiro had switched to non-alcoholic beverages.

Curious and with lowered inhibitions, Derek spoke up as the server dropped a fresh beer off at the table. "So what's with all the moving? You've been out of the Marines for what? A few years now?

And you're already on your third station in as many states." He glanced over at Kiro and back at Steve. "We don't want to have to treat our own."

Despite having expected the question, Steve's body tensed. "Treat your own?"

"Yeah." Derek leaned forward. "We want to make sure you're part of the team and not someone who will need rescuing because you went off on your own."

Steve stared at his root beer and took a sip while contemplating how best to answer. He leaned forward and rested both hands around the base of his bottle. Lifting his eyes to meet Derek's, he relaxed his shoulders and replied. "I'm not a discipline problem if that's what you're asking."

"Reckless, then?" Derek pushed, receiving a hard look from Steve in response. "I mean, why move so much?"

Kiro's eyes drifted back and forth between Derek and Steve, monitoring a swift influx of tension. "We're a tight-knit group here. We're like family. On shift, we trust each other with our lives. Off-shift, we do the same thing. Look." Steve's eyes narrowed in response as Kiro continued speaking. "We don't mean to pry, but..."

"I do," Derek countered with a single arched brow, earning a frustrated glare from Kiro. "I mean to pry."

"We just want to know who we're working with, that's all," Kiro explained, casting a warning glance toward Derek, who took another sip of his beer. "If you don't want to tell us, that's fine. But if it's something that will affect us on the job or put us in danger, then we have a right to know."

"Right to know, huh?"

"Yeah." Both Derek and Kiro answered in unison, apparently agreeing.

Steve nodded in understanding. He'd worked at fire stations where guys got along well out of necessity, but it always seemed forced. He'd also worked at some houses where they went out of their way to support each other. Well, one house, but it had been a while since his time in Chicago. Perhaps this one was similar. Taking a risk, he stared at his glass and started speaking. "It's for my brother."

"Your brother." Derek's tone was flat.

"Yes. My brother." Steve met his gaze with a glare that dared him to say more. "I've barely seen him since I got back," he mumbled into his glass.

"Since you got back?" Derek set down his beer. "Back from what? Vacation? Your last job? What?"

"From Iraq," Steve growled.

Kiro was lifting his glass to his lips and froze. "Wait. You haven't seen him since you were in the Marines?"

"Nope." Steve finished his drink. "Well. A few times, but that's it."

"That's been what? Two or three years?"

Steve's glare confirmed Kiro's math.

"What about your parents?" Derek leaned forward. "Don't they know?"

Steve huffed out a laugh. "My parents and I aren't exactly on speaking terms. And my brother," Steve set his glass on the table. "Let's just say he got away from them. I got letters and emails from him while I was deployed and saw him a time or two on leave. Since then, it's been less and less. Every time he calls or texts, I move to be closer so he can move in with me, but he's usually already gone by the time I get there."

Steve shook his head. "He fell into a dangerous crowd, and I haven't been able to locate him. They keep moving him."

"You mean he's in trouble with the police or something?"

"More like traffickers," Steve mumbled and shook his head to try to clear the thought from his head. "Fuck. Look. Just forget I said anything."

He started to rise when Derek reached across the table and grabbed him by the forearm to stop him. "This stays between us."

Steve almost shrugged him off but hesitated as Derek's expression changed from mistrust to genuine concern.

"And we can help," Derek said as he turned to Kiro, who nodded in confirmation. "Let us help."

Steve leaned in and gritted his teeth. His expression was stern, and his voice gruff. "How? How can you help? Every time I think I find him, he disappears. He'll call and set up a time to meet but then cancels at the last minute. Something comes up. It's as if they know I'm coming, so I'm always a step behind."

Derek tilted his chin toward the bar. "Drew can help you, then."

"Drew?"

"Sheriff Drew Strager. He's Jo Porter's brother."

Steve looked over to a man in a sheriff's uniform talking to the woman behind the bar then yanked his arm from Derek's grip. "Fuck that. I don't want him arrested. I want him to be safe."

"Okay." Derek pulled back, holding his palms out as he leaned back into his seat and stretched his legs out beneath the table. "I know you just got here, but you can trust him. He's good people."

"Yeah." Steve took one last look at the sheriff, sharing a joke with his sister. "That's what they always said about our parents." He stood up and dropped a few bills on the table. "Thanks for the drinks tonight. I'll see you both on Friday."

Derek and Kiro watched Steve walk out the front door.

Kiro turned to Derek and spoke in a low voice. His concern was evident. "Did he say trafficked?"

"Yeah, K." Derek reached into his pocket for his wallet and pulled out some cash to leave on the table. "He did."

Chapter 41

Dinner at the Station

"Heard anything about Nick lately?" Derek asked as he dished out Steve's plate, who was the last in line for dinner.

"No." Steve's curt response ended any further inquiry. He took the plate Derek handed him and sat down.

One bite of chicken, and he happily changed the subject. "Shit, Derek. The guys are right. You really are an excellent cook. What's with all the Creole cooking? And do you take requests?"

"My mom was from New Orleans," Derek added as he sat down across from him.

With his mouth full of food, Emerson gave Steve a friendly elbow to the arm. "You've been here a couple of months; find a girlfriend yet?"

Steve laughed as he washed his bite down with a Coke. "No way, man. Not interested in settling down. Hooking up? Sure. And I've noticed there's no shortage of good-looking women here in central Ohio."

The men laughed as they dug into their dinner.

"But if you have any recommendations," Steve said, "I'm happy to try them out."

Emerson held his hands up. "Nah, man."

"Thankfully," Tank raised a fork to his mouth. "I'm out of that scene."

Derek jumped into the fray. "You were never *in* that scene, Tank. Haven't you and Araceli been together since you were in diapers or something?"

Steve creased his brow, so Derek nodded toward Tank and playfully rolled his eyes. "High school sweethearts."

"Ahh," Steve replied. "How about you, Kiro?"

Kiro held up his hands. "I'm done as well."

"You're married, too?"

"Hopefully. Someday."

"You mean you still haven't proposed?" Tiny Tim wisecracked.

"So, technically, Celeste is still available, right?" Emerson joked, raising an arm to protect his face as Kiro glared at him.

"Don't even think about it, Roland."

Emerson grimaced when Kiro addressed him by his given name.

Derek explained to Steve. "Kiro and Celeste have had crushes on each other since they actually were in diapers but have only just started dating as of the last... what?" He shot an inquisitive look at Kiro. "A few months ago?"

"Been five months." Kiro corrected him, holding up his hand, with fingers splayed out for emphasis.

Derek placed his hand on his chest with attempted contrition. "I stand corrected. Five months."

Steve laughed as he shoved more chicken in his mouth.

Tank spoke up again. "If you do want recommendations, Derek can probably help. He can give you specifics about most of the single women in town."

"Some of the married women, too, probably," Tim joked.

Derek pointed toward Tim. "No. No. Even I have a code. No married women."

Tim held up his hands in surrender.

"I prefer out of town for that," Steve added. "Gotta live here."

Tank laughed. "Doesn't bother Derek, but it sounds like we've got another man whore among us."

Derek drew his hands up to his chest in an effort to look offended, then broke into a confident smile. "I prefer the term irresistible. Or charming. Handsome works, too. Definitely more so than all of you."

A chorus of yells erupted from the men as they tossed some well-aimed, wadded-up napkins at him. Derek laughed and turned his attention back to Steve.

"But I can offer you recommendations. What do you prefer? Blondes? Redheads? Brunettes? Short? Tall?" He paused to waggle his eyebrows. "Flexible?" Derek stuffed a large bite of food into his mouth while still grinning.

Steve shook his head with a laugh as he chewed, figuring it was probably best just to keep eating. They didn't need to know he preferred blondes or redheads, though mostly redheads. Especially tall redheads.

When he lifted his gaze, Derek had a smug yet proud expression. "Happy to help a new guy out."

"Oh. I can do well enough on my own, thanks."

As if on cue, the other men let out a collective *WHOA* in response.

"No, really. I'm happy to share." Derek offered.

"Uh... not really into that, thanks."

"Trade off then?"

Steve scrunched his face, hoping he was joking. "Nah. I'm good."

"You know," Kiro butted in, waving his palm back and forth between Derek and Steve, "you're both sounding pretty damned misogynistic. Women aren't commodities to share and trade, you know."

"Whipped!" Tiny Tim coughed into his glass. Kiro tossed a wadded-up napkin that landed right in Tim's drink.

"Hey!"

They all laughed as Tim grimaced and stuck his fingers in his glass to retrieve the sopping-wet napkin.

Derek couldn't resist. "I'm happy with the women I date."

"Yeah, but are *they*?" an ordinarily quiet Abhishek asked, adding more laughter.

"And do you ever see one for more than a couple hours at a time?" Emerson asked with a chuckle.

"Couple hours?" Tank joked. "That might be a stretch. How about ten minutes?"

"That's enough, Tank!" Derek glared at Tank, then broke out into a cocky grin. "Trust me, they're always happy. And It's always *much* longer than ten minutes, thank you."

Steve laughed and thought back to his unit in Iraq, obnoxiously joking about all the women they planned to see while on leave.

Men could be such dogs.

"It's all about setting expectations." Derek held out his hands as he carefully explained.

"Any repeats?" Steve couldn't hold back his curiosity.

"Sure," Derek confirmed, his grin widening. "Gotta have some regulars for holidays and when people are out of town."

"Yeah. That's a good idea," Steve agreed.

"Communication is key." Derek washed another bite down.

"*Stiga, be!*" Kiro tossed his arms in the air in mock exasperation as he muttered a long string of cuss words in Bulgarian.

Derek shrugged at Steve as they silently turned to Kiro.

"Now, imagine if you communicate enough to see her a second time." Kiro closed his eyes with a sigh. "It's pretty damned amazing."

Tim and Emerson both rolled their eyes. They were secretly nodding while mouthing the word *whipped* to each other.

"Amazing, huh? Any chance I can confirm that with Celeste?" Derek asked, his expression nonchalant.

Steve snorted a laugh.

Kiro sat up straighter. "You want to risk your junk for that, D? You know I'm very skilled with sharp objects. Never forget that."

Derek raised his hands in surrender. "I know. I know. She's off-limits."

"Got that right," he huffed.

Steve laughed at Derek and agreed. "You're right. He's definitely whipped."

"Et tu, Steve?" Exasperated, Kiro stood up to walk back to the counter for seconds. The shaking of his shoulders betrayed his laughter at the playful banter.

Emerson tapped Steve's arm with his elbow. "You know, if anyone ever tried to mess with somebody's wife or girlfriend, they'd have to fight all of us. We joke in here, but no one will ever touch Celeste. We just like seeing Kiro all riled up because he's an easy target. And," Emerson spoke louder to ensure Kiro heard him, "you're not that skilled with sharp objects. We've seen you play darts!"

They all laughed while Emerson turned back to Steve. "But we all love her like we do Tank's wife, Araceli, and their three little kids."

"Four." Tank corrected him, holding up four fingers.

"Sorry, four little kids now. And my Aimee. Tim and his girlfriend just broke up again, so he's living vicariously through you and Derek until they get back together, which, according to their usual routine, should be this weekend or next. Never lasts long."

"How long have you and Aimee been dating?" Steve asked.

Emerson hesitated. "Um."

"You are dating, right?"

"She hasn't said yes, not exactly."

"She turned you down?"

"Not really."

"Well?"

Emerson's shoulders slumped as he exhaled in defeat. "Ok. Fine. I want her to be my girlfriend."

Steve arched a brow. "Your chances will improve if you ask her out, man."

"I'll get around to it," he mumbled. Clearing his throat, he continued the conversation. "Anyway..."

Chapter 42

A Sighting

Steve laughed as Emerson provided the rundown of everyone's significant others. Judging by their descriptions, each sounded more impressive than the next.

The conversation drifted to other topics as the men sat at the tables finishing Derek's dinner. It was typically their favorite night since he was the best cook.

Steve and Emerson drew the short straws for dish duty and were just sitting down to watch TV with Abhishek when Sheriff Strager walked inside the fire station. While tall, the beginnings of a beer gut showed he wasn't in the same great shape as his firefighting brethren. Still, he stood as if he had the run of the place. His presence oozed authority with his mustache and hat covering his short, dark hair.

In a heated game of checkers, Kiro snapped his checkers several times across the board to reach the other side. He raised his arms in the air. "King me, baby!"

No one needed to understand Tank's muttered Spanish to know what he said.

"Good to see our first responders hard at work." Sheriff Strager said with a straight face as Tank reluctantly placed another checker atop Kiro's piece.

Elsewhere in the room, Derek was stretched out on a recliner, reading a book. Tim's long legs hung over the edge of the couch during a post-dinner nap. His snoring could easily be heard from across the room. When a well-thrown pillow landed on his head, he jumped up in surprise. "What the...?"

"Keep it down over there," Shek called out, aiming the remote at the TV to adjust the volume. "I'm trying to watch the game."

Emerson strode by the checkers' match and greeted Drew with a handshake. "You know we're just waiting around until you and your boys need rescued again."

Drew let out a hearty laugh. The Grant's Crossing police have always had an excellent relationship with the firefighters.

Tank gave a quick wave to Drew. "To what do we owe the pleasure of your company this fine evening, Sheriff?"

"I wanted to check to see how you were all doing." Drew laughed and said his hellos to those in the room who weren't half asleep. He nodded toward Steve. "Steve. You have a minute?"

"Yeah." Steve tensed up, knowing there would only be one reason Drew would want to talk to him in private. Mace and Andy had made some inquiries. As did Lynn, once she decided she wasn't pissed that Steve took it upon himself to go door-to-door to find Nick. "Let's take it outside."

From the table, Kiro waved to catch Derek's eye and nodded toward where Steve and Drew were talking. Derek folded over the corner of the page he was reading to look through the plate glass window separating the lounge from the garage.

Steve stopped next to the open door of the ladder truck. Drew handed over his phone, drawing attention to the picture lighting up the screen.

Steve didn't really hear what Drew said next. He just stared at a grainy picture of a thin man with straggly, shoulder-length blond hair.

It was his brother.

"That's Nicky." Steve's voice barely escaped his lips above a whisper. The picture wasn't very good, but there was no mistaking who it was. It looked like the other man in the picture was holding his brother up.

"This picture was taken this afternoon, Steve," Drew explained. "I'll send you an address, but it's in a sketchy part of Columbus. He's here, though. I spoke to someone who's keeping an eye on the house for us. He's working a case and can't blow his cover, so he can't pull him out right away."

"This is here? You mean he's close?"

Drew nodded. "Yes. He's here. Well, he's just outside of downtown Columbus."

"Tell them to get him out."

"They're working a bigger case that they can't jeopardize. I can't give you all the details."

"FUCK THE DETAILS," Steve yelled out. "He's not safe there, and this is the closest I've been in–"

Drew placed his hand on Steve's shoulder. "They're not expecting anyone else to be at the house for a couple of days. My source says he's being taken there to lie low for a few days at least. Something else is happening that might potentially blow the case wide open."

"He'll be there...so I can go get him."

"It's not that simple, but yes. You can go get him." Drew paused. "But Steve, you have to be careful. That's a nasty part of town."

Steve glared at the Sheriff. "And?"

"Just be careful, okay?"

Drew sent the picture to Steve's phone then left the fire station.

Derek and Kiro stepped out to check on Steve, who pulled up the picture on his phone and stared at his brother. His rough exterior softened when he saw his brother looking so thin, almost gaunt in the face. It looked like he hadn't seen a proper meal or a day without drugs in weeks, if not longer. His lackluster eyes were sunken in, drooping as if all hope was gone. "I'll get you out of there, Nicky. I promise."

Steve lifted his arm to check the time on his wristwatch. "I need to drive down to Columbus - just east of downtown near someplace called The Bottoms, wherever that is. And I can't go there on my motorcycle, and my car's in the shop. Shit. He's so thin. Where can I rent a car?" His thoughts were all over the place, betraying his usual calm demeanor.

"You don't need to rent a car," Derek responded. "I have a truck."

"I can borrow your truck?"

"Hell, no. I'll drive."

"I'm going, too," Kiro added. "But we'll take my SUV. Your truck is too new, D. It would stand out like a sore thumb in that neighborhood. I'll drive."

"You don't need to go. I can take care of my brother."

Derek clapped Steve's shoulder. "We know you can, but we're going, anyway." The alarm sounded on the overhead speakers for a multi-car accident. "We'll leave as soon as our shift is over."

Chapter 43

Crack House

THE BOTTOMS, COLUMBUS, OHIO

The bright sun was already high in the sky on a beautiful day when they arrived in an old, rundown neighborhood near the west side of Columbus. Houses with broken or boarded-up windows lined each side of the street. Many of the houses had lawns that hadn't felt the blade of a lawnmower in months, with grass growing higher than the cracked concrete porches or rusty chain-link fences.

Kiro stayed with his SUV, a fully stocked med kit at the ready, while Steve and Derek marched straight toward the door of an old, neglected, single-story bungalow with a dandelion-covered lawn. It was probably one of many neighborhood crackhouses, but most of the windows were still intact.

The creaking of rusty chains drew their gaze to a man napping on a swinging chair on the front porch. He wore dirty clothes that were at least a size or two too small for him, and it was clear he probably hadn't showered in a few days. He held a cigarette precariously close to the worn seat cushion with a long line of ash about to fall on the ground below him as the seat swung back and forth.

A voice called out from the swinging chair. "You sure you want to go in there?"

Steve glanced over to see the man tap his cigarette so the ashes fell on the porch. Not bothering to knock, Steve turned the bent metal door handle to find it unlocked. The foul stench hit Steve and Derek the moment they crossed the threshold. The thick, musty air was ripe with body odor, piss, and cigarette smoke.

Derek followed behind Steve, both taking a moment for their eyes to adjust to the loss of light. Steve took the lead, taking them past the small entry area to a large living room. Both men took inventory of all the windows and doors for potential exits while Steve focused on finding his brother. While Steve searched, Derek made sure neither of them was surprised by anyone.

The interior was quiet save for the man and woman going at it in a bedroom just off the living room, seemingly indifferent to the sunglasses-wearing, shirtless man with beer gut sleeping against the wall on the grungy, stained carpet that looked like it hadn't felt the touch of a vacuum cleaner in years. All the curtains were closed, and the blinds shut.

The only light in the room came from the ignored television. A half-naked woman was passed out on the couch, slumped over the side with part of a dollar sign tattoo visible on her lower back. The man next to her barely took notice of Steve and Derek as he leaned forward to inhale a line of white powder. He pulled himself up with a heavy sniff through his nose before wiping it upwards with the palm of his hand. His heavy lids barely lifted as he collapsed against the back of the putrid green couch with a half smile.

He'd have to be stoned out of his mind to be content in such squalid conditions.

Focused on finding his brother, Steve strode further into the dingy house. The living room turned into the dining room. When the floor creaked, a round, hairy man wearing an unbuttoned shirt covering a sweat-stained tank shot up out of his chair to face the intruder.

"Hey," he said, gritting his yellow, nicotine-stained teeth. "What the fuck are you doing here? You're not supposed to be here."

He stood protectively in front of the stacks of cash he'd been counting, and an ashtray full of butts collected the ash of what was left of his still-burning cigarette. He was slightly taller than Steve but probably hadn't seen the inside of a gym since a grade-school assembly.

Without a word, Steve grabbed him by the collar and shoved him against the wall, grimacing when the smelly man let out a loud belch in his face.

Derek stood behind him, acting as his second, equally intimidating and ready to jump in at a moment's notice if the man gave them any trouble. He kept his eye on the rest of the house, constantly monitoring for movement.

"Where is he?" Steve demanded.

"Fuck you," he sneered.

"Where. Is. He?" Steve repeated.

"Who?"

"Nicholas."

The man coughed a bit, attempting to clear his throat, then spit a glob of phlegm that narrowly missed Steve, earning him a right hook that landed square on his jaw. "There's no Nicholas here."

"Robert, then," Steve said, using his brother's first name that he never used. "Or RC."

"He's busy." The man let out a phlegm-ridden laugh that doubled him over into a full-blown cough. He hocked it up and spit toward a small trash can by the table.

He missed.

Steve shoved him back against the wall and shoved his knee into the man's stomach. "Last time, asshole. Where is he?"

The man worked to catch his breath, meeting Steve's glare. Still gasping for air, he must have decided to take Steve seriously because he nodded toward the back room, where a red light glowed from underneath the door. "In there," he said, struggling to find his voice. His lips curled up in a creepy smile that never reached his eyes. Spit sprayed out as he spoke. "He's got a visitor, so you'll have to wait your turn."

Fighting back the bile rising up from his clenched stomach, Steve punched him again without bothering to watch his limp body land on the floor in a heap. He wiped the man's spittle off his face with the back of his hand and wiped it off on the back of a chair. With a quick glance at the table, he snatched the tallest stack of bills and shoved them in his front jeans pocket.

Taking a deep breath, he turned toward the back room. He heard grunting sounds coming from inside. Steve threw the door open so hard it crashed against the wall, causing an old picture to crash to the floor. It revealed the only semi-clean spot in the entire house.

A balding man with his pants around his knees jumped back from the bed and yelled. "Hey!"

He dropped his used condom to the floor in a rush to pull up his pants. His angry eyes glared at Steve before gaining control of his expression and smiling down at the nearly-passed-out man lying face down with a pair of sweats around his ankles. The bald man pulled out his wallet and tossed some cash on the bed just as he caught sight of Derek in the doorway.

"Which one of you is next?" the man asked as he casually zipped up his fly.

Derek kept watch outside the bedroom door.

"Leave it," Steve growled.

"Leave what?" The man looked annoyed.

"Your cash. Leave it all."

"Hey. I paid the going price. Fair and square." He started to return his wallet to his pocket.

Thoroughly disgusted with the man, Steve stalked over and glowered at him. He produced a knife seemingly out of nowhere and held it in front of the man's face. The man went nearly cross-eyed as he focused on the sharp blade mere inches from his eyes.

In a low and steady voice, Steve lowered the blade down the man's body and spoke. "I don't give a flying fuck what you think was fair. I said leave it, or I'll make sure you leave something else."

Steve wasn't sure if the smell was already in the room or if the man just wet his pants. He guessed the latter.

The bald man's eyes widened in fear as he emptied the cash out of his wallet, stumbling backward until he bumped into a scratched-up chest of drawers. "Ow," he said as his face creased in a wince of pain.

Steve stepped back and glanced down at the man on the bed.

It was him.

Robert Nicholas Cook.

His brother.

"Nicky." Steve's voice came out as a whisper. He folded up the blade and stuck it in his back pocket.

The bald man chuckled. "He was a good f...."

Steve pounced on the man like a madman and pounded him with his fist until the man's face was beaten to a bloody pulp. He dropped him to the floor and turned around when he heard a moan coming from the bed.

Nick's eyes glazed over as his hand inched toward the cash. He clutched his fingers around it as if his life depended on it.

By the looks of him, it probably did.

Derek watched; a sad yet vigilant expression covered his face but his eyes kept moving, ever watchful for his friend's safety.

A tattoo on Nick's lower back drew Steve's attention. Similar to the woman's tattoo from the other room, it was a black line with three dollar signs above and the word JETT below in all capital letters.

"Fuck," he said, glancing up to notice some white pills on the dirty nightstand.

Steve took a rapid inventory of the room, finally resting his eyes on his brother. His expression softened. He sat down on the bed and helped his brother sit up. Pulling him against his chest, he rested his hand behind Nick's head to hold him close. "I'm here, Nicky."

"No. No. No," Nicholas groaned, his arm helplessly trying to grasp the bills that had fallen out of his hand.

"It's okay, Nicky." Steve comforted him in a gentle voice. "It's okay."

Frightened, Nick pleaded again, his voice weak. "No. Please, no." His arms shook, and he lacked any strength to push himself away because he was still too high on who knew what.

"Shh. You're alright, Nicky. I've got you." Steve placed a hand on his brother's cheek to look at him. "I'm going to get you out of here, okay?"

In that instant, his brother's deep blue eyes focused back on him with a faint flicker of recognition.

"Stevie?" Nick whispered as his head dropped back, his limp body held up only thanks to the strong arms of what was probably nothing more than a blur of a man sitting next to him.

Steve gave Nick a gentle squeeze and lowered him back to the bed. He pulled the pair of sweatpants up Nick's legs to his waist. Seeing a shirt hanging on the side of a chair, he grabbed it and pulled Nick to an upright position. He rested Nick's passed-out head against his chest as he eased the far-too-large shirt over his brother's slender shoulders, not bothering to button it up.

A flash of leather caught his eye in the open nightstand drawer. Steve reached in to pick up an old, well-used wallet. His heart sank. It was the wallet he gave his brother before he'd left for the Marines. Inside was Nick's expired Illinois driver's license with their great aunt and uncle's old address and a few other things he could check out later.

Standing up, Steve stuck it in his own front jeans pocket, then grabbed the wad of cash Nick's fingers could no longer grip and stuck it with the other money he'd already taken off the table in the other room.

Knowing there was no chance Nick would walk out of his own accord, Steve gripped one arm and picked him up to carry him over his shoulders in a firefighter's carry, leaving his other arm and legs dangling behind him. "Let's go, Nicky."

Derek led them toward the front without a word, ensuring no one blocked their exit. The man Steve punched in the dining room was still out cold, slumped against the wall. The man and woman on the couch remained oblivious to everything around them. The resting man on the porch opened his eyes enough to watch them take a few steps but didn't say a word to the two strange men who carried the third man outside.

Kiro rushed to open the back of his SUV, having already folded down the seats. Derek jumped inside first while Kiro helped Steve lower his brother off his shoulders. Derek helped pull him in, already checking his pulse and blood pressure as Steve clambered inside.

Kiro closed the door behind them and climbed into the driver's seat to start the engine as another car drove toward the house. He pulled away, never sparing a backward glance as the car turned into the driveway.

"Pulse is weak, but all things considered, he's okay," Derek announced, lifting Nick's eyelids as the SUV bounced over the pothole-ridden street. "Pupils only slightly reactive."

Nick coughed, but his eyes remained closed.

"It's okay, Nicky. You're safe," Steve assured his brother, brushing his long blond hair off his forehead with his fingers.

Steve grabbed his brother's hand as he watched Derek work. The back of Kiro's SUV wasn't spacious for three adult men, but it was what they had. He grappled with the fear of what may happen to his brother, fighting back the anger that had him wanting to kill each and every person who had ever hurt Nick.

A few miles away, they stopped at a red light. Kiro turned around in the seat, concerned for their patient. "How is he, D?"

Steve put an oxygen mask over Nick's nose and mouth so he could breathe a little easier, thanks to the portable tank they'd brought to get them back to Grant's Crossing if he didn't absolutely need to go straight to a hospital. Steve wanted to avoid calling the police if they could.

Behind the mask, they could see the remnants of a black eye and a bruised cheek on Nick's face. Bruises on his neck shaped like fingers were also visible. His wiry frame had more bruises on his torso as if he'd been kicked rather than just hit. He smelled like he hadn't had a proper shower for a while, and his long, dull hair looked oily and stringy and probably hadn't been combed in days.

"He's okay," Derek said. "He's got bruising all over. I'm worried about his ribs. He needs to come down from the high before we really know anything. Any idea what's in him?"

Steve shook his head. "There were pills on the nightstand, so an opioid of some sort, maybe?"

Derek nodded. "Probably."

"What did they do, give him enough to keep him unconscious?" Kiro wondered aloud as he pressed the accelerator and turned onto the freeway.

As certified paramedics, Steve, Derek, and Kiro treated patients on drugs. Fortunately, this wasn't an overdose situation, but it was still serious, not knowing what he was on or for how long.

"Or he wanted to take something to forget where he was," Steve muttered as he examined Nick's ribs. "I don't feel any breaks, but that doesn't mean there aren't any. Needs an x-ray to be sure nothing's broken."

Derek and Kiro both agreed.

"Hand me the stethoscope," Steve commanded.

Derek handed it over without question. Steve didn't care whether they understood why he wanted to double-check his brother's vitals. He just needed to hear his brother's heart for himself.

"Steve." Derek lifted one of Nick's sleeves.

Steve looked up with watery eyes. "What?"

"Look at his arm."

His head snapped down as he pushed up his brother's left arm sleeve. Nick's arm was covered in horizontal scars, the kind that could only have been self-inflicted. They were all straight across the width of his arm, leading from his wrist to his elbow. Most had already healed.

"They're old."

"Not all of them."

Steve's heart sank upon confirming Derek's assessment.

Derek lifted the sleeve even higher to reveal track marks made by someone who was clearly not a medical professional. Steve secretly hoped they weren't put there by Nick himself but rather by someone who wanted to keep him unable to fight back.

He pressed his lips together and cupped his hand to his brother's face, brushing his straggly long hair off his forehead. "Oh, Nicky. What happened to you?"

Derek handed a splint to Steve. "He needs fluids. Get this on him so his elbow doesn't move. I'll get the IV going."

Once Steve secured the splint on his brother's arm, Derek expertly inserted the needle and taped the line in place. He then tied the bag up to the back of the passenger seat. Not the ideal setting to move a patient, but they made it work. Steve had witnessed plenty of Corpsmen work in worse conditions in Iraq.

With Nick and his arm secure, Steve grabbed the blanket they'd brought with them and did his best to cover his shivering brother to keep him warm. He shifted so his brother's head and shoulders rested on his lap.

Steve nodded to Derek, who turned to Kiro. "How far out are we, K?"

"About 40 minutes without a siren," Kiro said over his shoulder as he drove over a rough patch of pavement.

The movement startled Nick, whose eyes popped open in surprise. "No!"

Derek's eyes snapped toward his splinted arm, concerned a struggle may cause more harm than was already apparent.

Steve tightened his hold on his brother. "Shh. You're safe now, little brother. Just hold on." He met Derek's gaze with a nod of thanks. He dropped his head again to observe his brother, who was already drifting back out of consciousness. "You're safe," he whispered. He dropped a kiss on his brother's forehead and held him close the entire way home.

Steve's own hands were shaking. He clenched his fists a few times to still them, all while taking a deep breath or two to calm his own racing heart. Lifting his gaze, he caught Derek watching him. Steve narrowed his eyes but received an understanding nod in return. Derek rechecked the IV bag while Steve clutched his brother tightly for the long ride back to Grant's Crossing.

Chapter 44

Tossing and Turning

Steve woke up as the dawn's light filled the living room of his sparsely furnished apartment across from the town hall on the Square. Yawning, he stretched his arms above his head and sat up on the couch where he spent the night after getting his brother settled in his bedroom. After scrubbing his face with his hands, he stood up to check in on his brother.

The apartment was perfectly located, right in the center of downtown Grant's Crossing, and within walking distance of both the fire station and what little nightlife the town offered. The night sky was just starting to lighten as the sleepy town showed its first signs of life. He filled a fresh glass with water, noticing as he entered the bedroom that his brother had drunk at least half of the last one. He could give him another IV of fluids to help keep him hydrated and put some nutrients in him if need be, but all things considered, Nick was doing okay.

Steve's brother slept on and off all day and night, waking up long enough for a little soup. It was mostly broth, since Steve didn't want to put too much into his stomach, not knowing what else was coursing through his brother's system. Nick hadn't really spoken yet, but Steve figured that would come in time. Each time Nick woke, he was disoriented by his new location.

Steve set the glass on the nightstand next to the framed picture of them at Busch Stadium back when Nick was still in high school. He picked up the old glass and returned it to the kitchen. A minute later, he heard a sound and returned to the bedroom. Nick was tossing and turning.

"Damn," Steve muttered to himself as he sat down on the edge of the bed and placed a hand on his brother's shoulder. "Nick." He spoke in a low voice and gave his shoulder a gentle squeeze. "Nicky, you're having a nightmare."

Nick sat up with a sudden inhale, forcing Steve back. Nick's arms shot up in front of his face as if trying to fend someone off. "No! Don't!"

Steve gently placed his hands on Nick's upper arms, attempting to calm him. "It's okay. Nicky. It's okay."

His brother's eyes opened wide like a deer in headlights. Steve did his best to remain calm, to counter the panic on his brother's face without revealing his own hurt.

Nick had been a vibrant, happy, eternally optimistic boy at one time. Now, the man before Steve was a shell of the brother he once knew back home in St. Louis.

Steve was grateful they were finally together. He didn't see a guitar in that shit hole they found him in, so he'd have to see about picking one up for him. He wanted Nick to have his music. Nick could always trust his music.

Nick turned his head away and tried to protect his face despite Steve's assurances that he was safe. His breathing was short and rapid.

"I'm not going to hurt you, Nicky. Nobody's gonna hurt you. You're safe."

"What? Where?" Nick looked around the room, his head turning right and left, then up at the ceiling and back down, trying to get his bearings.

"Nicky. Look at me. It's me, Steve."

It took a bit, but Nick lowered his arms away from his face. His eyes turned toward Steve but looked more through him than at him.

"Nicky?" Steve worked to keep the concern from his face and his voice soft and not threatening as he spoke calmly to his brother.

Nick finally met Steve's gaze. His eyes seemed to focus on Steve's face, resting on his eyes. "Stevie?" His breathing slowed and finally evened out.

Steve smiled. "Yeah, little brother. It's me."

"Where?" Nick's eyes darted around the room again. "How? What happened?" His eyes returned to Steve, and he panicked. "Stevie, I'm not supposed to be with anyone else. If Mac comes back, he'll send those men... and then they'll..."

Steve cut him off. "Nobody's coming back. Mac's not coming back. You're safe here, Nicky."

Steve's stomach sank. So many people had hurt his brother: his parents, their uncle, Mac, the supposed boyfriend who left him in Detroit, and the traffickers who brought him here.

"This is my home, which makes it your home, too. You're safe now. No one is coming after you, alright?" He angled his head to make eye contact with Nick again. "Nicky?"

Nick gave a quick nod as if unsure whether to trust Steve or his own senses. Nick looked back at his brother as tears fell down his cheeks. "I can stay here?"

Nick shook, reminding Steve of a small child who felt helpless and needed comfort during a thunderstorm. Steve's heart broke at the sight of him. He pressed his lips together and used his thumb to wipe the tears off Nick's face. "As long as you want."

Nick gave half a nod as Steve gave his brother a chance to survey the barely lit room with curtain-covered windows and a clean bed that smelled a lot better than the house where Steve found him hidden away. Even in the dim morning light, the room looked a little untidy, but it was clean.

Nick's fingers grabbed at the fabric of the Harley Davidson T-shirt he was wearing. "This... isn't mine."

"No. It's mine." Steve gave his brother a bath when he got home yesterday and gave him a pair of shorts and a T-shirt to cover him for the time being. Nick was so thin they practically fell off him. Steve planned to get some clothes for him later but didn't yet want to leave him alone. He had only been out of the apartment for a quick trip to the dumpster to toss out the clothes he found Nicky in the day before. He wanted to burn them, but he didn't have the means or the time. "But you can have it."

Nick crossed his arms across his chest and rubbed his upper arms. "I'm c... cold." This time, he shivered from the cold as he looked toward the window.

Steve grabbed the blanket on the end of the bed and wrapped it around his brother's shoulders. With shaky hands, Nick tightened it around himself and leaned his head into Steve's shoulder.

"They wouldn't let me call you, Stevie." Nick's voice was barely audible. He sniffed and wiped his nose with the back of his hand. "I tried to call you."

"I know you did." Steve rubbed his hand up and down his brother's back to warm him up.

"But you still found me."

"Yeah."

Nick turned his head toward the window. "Can we leave Detroit? I can't stay in Detroit. He'll find me."

"We're not in Detroit. We're in Grant's Crossing. We're in Ohio."

"Oh."

Steve grabbed Nick's shoulders to pull back and see his face. "We're right above a bookstore." He did his best to stay optimistic and knew how Nick loved to read as a kid. "The people are really nice and can help you pick out some books. You still like to read mysteries, right?"

A simple nod was all the reaction Nick gave.

"Are you hungry? Want me to make you some eggs? Or some toast?" Steve offered.

Nick furrowed his brow, taking a few seconds to process the question. His lips curled into the start of a smile. "With raspberry jam?"

For a split second, Steve thought he saw a hint of the brother he once knew.

"Yeah." Steve smiled. "With raspberry jam."

"It's my favorite." Nick still sounded like a little kid.

"I know. Mine, too."

He leaned his head against Steve's chest again. "I missed you, Stevie."

"I missed you, too, Nicky." Steve held his brother tight. "I missed you, too."

Chapter 45

I Don't Know How

Steve jolted upright to the frantic sounds of a buzzer. Blinking a few times to wake himself up from an unplanned nap on the couch, he jumped up and pushed the button for the intercom to the outside entrance. "Yeah?"

"Steve." A low voice came through the speaker. "It's Derek."

Steve buzzed him in, then went back to pull the bedroom door so it was barely open, not wanting to disturb his brother, who had fallen back to sleep after Steve's return from Cafe Mocha, the local coffee shop on the square. Convinced Nick was safe, Steve opened the front door.

As the footsteps grew closer, he heard more than one voice. Steve stuck his head out into the hall to see two other men behind Derek. "You brought people with you?"

Derek motioned to the two men to wait outside the door. He stepped inside the apartment and closed the door behind him.

Steve glared at the door, then got in Derek's face. "Who are they?" he asked, his voice seething with anger at having strangers so close to his brother.

"Logan Shepherd and Matthew Lees." Derek held up his hands while answering. "Logan and I grew up together. He volunteers at a

250

local shelter working to help the LGBTQ community here, which isn't always the most welcome outside of Ohio's major cities, though it's getting better."

Steve nodded brusquely. "And the other one?"

"Matt is a medical doctor who volunteers at the same shelter. He's based out of Grady Hospital over in Delaware but spends most of his time at a local rehab center that helps folks with anything from drug and alcohol addiction to mental health services. It's the same clinic where Tank's wife, Araceli, works. She's an RN there. I think you should talk to them because they can help your brother in both the immediate and long term."

Sensing a flash of movement, Derek turned toward the bedroom. They heard someone getting sick.

"Shit." Steve tore through the bedroom and into the bathroom to find Nick hunched over the toilet, losing everything he'd eaten earlier that day for breakfast. His body spasmed, arching his back each time it emptied what little he had left in his system. When he finally stopped heaving, he spit a few times and leaned back on his knees with a sniff. Steve flushed the toilet, then dampened a washcloth to gently clean Nick's flushed face.

"It's okay, Nicky. You'll get through this," Steve said as Nick leaned against his brother's shoulder for a few minutes, taking shallow breaths and swallowing over and over again. "And I'll be right here with you."

Steve pushed his brother's hair back from his face. "Do you think you're done? Want to go back to bed?"

Nick nodded and let his brother help him back to the bed. Steve pulled the blankets back up to his shoulders to ensure he didn't get cold again, then set an empty wastebasket next to the bed, just in case. When he was satisfied his brother was okay, he went back out and pulled the bedroom door mostly closed behind him.

"Sorry about that."

"Don't be." Derek's concern was genuine. "How's he doing?"

Steve scrubbed his face with his hand. "Okay, for the moment, but honestly? I don't know. You saw where he came from."

"They can help. Will you at least talk to them?"

"I..."

"They can get him the help he needs, Steve." Derek motioned to the bedroom. "You've got tomorrow off, but you'll need someone to stay with him when you're back on shift. This is too much for one person."

Steve wasn't ready to agree. Instead, he pointed to the plastic bag Derek was holding. "What's that?"

"Oh. It's for you." Derek handed over the shopping bag he'd brought with him. "Well, for Nick. We guessed him to be about Kiro's size, so we picked up a few things. I figured you've already tossed what he wore home."

"Yeah. I did." Steve unpacked the bag on the table and fought to hold back the emotion that swamped him. Inside were new socks, underwear, a pair of sweats, and a couple of T-shirts. He'd also brought the basics for a shaving kit.

"It's not much," Derek went on, "but it's a start. I figure he's probably already using your stuff for now. We can get more later."

"Let me pay you back." Steve turned back to the coffee table for his wallet.

"No." Derek held up his hand to stop him. "No need."

"But..."

"No." Derek refused his offer. "And there will be more. Kiro will bring dinner over later." Derek laughed. "He told his mom that you had company and, despite your last name, you couldn't actually cook."

"I can cook," Steve deadpanned.

"I've eaten your cooking at the station. What can you make beyond spaghetti?"

"Um..."

"Right," Derek confirmed. "Anyway, she offered to cook for you both."

Steve laughed. "Thanks." A noise drew his gaze toward the bedroom. Satisfied Nick was still resting, he returned his attention back to Derek.

"So," Derek asked, "can they come in now?"

Steve's laugh disappeared as he nodded.

Derek ushered the two men inside, one of whom looked like an NFL linebacker.

"This is Logan Shepherd." Steve shook hands with a slightly suntanned, well-dressed man with black hair and dark brown eyes, broad shoulders, and standing at least a few inches taller than he was.

"And this is Dr. Matthew Lees."

"Matt," said an equally tall but far more slender Asian man who wore his hair in a short ponytail.

Before either man made it beyond pleasantries, Derek gave one more assurance. "You can trust them, Steve."

Steve glanced over at Derek without a word.

"Let's sit down." Logan motioned toward the table. "So we can figure out how best to work with you and your brother."

Steve liked that the first words out of Logan's mouth were to let him know they were on his side rather than just offering charity or pity. They sat down and started talking about Nick's background. Steve noticed Matt set a backpack on the floor beside him but said nothing.

Logan and Matt asked pointed questions, which Steve answered as best he could, though usually they had to dig a bit to get their answers. He wasn't making it easy, but then again, he'd never shared this much about his brother beyond what he'd told his fellow Marines, and even that wasn't much. Over the next quarter hour, he related what he knew of his brother's life since they'd both left their hometown. It embarrassed him that he could only tell them about Nick's life from afar.

When he described the ongoing search that led him to Detroit and then down to Columbus, Steve's voice grew angrier. "He was moved by a guy who controls people with fear. They're all afraid of him. I've heard the name Mac, but he's dead now. I've heard the name Jett a few times but nothing else."

Steve glanced up just as Matt and Logan exchanged a knowing glance. "What? You know them?"

Matt shook his head as Logan met Steve's gaze.

"We've heard of Jett," Logan said. "He's supposedly the man behind a rather sizable human trafficking ring in the region. The Toledo Police Department has had some luck catching some of the lower-level players, but no one ever gave up any information on Jett."

Matt took up the explanation. "They're known for preying on the LGBTQ community, or anyone marginalized, but especially those who have run away or been kicked out. They pretend to help them at first by offering them food and shelter. After a while, they suggest drugs," he held up his hands to make finger quotes, "to take off the edge. Then they take payback in the form of prostitution while they're either passed out drunk or high as a kite."

Steve felt his stomach churn as he pictured Nick in that house where they found him.

"Jett likes to see his name in print." Logan sighed in sad frustration. "He marks everyone he considers his property."

Steve's head snapped up. His eyes bounced from Logan to Matt and back to Logan. "He what?"

"Marks them."

"Shit." Steve closed his eyes and released a long exhale. "With a tattoo on their lower back."

Logan continued. "His name, topped..."

Steve cut him off. "Topped with three dollar signs."

"The number of dollar signs varies," Logan confirmed. "Does Nick...?"

"Yeah. It's on his back. Just above the pants line so it's visible if he's not wearing a shirt."

The four men went silent for a long minute.

Matt cleared his throat. "Have you taken him to see a doctor yet?"

"No."

"May I meet him?" Matt asked as if gauging Steve's reaction. "Usually, when someone has come out of a trafficking ring where prostitution is prevalent, we like to make sure they're hydrated and then put them on an antiviral regimen to help stave off..."

"HIV and AIDS." Steve finished, the life now gone from his voice. "I know."

"Yes."

"He's still pretty skittish around me. I don't know how he'll feel about another stranger."

"I just want to check on a few things. It'll be nothing invasive and nothing he doesn't want done. The last thing we want is to give him more cause for fear."

Matt looked directly at Steve when he spoke. "I don't want to hurt him, Steve. He's been through enough."

Steve's tight expression never changed.

"He's got a long road ahead of him. You know that, right?" Matt asked. After a moment, he added, "Tell me this. Did he sleep last night?"

Steve blinked. "What?"

"You brought him here yesterday. Has he slept?" Matt repeated himself. "Or has he had nightmares?"

Steve's eyes darted back and forth between the three men sitting at the table with him. "Nightmares."

"We can help with that." Logan inserted himself back into the conversation. "We all have them."

Steve noticed Logan's pointed glance at Derek, who showed no outward reaction.

"What your brother has been through is something no one should ever have to experience. We can help him with that." Logan nodded to Matt.

"Right," Matt added. "We can help him off any drug dependence he has and then help him to come to terms with what he's been through. Starting that process will help him move forward."

They heard a yell, a crash, and a loud thud from the bedroom. They all jumped up from the table. Steve ran inside with Matt right on his heels with his backpack. Derek stood at the door with Logan, the only one with no medical training.

"It's okay, Nicky. I've got you." Steve kept his voice calm as Nick struggled to keep an invisible terror away. The lamp had fallen on its side atop the nightstand.

Matt pulled a syringe out of his med kit. "It'll help him sleep." When Steve nodded, he deftly stuck the needle in Nick's arm, instantly calming him.

Leaning his head against his brother's chest, Nick's eyes stayed open, staring at everything and nothing while his breathing evened out.

Steve just held him, his arms wrapped tightly around his brother as his expression finally cracked, showing concern and fear. He was a man who had made it through the most dangerous combat situations, through firefights in Iraq and Afghanistan, but when it came to helping his brother, he was helpless. He had no idea how to process the feeling. He knew what to do to extract Nick from the people who had been so cruel to him for so long, but he had no idea what to do now that he was out.

Matt spoke in soft tones, assuring Steve it was going to be okay.

Logan spoke in a low voice as they stood back from the doorway.

"Talk to him, Derek. This is too much for one person to take on alone."

Derek gave Logan a silent nod of agreement.

"We can help you, too, you know," Logan added quietly.

Derek flashed an angry glare at Logan, who wasn't the least bit intimidated. "You know we provide space for and help a lot of veterans who need help readjusting to civilian life. Queer and otherwise."

Nick's eyelids drooped as they got him back on the bed and under the covers. "That should help him sleep soundly for a while," Matt advised Steve while taking Nick's vitals.

"I've been looking for him for so long, and now that I've found him," Steve confessed in a gravelly voice, "I don't know how to help him."

"We do, Steve," Matt assured him. "And we can."

Chapter 46

Sugar

IN THE FEW MONTHS HE'D LIVED IN GRANT'S CROSSING, STEVE fell into the habit of joining Kiro and Derek for breakfast. It didn't hurt that Kiro's parents owned Baba's Diner, a great place for breakfast and lunch across the square from Steve's apartment.

Breakfast was always delicious; and Kiro's mom, who was quite the force to be reckoned with, never let them pay though Steve and Derek always snuck some bills into the tip jar when she wasn't looking. Steve was sure she caught on, but she never said anything. When she did speak up, though, everyone listened. Apparently, they'd all learned that whenever an Eastern European mom speaks, they had to listen.

After they were done eating this morning and Derek went home, Steve joined Kiro for a quick walk across the square to Cafe Mocha, the coffee shop run by Kiro's girlfriend, Celeste.

Celeste was a tiny black woman with mostly black, with a little bit of red, natural hair going out in all directions, and enough energy to fuel a small town. She owned the coffee shop, so maybe she did fuel a small town. Steve chuckled at the thought.

While Kiro talked to his girlfriend, Steve decided to get another coffee to take home. He got in line behind a tall, redheaded woman with an eye-catching hourglass figure. She had hips he could picture himself holding onto, a slender waist to wrap his arms around, and a chest to die for. What he wouldn't do to get his hands on those...

He heard a throat clearing. His eyes snapped to the most gorgeous green eyes he'd ever seen. She arched a brow. The look said she was not at all amused, but he couldn't resist grinning back at her. No need to pretend he wasn't looking at what she thought he was looking at.

Because he absolutely was.

Dropping his gaze to her mouth, he skimmed his tongue across his teeth. He felt the bar from his pierced tongue clicking as it passed from tooth to tooth and back. His grin grew wider when he saw her cheeks flush to a color that came close to matching the color of her long, wavy, red hair.

"Can I help you, ma'am?"

Their eyes remained locked until Steve tilted his head toward the barista behind the counter, trying to get her attention.

"Oh right. Yes," she prattled. "A large cafe latte, please, with an extra shot."

"You bet. We'll get that right up for you."

She paid for her drink and stepped away to the pickup counter. Steve's eyes followed her as she walked.

"And for you, sir?"

"I'll have the same."

"Another large cafe latte with an extra shot of espresso."

Steve paid for the order and stepped aside, seeing Kiro and Celeste exchanging those goofy grins new couples always share. He never understood the appeal.

Growing up, his parents were his only real example of a relationship, and he couldn't imagine the two of them actually liked each other, much less showed it in public. To them, a relationship was just an obligation, something society expected of them. They got married and had kids as if checking off a to-do list.

No. He didn't want to be like that.

Clearing his head, he stepped away and returned to check out the redhead's profile in the form-fitting jeans. He dropped his gaze to the high-heeled black boots that made her seem almost as tall as he was.

God, he loved tall women.

An older couple entered the shop and started looking about for a table. Steve caught their eye and held a chair for the woman, who smiled sweetly as she thanked him. The man he assumed was her husband offered a nod of thanks as he got in line to place their order.

A trio of older ladies watched this exchange. "You're such a polite young man, helping her to her seat," the slender black lady with her hair in a gray chignon commented with a flirty smile.

"Yes," a lady with a short black pixie cut agreed with a giggle. "Oh. And look at all these tattoos. Remember when Stanley was in the service? He had a lot of tattoos."

Steve turned and suppressed a laugh as the older lady pointed to his arms, which weren't covered beyond the length of the shirt sleeves he'd rolled up to his elbows.

"Sexy," the third lady, a round woman with a primarily gray shoulder-length bob, added while lifting her eyebrows at him. "Maybe I can buy him a coffee with my Golden Buckeye card."

"Now stop your flirting, Lizzie," the chignon lady scolded her. "He probably has at least three girlfriends already. He doesn't need a fourth."

The round woman looked up at him and batted her eyelashes. "Oh, I don't know, Berneta. I think he could handle me."

Steve flashed her his best smile.

"See? He likes me already."

"Tell me something," the pixie-cut lady spoke directly to Steve, slowly poking his bicep as she spoke. "Do you ever go to Jo's for dinner?"

"Yes, ma'am. I do." He wasn't sure where she was going with this, but he'd play along.

"Then will you promise me a dance the next time I see you there? My name's Abigail." Like her friend, Lizzie, she batted her eyelashes at him. "I'd be happy to free up space on my dance card for you."

Lizzie rolled her eyes. "What would Stanley say?"

Abigail waved her off. "That he'd want me to enjoy life and dance like no one is watching."

Berneta raised an eyebrow. "Best if they don't. I've seen you dance."

Steve laughed. "It would be my honor to dance with you, Miss Abigail," he said with a polite dip of his chin.

Abigail swooned. "Oh, thank you."

Berneta clicked her tongue. "That's enough flirting, ladies. Let's get in line."

"Bye!" Abigail wiggled her fingers at him.

He flashed another smile and waved back. "Bye, Miss Abigail."

"Large cafe latte with an extra espresso shot," a barista behind the counter announced.

Steve watched the redhead pick up her drink. His coffee was called out just after hers, but he gave her space to walk over before picking up his own.

His eyes followed her as she moved over to add sweetener, then grabbed a thin wooden stir stick to mix it. As soon as she dropped the stick into the small metal bucket on the counter, he moved in.

"Excuse me." Steve leaned in far enough to trap her between him and the counter.

She turned around, nearly standing face-to-face with him. Any closer, and they'd be touching. For sure, they would have been called out at a middle school dance for not having eight fingers' worth of space between them, though she certainly didn't look like any middle school girl he'd ever known.

Steve met her green eyes and dropped his own eyes down to her mouth and back. She smelled of lavender. He leaned in, his grin widening the closer he got to her, so close she bit her lower lip as she stared right back at him.

"Sugar."

"Don't call me..." she whispered as she tried to lean back but met the counter instead. Her free hand, not gripping her coffee cup, shot back to grip the counter behind her to maintain her balance as she leaned backward.

"*Flexible.*" Steve thought as he reached around her. "*Nice.*"

When his grin grew ever more confident, she narrowed her eyes. He knew exactly what effect he had on her.

Never once taking his eyes off hers, he pulled his arm back and held something up in his hand. Her eyes shifted to focus on the two white packets he held between his fingers.

"Sugar."

She stood in front of the condiment display on the counter right behind her. "Ah." Unable to find her actual voice, her response came out breathy.

For a few seconds, he didn't move. He just gazed into her eyes. She broke eye contact, clearly taking in the edges of tattoos peeking out from behind the unbuttoned henley that hugged his broad shoulders.

He now sported pierced ears and a pierced eyebrow. She was hot, so maybe he'd get to take her on a tour of his other piercings, including a few below the belt. If nothing else, he could explore the more adventurous side he'd developed since being discharged from the Marines.

He licked his lips, again revealing his pierced tongue. A breath escaped hers. He had a lot of fun with that particular piercing.

Oh, what he could do to her.

His grin widened, not minding that she was taking him in.

He took a step back and made no attempt to hide the fact that he was checking her out. His eyes traveled all the way down her legs and back up her torso, resting a second on her chest before returning to her eyes.

"Excuse me, please."

As if caught with her hands in the cookie jar, the redhead's eyes widened for a split second. She stepped aside to make room for a woman wanting to reach the sweeteners behind her. She narrowed her eyes toward Steve while scanning for a table.

Kiro paused next to the redhead. "Glad your dad's getting better. Give him my best, would you?"

"I will, Kiro. Thanks."

Kiro smacked Steve on the arm to leave. On their way out, Steve waved at the trio of older ladies, sending them into a fit of giggles worthy of grade school girls.

Chapter 47

Rehab

Delaware County Rehabilitation Clinic, Delaware, Ohio

The doors to the Delaware County Rehabilitation Clinic opened with a whoosh. A glance ahead revealed the welcome desk. With a plastic shopping bag in hand, Steve gave them his name.

"Good morning. I'm here to drop something off for my brother, Nicholas Cook." Steve placed his hands on the counter and leaned forward. "He checked in the day before yesterday."

"Steve," a voice to his right drew his attention. He stood up straight and took Matt Lees' extended hand in greeting.

"Hi, Matt. How's my brother doing?"

"He's settled in," Matt said, giving no additional details.

"Think I can see him?"

"I'm sorry, but not for another few weeks, at least."

Disappointed, Steve nodded in acceptance.

"We like our patients to be here a few weeks to settle into the program before allowing any visitors. It's nothing personal, Steve." Matt assured him. "They need to be free from the outside influences that are potentially what brought them here in the first place."

Steve grimaced at the thought but knew it made good sense. "But he's doing okay? He's eating? Nobody's hurting..."

Matt rested his hand on Steve's arm and led him to the side of the room, where they could have a modicum of privacy. "Yes. All that. I promise he's being treated well, but you need to remember he just got here. Give him time to adjust. This is a big change for him."

"Okay." Steve glanced down at his bag and held it up. "I uh... brought some extra clothes. He didn't really have anything when we found him. Thought maybe it would help."

"That I *can* take to him." Matt smiled and accepted the bag of clothes.

"Thanks."

"Steve. We're taking good care of him. He's just got a lot to work through."

"I know. I'm just...." Steve paused and scrubbed his face with his hand.

"You're worried about your brother."

"Yeah."

"He's in excellent hands, and more important, he's getting the help he needs."

Steve hesitated, then nodded in resignation. "Thanks, Matt. Tell him I stopped by?"

Matt shook his hand without responding.

Steve took a deep breath as he climbed onto his motorcycle. He drove it home and then walked the few blocks to the fire station to help clear his head. Going straight to the locker room, he stuck his backpack inside his locker and sat down on the bench for a few minutes, unsure how to feel. He was used to conflict but wasn't accustomed to being conflicted.

He had been on a mission to find his brother all these years.

He found him. He accomplished his mission.

And now, he wasn't allowed to be with him. He wavered between being angry at not being able to see his brother and worried about how he was doing versus knowing he was safe and not being taken advantage of by someone wanting only to use him for their own gain.

Steve took a deep breath and stood up. He closed his locker and did his best to deal with relinquishing control to the doctors and therapists at the rehab center, who all promised to take good care of his brother. Deep down, he knew they would, but it didn't stop him from worrying. He'd always been there for his little brother.

Until he wasn't.

But now he's back.

He heard Kiro and Emerson talking outside the locker room and thought it best to walk over to start his day.

"Morning, Steve."

"Good morning."

"Got something on your mind?" Kiro wondered. "You look a million miles away."

"Yeah." Steve knitted his brow. "I'm curious about something."

"What's that?"

Pushing his troubled thoughts to the side, he curled his lips up in a mischievous smile. "Are all the retirees in this town so forward?"

"Huh?"

They strolled down the hallway into the lounge to fix cups of coffee.

"The old women at the coffee shop the other day. Are they always like that?"

"You mean the Tres Widows?"

"The trace what?" He grabbed a mug and filled it with coffee, emptying in a couple of sugar packets. Tossing the empty wrappers into the trash, he added milk and stirred.

"The Tres Widows," Kiro repeated while filling his own cup. "Lizzie, Berneta, and Abigail. They've been friends since grade school, and they've all outlived their husbands. Hell, they're practically as old as the town itself." He set the carafe on the burner and grabbed a glazed donut from the box on the counter. "You have to be careful around them, or you'll end up on a date."

Steve choked on his coffee. "What?" He wiped his mouth with the back of his hand.

Kiro shoved half of his donut between his teeth in time to see the panic on Steve's face. "Oh shit. What'd you do?"

Steve surveyed the room, afraid the three women would appear out of nowhere. "I uh..."

"Which one?"

"Abigail?" His voice cracked as he cleared his throat just as Emerson walked up.

"Abigail?" Emerson paused for a split second, then burst out laughing. "Wait. Does Steve have a date with one of the Tres Widows?"

Steve raised his hands, immediately going into damage control mode. "What? How? Don't..."

"Fresh meat," Emerson coughed out.

Steve extended his hand toward Emerson. "Wait. No. I..."

"Let me guess," Kiro said, smirking. "Drinks at Jo's?"

Emerson's hand landed on Steve's shoulder. "Yeah. What is it? Dinner? Dancing?" He could barely get the questions out before doubling over in laughter.

Steve mumbled something unintelligible.

"Say again?" Emerson said.

Steve dropped his head. "Dance at Jo's."

Kiro gave a slow nod while feigning concern. "That's not so bad, all things considered."

Emerson nodded in agreement. "Yeah. You got off pretty easy." Emerson patted Steve on his back and walked away, no longer able to suppress his laughter. The other men looked up when Emerson made a loud announcement. "Hey guys, Steve has a date with one of the Tres Widows!"

Steve closed his eyes and slumped as soon as he heard boisterous laughter break out in the lounge area. "I am never going to live this down, am I?"

"Nope," Kiro popped the rest of his donut in his mouth. "She'll hold you to it, too." Kiro walked away with a grin.

"Well, shit." Head dropped, Steve stood alone at the counter, psyching himself up for a day of endless mockery at the hands of his fellow firefighters, when the image of a tall, gorgeous redhead suddenly filled his thoughts.

He walked into the lounge with a smile, offering a formal bow to a rousing bout of applause and whistles.

Chapter 48

Agent Yards

That afternoon, the sheriff's SUV pulled up just as the fire engine was returning to quarters. On the street, a black Mustang parked just beyond the station, the driver of which walked directly to Sheriff Strager. Based on how they greeted each other, they were well-acquainted.

The men were putting their gear away and restocking all their supplies, having just returned from a house fire. The ambulance was still on its way back from the hospital, expected to arrive soon. Steve was stowing away his gear just as Drew and the other man appeared behind the open storage compartment door.

"Hi, Drew." Steve greeted him with a quick handshake while still securing the compartment door. "Sorry I haven't stopped by."

He turned and looked at the other man for the first time. He wore faded blue jeans, scuffed-up boots, and a tight black T-shirt. It was cloudy but bright enough for his cheap, plastic sunglasses, which he pushed up and off his face, giving Steve a better look. A badge dangled from a silver chain around his neck.

Steve knitted his brow, trying to place the now familiar-looking face, and then it hit him.

The sleeping man on the front porch of the house where they found Nick.

He narrowed his eyes.

Drew spoke first. "Steve, I'd like you to meet Agent Tyson Yards."

Tyson offered a cocky smile as he extended his hand to Steve, who countered with a quick drop of his chin.

He only hesitated a split second before extending his hand. "Nice performance you put on the other day."

"Yeah. I've gotten pretty good at looking like a stoner." The man's voice was just as cocky as his smile. "The best part is no one notices how much you can see when you're just sitting around."

"I wondered if someone was going to be there when Drew gave me the address."

"Sounds like you gave Dominic quite the surprise. He's probably still nursing a bruised jaw."

"I don't know what you're talking about, but he seemed like a nice guy," Steve deadpanned.

Drew shook his head as Tyson grinned. "You two talk. I'm going to take off and be grateful you weren't in my jurisdiction." Drew patted Steve's shoulder and walked away.

Steve's gaze followed the Sheriff then he turned to finish his work. Agent Yards started talking again as Steve stowed the rest of his gear.

"Yeah. That guy's an ass, but he caught some heat for losing a sizable chunk of their weekly deposit." Tyson took a step closer to the fire engine, picking at imaginary dirt with his fingers. "You wouldn't know anything about that, would you?" He raised an eyebrow and directed a sideways glance up at Steve.

"Nope." Steve's expression gave nothing away as he concentrated on hanging his turnout jacket on a hook above the compartment he'd just closed.

The corner of Tyson's lip curled up in an appreciative smirk, then disappeared just as fast. "Look. I'm sorry about your brother. Runners come in through the back, but they just run errands. I didn't even know someone was there. He wasn't supposed to be...."

"Don't." Steve held up his hand to cut him off. "You chose to leave him there. We had to do your job."

"I had no choice." Agent Yards stopped short and pulled back as Tank and Emerson walked by, each nodding to Steve, who lifted his chin in their direction. "I had to maintain my cover."

Steve glowered. "Bullshit."

Tyson held up his hands and took a step back. "I'm glad you got him out. How's he doing, anyway?"

"How do you think he's doing? He's fucked up. He just went into rehab."

Tyson pressed his lips into a straight line. "For what it's worth, they busted the place the night before last. The guy you allegedly didn't punch? He gave up a mid-level guy in the trafficking ring we've been investigating. Because of him, we were also able to break up three more houses controlled by people who report to the brains behind the organization. A man named Jett."

Steve feigned ignorance.

"A lot of people are getting help now as a result. Maybe your brother can help us, too."

Hackles raised, Steve clenched his fist and glared down at Tyson. "Leave my brother out of this. You don't need him."

Tyson turned his gaze toward the ambulance, pulling into the station. Kiro and Derek eyed Agent Yards with suspicion as they exited the vehicle.

"This guy, Jett. He runs the whole thing. He's the one we want to bring down." He stuck his hands in his pockets. "Jett is slick but arrogant. He's a narcissist, so he likes to see his name in print."

Steve clenched his teeth at the thought of his name tattooed on his brother's back.

"Someday, he'll get too cocky, and we'll get him." Tyson offered an expectant look toward Steve, whose stomach churned at the thought.

"So you're saying the only way to catch him is if *he* makes a mistake?" His tone was cutting, but the implication that the feds weren't good enough to catch him on their own was clear.

Derek and Kiro slowed as they neared the conversation. "Everything okay?"

"Yep," Steve answered.

"That's one way." Tyson gave a hard stare in return. He reached into his back pocket and pulled out a business card. He flicked it back and forth between his fingers. "Here's my card. If your brother wants to talk or if you ever need help with anything."

Steve grunted, ignoring the card. "Pretty sure you probably need mine."

"I'm the one who found him, you know."

Steve knew he was grateful to finally find his brother, but he gritted his teeth, unable to shake his overwhelming contempt for the man who stood before him. Lawman or not, he turned and leaned closer to him. His muscles were tense as he clenched his fists. "Yet knowing who he was, you left him there. Tell me. Agent. Yards." Steve spit his name out with disgust, but Tyson stood his ground.

Derek and Kiro stood by, ready to step in at a moment's notice.

"How many other men assaulted my brother while you sat there and napped, huh?"

Tyson narrowed his eyes. "Don't you fucking..."

"Look," Steve cut him off with a lighter tone. "I've got work to do." He backed off and extended his hand, which Tyson reluctantly accepted. "Thanks for stopping by."

Tyson stood there with his business card still extended as Steve and Kiro walked away. Derek took a step closer, projecting a similar level of contempt. He glanced down, snatched the card out of his hand, and stared down at him with heated indifference. "You're done here."

Tyson stared back for a few seconds before stalking off, mumbling something about fucking ungrateful firefighters. Derek followed him until he was outside the station.

Yards' Mustang flashed its lights and beeped when he held out his keys. He slipped inside and slammed the door shut. Revving the engine a few times, he tossed a final glare back at the fire station and peeled out, screeching his tires so loudly he drew the eyes of the people strolling down the sidewalk.

Derek turned around and walked back inside. "K. Where's Steve?"

Kiro looked up and tilted his head back to the back of the station. "Cold room."

"Thanks." Derek headed down the hall to the back of the station, where Steve was lying on his bunk with his arms folded behind his head, staring at the ceiling.

Derek eased himself down on the bunk next to Steve's. "Got his card." He held up the card and then set it on the table between the two beds.

"He let it happen," Steve spoke slowly. Softly. Pain permeated every syllable of every word. "He was there. He knew Nicky was a victim, and he let it happen."

Derek listened without speaking.

After a few long moments, Steve breathed in a long breath and swung his legs off the side of the bed to sit up. He ran his hands through his hair and down his face before his eyes met Derek's. The fire he typically controlled now threatened to break through the surface, a rage that had simmered since long before he ever found his brother.

"I want to break every bone in his fucking body," he snarled. "I'm trying to fight it, but part of me wants to go back and just..." he held up a clenched fist, "rip the throats out of everyone who ever hurt my brother." He stared at the floor as he took in a long breath. With an exhale, he stared at his hand and watched it unclench, his knuckles white with tension. "It won't change a damned thing, but..." his voice trailed off. He gritted his teeth and dropped his chin to his chest. "Nicky never deserved that, you know?"

Resting his arms on his knees, he slouched forward, looking defeated. He lifted his eyes just enough to ask, "He said they cleared the place out and three other houses, too, but... how many other people had to go through that while Yards just sat there?"

Derek didn't answer. He just shook his head and reached his hand across to his friend's shoulder in support.

Chapter 49

Redhead

DESPITE A FAIRLY UNEVENTFUL NIGHT, STEVE ONLY MANAGED to get a little sleep at the firehouse. After passing on hanging out in the lounge with the other guys who watched a game on TV, he opted to remain in the cold room for a chance at some shuteye.

The only calls they had were focused on Central Ohio's lack of cooking skills.

A burned bag of microwave popcorn set off the fire alarm that required them to inspect an entire four-story office building before declaring it safe and allowing the employees back inside.

An hour after they returned to the station, a panicked bachelor's dinner went up in flames thanks to using an oven that probably hadn't been cleaned since before Jimmy Carter was president. A delivery driver arrived with a replacement pizza before they'd even pulled away.

Calls like those quickly fell into the *'stick with carryout'* category, but that's why they all worked the job they did.

The following morning, Steve joined Derek and Kiro for breakfast at Baba's because there was nothing better than Kiro's mom's cooking after a long shift.

Though he never questioned it out loud, Steve often wondered why Kiro's mom got the credit for the cooking when Kiro's dad ran the kitchen. Regardless, the food was always delicious.

After saying his goodbyes, including an obligatory hug from Kiro's mom, Steve walked across the square to go home and shower. Once clean, he planned to sleep a few more hours.

Thunder rumbled in the distance. He lifted his eyes to the overcast sky. Maybe he'd sleep first.

He was so accustomed to spending all his spare time looking for his brother. Now, he could relax for a couple of months while Nick went through rehab and treatment to deal with everything those assholes put him through. Not that he knew how to do that.

Everything was changing.

As kids, Steve and Nick were like two peas in a pod. They shared everything, good, bad, and indifferent, despite a five-year age difference. He hoped they could pick that up again. Steve couldn't wait until they could go out and enjoy each other's company. He wanted to catch up. Talk about anything and everything. Be friends again. Be brothers. Watch movies. Listen to Nick play the guitar. But with as much as Nick had to work through, Steve had plenty to think about as well.

One day at a time.

In the meantime, he'd get some rest. He hadn't just relaxed in so long; he wasn't sure how to do it.

Would he stay here in Grant's Crossing? Would Nick even want to stay here? Steve's impression was that Nick might not even know what he wanted since other people had forced their decisions on him for so long.

"Ma'am." He stepped aside to make room for an older lady walking her dog on the pathway carrying a cup from Cafe Mocha.

Maybe he could get some coffee before he returned home.

Maybe the redhead would be there.

Maybe he'd get her number and... well. The mere thought of her made his jeans tighten.

He held the door open for an exiting student, then stepped inside to be greeted by the sounds of the cappuccino machine steaming some hot milk for a latte. He inhaled deeply, taking in the robust and ambrosia-like scent of coffee.

For a weekday morning, it was surprisingly full of students working on their laptops. Grant's Crossing wasn't a college town, but the nearby cities of Delaware and Columbus were, so they were probably commuters. He joined the line, but gunshy from his last visit, he made a quick scan of the room to confirm that the Tres Widows were not present.

He arrived at the counter and placed his order. Kiro's girlfriend, Celeste, wasn't behind the counter when he walked in, but she was probably in the back, taking care of the books. He ordered a latte for the short walk home that took him right by the front window display of Between the Lines bookstore.

He glanced inside and saw a lady leaning into the window display from the inside. She was adjusting a few of the books that were part of an autumn-themed display. All the books were yellow, red, orange, or brown, a perfect color palette for this time of year. They even complimented the hair color of the woman leaning into the display. She wore a green, v-necked top that gave him an excellent view of everything she had to offer.

He took a step back for a more careful look. Was that...? Was that the redhead from the coffee shop?

She finished her task and stood back up without noticing him watching from the sidewalk. She grabbed a couple more books and leaned back to set them on the table.

He grinned while thoroughly enjoying the show. The shop wasn't open yet, so she had to work there. On a whim, he stepped closer to the window.

His movement must have startled her because she dropped a book and caught herself, gripping the half wall she was leaning over.

She froze when her eyes met his. Steve grinned and checked her out, though the half wall rudely obstructed part of his view.

He raised his hand in a wave, but his grin widened in response to the dirty look she gave him. Her narrowed eyes fueled his desire to stay and watch. Fine. It fueled more than that, but he was patient. Feeling a few drops of rain, he glanced up at the sky and made a mental note to walk down to the shop later in the day. Offering her one last cocky grin, he abandoned the view in favor of getting out of the now-falling rain, stepping down the sidewalk to a keypad on the outside wall. He plugged in his code, and the door clicked open. Fortunately, he made it inside and jogged up the stairs just as the downpour started, not believing his good fortune that his mysterious redhead was so close.

He yanked out an envelope wedged between the door and its frame as he opened his door. It had his first name on it, so it was probably just a note from Ken Bailey, his landlord and the owner of the bookshop below. He dropped it on the table and figured he'd get a few more hours of sleep before reading it. He could only sleep so well on his bunk at the station. As a Marine, he learned it was best to get some sleep whenever he could.

Just before taking a nap, he called the rehab clinic, mainly to ensure Nick was still there. He couldn't shake the nervous feeling of calling one day and being told Nick was no longer there. He feared being told Nick had checked himself out or, worse, had been taken. The lady on the other end assured him all was well and that he could visit the following week.

After a few hours of sleep and a long, hot shower, he padded out to the kitchen for something to drink. The day had turned dark thanks to the late summer thunderstorm. Though the rain had slowed to a sprinkle, he could still hear the water splash every time a car drove by on the street below.

He remembered the letter just as he opened the refrigerator for a bottle of root beer. Unscrewing the cap, he opened the letter and started reading.

It wasn't from Ken. The name on the bottom just read 'Tara.'

Who was Tara?

It looked like a trip to the bookstore would happen sooner rather than later. Figuring he probably shouldn't wear just a towel, he slammed the letter on the table and put on a pair of jeans and shoes. He could stop there before meeting the guys for dinner at Jo's.

He snatched the letter and his T-shirt and stormed down the stairs toward the back door to Between the Lines bookstore.

He made it within ten feet of the door when his redhead walked through. The sight of her knocked the wind right out of him, stopping him dead in his tracks.

It stopped her, too.

Damn, she was gorgeous.

He watched her eyes scan every inch of him from head to toe and back up when he realized he was giving her quite a show with his shirt in his hand rather than covering his body.

He curled his lip up into a crooked smile. "Hey, Sugar."

Chapter 50

Fellow Veterans

STEVE STEPPED INTO JO'S TO MEET DEREK AND TANK FOR dinner. Hopefully, Mike would join them. His new friends weren't Marines, but they had all served in combat. They understood what it was like to readjust to civilian life.

Steve swallowed the last bite of his cheeseburger and pushed his plate back. "You ever feel lost now that you're home? Now that there's not a mission calling us out to fight?"

"Every damn day," Derek mumbled from the seat next to him.

Steve met his gaze with a nod.

Mike Porter came over and collected all their dinner plates. Steve sat back in his seat as Mike set them in a plastic bin for dirty dishes. He reached behind the bar to grab four more bottles of beer and distributed them around the table before sitting down to join them. He tapped their bottles before taking a sip.

"I'm not sure what to do now that I've found my brother," Steve said. He took another swig and continued. "I've always taken care of him as best I could, which was pretty awful considering all he's been through. I mean, I thought I was doing the right thing. I tried to protect him from my Mom and Dad and well - that didn't turn out so well. Dad's dead and Mom's in jail for life."

Steve hadn't opened up to all the men at the station, but he had to the other guys who had served, so his parents' whereabouts weren't a surprise to them.

"I took him to live with our great aunt and uncle, who are some of the nicest people you'll ever meet, but they didn't need to take on a guy already out of school. Nicky was safe there. So, I enlisted. Nicky moved to Chicago, and he stopped being safe." Steve didn't often ramble at these gatherings, but he was more contemplative tonight and couldn't stop the words from flowing.

Derek clapped him on the shoulder in an offer of support.

Steve kept talking. "I had no idea what he was doing there. He said he was in hospitality at some hotel. He said he had a boyfriend. He said things were going well. I wanted for us to share an apartment together and it was about to happen, too, and then he went away."

Steve scanned the thoughtful faces around the table. They were all listening intently. "This time, he really is safe, and he really does have people who can help him. Much better than I ever could."

Tank leaned forward and looked him in the eye. "No, Steve."

"No, what?"

"He has all that help *because* of you," he explained. "You're not to blame for all that shit that happened when you were a kid." Tank leaned back in his seat. "And you told us you would have been arrested had you taken him when he was still in high school. You weren't able to take care of him. *Dios mio.* You were barely able to take care of yourself. Firefighters don't get paid enough right out of the academy to support a family. I can only take care of mine thanks to a pension and disability."

Steve rotated his bottle on the table. "I just want to kick in walls. I want to punch people's faces in." He scoffed. "Starting with that damned undercover agent. It probably wasn't even his fault what happened, but fuck, man. He was supposed to take care of the ones he knew were victims."

"I always want to punch something," Tank agreed. "If I'm not knocking down doors at a fire, firing a weapon at the range, then I…" He struggled to find the right word. "I'm just restless."

"I recommend fucking," Derek said with his beer bottle poised for another drink.

Mike and Tank both tossed him friendly glares, to which Derek shrugged.

"Drinking works, too." Derek took another pull from his bottle.

Steve caught Tank exchanging a worried glance with Mike, who shook his head. He thought back to the times he and Lynn hooked up simply because they were both in the same place at the same time. "Derek's not wrong. Fucking works, too, but only as a means to an end."

Tank broke out laughing. "Well. I do have four kids now."

They all laughed as a handful of customers at the bar cheered. Steve glanced at the TV to see a runner rounding the bases after hitting a home run. "I don't know. Maybe I'll always have to deal with this, but I just have this rage inside me that's just itching to blast out of my chest and bowl people over, you know?"

Tank nodded. "Yeah. I know."

"So, how do you get past it?" Steve leaned forward and held his bottle with both hands. "All I've done since I was discharged is fight fires and search for Nick."

"Simple." Tank shrugged. "Araceli. My wife has talked me down; I don't even know how many times. Especially when I first got back and had to go through all that therapy. Shit. I spent six months at Walter Reed before I could even come home. Celi kept our family together." He paused to smile. "Our parents are all here and love watching over the grandkids who are surrounded by a million aunts, uncles, and cousins. We have a great support network, but I still have days when I have to just step away and get my head back in the game."

"Jo was the same for me," Mike added. "With two of her

brothers in law enforcement and me over in Desert Storm, then Bosnia, she had all those years always wondering if her brothers or husband would make it home or if someone else would come knocking at their door instead." He blew out a lengthy exhale. "I hated how much relief she showed every time we could chat or video call each other. And that was from Bosnia. In Desert Storm, it was letters or nothing."

Tank tapped his bottle with Mike's.

"My dad had that visit," Derek said without making eye contact with any of them. "When Joey…"

Tank reached out and set his hand on Derek's forearm, receiving a knowing nod in return.

Through bits and pieces told when they got together, Steve knew about Derek's best friend and, for all intents and purposes, his brother, Joey Parker, who didn't make it home from their last deployment. He'd also learned that while a combat medic, Derek had saved Tank's life. He'd never seen it affect his work, but he knew Derek often found comfort with the bottle or whatever woman he dated for the evening.

"I have Nicky," Steve said. "I don't have the same network you guys have. And now that he's in rehab, I don't even have a mission."

"Yeah, you do." Derek sat up and turned in his seat to face Steve.

"What?"

"Yeah, you do," Derek repeated. He extended his arm around the table. "You have a support network. Nick may be your only blood relative here, but you have us. We know what you've been through. We've all spent time in the sandbox." Derek nodded to Tank. "Tank and me? We served countless missions together in Afghanistan. We know what it's like to be deployed and have to do things we didn't want or were afraid to do, but we did them." He leaned back in his seat. "And you have the guys at the station. That's as strong a family as any I've ever known."

Tank snorted out a laugh. "A little more unruly and eclectic–"

"Like your kids," Derek added.

Tank laughed without disagreeing. "Yeah, but they're some of the best men I've ever worked with."

"Hear, hear." Derek tapped his bottle against Tank's in agreement.

Tank turned serious again. "Your fellow Marines may have had your back while you served, Steve, but we've got it while you're here. You're family now, and I hope, in time, you'll come to think the same of us."

Chapter 51

A Little Knowledge

THE NEXT MORNING, STEVE CAUGHT A RIDE TO THE LOCAL impound lot after discovering his bike had been towed from its usual parking spot behind the bookstore.

Steve shook his head. Small towns.

"Thanks." Steve shook the hand of the middle-aged man who released his motorcycle out of the impound lot behind Aiden's Auto Shop. He got it out for only the cost of the tow—not that bad, all things considered.

The man pointed to the bike as he walked Steve over to where it was parked. "I went ahead and changed the oil for you. Gave it a tune-up, too. Looks like it had been a while."

"What? I didn't want anyone working on...."

"Hey." The man held up his hand. "The request was called in and paid for. We don't get to work on too many of these. Trust me; it was a pleasure. You should feel a better reaction when you squeeze the clutch. Felt like it was sticking."

Steve glanced back in surprise. "Yeah. It had been sticking a little. Haven't had time to bring it in." Steve climbed on his bike and started the engine, revving it a few times. "What's your name?"

"Francisco Serratos, but everybody calls me Frankie."

The engine sounded good. Steve extended his hand again. "Thanks again, Frankie."

They'd treated his motorcycle pretty well, too, thank goodness. From what he understood, Frankie was the one you wanted to take care of your vehicle if it ever needed to be towed anywhere.

Well-treated or not didn't change how pissed Steve was that he had to rescue his bike at all. He pulled on his helmet, revved the engine, and drove off.

Steve parked his motorcycle in the station lot before his shift started, knowing it would be safe there. He carried his helmet inside and slammed it on top of his locker. He opened his locker door hard enough to make a clanging noise that reverberated throughout the room.

"Who pissed in your Wheaties today?" Kiro looked up at Steve, who hadn't even seen him sitting there tying his shoes.

"Damned redhead had my bike towed from behind the shop. Had to get it out."

"Redhead?"

"Tara, something?"

Kiro cleared his throat. "Huh."

"Actually," Steve confessed, "it was someone from the shop next door who had it towed. Not the redhead."

"That sucks. Where'd you park it?"

"Behind the bookstore."

"In the alley?"

"Yeah."

"In a marked spot?"

Steve shot his arms up and snapped. "What's with the twenty questions?"

Kiro shrugged.

"Yes. It was in the alley." Steve explained slowly. "No. It was not in a marked spot, but I've had no problems before. I can't wait until Ken gets back. He'll take care of it for me."

"Ken Bailey?"

"Yeah, why?"

Kiro gave him a blank stare.

"What?"

"You haven't talked to Helen recently, have you?"

"Not in the last couple of weeks, no." He shoved his bag in his locker and closed the door. Much quieter this time. "Why? I haven't seen her. I've only been down in the shop once since finding Nick."

Steve wondered if he should see if they needed help with anything. It would allow him to give Tara a piece of his mind.

"Remember the car accident we had a couple of weeks ago?"

"Which one?"

"The multi-car pileup on Browning Street," Kiro explained. "Kid was texting and T-boned another car. It caused a three-car accident?"

"Yeah. I remember. We had to use the jaws of life on two of the cars."

"Right."

Steve sat down on the bench in between the rows of lockers. "Why do you ask?"

"Derek and I took the guy he T-boned to Grady Hospital."

"Okay?" Steve wasn't sure where Kiro was going with this.

"That was Ken Bailey."

"What?" Steve shot to his feet.

"Yeah."

"Shit. I didn't know. I didn't even see him."

"Got him out after disassembling half the car."

"I remember seeing you working on it, but I didn't see the driver." Steve scrubbed his face with his hand. "How's he doing?"

"He's okay. He had broken bones all over the left side of his body. Was even in a medically induced coma for a few days. Not much was damaged internally. He was lucky. "

"Wow." Steve exhaled, looking deflated by the news. "I didn't know."

"Figured. I think he's getting out soon." Kiro said matter-of-factly. "But there's something else you should know."

Steve shook his head. "What's that?"

"The redhead? Tara?" Kiro leaned back.

"Yeah? What about her?"

"She's his daughter."

Shit.

He sat down again as Kiro continued. "She came down from Chicago to help them keep their bookstore going. Helen's pretty much been on her own since school started up."

"Fuck."

Kiro nodded. "So, you might want to cut her a little slack."

"I should go down tomorrow to see if she needs anything. How do you know all this? Is it a small-town thing?"

Kiro chuckled. "Yeah. It is a small-town thing. But my parents live next door to the Baileys. Mom drove Helen to the hospital that night and stayed with her while Ken was being treated."

"I still can't get over how people here go out of their way like that. To help others." Then again, maybe he could. Derek and Kiro had helped him with Nick. "Except for my cousin, it was never like that growing up."

"Welcome to our small town, Steve. Anyway, Tara and Celeste were best friends growing up, then college roommates at OSU. They may live in separate cities now, but when they're together? It's as if they were never apart."

Steve groaned.

"What?"

"I might have pissed her off."

"Tara?"

"Yeah."

Kiro's expression turned grim. "You shouldn't do that."

"Probably not." Steve tilted his head and arched his eyebrows for a quick second. "Because she's fucking hot."

Kiro snorted out a laugh as he stood up.

Steve shot him a dirty look. "Not a word."

"Like I'm keeping that a secret." Kiro pulled his phone out of his pocket and laughed his way out of the locker room.

"Kiro," Steve called out behind him, chasing him down the hall to the lounge. "KIRO!" He yelled out to the sound of more laughter.

Chapter 52

Car Accident

THE SIRENS BLARED IN THE POURING RAIN AS THE LADDER truck from the Grant's Crossing Fire Department sped down the road, slowing down to work its way through a handful of cars that all appeared to have stopped suddenly to avoid playing a direct role in a car accident in the next intersection.

Two sheriff's deputies were already on the scene, trying to divert drivers away from the accident while also getting people to slow down despite the rain having eased up. Behind the wheel, Emerson turned off the sirens but kept the lights flashing while Steve, Tank, and the other firefighters jumped out.

A truck had crashed into the back of a smaller, stopped vehicle, smashing the front end when it forced it to spin around into a telephone pole. The airbag deployed, saving the driver from serious injury, but the impact jammed the driver's side door shut. While the firefighters worked to force it open, Kiro and Derek rushed over to the other side and, after Steve smashed the window for them, leaned in to take care of the stunned, albeit responsive driver.

Kiro had put a neck brace on the young man by the time they could pry open the driver's side door. The driver made it through with no life-threatening injuries. He was shaken up and had cuts on his forehead and temple from slamming against the steering wheel and driver's side window.

Steve spared a glance back to see the police interviewing the truck driver. It looked pretty straightforward.

But then again, they all did.

At first.

Once the investigation started, more details would confirm whether it stayed that way. The truck driver, by all accounts sober, was fully cooperating. Another deputy walked over to the firefighters to explain that the pickup truck driver had been unable to stop on the wet, downward-sloped road. He hydroplaned into the car.

Steve quickly learned this was a familiar spot for accidents, thanks to a nearly blind turn coming into the intersection just outside of town. He'd only been in Grant's Crossing a few months, but he'd already seen his fair share of accidents where the victims barely made it to the hospital or were pronounced dead at the scene.

"That was fast." Emerson leaned over to Steve and tapped his arm, pointing to the tow truck pulling into the scene for the smaller vehicle. They'd barely gotten the young driver onto a gurney.

A large man hopped out of the tow truck and stormed toward Derek and Kiro, who were treating the victim. Cussing up a storm, he called the young driver by name. The man's expletive-laden rant was full of off-handed remarks that implied he had significant objections to the young man's lifestyle.

The young man flinched and called him Dad. He grew more and more agitated as Kiro and Derek tried to treat him for the trauma of the accident and now for the additional trauma of his father's laying into him.

"Shit," Steve muttered within earshot of Emerson, both of whom kept their eyes on the man, whose arm movements became more and more animated as he blamed the entire accident on his son.

His son recoiled, trying to protect himself the closer his father got to him.

Steve recognized that reaction. He had seen the same one with his brother.

"Damn it, Johnny. I knew it. If you weren't so damned irresponsible..." the kid's father raged on and on.

Steve had enough. A quick look around showed the deputies still had their hands full with the other drivers, trying to keep traffic moving around the accident. Steve ran over and put himself between the raging father and the son the paramedics were treating. "That's enough!"

"He's my kid." The man yelled at Steve, who got right in his face.

"I don't give a shit who he is. You need to stand back until the medics have taken care of him." Tim and Emerson joined him and formed a wall between the father, who was on the verge of throwing punches, and his son.

The son visibly cowered on the gurney behind them while Tim and Emerson physically restrained his father.

"No. I can go home," his son's shaky voice squeaked out while blood ran down the side of his face. "I don't need to go."

Thinking of his own brother, Steve turned toward the gurney where Derek and Kiro were encouraging him to get himself checked out. "Can I talk to him?"

Derek nodded and stepped aside for Steve to lean in. Steve kept one eye on the kid's father to ensure he didn't break through their makeshift barricade.

"Hey." Steve offered an encouraging smile. He kept his voice much softer than he used with the kid's father. "I know what it's like to have it tough. It was like this back home with my own parents. But with an accident like this, you really need to be checked out by a doctor. You don't yet know the full extent of your injuries. Please let us take you in, okay?"

"But my dad…" he spoke with a shaky voice. Whether that was from the accident or his dad, Steve couldn't tell. Both were strong possibilities.

"We'll take care of your dad." Steve wasn't sure what he meant by that, but he had plenty of ideas, some of which were even legal.

"I don't know." The boy's frightened eyes kept darting over toward his dad, who was still yelling from the other side of Tim, Emerson, and now Shek.

"Would it help if I came with you?" Steve lifted his chin in the direction of Derek and Kiro. "They're really good and will take great care of you, but if you want, I can come along, too."

Steve was next in line to work the ambulance if Derek or Kiro ever had additional training or a day off. He was also the first one to go with them if a patient were injured badly enough to need extra hands on the way to the hospital.

"Yeah. Okay," the young driver responded with a little more confidence.

"We'll get him in if you want to go up front, Kiro." Steve offered, figuring the quicker the exit, the better. With a nod, Kiro went up front to drive as Steve and Derek loaded the gurney and locked it in place inside the ambulance.

Once inside, Derek started working on the kid's facial lacerations again from the captain's chair as Shek walked up and closed the doors behind them and pounded it twice, so Kiro knew he could take off. Steve removed his helmet and turnout jacket so he could move around easier as the sirens started and they started moving.

Derek handed an IV pack to Steve, who opened it and pulled out the needle to start an IV after he put on a pair of gloves.

"No. No. No," the boy said. "Don't stick me."

"It's just a saline solution. Nothing to worry about." Steve spoke softly as he cleaned off his elbow. "So your name's Johnny, right?" Steve gently straightened Johnny's arm.

"Jonathan. I hate Johnny." He breathed out, sounding slightly panicked. "Only my dad calls me that, and I hate it."

"Jonathan it is, then." Steve reassured him.

"John works, too." He winced as Derek swabbed the cuts on his head. "My friends call me John."

"Sounds good, John. I'm Steve." John's arm relaxed while Steve spoke. He tilted his head toward Derek. "And this is Derek."

Steve got the needle in without John even noticing. He taped it to his arm and got it started. Whether or not a head injury was serious, which they often were, they bled a lot, so they relied on saline solution to keep everything flowing.

"What's that?"

"This is the saline solution I mentioned," Steve explained as he checked the bag to make sure it was flowing as it should, then started examining his wrist. It might have been broken, judging by the way John winced when he applied even the slightest bit of pressure. Derek relayed his vitals and injuries ahead to the hospital so they knew what to expect.

"But I didn't feel a thing."

"That's the idea." Steve shot a confident smile to his visibly relieved patient. Grabbing a splint, he secured it around his wrist, which would have to be x-rayed at the hospital.

"Will they tell my dad where you're taking me?"

Steve met his eyes with a nod. "Probably. They'll tell him we're taking you to Grady Hospital."

"What happens when he gets there? He'll just yell and scream like he always does." John started breathing heavily again.

"Do you want me to stick around?" Steve made more of an effort to keep him calm.

John lifted his head. "You'd do that?"

"Of course."

He let his head fall back on the gurney. "You sound like my cousin. He was a Marine. He could always stand up to my father." John looked like he was fighting back tears.

It broke Steve's heart that this kid was terrified of his own family. Is that what he and Nicky were like all those years?

"Your cousin's a good man. I served in the Marines, too." Nodding toward Derek, he couldn't resist adding. "He was just in the Army. I mean, he was a Ranger, which scores him a few extra points, I guess, but he's definitely not as cool as your cousin and me."

Derek shook his head with a smirk. "Maybe you boys should stop chatting. We're about there."

"See?" Steve laughed. "Can't even multi-task."

John breathed out half a laugh.

Steve turned serious. "Look, John. I'll stick around with you tonight. I'll make sure you get home, too, when they say it's okay for you to leave. Where do you live? Delaware? Radnor? Grant's Crossing?"

"Grant's Crossing."

"Perfect. Me, too. And how old are you?"

"Eighteen. I graduated last Spring." He fought back tears. "I'm old enough to be kicked out, but I'm still on my dad's insurance while I'm looking for a full-time job."

Kiro brought the ambulance to a stop, silencing the sirens as he pulled up to the Emergency Department at Grady Hospital.

"Hey." Steve understood how that worked. "If you need anything, anything at all, you just let me know. I'm Steve Cook. You can ask for me at the fire station. I also live above the bookstore on the square. You can find me there if you're ever in a bind."

For a split second, Derek's brows arched at the mention of where he lived, but to his credit, he stayed silent as he worked. He made eye contact with Steve from where he sat behind John.

Under normal circumstances, Steve would never let anyone at a call know where he lived, but in a small town, everybody probably knew anyway. He felt protective of this kid and wanted to make sure he had options his own brother did not.

Steve returned the look and dared him to challenge him, but Derek only nodded as Kiro opened the back door to transfer John from the ambulance to the emergency department.

Chapter 53

The Walk Home

Steve stood by Kiro, his empty bottle in hand.

"I think they're about done," Kiro exclaimed, watching his girlfriend and some friends part ways after their girls' night out.

Steve rolled his eyes since Kiro had been counting down the minutes all night before he could join Celeste for the rest of the evening.

Steve ordered the next round for him and Kiro as Kiro greeted Celeste at the table with a kiss. Steve would be a third wheel at least long enough to finish his second beer before heading home. He wasn't in the mood to be alone in his apartment tonight.

He paid the bartender, an older man with a ponytail Jo and Mike had just hired, then took the drinks to the table. Steve placed his jacket on a seat at their table and reached across to shake Celeste's hand. Somehow, he'd never actually been introduced to her until now.

Steve looked up and froze. He fought to regain his usual cocky countenance. He had only seen Tara dressed in nice slacks or a casual dress, her typical work clothing at the bookstore. Tonight, she wore a low-cut, olive green dress that hugged her waist and dropped into a flowing skirt that made it almost to her knees. She certainly didn't wear heels to work since she was on her feet all day but for tonight? Her feet were balanced on thin, black spikes.

Her smile disappeared the moment they made eye contact.

Clearly, she wasn't happy with him. Maybe he shouldn't have ogled her through the plate glass window at the bookstore.

Steve glared at Kiro and Celeste, who failed to disguise their amusement.

She cleared her throat, drawing Steve's attention.

"Tara." Why did his voice sound lower than usual?

"Steve."

"I didn't know you'd be joining us."

"Girls' Night Out." She sat down in the chair next to his.

Tara and Celeste put their heads close together and exchanged a few quiet words followed by laughter.

"Derek, Kiro, and I were shooting pool on the other side of the bar," Steve admitted.

"Keeping tabs on your girl, Kiro?" Tara smirked at him.

"Am I that obvious?" For a second, Kiro looked worried but quickly recovered. He cleared his throat.

Tara held her thumb and index finger close together. "Just a little."

Kiro turned to Steve, who grinned as if sharing an inside joke. "We actually haven't been waiting for long. Have we?"

"Tim was right about you." Steve took a pull of his beer, staying nonchalant.

"Right about what? Oh." Kiro sent a friendly glare toward Steve.

"Tim?" Tara asked.

"One of the guys at the station," Steve explained. His eyes lingered on hers for a second or two longer.

"Oh." She cleared her throat. "Tim Ellis?"

"Yeah."

"I see you got your motorcycle back." Tara turned to Steve.

"Yeah. Don't have it towed again." His blue eyes peered right into hers; then he softened his gaze. "Please."

She narrowed her own. "Well, make sure you don't park it in the loading zone again."

"Sure thing, Sugar."

Tara leaned closer. "And don't call me sugar. You're not fixing a cup of coffee this time."

"I think you like it." He never took his eyes off hers. She rolled her eyes at him.

Tara smiled across the table at Kiro and Celeste. "I think I'm going to head home."

"Gurl." Celeste stood up to give Tara a hug. "I'm so glad we did this."

"Me, too. Goodnight, Kiro." She turned her head. "Steve."

Celeste paused. "Wait. Where's your jacket?"

Tara waved her off. "I walked off without it this morning. It's okay. I'm not going far."

"In those?"

"Sure." Tara looked down at her high heels. "I walk in these all the time."

Steve pulled out his wallet and dropped a couple of bills on the table. He grabbed his jacket off the back of his chair. "Then I'll walk you home."

"You don't need to."

"Let me walk you home." He extended his hand so she could walk out first. "Please?"

She shared a look with Celeste and reluctantly agreed.

With a nod, he wished Celeste and Kiro goodnight, both of whom were unsuccessfully suppressing smiles.

Steve shook his head as he followed Tara outside.

Tara was hurrying out of Jo's. Steve had to jog to catch up to her. "Hey, Sugar. Slow down."

Doing an about-face, she snapped. "Would you stop calling me that?"

"I just want to make sure you get home safe."

"Any chance you can do it without being an incorrigible ass? I mean, why are you like that?"

He shrugged. "Talented, I guess."

She rolled her eyes but laughed anyway. He couldn't resist laughing, too.

A minute later, she rubbed her hands along her upper arms but kept walking.

"Hold up." He held his jacket out for her to wear.

"What?" She only hesitated a moment before sliding her hands through the sleeves as he pulled it up over her shoulders.

"Thank you." She pulled it shut in the front. It was way too big on her, but he liked seeing her in it. He stuck his hands in his jeans pocket to stave off the evening chill.

"Kiro said your dad was in an accident a while back?"

"A few weeks ago. Yes."

"I worked on the other car, so I didn't know it was him. How's he doing?"

She glanced up at him. "He's out of the hospital but won't be able to work for a while." She exhaled audibly. "They needed me, so I came home to help." She paused at the end of the sidewalk before they crossed the street. "I was supposed to go on vacation next week."

"Is that right? Where?"

"It wasn't any place fancy."

"That doesn't matter. Where were you going to go?"

"Mackinac Island. They have the Grand Hotel up there." She laughed and met his gaze with a half smile. "So maybe it was going to be fancy. It looked so beautiful up there... at least in the pictures." She continued walking.

"It *is* beautiful."

"You've been there?"

"Yes. I filled in for the fire department up in St. Ignace when they lost two firefighters in a fire. I volunteered to fill in for a few weeks."

"Is that how you ended up here in Grant's Crossing?"

"That's a long story."

Tara stopped walking. "Well, we have three more blocks to go."

Steve stared down and rubbed the toe of his shoe on the ground as if putting out a non-existent cigarette.

"More like three and a half blocks, if you want to be exact," she smiled.

He took in a deep breath and stared back at her for a few moments. Then he started talking... about growing up outside of St. Louis, his time in the service, to taking care of his brother.

By the time they reached her parents' house, he'd shared more than he'd originally intended, but it felt right. Being with her felt right.

Comfortable.

He walked her up to the front porch, where she turned around and faced him. "Thanks for walking me home." She glanced up at him as if waiting for something. Prominently displayed in the front window was a flag with two blue stars, indicating they had two family members actively serving in the military.

"You're military?"

Tara glanced back at the window. "Yes. My sister and one of my brothers are in the Navy."

His eyes fell to her lips. For a few seconds, he let his mind wander to thoughts of pressing his lips to hers. They looked soft and inviting, and he wanted nothing more in that moment than to reach a hand behind her neck and pull her close. He wanted to hold her body against his and claim her as his.

"Oh." She slid out of his jacket and handed it back to him. "Thanks for this."

Yanked from his thoughts, he blinked and stood up straighter, hoping she didn't pick up on what he was thinking. "You're welcome."

Her green eyes narrowed for a moment. It was as if she could see straight into him. Mind, body, and soul.

Steve cleared his throat. Maybe she did pick up on his thoughts.

She curled up a lip on one side, but in a flash, she muttered a quick goodnight and slipped inside the door.

"Goodnight," he said to the closing door.

He waited a few seconds, then trotted down the front steps. He followed the sidewalk to the narrow driveway that led to a detached garage behind the house. Turning around for one last look, he started for home.

Steve pulled on his jacket and shrugged his shoulders up and down to pull the collar up around his neck. He didn't know why he'd told Tara everything he did. Maybe it was easier to open up to a stranger. Whatever it was during that walk home, opening up to her lightened the immense weight on his shoulders, even if just a little bit.

It was a cool night, yet he felt warm and comforted at having been able to share his history with Tara. He rarely talked about his personal life. It was usually too gritty for polite company, but somehow, he knew she wouldn't judge him for it.

There are some parts he'd never tell her, of course, because they were for Nick to share, not him, but he trusted her with what he could.

Sugar.

Catching a whiff of her perfume on his jacket collar, he chuckled as he rounded the corner back to his apartment.

Chapter 54

Surprise Visitor

Turning down Washington Avenue in front of the bookstore on his way back home, Steve caught the movement of what looked like a foot sticking out of the small recessed entryway that led to his apartment. As he grew closer, a young man sitting on the ground in the doorway came into view. He was clutching a duffle bag for dear life, but it looked like he'd nodded off to sleep.

Steve gave him a wide berth and stepped out onto the street so he could view him head-on. The man was in rough shape. His wrist was already in a cast; it looked like he'd been through one hell of a fight.

Stepping closer, Steve recognized him as the kid from the car accident earlier that week. He rushed over and crouched down beside him. "John." He squeezed his shoulder to rouse him. "Jonathan."

With a yelp, John jumped to his feet, protecting his face with his arms. He squeezed his eyes shut, then reopened them. He snatched up his bag and clutched it against his chest like a shield. He also wore a backpack.

Steve took a step back and held his arms up, palms out. "It's me, Steve Cook."

John narrowed his eyes and looked him up and down.

"I'm not going to hurt you."

John closed his eyes and slouched, falling back against the door with a relieved exhale.

"What happened?"

John looked up at Steve with tears in his eyes. "Me and Dad..." he said, starting but unable to complete the sentence.

"What about your dad?" Steve's eyes darkened with anger. "Did he do this to you?"

He just nodded, still shaking in fear as his tears fell.

"Son of a..."

Taking a deep breath, Steve closed his eyes for a moment, figuring his own anger at the kid's father wouldn't help the immediate situation.

"Let's go inside." Steve put a reassuring hand back on John's shoulder and entered his code to open the door. "Top of the stairs. First door on the right."

John trudged up the stairs but faltered just shy of Steve's doorway. His eyes darted left and right.

Sensing his hesitation, Steve moved past him and opened the door. "Go on in."

Steve followed John inside, dropping his wallet and keys on the coffee table. He gestured toward the kitchen table. "Have a seat."

John sat down, still holding his bag close. Steve tossed his jacket on the couch and then disappeared into his bedroom. He returned with his large, well-stocked first-aid kit.

"Drop your bags anywhere." He pulled out a chair and sat beside John, who set his bags on the floor by his feet.

Steve gave John a visual once over. "Let's take a look. Where does it hurt the most?"

"Everywhere?" John fought his tears but wouldn't make eye contact with Steve, who stopped what he was doing and looked straight at him.

"Hey."

John stared at the floor, still withdrawn.

"Look at me." Steve's voice was gentle. John raised his eyes to meet Steve's. "It's okay. You're okay."

Steve stood up to run water over a washcloth. He sat back down and gently cleaned John's face to figure out where the cuts actually were. He had a couple of minor lacerations over his left eye, the remnants of a bloody nose, and a heavy dose of leftover fear.

Steve held up his fingers. "How many fingers am I holding up?"

"Three." John sniffed again and wiped his nose with the back of his shaking hand.

"Good." He had John follow his fingers back and forth and up and down.

John flinched when Steve touched the bridge of his nose. Steve butterflied a couple of cuts and was happy John's nose wasn't broken.

John shuddered out a breath.

Steve looked up with a knitted brow. "I don't like the sound of that. Did you take any hits to your chest or stomach?"

John looked away.

"Did you?"

"Yes."

"Fuck."

For John's sake, Steve worked hard to control the anger that was boiling in his chest at what John's father did to him. "Can you try to take off your shirt?"

Seeing him flinch when he did, Steve helped him remove his shirt, which revealed bruising all over his torso.

"Shit." He pulled out a stethoscope and listened to his breathing, then examined his ribs. The area around one seemed particularly tender. "You might have a cracked rib. You really need an X-ray... and an actual doctor."

"I can't go to a hospital. Dad would find out."

The panic on his face made Steve's stomach drop. "Only if you made an insurance claim." He released a long breath. "No hospital. Lucky for you, I know someone who makes house calls."

"I hope you don't make this a habit," Dr. Lees said as he followed Steve into his apartment.

"Thanks for coming over, Matt."

"Anytime."

Fear was etched on John's face as he sat there holding an ice pack against his eye. His other hand held a wrapped blanket around his shoulders.

"John?" Steve's voice went soft again. "This is a friend of mine, Matt Lees. He's a doctor who can tell us if we need to take you in for X-rays or not."

Steve looked up at Matt, then back over at where John was sitting. "You can trust him."

John's nervous eyes darted back and forth between the two men. "Do you... trust him?"

"He's helping my brother, so, yes."

Though still nervous, he seemed to relax a bit. "Okay."

"May I take a look?" Matt asked John, not wanting to make any moves without first getting his express permission.

John glanced up at Steve, who nodded in encouragement.

"Alright."

Steve pushed his first aid kit out of the way to make room for Matt's pack.

"Thanks." Matt sat down and examined John while Steve ran through everything he'd already done to treat him. "You couldn't have gone to a better person for help, John. Breathe in slowly."

John breathed in. "Now, breathe out."

He exhaled.

Matt had him do that a few times before determining it was probably just bruised.

"I stopped by the fire station, and they said you weren't there." John struggled to get the words out.

"I wasn't on shift today," Steve answered.

"So I came here. I'm sorry." Tears fell down his cheeks. "I didn't have anywhere else to go."

"Hey. It's no problem." Steve sat down next to him. "Never be sorry for coming here, John. You did the right thing."

"Have you notified the authorities?"

John's eyes widened at Matt's question. He shook his head. "No. What could they do?"

"They would have a record of the assault, and you'd be within your rights to press charges," Matt explained. He continued as John just stared. "It would also help establish a pattern should you ever need a restraining order."

"A restraining order?"

"You can also file a report without filing charges."

"You don't have to decide right now, John," Steve offered, attempting to calm him.

"Are you staying here in the meantime?" Matt asked as John appeared ready to panic again.

"I don't know... I don't have a place to stay. I..."

"Yes. He can stay with me until we figure something out. It's too late to find anything tonight anyway." Steve turned to John, his face resolute. "Look. I said you could come to me anytime, and I meant it. You don't have to figure this out by yourself."

John looked up at Steve as more tears fell. His voice cracked when he spoke. "He told me he wished I wasn't his son." He collapsed against Steve's chest and just cried.

"I've got you." Deflated, Steve wrapped his arms around him and held him while the tears flowed.

His thoughts wandered to his brother. He wondered what

would have happened to his brother had someone been able to take him in like this... had *he* been there to take him in. He swallowed his regret, knowing it was far too late for that now. He couldn't change the past. His brother was getting the help he needed now. Steve needed to concentrate on what he could control, which was a hell of a lot more than he could have done eight years earlier.

One glance at Matt confirmed the genuine anger they shared over this kid's dad.

"It's okay," Steve said, attempting to offer him comfort. "I'm glad you're here, John. I'm glad you're here."

Chapter 55

Proud of You

TARA SAT A FEW BOXES OF COOKIES DOWN ON THE TABLE IN THE firehouse break room. "Thanks, boys." With Kiro's help, she had talked the firefighters into helping her move furniture and displays for an upcoming event at the bookstore.

"I knew you'd help her out with Homefest," Kiro said of the town's upcoming Homecoming Festival.

"Yep." Steve's gaze followed Tara as she walked through the door and out of the station. As he bit into a cookie, he thought about how good it would feel to sink his teeth into her neck, or her chest, or her thighs. As she walked past the plate glass window that separated the lounge from the garage area, his eyes made one last survey of her curves, eyeing her all the way down her long legs and back, stopping at the curve of her ass that he knew was just calling his name.

"And painting her store," Kiro couldn't resist adding.

"So? Emerson'll be there, too."

"Sure, but like you, the girl he likes will be there."

"I'm a first responder. I like to help the community," Steve said.

Kiro laughed. "And they said I was whipped."

"You are," Tim and Emerson called out from the other side of the lounge.

Kiro scoffed, but still shot them both a friendly glare.

Steve shifted in his seat and shoved the rest of the cookie in his mouth as he felt a hand on his shoulder. With his eyes still trained on the closing door, he tilted his head up as Derek spoke. "Guess you're off the market, huh?"

Steve chewed the rest of the cookie and swallowed. He turned his head toward Derek but kept his eyes on the TV. "Just watching the game."

"Uh-huh." Derek laughed but kept his voice low. "Say what you like, but that just leaves more for me." He patted Steve's shoulder again.

Steve turned his head in time to see him picking up the carafe to pour himself another cup of coffee. As he turned back to the TV, he caught sight of Kiro, who was clearly on the same wavelength as Derek.

Kiro snorted out a laugh, then pressed his lips together to give the appearance of a straight face, earning him a front-row viewing of Steve's middle finger.

Two back-to-back fires kept them working all night and into the morning, well past the end of their shift, but that was how it was with firefighters. They stayed on the job until the job was done.

After taking showers to remove the soot and grime off their weary bodies, Steve shuffled into Baba's Diner with Derek and Kiro for some well-deserved breakfast. As usual, Kiro's mom just dropped food off at the table and ordered them to eat. Logan joined them.

Once their stomachs realized they were no longer being neglected, Steve mentioned John and told them how he showed up on his doorstep the other night.

"There's a waitlist for the local shelter for displaced youth," Logan said. "But John's in a gray area because he's already eighteen.

He might be able to go there for a few days, but he'd ultimately need to get an apartment. The challenge now is finding him a job."

Steve scraped the last food on his plate onto a fork, shoved it in his mouth, and downed the rest of his orange juice. "He said he was looking for another job."

"I think I can help with that." Logan emptied his mug of coffee before continuing. "I'm working with area employers to set up job training opportunities so everyone in our program can earn a decent wage while gaining useful skills."

Derek held up a hand and grunted while taking a sip of coffee. "Yeah. My dad told me how he's going to start something up where they can start working on my dad's demo crews and then, little by little, start learning construction skills. Dad likes the idea because it helps him find people willing to learn the trade but who can start part-time until full-time work opens up."

Logan smiled. "Yes, your dad is helping pilot the program. He's been really supportive. And..." He held up his hand for emphasis. "I have an uncle who has a studio apartment above his auto shop that John can probably use."

"Oh, yeah?" Steve perked up. "Maybe that's an option for John. Kill two birds with one stone. Has the program started up yet?"

"We're sending him some candidates to interview in the next couple of weeks."

"Perfect."

***

Steve grabbed some food to go and said his goodbyes. He figured John would be hungry, and he didn't have time to get groceries before going on shift the day before, so his fridge was bare.

Stepping into his apartment, he found John asleep on the couch. The lights were out, but the TV was on whatever station he'd been watching.

Steve snickered and placed the food on the table. He walked over to the couch and gently tapped John's shoulder. When John didn't move, he nudged his shoulder a little harder.

"Go away," John gave the typical teenage response, then rolled over to face the back of the couch.

Steve chuckled and pushed against his shoulder one last time. "John. Wake up. I brought food."

John turned over and opened an eye just as Steve, wearing a leather jacket, stared down at him. He cried out and sat up with a start. "Don't do that. You scared the crap out of me."

So much for being shy.

"You sleep like the dead. Get up." Steve hung his coat on a hook on the wall and tossed his backpack into his bedroom. He returned to open the fridge and found it full of food.

"What's this?" He asked as a still-sleepy John sat down at the table and opened the bag from Baba's. He unwrapped a thick sandwich filled with meat, cheese, lettuce, and tomatoes on a baguette and took a big bite. "I picked up a few things yesterday while you were on shift. Least I could do since you took me in."

Steve grabbed a bottle of root beer and popped the top as he looked around his spotless apartment. The pile of once-dirty dishes was in the dishwasher or drying on the rack on the counter.

"I cleaned up, too," he spoke around a mouth full of food. "Hope that's alright. No offense, but you're a slob."

Steve surveyed his apartment only to realize every space was much cleaner than it was the day before. "How'd you get around?"

"Oh, the lady downstairs helped me out. Tara. The pretty one?" he gulped down another bite of sandwich.

Steve swallowed and tried not to let his thoughts wander as John spoke.

"I walked down to get a book and ended up helping her receive a delivery. I told her I was staying with you for a while and needed a job, but she didn't have any full-time positions open. She offered to give me about ten hours a week cleaning, stocking, and unloading, so that's a start, right?"

A small burst of pride he had no right to claim filled Steve's chest at John's willingness to take it upon himself and find work despite having been kicked out of the only home he'd ever known. That's not to mention having to talk to people with a bruised face with butterfly bandages over one eye.

"Anyway, she took me to buy groceries, and then we stopped by my house." He stopped eating for a moment. His eyes stared blankly at the wall as he spoke. "Dad was at work, so I grabbed as much stuff as I could." His voice cracked, and his hand jumped to his cheek to wipe a tear off his face. "He'd already boxed it up."

Steve leaned back against the counter and remained silent so John could take a moment to collect himself.

"Anyway, Tara and I made three trips before it was almost time for Dad to come home. I'll eventually need furniture."

"She helped you move your stuff?" It surprised Steve that Tara was willing to help John on the spot. The fact that his dad already had his stuff in boxes didn't surprise him at all.

"Yeah. Her car could only hold so much, but we packed it full each time. Most of the stuff is in a storage room downstairs. She gave me a key to get to it when I wanted."

"Look. It's not my place or anything, but I'm proud of you, John."

John sat up a little straighter and ran his hands through his sleep-messed hair.

"Really?"

"Yeah. What you did yesterday took guts. It takes a lot of courage to walk outside with a black eye and cuts on your face, but to go back home?"

"I think I got all the important stuff. I wish I had the guts to confront my father, but he scares me too much."

"It took me a long time to stand up to mine, too. Someday, though, you'll find that courage."

"Yeah." John's eyes glazed over for a few seconds. He blinked again and breathed deeply for a long minute before exhaling. "Now, all I need is another job so I can get my own place."

"I think my friend, Logan, has some ideas for that," Steve said with authority. "In the meantime, I can pick up an air mattress for the second bedroom. It's not fancy, but you wouldn't have to stay on the couch. You can stay here as long as you need to get stuff sorted out. Then we can find you a place of your own."

"Wow. Thanks, Steve."

"You bet."

Chapter 56

It wasn't Nothing

AFTER A LONG NAP, STEVE MADE SURE JOHN WAS OKAY, THEN jogged downstairs in time to catch Tara flipping the sign in the front window around to 'closed'. Her hand shot up to her chest when he knocked on the plate-glass window. He shrugged and mouthed a quick sorry, but he couldn't stop himself from laughing at her reaction.

She narrowed her eyes for a few seconds, then unlocked the door. She pushed it open enough so he could hear. "Mr. Cook?"

"Miss Bailey." His response was just as formal as hers. "Mind if I come in?"

"We're closed." She pressed her lips together in an effort not to smile.

"I promise not to buy anything."

After debating for a few seconds, her smile broke free, and she welcomed him inside. "Come on in."

She opened the door wide enough for him to walk inside.

Steve nodded toward Tara's coworker who gave a quick return wave, then turned his attention back to Tara. "So, what do you have planned for dinner?"

Tara crossed her arms. "Inviting yourself over, are you?"

His grin widened. "Asking you out, actually. You have to eat, right?"

"Mmhmm."

He extended his arm toward the park across the street. "I was heading over to Jo's and...well... come on. Let me buy you dinner. Although..." He looked her up and down.

"What?" She placed her hands on her hips.

He motioned with his hand. "Sweater, jeans, boots..." He shook his head and inhaled through his teeth. "You might be a bit underdressed." He recalled her Girls' Night Out when she wore a dress and heels.

She breathed out a sigh but froze when she noticed his red Cardinals shirt. "If you have to wear a shirt for a baseball team outside of Ohio, you could at least wear something with the Chicago Cubs on it."

"The Cubs?" He grasped his chest as if gripping a figurative knife. "You wound me."

"You're a jerk. You know that, right?"

"I do," he agreed. "I really do."

She laughed. "But if you're so desperate for company, I'll go grab my purse and lock up."

"You don't need your purse. Dinner's on me."

"But..."

"But nothing. Just get your jacket," he smirked, "or do I need to head back to my place to grab an extra?"

"Still a jerk," she called back over her shoulder.

Steve laughed as she headed back to the office for her jacket.

Steve and Tara sat in a booth toward the front of Jo's with a window that looked out at the square. Within a few minutes, they had their orders placed.

"Look," Steve held out his hand and paused a few seconds before finding the right words. "John told me how you helped him."

"It was nothing–"

"It wasn't nothing, Tara." He cut her off. "It..."

Steve struggled for words so Tara spoke up instead. "How often do you take in lost souls?"

"I don't..." He cleared his throat, dropping any pretense. "I just do what it takes when somebody's parents are too chicken shit to do it themselves, that's all. He deserves better."

"Yeah. He does. He's lucky you were there for him."

"It meant a lot to him, Tara, what you did. And..." he swallowed, thinking of how his brother and John were so similar. "And to me, too."

Tara smiled. "You're welcome."

Steve spent the rest of the meal getting to know Tara a little better. After they finished eating, they watched the last of the ballgame, showing two teams neither of them followed on one of the large screen TVs on the wall. Steve was still dismayed that Tara was a Cubs fan, but at least she enjoyed live sports. He knew her time in Grant's Crossing was limited. She would be returning to her life in Chicago sooner rather than later, but maybe he could talk her into going to a hockey game when the St. Louis Blues were in town.

"You and your St. Louis teams," she said, shaking her head.

"I'm from there, remember? Besides, it sure beats liking Chicago teams."

"And I live there, remember?"

"Don't remind me."

The game ended, and music started playing. Some couples worked their way to the small dance floor in front of the jukebox.

"That's a good idea." He turned to Tara

Curling up a lip in a lopsided smile, he stood up and held out his hand. "Care to dance, Tara Bailey?"

Blinking off the shock of the question, she slipped her small fingers into his larger hand and lifted her eyes. "I'd love to."

His eyes lit up as she stood to follow him. They held hands for the short length it took to get to the dance floor. He turned and placed his hand on the small of her back to pull her closer. He felt her hand hesitate as it found his shoulder but smiled to himself as she relaxed into him when they started moving to the music.

"I'm a horrible dancer," Tara confessed.

"Just follow my lead." He hoped she couldn't feel his racing heart. He couldn't remember the last time he felt even remotely nervous around a woman. "Though I usually fake it and hope nobody notices. I can only sway back and forth." His cheek nearly met hers as he shared what sounded like a secret.

When the music ended, they both still held each other. He didn't want to move apart and held his breath, suddenly as nervous as a middle schooler asking a girl to dance for the very first time.

He gently tipped her chin up and met her gaze. The rest of the restaurant disappeared. Nothing existed but Tara.

Her gorgeous green eyes were going to be the death of him, but right now, Steve wanted to lose himself in her eyes. His own eyes dropped to her parted lips, feeling butterflies flutter through his middle. He wanted nothing more than to feel her, taste her. Her lavender scent filled his senses, driving his desire higher. He tilted his head and leaned in to kiss her when a high-pitched voice called out.

"STEVE!"

He closed his eyes and dropped his chin to his chest. "Shit."

"Oh, Ste-eve," Miss Abigail sing-songed.

He exhaled and led Tara back to their booth. "I'm sorry, but I have a promise to keep."

A row of hand-made signs welcomed Steve the following morning when he arrived at the station. Each firefighter held up a number to rate his dancing ability the night before with Miss Abigail.

Word had apparently gotten out to the entire B-shift about his dance with one of the Tres Widows, and from what he could see, Kiro was right. The men of GC Fire had no intention of letting him live it down. The numbers ranged from seven to nine except for Derek, who held up a two. Steve greeted them all with a middle finger and a smile.

He'd eventually get back at all of them, but when the siren went off for an apartment fire, he decided it could wait.

Chapter 57

Not Your Fault

When Kiro walked into the treatment room, the doctor was stitching up a laceration above Steve's eyebrow. "They say the fire is out. Just working through the inspections and clean up."

More cuts were on Steve's face, and his left arm and torso were covered in bruises.

Kiro scrutinized his injuries. "Did you fall? Or single-handedly break up a bar fight?"

Steve thought back to when the floor of a burning home gave out beneath him, sending him to the basement where his fellow firefighter had to help him to safety.

He lifted the mask off his mouth and nose. "Fuck you," he wheezed and then coughed a few times.

Kiro leaned against the wall and crossed his arms, casually watching the doctor care for Steve's injuries. "I think you owe Derek and me a drink after today."

Steve coughed again and spoke in a scratchy whisper. "Then I owe Tim two drinks. He got me out. Is he okay?"

"Mask on," the doctor ordered.

Steve growled in response but complied.

"He's about like you," Kiro held up his hand and made a circle in front of Steve, "minus the whole bar fight look; but yeah, he'll be fine."

Steve nodded.

"Tara's here."

"Why?"

Kiro caught the increase of Steve's heart rate on the monitor and didn't try to hide a smirk. "She's worried about you."

Steve grunted.

Kiro rolled his eyes. "Why don't you talk to her? And why are you being such a dick to her, man?"

The X-ray technician brought in the X-ray of Steve's arm.

"What? A dick because we haven't spent every waking moment together?"

"She likes you. So...word to the wise. Never let Tara think she means nothing to you, and you sure as hell had better not ghost her. Apparently, you mean something to her, though for the life of me, I don't understand why... considering you're being a total ass."

Steve glared at Kiro. "She means something to me." His voice came out as a raspy shell of its former self.

"I mean, it's been what? Two weeks since you guys went out, and you can't even bring yourself to talk to her." Kiro stated.

"Looks like it's not broken," the doctor interrupted their conversation. "You're going to have to wear a brace for a while with the sprain. That means light duty for the next few shifts."

Steve spread his arms wide. "I've gotta work, Doc." His wheeze broke into a cough.

"Not this week, you're not." The doctor left, only to be replaced by a nurse.

"Put the mask back on, Mr. Cook." The nurse fitted it back over his nose and mouth with a glare that rivaled any his fellow Marines could give. "I'll be back in a while to check on you, but you're here for another couple of hours, so sit back and make yourself comfortable."

Kiro nodded to the nurse as she left. "So, should I send her back here?"

Steve furrowed his brow. "Huh?"

"Tara." Kiro extended his hand toward the waiting room. "Tall redhead, remember? She's worried."

Steve shook his head. "No."

"No?"

Steve coughed again. "No. Tell her I'm fine. I don't want her to see me in here."

"Really?" Kiro laughed. "You're playing the pride card?"

"Get outta here."

"Yep." Kiro turned but paused with his hand on the doorframe. "Tara's great, Steve. Don't fuck it up."

Steve woke up the next morning and swung his legs over the edge of the bed. At least he was feeling better. He still coughed a bit, but not as much as the night before. He scrubbed his face with both hands, stopping to study the brace on his left wrist.

Kiro was right. He'd ghosted Tara. And he was still angry about falling in the fire so he didn't want to see her.

His anger had always served him well. It always kept him going, kept him alive. He was angry at his parents for not caring enough about their own children. Angry at the Iraqi insurgents. He was angry at anyone who ever laid a hand on his brother. And he was angry at John's Dad.

Besides, not getting attached to anyone came naturally to him.

Now, he was angry at himself for not calling her since they went out.

He took a shower and drove to the rehab center to visit his brother for his second to last allotted bi-weekly visit before Nicky's release day, which should be just after Thanksgiving. Steve wished they got to see more of each other, but Nick needed to get the help he needed without unnecessary distractions. Sadly, Steve counted as one of those. He just needed to be glad they could see each other occasionally.

His smile was broad as he greeted his brother with arms spread wide. Nick clung to him for a couple of minutes.

"Stevie." Nick's light blue eyes still darted around the room with each visit, half-expecting someone from his past to jump out and surprise him. They sat in the corner of a warmly colored room on two comfortable couches with an end table between them.

Steve liked this room. Everything was warm and inviting. It was almost funny that the living space in the rehab center felt more like home than the living room they had growing up. Here, the furniture yearned for people to take a nap on them or curl up to watch a movie. As kids, they were barely allowed to touch anything in the family spaces of their house. They certainly weren't allowed to make a mess. Nick told him he sometimes spent time here in the evenings with the other residents, though most people tended to stay in their rooms.

Despite the cozy accommodations, Nick never really relaxed until halfway through his hour-long visit. Steve remained patient, but he wondered if Nick would ever shake the feeling that the men who forced him into that downward spiral would come back for him. He hoped so.

"You look good, Nicky."

"Thanks." Nick's shy smile made a brief appearance but disappeared just as quickly.

They talked about the small things: how Nick was doing, the new therapist he liked, and why Steve had stitches above his eye and his wrist in a brace.

"I'm doing fine," Nick said, tapping his fingers on the table to a beat only he could hear. "I promise."

Steve pulled out his phone and showed him some pictures from the Halloween party at Jo's a few weeks earlier. Nick always enjoyed dressing up for Halloween as a kid. Steve's voice caught as a picture of him and Tara appeared on the screen.

"Tara," Nick said in a whisper. He put his fingers over the picture. "She's pretty."

"Yeah." Steve's heart raced. "She is."

Nick flipped through some more pictures. "I'm getting better," he said out of the blue.

"I know you are."

"You don't need to keep watching me, you know."

"Yeah, I do. I'm your big brother. It's what I do."

"I mean, I'm fine." Nick took a breath. "Actually, I'm messed up. I know that."

Steve swallowed. "You're not..."

"Yes, I am, Stevie." Nick rocked back and forth a few times. "And it's okay. I didn't think I was messed up before. I just was."

Steve frowned. "None of that was your fault, you know."

"Some of it was." Nick smiled and looked away, his eyes distant. After a few seconds, he turned his gaze back to Steve. "You never gave up on me."

Steve leaned in and squeezed his brother's shoulder. "Never, little brother."

"So, why are you giving up on her?"

Steve pulled back and knitted his brow. "What?"

"On Tara. You're not talking about her today. Why are you giving up on her?"

How had his brother picked up on that?

"I'm... I need to make sure you're okay first."

Nick lifted his head up and down slowly. "You have no way of knowing if I will be, but you can know I'm going to try."

Pride filled Steve's chest as his brother spoke.

"For the first time, Stevie, I feel like I actually have a chance." Nick held out his hand. "Let me see those again."

Steve opened his phone to the pictures from Halloween and handed over his phone.

Nick found a picture of Tara in full costume, leaning her head back and laughing. He placed the picture in front of Steve. "Do you have a chance with her?"

Steve's eyes roamed between the picture of Tara and his brother and then back. "She's not staying here."

"Where's she going?"

"Chicago, of all places." Steve laughed. "She's a Cubs fan."

Nick brought his hand to his mouth. "No, Stevie!" He tried and failed to cover his laughter.

"I know. I know."

"You don't have to wait for me to get better for you to be happy, you know."

Steve stared at the picture of Tara, wondering when his brother got so wise. He wasn't one to get butterflies, but he'd be damned if they weren't dancing in his stomach again at the thought of being with her.

Steve's voice was still scratchy. "I don't think I have a chance."

"I like her."

"I do, too."

"No. You don't."

Steve perked up indignantly. "Yeah. I do."

"No. It's more."

Steve was still staring at his brother when one of the counselors walked into the room with her hands clasped together. "Time to go, Nicholas."

Nick rolled his eyes. "They never call me Nick."

Steve stuck his phone in his pocket.

"Bye, Stevie." Nick stood up. "Love you."

"I love you, too, Nicky."

"Go out with her. Be happy, okay?"

"I want you to be okay first, a'ight?"

Nick pulled back and smiled. "Ah-what?"

Steve hugged his brother again and waved as he disappeared behind the doors that led back to the residential area of the rehab center. He walked outside and sat down on his motorcycle with renewed confidence.

Chapter 58

Thanksgiving

Derek came into the room after taking care of the dinner dishes. "Tank, next time you cook, can you at least leave one dish unused? I swear I just washed every single dish in this station."

"Price of greatness, Doc."

Steve laughed at the banter, grateful he wasn't on dish duty tonight. Tank was a sure thing for taco night, but he was an absolute mess in the kitchen.

Derek sat down at the table with Kiro and Steve, displaying his pruned fingers in exasperation. "So, what are your plans for Thanksgiving?"

"Two meals," Kiro said. "I'll be splitting my time between my parents and Celeste's aunt and uncle. I'm starting with mine. Otherwise, Mom'll make me eat another full meal if she doesn't personally witness me consume the first one."

Steve and Derek both laughed.

"Don't laugh. Bulgarian moms are like that. Derek knows this."

Derek acknowledged Kiro with a nod.

"It's a Balkan thing. She just doesn't want me to go hungry. Maybe I can get by with a few leftovers with Celeste's aunt and uncle. I'm sure I'll still be waddling around on Saturday when our next shift starts."

Still laughing, Derek jutted his chin out from across the table. "How about you, Steve?"

Steve let out a long exhale. "I haven't celebrated Thanksgiving since before I enlisted. Well, except for the meals they provided us on base."

Derek and Tank both nodded in agreement, having eaten some of those same meals. "How old were you when you enlisted?" Tank asked.

"Barely twenty-two." Steve scrubbed his face with his hand. "Wow. Can't believe it's been eight years."

"Will Nick be able to join you?" Derek wondered aloud.

Steve's mood dipped, and he shook his head. "I wish, but he won't get out of rehab until this weekend or next week."

"That stinks."

"Yeah. Thanksgiving has never really been a big deal, anyway, but I really wanted to see him, you know? I'm just glad he's coming home soon."

"How's he doing?" Derek asked.

"Pretty well, all things considered," Steve said, smiling at the thought. "The times I've seen him, he's looked really good." Steve offered a grateful look to Derek, who had been with him every step of the way since finding Nick. Kiro, too. "Thanks to you two."

"Thanks, but we weren't the ones who negotiated his release."

Steve chuckled at Derek's description of how Steve threatened two of the men inside the house in which they found his brother. His only regret was how quickly he knocked the second guy out.

Derek and Kiro didn't know him from Adam when he arrived in Grant's Crossing. Still, they jumped into his fucked-up world and, without question, drove him down to Columbus to pull his brother out of a really shitty and potentially dangerous situation as if it were nothing.

"So..." Derek nudged him. "Do you have any plans for tomorrow? If you want, you're welcome to join us. Football, food, then Friday, I'm helping Dad demo a house."

"Demoing a house? Thanks. Sounds tempting, but..." he tried to contain his smile. "I'll be spending Thanksgiving with the Baileys."

Big grins broke out on Derek and Kiro's faces. "Oh, yeah? Tara's family?"

Steve returned their laughs with a stern look. "Enough." He tried to tamp them down. "They're just taking in strays."

"But you've gone out with her a couple of times now, haven't you?" Kiro asked.

Steve grinned. "Yes, I have."

Behind him, he could hear Tank using his voice to imitate a loud bass sound. "Da da dum dum dum."

Then they all sang the chorus to the Queen song "Another One Bites the Dust."

Steve scrubbed his face with his hands and shook his head at the good-natured ribbing directed his way.

Tank dropped his hand on Steve's shoulder as he walked behind the table. "Welcome to the club, buddy."

The alert sounded, lifting all their heads like prairie dogs, they listened to the address of a car accident.

"Ahh. The sound of job security." Tank patted him on the shoulder again as they all jumped up to head out to the truck and ambulance. "Let's go, men."

Exhausted like the other men were after a night full of car accidents and one minor house fire, Steve finally got back to the station for a shower a little after 11 am. His body yearned for a nap, but he pulled his phone out first and texted Tara.

Steve: Shift ran over

Tara: Dinner at 12

Steve: May need a nap first

Tara: Skip the nap - have a surprise for you

Steve: Surprise? I'm really tired.

Tara: You'll love it. Promise.

About ten minutes later, Steve pulled his motorcycle in front of the Bailey family home. He cut the engine, walked up the sidewalk, and knocked on their front door.

A deep voice called out. "I'll get it."

A few seconds later, a man with a military haircut opened the door and stood in the doorway. He had the same red hair as Tara, but his eyes were blue instead of her intense green. He scrutinized Steve from head to toe as if weighing and measuring his overall worth.

"You must be Steve," he said sternly while sizing up the man standing before him.

"That's right."

With a grunt, Tristan pressed his lips into a line. "You're dating Tara?"

"Yes."

"You hesitated. Why?" His gruff voice demanded.

"And you are?" Steve stood his ground.

The man in the doorway did the same. He crossed his arms over his chest. "I'm her brother."

"Tris!" Tara's voice cut through the tension. "Let him in."

Tristan broke out into a smile and extended his hand. "Tristan Bailey."

"Steve Cook."

"Come on in, Steve."

Steve stepped into a room full of smiles and set his bag and motorcycle helmet down near the door.

"Figures a jarhead wouldn't know when to back down."

"Squid, huh?"

Tristan narrowed his eyes. "Yeah. Always have to cart you guys around," he tsked with a shake of his head.

Steve smirked and eyed him sideways, but the glint in his eye made it clear he was joking. "Yeah, so you can kick back and relax on your luxury liners while we do all the real work."

Tristan broke out into laughter and slapped his hand on Steve's shoulder. "Come in and meet everybody. This is my wife, Emily." She stood up and greeted him with an enthusiastic hug, which he happily returned, figuring it was best to go with the flow. "Watch out, she's a hugger."

"This is our Grams, Evelyn." Steve nodded at the petite woman as she sauntered up to him.

"Oh no. You can't get away so easily." Grams greeted him with a hug, too.

Tara wrapped her arms around his neck to lean up for a quick kiss.

Steve wrapped his arms around her waist and dropped his voice so only Tara could hear. "Hey, Sugar."

"Hey," she said, meeting his lips for a kiss.

"None of that, now. Yuck."

She made a face at her brother. "Shut up, Tris."

"Yeah," Emily gave her husband a friendly elbow to the ribs. "Shut up, Tris."

Tristan feigned shock at his wife's comment, then gave her a loving smile.

"Good to see you," Steve spoke in a low tone.

"Good to see you, too." Tara smiled up at him.

The sound of a throat clearing pulled them out of their shared daze.

"Oh." Tara extended her arm. "This is our younger brother…"

"We're both her younger brothers." Tristan laughed while wrapping his arm around Emily's shoulders.

"By a whopping seven minutes, Tris."

"Still younger."

Tara cleared her throat and resumed her introduction. "This is our younger brother, Theo."

A barely-old-enough-to-legally-drink Theo stood up to shake Steve's hand and pat him on the back in a half-man-hug. He sported blue jeans and a green Ohio University sweatshirt with his thick dark red hair pulled back in a short ponytail. "Good to meet you, Steve."

"You, too."

Steve leaned over to shake Ken's hand, where he sat off to the side of the room in his wheelchair. "How are you doing, Ken?"

"Fantastic, Steve." His grin was mischievous, but he lowered his voice and motioned for Steve to lean closer. "Remind me to show you some wheelies later. I've been practicing." He waggled his eyebrows in excitement.

"You will do no such thing, Kenneth."

"Busted!" Ken pretended to rein in his smile as his wife, Helen, scolded him.

"You're getting rid of that thing soon, right?"

"Yes, Steve. He is." Helen pulled him into a warm embrace, both of them smiling. "It's so good to see you, honey."

"Thanks for having me…" Steve's comment trailed off when his eyes met a shy smile just a few steps behind Helen. "What…" He stopped momentarily, not caring that his jaw just hit the floor. "Nicky?"

Holding his hands on Helen's upper arms, he pulled back from his hug and stared right at her, wide-eyed like a deer in headlights. Despite a hint of tears in her eyes, she was grinning from ear to ear.

"What? How? When?" He attempted to ask but broke out into a huge smile.

"Go!" Helen nudged him toward his brother.

"Nicky!"

"Stevie!"

Steve stepped around Helen and pulled his brother into an enormous hug, which Nick enthusiastically returned. They held the embrace for a long minute to the sound of sniffing behind them, thanks to their emotional reunion inside the Bailey family's living room.

"You're home," Steve's voice cracked, "I can't believe you're here." He pulled back just long enough to double-check his own senses, grasping Nick's grinning face with both hands before pulling him back into another hug. "God, I'm so glad you're here."

"Thanks, Stevie," Nick whispered so only Steve could hear. "Thanks for finding me."

"Anything for you, little brother. Anything for you."

He pulled back again, leaving one hand on his brother's shoulder. He wiped his eyes with the palm of his other hand. And when he turned around, he saw everyone staring at them. There was not a dry eye in the house.

Steve had never been the emotional type, but when he shot a grateful look toward Helen, Tara, then back at Helen, he couldn't even speak. With a swallow, he found his words. "Thank you."

His voice cracked again, but he didn't care. His brother was home, and they were together.

"Well, we all know what we're thankful for this year, don't we?" Helen clapped her hands together with a sniff. "Theo? Tristan? Make sure the table's all set. Dinner's going to be ready soon. Tara? Fix the glasses."

The three of them snapped into action as Helen dabbed a tear from her eye on her way back to the kitchen. Steve couldn't resist pulling his brother into another hug, not letting him go until they were all called to dinner.

Epilogue

Grant's Crossing - Black Friday

"Thank you very much." Tara handed the bag full of books to her customer with a smile and took care of the next customer in line. Four hours into Black Friday and they'd been taking care of customers nonstop since they opened the doors at nine o'clock that morning. Helen ran the register all day while Tara bagged up customers' purchases. The whole family was helping customers choose books or restocking and rearranging shelves as the stock ran low. Even Tara's dad was back in the store, though he mainly stayed in the office to learn the new billing system and, of course, man the phones for pick-up orders, enlisting his sons as runners.

Steve and Nick walked into the sounds of "White Christmas" playing overhead. The line was about six people long. Nick opted to look around while Steve stepped up to the edge of the counter.

Tara turned to flash him a smile. "I've barely had time to breathe, we've been so busy," Tara said. But she turned to flash him a smile.

Tara let out a slow exhale as the last customer in line walked out with a bag full of books.

"I'll be right back," Tara's mom slipped out behind her.

Tara turned to face Steve when a middle-aged lady approached with another couple of books.

"Excuse me." The woman said as she set three paperbacks on the counter.

"Yes, ma'am," Tara greeted a lady with a light blue knit cap still pulled down over her ears.

"I was told you could help me."

Tara smiled. "Of course."

"The young man over there suggested a book, but we couldn't find it on your shelf."

"I can look it up." Tara offered. "What's the title?"

"Oh, shoot." She scrunched her face. "Now I can't remember."

"No worries." Tara looked up and spotted her brother. "Theo?"

"Yeah," He peeked his head around the shelf. "What was the title of the book you were helping this lady find?"

Theo walked up with a confused expression on his face.

"Oh, not him." The lady smiled and pointed in the direction of the man she couldn't see. "The other young man with long hair."

Now it was Tara's turn to look confused.

"He's tall with blond hair?" The lady added.

"Nick?" Tara looked around to see Nick heading toward the counter. "Hey, Nick?"

Startled, he lifted his face to meet Tara's. "Um. Yes?"

"Were you helping this lady with a book?"

"Um..." Worry flashed across his face, but then he smiled at the lady. "'Term Limits' by Vince Flynn."

"That's it." She said, relieved. "'Term Limits'."

Tara couldn't hide her surprise that Nick had jumped in to help. She exchanged a proud smile with Steve.

He shrugged. "I read it a few weeks ago."

"Thank you, young man."

"You're welcome." Nick dropped his eyes, but his shy smile returned.

Tara checked the computer and confirmed they didn't have any in stock but placed the order. "We'll call you when that gets in next week."

"Thank you."

And another happy customer walked out the door.

"Hey, Nick." Nick walked up to the counter during a lull in customers.

"Not sure what your plans are here in Grant's Crossing," Tara said, "but are you looking for a job? We could use the help."

His face lit up. "Really? I mean. Yes."

"Great! You're hired."

Nick shot a nervous glance at his brother before responding to Tara. "Thanks!"

"Can you start today?"

"Um." His eyes flicked back and forth between Tara and a snickering Steve. "Haven't I already?"

Between the Lines Bookstore - Six months later

Nick smiled sweetly at Helen Bailey before leading the trio of older ladies back to the romance section to help them find the latest book written by Helen's daughter-in-law, Emily. It was an instant bestseller that they couldn't keep on the shelves.

Nick started working full-time hours after the new year and was settling in well. He worked with Lydia, who became a manager after Tara returned to Chicago. He smiled and looked out over the shop until the Tres Widows approached the counter with their books.

Steve walked up to the front door to Between the Lines wearing a backpack over one shoulder after his usual post-shift breakfast at Baba's.

"Long night, huh?" Helen asked.

Steve scrubbed his face with his hand. "Very."

"Well, you made it home safely, so now you can take it easy." She headed to the back of the store and called over her shoulder. "Nothing a good nap won't cure."

Steve spoke to Nick for a few minutes before stepping over to hold the door open for the Tres Widows who were leaving the bookstore.

Abigail spoke up in a flirtatious tone. "Hi Steve," Abigail singsonged in a flirtatious tone as she and Lizzie exited through the door he held open for them.

He turned on his charming smile. "Hello, Miss Abigail."

"Not now, ladies," Berneta followed behind them with her purchase. "We still need to get over to Strings Attached for the yarn sale."

"Bye, Nick." Abigail turned to wave to Nick, who waved back in confusion.

Steve turned back inside and grabbed his pack off the floor. "Be careful, little brother. You might have a dance later."

Nick's eyes popped wide open like a deer in headlights. "What?"

Steve laughed. "Remind me to tell you about Miss Abigail sometime."

THE END

Continue reading for excerpts from all my Grant's Crossing novels!

All my novels are available online wherever books are sold. Also available at your local library in print and via the Libby app. (If not yet at your library, please click "notify me" in Libby to let them know you want to read it.) Wayward Guilt is also available on

Hoopla via your local library across the US, Canada, Australia, and New Zealand.

Thank you for reading my books! If you liked the story you just read, please take a moment to rate it and leave a few words. Even something as simple as "I enjoyed this book!" is a huge help in places like Amazon which bumps books up in their algorithms once it hits a certain number of reviews.

Sign up for my monthly (ish) Leaux Cay newsletter for the first three chapters of Wayward Guilt and a Safe Now Bonus Epilogue with all the B-shift Grant's Crossing Firefighters!

https://www.hmsbrown.com/p/newsletter-sign-up.html

Continue reading for excerpts of my other novels

Wayward Guilt, Heroes of Grant's Crossing Book 1,
https://books2read.com/u/38WRM7

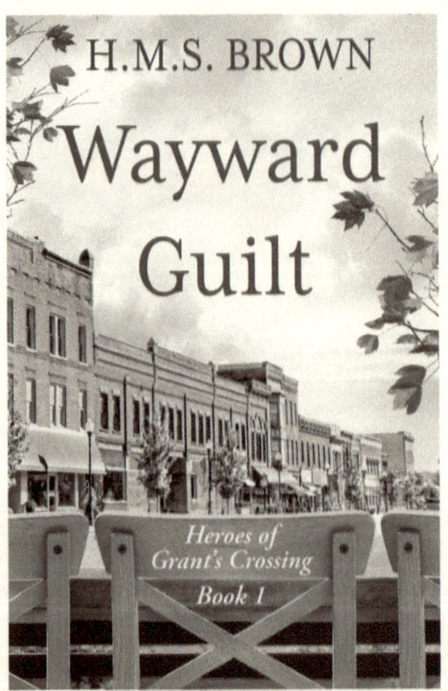

. . .

Derek's Story continues in **End of a New Life, Heroes of Grant's Crossing Book 3**, available Summer 2025. Add it to your Goodreads TBR: https://www.goodreads.com/author/dashboard?ref=nav_profile_authordash

Want more about Tara and Steve's story? Turn the page for an excerpt from **Don't Call Me Sugar, a Grant's Crossing Romance**. https://books2read.com/DCMS

H.M.S. Brown - Author - https://linktr.ee/grantscrossing

Excerpt - End of a New Life - Heroes of Grant's Crossing Book 3

Grant's Crossing, Ohio - August 2015

"Have you heard from him?" Kiro Marinov turned the lock and opened the door so he and Tank could step inside the carriage house. "He was supposed to meet us for dinner but never showed."

Tank jogged up the stairs and pounded on the door to Derek Mitchell's one-bedroom apartment. "Hey, Doc. You there?" Tank turned to Kiro. "Do you have a key?"

"Yep. Abe gave it to me a while back in case I needed to check up on him." Kiro unlocked the door. Flipping on a light, they both walked into the tidy apartment. The only things out of place were the empty beer bottles on the counter and coffee table.

"Shit." Tank rushed into the bedroom, checking both the bathroom and walk-in closet to make sure he wasn't there. "He's not here."

One look through the window revealed a conspicuously missing truck. "Tell me he didn't drink and drive."

"He might have," Kiro said, sounding defeated. "I just hope I'm wrong." He darted downstairs with Tank on his heels. "Come on. I'll drive."

"Where are we going?" Tank asked as Kiro pulled out of the oversized driveway.

"It's just a hunch, but," Kiro shook his head and turned toward the edge of town. "How long has it been since...."

Tank looked upward long enough to confirm the math. It had been one year since Joey Parker was killed in Afghanistan. "Yesterday would have been one year to the day."

"Right, but we were all on shift." Kiro turned into the main entrance of Grant's Crossing Cemetery. The gravel crunched under his tires as he navigated the narrow lanes to the newer section. "There it is."

The last remnants of the late-setting sun shone down through the leaves and highlighted Derek's blue Silverado parked diagonally across the lane. While it looked undamaged, the grill rested solidly against the trunk of a large oak tree. The driver's door hung open, and empty beer cans were strewn about on the ground below it.

Before Kiro even stopped his SUV, Tank jumped out and sprinted to the other side of the tree to Joey Parker's gravesite. "No. No. No. No. No. Shit. KIRO!" Tank called out around the side of the wide oak tree. "OVER HERE!"

Kiro ran around in time to see Tank drop to the ground where Derek was sprawled across Joey Parker's grave, face down in the damp grass. More beer cans were tossed on the ground.

Some were smashed.

All were empty.

A quick glance revealed four coins totaling .41 cents that Derek had placed on top of Joey's headstone.

A penny for visiting his grave.

A nickel for having gone through boot camp together.

A dime for having served together.

And a quarter for having been with Joey when he died.

Derek had served as the combat medic on Joey's final mission in Afghanistan.

Kiro wiped his brow in the mid-August heat and joined them just as Tank rolled Derek over on his back, not even earning so much as a faint groan from his unconscious friend. Reaching down to feel his pulse, Tank haphazardly wiped some of the dirt off Derek's face. "He's breathing, but his pulse is weak. Let's get him out of here."

Kiro helped lift him enough so Tank could carry him over his shoulders. Tank grunted as he stood. Derek's limp body draped down Tank's back as he took him to Kiro's truck. Kiro ran ahead to open the cargo door and fold down the seats. A moan escaped Derek's mouth as Tank carefully placed him in the back of the truck and climbed inside.

"Keep him on his side," Kiro shut the door and jumped in the driver's seat.

"Yeah. Yeah. I've got it." Tank said, then concentrated on speaking to Derek to try to rouse him from his worse-than-usual drunken stupor.

Kiro broke all sorts of speed records on the short drive back to the Brockmoor carriage house. He was grateful they didn't pass any police along the way.

Despite his Ranger and firefighter training, Tank still struggled to get Derek upstairs to his apartment. He eased Derek onto the bed, turning him on his side to keep his airway open. "Pretty sure you weighed less in Ranger school, Doc."

Kiro kneeled down beside the bed and opened the med bag he kept in his truck. Taking his friend's vitals, he felt better when another groan escaped Derek's lips. "Tank, grab the trash can out of the bathroom. Whatever he drank will probably come back to haunt him after a while."

Tank retrieved the trash can and set it on the floor by the bed. Then he took off Derek's shoes. "Well?"

"What do you think?" Kiro threw up his hands. "He's weak, dehydrated, and drunk off his ass."

"Guess we just wait now, right?"

"Yep. Let him sleep it off." Kiro responded without enthusiasm. "Not much else we can do except make sure he keeps breathing and doesn't choke when he gets sick."

"Jesus, Doc." Tank gently rested his hand on Derek's shoulder. "Why are you doing this?"

"I'll stay and watch over him," Kiro offered.

"Got a banana bag handy?"

"Yeah." Kiro tilted his head toward the small refrigerator in the corner of the room. "He's gonna need fluids and nutrients."

"Ok. I'll head back to the cemetery to clean up Joey's gravesite and figure out how to bring his truck back. I shouldn't be too long."

"No need to come back. I'll watch him tonight." Kiro offered, his expression as grim as Tank's. "Get back to your family. We can get his truck later."

Tank's shoulders sagged as he dropped a hand to Kiro's shoulder. "Thanks, man."

"Of course." Kiro settled on the floor against the wall and scrubbed his face with his hands. A book on the nightstand caught his eye. "You and your spy novels, D."

Keeping Derek's bookmark in place, he opened the book to the first chapter and started reading.

Please add End of a New Life, the third and final installment of Heroes of Grant's Crossing to your TBR. Coming Summer 2025. https://www.goodreads.com/book/show/204551136-end-of-a-new-life

Continue reading for an excerpt from Don't Call Me Sugar, a M/F Grant's Crossing Romance featuring Steve Cook from Safe Now. https://books2read.com/DCMS

Excerpt - Don't Call Me Sugar - A M/F Grant's Crossing Romance

Chicago, IL

"I can't believe I let you talk me into going clubbing with you tonight." Tara Bailey adjusted her dress that barely made it halfway down her thighs. Her wavy, red hair hung down well beyond her freckled shoulder blades, covering some of what her backless, green dress did not.

"If I'm driving downtown, you're going out with me," Becca admitted as she smoothed out her own dress. She flipped her long, black hair behind her shoulders. "And giving you an excuse to wear those heels was all the convincing you needed to get out of those yoga pants you've been living in lately, so no complaining."

Tara grinned and shimmied her shoulders, unable to resist making sure everyone and their mother saw the gorgeous red soles on the pair of heels she loved so much. The same shoes she'd saved for months to afford but rarely wore except for very special occasions.

Her first time clubbing since her breakup definitely qualified as a special occasion. With three-inch heels, she was an inch or so shy of six feet tall and most definitely stood out in the crowd.

"Besides, your dress makes your green eyes pop." Becca smiled as they drew closer to the bouncer at the entrance. "Face it, Tara. You look hot tonight. The men will line up to dance with you. Oh!" Becca tapped her arm and surreptitiously pointed to a man towards the front of the line. "Maybe even him."

Tara didn't bother to be subtle while checking him out from head to toe. Then she caught the woman wrapping her arm through his. Her smile dropped. "Looks hot, but I think he has eyes only for that blonde up there. She's just as hot."

Shorter by several inches, Becca missed the blond. She grabbed Tara's shoulder to balance herself on her tiptoes. "Damn. You're right."

"Yeah." Tara exhaled and leaned towards Becca so she could be heard over the sound of the music that made its way outside. "Last thing I want to do is encroach on someone else's date."

"Good point." Becca smiled as she approached the bouncer, who held them back until a couple holding hands exited the building. "But we can still dance."

"Yes, we can."

Motioned inside, Tara and Becca shared a grin as they walked into their favorite nightclub, Club 72. It was an upscale nightclub with an enormous dance floor and Chicago's best DJ on the weekends.

Tara liked it because it reminded her of her family's bookstore back home, which was established in 1972, the same year as this club. Though she was confident the owner of this club had put more effort into updating it than her parents had with their shop back home in Grant's Crossing, Ohio.

Both Tara and Becca loved a good cocktail or glass of wine but weren't otherwise big drinkers. A big night on the town though warranted at least a drink or two before hitting the dance floor. As they always did, they started by heading to the bar before taking a lap around the perimeter to see who was there and what everyone was wearing.

"I'll get the first round." Tara offered as she reached into her tiny purse that held her ID and credit card, phone, lipstick, and enough cash for a cab ride home if the Lyft was too expensive when they left for the night. "The usual?" she raised her eyebrows with a glance towards her friend.

Receiving a nod, she ordered their drinks and handed the Manhattan to Becca while keeping the Old Fashioned for herself. They meandered through a crowd of ladies gathered for a bachelorette party, admiring their dresses as they passed by. She caught the eye of the bride-to-be and couldn't resist offering her congratulations. "And you look fantastic in that dress." Tara nearly yelled to be heard over the music blaring in their ears.

"THANK YOU!" the lady yelled in return. Glancing down, her eyes widened when she caught sight of Tara's red soles. With a big smile, the bachelorette added, "And I love your shoes!"

Tara's face lit up. "Thanks!"

With a renewed spring in her step, she and Becca twisted and turned through the hoards of people to step up on the table-filled platform that surrounded the dance floor on three sides. As if they'd just hacked their way through the jungle with machetes, they finally reached a clearing that had an open high-top table.

Becca held up her drink and spoke loudly enough to be heard over the loud music and the steady beat they could feel up through the floor. "Here's to a fun night out with friends and an entire club full of good-looking men."

Relieved to be just outside of the people traffic, Tara clinked her glass against her friend's. "And here's to the best roommate a girl could ask for, happily sacrificing to come out and be my wing woman!

Becca smiled and drank to the kind words Tara offered her.

Tara took another sip as her other hand rested atop her purse. "Let the people watching begin!"

After an hour of dancing, they found a table and cushioned bench off to the side with another round of drinks. Both looked like two-fisted drinkers with a cocktail in one hand and a with a glass of water in the other, not wanting to be hungover in the morning.

Holding her cocktail, Tara rested her hand on her tiny purse. A vibration drew her eyes to the table. Releasing her drink, she reached inside and pulled out her phone to find it blowing up with calls and text messages.

"Everything alright?" Becca creased her brow out of concern.

"I'm not sure." Tara scrolled through her phone and noticed most of the calls were from her mother or an unknown central Ohio number. There's no way she could call from inside with the music playing, so she opened her texts to find several from her mom, written in complete, grammatically correct sentences, all words perfectly spelled out. Her mom never did get the hang of texting, but she at least knew how.

The last few messages made her heart race.

Mom: Your father has been in a car accident.

Mom: It is serious.

Mom: I'm on my way to the hospital now.

Mom: Call me as soon as you get this.

Her eyes watered as she drew her hand to her chest. She tried to catch her breath, but was on the verge of hyperventilating.

Becca grabbed her drink and set it on the table next to her own. "Tara! What's wrong?"

"My...my dad."

Tara couldn't bring herself to speak. She held her phone out for Becca to read.

"Come on. Let's get out of here." Becca stuck Tara's phone into her purse and hung the tiny strap over her own shoulder. She grabbed Tara's hand and led her outside the front entrance so they could hail a Lyft.

Once inside the car, she pulled the phone out and handed it to a still-stunned Tara. "Call your mom."

Tara took a deep breath and fought back the tears as she dialed her mom.

"It's going straight to voice mail."

"Keep trying."

Tara kept dialing and redialing. She tried calling her brothers and sister, but with two of them at sea with the Navy and the other a senior at Ohio University who was probably partying on a Saturday night, she had no luck.

"Shit." She redialed her mother's number.

The Lyft driver pulled up to the curb and stopped. Becca thanked the driver and ushered Tara out of the cab and to the elevator in their building.

Finally, her mom answered. "Oh, Tara. Where have you been?"

"Mom!" Tara cried, grateful to hear her mother's voice. "How's Dad? What happened?"

"He's been in a car accident." Her mother's voice shook. "I'm at the hospital now. Honey, it's serious."

Tara's shock gradually changed to concern as her mother described the accident. Her father was currently in surgery for a handful of broken bones and internal injuries.

"Geez, Mom. Are you ok? Were you in the car with him?" Tara's eyes snapped up when the elevator bell dinged on the fifth floor. She let Becca guide her through the door and down the hall to her apartment.

"I'm fine," her mom said, giving Tara an opportunity to breathe. "I was at home when it happened. Anna Marinova came over and drove me to the hospital. My hands are still shaking."

"So Kiro was there?"

Becca kept a hand on Tara's shoulder for support.

"Yes," her mom continued. "They say he was lucky because the car mostly hit the back seat and swung him around rather than hitting his door directly."

Tara said a silent prayer of thanks for her friend, Kiro Marinov, a paramedic with the Grant's Crossing Fire Department. He must have called his mom after getting her dad to the hospital. Tara's hand flew to her face as she fought back any thoughts about how much worse it could have been. She turned her gaze towards the ceiling, closing her eyes to keep her tears at bay.

Her mom coughed a sob over the phone. "Had they hit his door directly...."

Her eyes flew open. "Don't even think it, Mom. You just said they didn't." Tara did her best to come across as brave. "Let's be grateful for that."

"You're right, honey," her mom reluctantly agreed. "We should be grateful. Bones will heal." She breathed a humorless laugh. "Perhaps a bit more slowly at our age, but they'll heal."

Tara smiled at her mom's attempt at an optimistic outlook. "So, how are you, Mom? Really. Is there someone there with you right now?"

"Um... I'm... yes. Anna is still here with me." Her mom's shaky voice made her come across as so unsure of herself right now. So much for the optimistic outlook. Gone was the constantly upbeat woman who always cheered everyone else up when the chips were down.

Tara switched to her problem-solving self. "What else can I do, Mom? What else do you need?"

"I don't even know yet."

Tara forced herself to keep calm as her mom listed off the long list of her father's injuries. A driver more interested in texting had run a red light and t-boned her father's car, smashing him into the corner of the car in the lane next to him. The third driver was treated and released with only superficial injuries, but her dad landed in emergency surgery and his car was probably totaled.

"Of course. I can probably rearrange my vacation time and be there in a few days. I'm sure I can stay for a week or two." In her mind, she kissed her Mackinac vacation goodbye. Tara thought of her siblings. "Have you talked to Tristan or Theo yet? What about Tiff? Do they know what happened? I haven't been able to get through to any of them."

"I spoke to Theo, but not yet Tristan or Tiffany. I should really call Tristan's wife." Her mom sounded panicky. "She should know what happened."

"I'll call Emily for you. Don't worry about that. Tristan's at sea for another couple of months anyway, but you're right. We can get word to him and Tiffany."

"Oh yes. You're right, honey."

"Lydia can run the shop today, but without your father there..." her voice trailed off.

Shit.

"We really need your help. Can you please come home?"

Don't Call Me Sugar, a Grant's Crossing Romance, can be found wherever books are sold online. https://books2read.com/DCMS

Have a library card? All my books are readily available on Hoopla & Libby. Please request them at your local library if not already on the shelves as a paperback or digitally via Libby.

Click on my link tree for the following Leaux Cay fun!

H.M.S. Brown - Author - https://linktr.ee/grantscrossing

Sign up for my newsletter because you want a chance to win free ebooks!

Thanks so much for reading my book! I hope you loved Steve and Nick. Leaving a written review on Amazon or Goodreads or Bookbub - even just a few words - is a huge help to an indie author like me!

THANK YOU!

Acknowledgments

Thanks so much to my friends and family for continuing to support my writing adventure, even if it does mean I'm sitting in front of the TV with a laptop or spending my lunch hours in a meeting room to get lost in the world of Grant's Crossing.

As always, Mom and Dad are ridiculously supportive of me, talking my book up to anyone who will listen to them. Like the Tres Widows can get a dance date at a coffee shop, my mom can get someone to buy my books!

Dan and Duchess - your input to this novel was invaluable. Thank you for keeping my story honest.

Amy, Deb, Kristy, and Rachel - I'm so glad I met all of you. You're the best support group a writer could ever imagine!

Jeremy - I can't wait to someday read your fantasy stories. I appreciate you so much for keeping my writing group an actual group!

Liberty - you're the best at providing feedback on the most random things at the most random times. Your writing is beautiful. One day, we'll both randomly win the recognition we seek!

Andrea - Amazing how a silly word game can keep us together. Cubs game this season?

Amy - your editing has made my books so much better than I ever thought they could be. Thanks for pushing me to always be better.

To everyone who's read my books and shed tears with the men and women of Grant's Crossing, thank you so much! I love that you've joined Derek, Tank, Steve, Nick, and all the others on this heroes journey, and hope you stick around for more.

Steve and Nick have had it rough, but things are beginning to look up for them. I have more plans for Nick that may or may not include a certain character from this book and Wayward Guilt because a couple of my guys just need their happy endings.

But, before that happens, I need to give Derek another run at dealing with the loss of his best friend in Heroes of Grant's Crossing Book 3: End of a New Life. It'll be a rough ride, but the people of Grant's Crossing have a never ending supply of love and support. Thank goodness, because he'll need it!

In the meantime, if you enjoyed my books, please consider leaving a written review on Amazon and Goodreads. Even typing a couple of works saying you loved the book (even though I made you cry) is a huge help and will go a long way into getting discovered by other readers. While you're there, feel free to give me a follow and add my next book to your TBR.

About the Author

H.M.S. Brown stumbled into writing during lockdown in 2020 after complaining to her mom about a romance novel she didn't like. When her mom challenged her to write her own book, Grant's Crossing was born.

When not cheering on the Columbus Blue Jackets, H.M.S. Brown can be found at a neighborhood cafe working on her next story or at her day job so she can maintain a roof over her library and yarn stash.

Safe Now is H.M.S. Brown's companion novel to Wayward Guilt and Book 2 of her Heroes of Grant's Crossing series. Book 3, End of a New Life, will hit the shelves on Summer 2025.

You can find all of H.M.S. Brown's novels at your local library and wherever books are sold online.

Official Website: www.hmsbrown.com

facebook.com/AuthorHMSBrown

x.com/GrantsCrossing

instagram.com/grantscrossing

goodreads.com/hmsbrown

bookbub.com/authors/h-m-s-brown

bsky.app/profile/grantscrossing.bsky.social

amazon.com/author/hmsbrown

youtube.com/@GrantsCrossing

linkedin.com/in/rpcvbg

tiktok.com/@grantscrossing

www.ingramcontent.com/pod-product-compliance
Lightning Source LLC
Chambersburg PA
CBHW031845310726
48972CB00005B/1423